Peter May was born and raised in Scotland. He was an award-winning journalist at the age of twenty-one and a published novelist at twenty-six. When his first book was adapted as a major drama series for the BBC, he quit journalism and during the high-octane fifteen years that followed, became one of Scotland's most successful television dramatists. He created three prime-time drama series, presided over two of the highest-rated serials in his homeland as script editor and producer, and worked on more than 1,000 episodes of ratings-topping drama before deciding to leave television to return to his first love, writing novels.

His passion for detailed research for his books has taken him behind the closed doors of the Chinese Police force, to the kitchen of a three-star Michelin chef, and down the Paris catacombs; he has worked as an online private detective, was inducted as a Chevalier of the Grand Order of Gaillac wines and earned honorary membership of the Chinese Crime Writers' Association.

He has won several literature awards in France and received the USA's Barry Award for *The Blackhouse*, the first in his internationally bestselling Lewis Trilogy, and the ITV Crime Thriller Awards Book Club Best Read for *Entry Island*.

He now lives in south-west France with his wife, writer Janice Hally.

BY PETER MAY

The Enzo Files

Extraordinary People
The Critic
Blacklight Blue
Freeze Frame
Blowback
Cast Iron

The China Thrillers

The Firemaker
The Fourth Sacrifice
The Killing Room
Snakehead
The Runner
Chinese Whispers

The Lewis Trilogy

The Blackhouse
The Lewis Man
The Chessmen

Standalone Novels

Entry Island
Runaway
Coffin Road

Non-fiction

Hebrides with David Wilson

PETER MAY

SNAKE HEAD

riverrun

First published in Great Britain in 2002 by Coronet Books
This paperback edition published in 2017 by

r

riverrun

an imprint of

Quercus Editions Ltd
Carmelite House
50 Victoria Embankment
London EC4Y 0DZ

An Hachette UK company

A CIP catalogue record for this book is available
from the British Library

ISBN 978 1 78206 232 5
EBOOK ISBN 978 1 78206 555 5

10 9 8 7 6 5 4 3 2

Typeset by CC Book Production

Printed and bound in Great Britain by Clays Ltd, St Ives plc

For Dick and Michelle

The science in this book is real, and only too possible.

PROLOGUE

Half an hour ago a frozen sun shone in the palest of clear blue skies. Pink faces were wrapped against a temperature of minus forty degrees centigrade, tiny coloured ice particles dancing in clouded breath. Now the sky has darkened, suddenly and out of nowhere, wind shaving the peaks off seventy-foot pressure ridges driven up by colliding floes. The weather window has narrowed with the unpredictable Arctic winter and there is an urgency in the figures, thickened by twenty pounds of bright red protective clothing, who crowd the ice. For while the dead will wait forever, the living know that life is short.

Petrels circle the ice-breaker, plaintive cries whipped away on the edge of a wind that tugs ever more fiercely at the walls of the decontamination tent. The steel cables of the lift-arm whine and scream as the ice shifts and the submarine cants slightly to its port side where the supports they have laboured so hard to put in place prevent it from toppling back to its icy grave. A frozen crust has attached itself already to the soft orange coral accumulated along its hull.

From the tent, five figures emerge in slow motion, like spacemen negotiating a moonscape, clumsy and encumbered by their protective STEPO outfits. Beneath, they are encased in tear-resistant thermal body suits. Filtered air blows down over the faces of The Team, pale and anxious, peering out from behind clear, curved faceplates. Each of them has brought his or her own discipline to The Project: microbiology, virology, medicine, medical archaeology, pathology. Nearly twelve months of planning are nearing their moment of fruition. The tension of The Team is palpable.

'We all live in an orange submarine, orange submarine . . .' Doctor Ruben's tuneless voice crackles in their headsets.

'Shut up, Philip!' Doctor Catherine Oxley's voice carries the authority of the Team Leader, but it is also tight with stress. She wonders why it is that all the pathologists she has known share the same juvenile sense of humour.

The Seadragon looms over them. At first, when the vessel was raised from the water, Catherine had been surprised at how small she seemed, how it was possible that twenty-two men had once lived and worked — and died — aboard her. Now she seems huge, rising up out of the ice like the carcass of some giant beached mother whale with twenty-two Jonahs in her belly.

They clamber up the scaffolding erected by the crew, thickly gloved hands emerging from red sleeves reaching out to help them at each step. Everything is coated in ice and treacherous underfoot. Each movement is meticulously, painfully slow. As they climb the conning tower they can see the muzzles of the four torpedo tubes slightly proud of the foremost bulkhead. The engine-room hatch is rusted solid and no attempt has been made to open it. A sheet-metal screen around the chariot bridge is almost eaten through. The mounting behind it where the portable wireless aerial would have been disassembled prior to diving for the last time, is obscured by more than eighty years of accumulated coral. The main hatch has been cleaned off and shot with lubricating fluid and anti-freeze, but remains unopened.

Catherine watches as Doctor Ruben and Professor Marlowe get stiffly down on their knees and grasp the handwheel that locks the hatch in place. To their surprise it turns almost easily. The crew have done a fine job. But prising it loose from its seal proves more difficult. Doctor Arnold squeezes on to the bridge to help. Catherine looks away for a moment at the detritus of The Project littering the ice, at the red-suited crewmen, like slashes of blood against the white, standing in groups looking on, many of them just kids, student volunteers. Funding had been a nightmare. And she looks at the sky, almost black now, and knows that they have an hour, maybe less.

In almost twenty years of medical archaeology she has recovered many bodies from many graves. But for the first time she feels an uneasiness about the opening of this unintended tomb, and tries hard not to visualise the horrors she expects to find locked in its dark interior.

She turns back as the hatch finally breaks free, and gases escape with a moan from inside, making all the hairs rise up on the back of her neck.

They stand there for a moment, staring into the inky blackness, before Catherine snaps on her flashlight and picks out the rungs of the ladder that will take them down into the body of the submarine. She manoeuvres herself carefully to make the descent. At the bottom there is nearly a foot of water. Although the Seadragon was never holed, the salt water has, over all the years, eaten its way through rivets and joints, slowly seeping in to violate her icy sanctity. The air is steamy cold and fetid and Catherine is glad she does not have to breathe it in. She is aware of The Team following behind her, flashlights holding moisture in their beams, bringing light to decades of darkness. Catherine moves *forward into the battery compartment. She points her flashlight up at the capstan and windless motor above her head, then pans down and starboard to pick out the crewmen's personal lockers. She has conducted a virtual tour of this Canadian-built H-boat submarine many times, but the reality is very different. She turns, knowing that she is moving into the Chief and PO's mess, and is unable to prevent a small scream escaping her lips as a mummified face peers up at her from the table, pasty white, with shrivelled eyes and sunken nose, the dark staining of blood and vomit, like a shadow, still visible about the mouth. The uniform is preserved almost intact, but where the feet and lower legs have been in the water, the flesh is long gone, leaving the bones pale and white and washed clean.*

'Jesus . . .' She hears Marlowe's whispered oath from the fore-ends and turns back, wading quickly forward to see, in the criss-crossing shafts of light, the shrunken bodies of the ship's crew swaying gently, silently, in hammocks rigged in the torpedo tube and stowage area. They are wrapped in blankets and coats, the horrors of a death that took them without mercy nearly a century before, frozen on their faces, like their beards and moustaches, for eternity. She shivers, wrestling in her mind with a sense of foreboding, knowing that the disease that took these men so horribly is certain to return, one way or another. It is only a matter of time.

CHAPTER ONE

I

Deputy J. J. Jackson, known to his colleagues at the Walker County Sheriff's Department simply as Jayjay, stuck another matchstick between his front teeth and began chewing on it. He unzipped his fly and issued a yellow stream into the dry bed of Bedias Creek. Steam rose from it in the cool morning air, and he made a bold effort to make sure that most of it crossed the county line into Madison. Somewhere to the north, beyond the trees that broke the monotony of the flat Texan landscape, prisoners were being called out of their cells at the Ferguson Unit to face another day of incarceration. And he was free to piss in the breeze, clocking off in just over half an hour, to bring to an end the long red-eye shift, and with it the prospect of an empty bed. He spat out the matchstick and regretted that he had ever given up smoking. He was sure to die of wood poisoning.

The Dixie Chicks played from the open door of his black and white. Strictly non-regulation, but hell, you had to have something to keep you awake. He squeezed his ample frame in behind the wheel and eased his patrol car out on to the deserted Highway 45. He was flying now, south, into the wild blue. Day was when Martha would have had hot pancakes and syrup, and a plate of grits on the table when he got home. But since she'd run off with that air-con salesman he'd taken to driving into Huntsville for breakfast at the Cafe Texan, opposite the County Courthouse on Sam Houston Avenue. He always sat in the smoking room just so he could breathe in other people's cigarettes. Nothing you could do about second-hand smoke, he could tell the doc.

He sang along with the Chicks for a few bars.

Up off the highway on the right a Mexican fast food joint stood proud on the bluff. Much as he liked that beer with the slice of lime stuffed in the neck, Jayjay avoided Mexican food whenever possible. It gave him bad heartburn. But today he turned off and followed the bumpy road up to the parking lot, a big empty stretch of dusty tarmac. Empty, that is, except for a large refrigerated food container hooked up to a red, shiny trailer tractor. Not unusual. Truckers often pulled off to snatch a few moments' shut-eye during an all-nighter. But the door on the driver's side was lying wide open, and there was no sign of anyone around. There were no other vehicles in the lot, and the restaurant wouldn't be open for hours yet.

Jayjay left his engine running and got out of the car. He had no idea why the truck had drawn his attention. Maybe it was because the driver had made no attempt to slot it anywhere between the faded white lines. Maybe it was just instinct. Jayjay held a lot of store by instinct. He had had an instinct that Martha was going to leave him at least two years before she finally got around to it. Although that might not have been so much instinct as wishful thinking. But, hell, there was something odd about this truck. It looked . . . abandoned. He pulled the brim of his Stetson down, stuck another matchstick in his mouth and clamped his open palms on his hips, the forefinger of his right hand touching the leather of his holster for comfort.

Slowly he approached the open door of the truck, glancing a touch nervously to left and right.

'Hey y'all,' he called. And when there was no response, 'Anybody there?' He stopped, staring up into the empty cab, working the matchstick from one corner of his mouth to the other. Then he pulled himself up into the cabin and checked in back where the driver would usually sleep. Empty.

He eased himself down on to the tarmac and looked around. Where the hell could he have gone? The Dixie Chicks were getting into some R&B back in the car. A slight breeze stirred the dust in the lot. Sun rising under early morning cloud dimpled it copper pink. Later, as the same sun rose, it would burn it off.

Jayjay walked the length of the trailer, past rows of tyres as tall as he was, painted black walls, treads he could almost get a fist into. GARCIA WHOLESALE, it said on the side. Fresh painted. New.

Round the back the tall doors of the trailer stood slightly ajar, and he began to get a bad feeling. He took his gun from his holster, crooking his arm and pointing the weapon at the sky. 'Hey!' he shouted again. 'Is there anybody in there?' He didn't

really expect a reply, but was disappointed to be right. He spat
out the match and pulled the left-hand door wide. It was heavy
and swung open slowly. He was immediately hit by the smell of
something rotten. Whatever cargo this thing was carrying had
been left unrefrigerated and was well past its sell-by. He could
see boxes of produce piled high: tomatoes, eggplants, avocados,
cucumbers. He grabbed a handle on the inside of the door and
pulled himself up. The smell was almost overpowering now,
thick and sour like vomit and faeces. Jayjay blenched. 'Jesus . . .'
he hissed. Boxes had collapsed from either side and he had to
pull them away to make any progress into the interior of the
trailer. Tomatoes and cucumbers rattled away across the riveted
steel floor, and a naked arm fell from between two boxes, an
open palm seeming to beckon him in. Jayjay let out an involuntary yelp and felt goosebumps prickle across his scalp. He
holstered his gun and started tearing at the cardboard. Another
column of boxes toppled around him revealing that only the
back quarter of the truck was carrying produce. It was too dark
to see clearly into the space beyond, or the body lying at his feet.
He was gagging now on the stench. He fumbled for the flashlight
hanging on his belt. The beam that pierced the dark shot back
through him like a frozen arrow. The scream stopped in his
throat, too thick to squeeze past constricting airways. Bodies.
Dozens of them trapped in the light, fixed in death. Arms and
legs entwined, faces contorted terribly by some dreadful struggle
to hold on to life. Vomit and blood and torn clothes. Ghostly
pale Asian faces, wide-eyed and lifeless, like photographs he had
seen of mass graves in concentration camps. Jayjay staggered

backwards, stumbling over boxes, feet skidding away from him on the slime of burst and rotting tomatoes. He hit the floor with a force that knocked all the breath out of him. For a moment he lay still, wondering if he had slipped through a crack in the earth and fallen into the devil's lair. And in the distance he heard the Dixie Chicks still doing their thing.

II

Wang's Diary

All my knuckles are broken and bleeding, so I can barely hold my pencil. I have smashed them on the door until I can lift my arms no more. It is difficult to breathe now and the heat is insufferable. The battery in my penlight is almost done and I can no longer see the faces around me. I no longer want to. They only reflect the fear and despair I know is on mine. Cheng has passed out. I do not know if she is still breathing. The grip of her fingers on my arm has gone slack. Poor Cheng. My *yazi*. All she wanted was a better life, to reach *Meiguo*, find her Mountain of Gold. It is all any of them wanted. How cruel to have come this far, and be separated from the land we sought by rubber and metal. And death. I can feel it pass under me. Tyres on tarmac. American soil. Why will no one hear us? Why won't they stop? Please, if someone finds this, tell my mother and father that I loved them. Tell my little girl that she was my last thought. Tell her —

III

Doctor Margaret Campbell stood before a class of nearly twenty students in a lecture room at the George J. Beto Criminal Justice Center in Huntsville. The center stood on a hill overlooking the death house in the Walls Unit of Huntsville Prison, where George W. Bush had given all of fifteen minutes consideration to the case of each prisoner he had sent for execution there during his time as State Governor.

The Criminal Justice Center was a part of the Sam Houston State University, and another seventeen students were watching Margaret on closed circuit television from a facility called The Woodlands, nearly thirty miles away down the highway towards Houston. Any one of them could hit a remote unit on the bench in front of them and have their picture and voice relayed to the lecturer. She, in turn, could direct the camera towards herself, or towards the screen at the front of the room on which she was at that moment projecting an image of a woman hanging by the neck from the ceiling of a garage.

'When the officer failed to show up for his shift, and they couldn't raise him on the telephone, the desk sergeant sent a couple of patrolmen round to the house to see what was wrong. They knew his wife was away visiting her parents that weekend, and thought maybe he was just sleeping off a night of excess.' Margaret chuckled. 'Well, excess was right, and the sleep was permanent. When they couldn't raise anyone in the house, the patrolmen went round peering in the windows.' She prodded the screen with a pointer. 'And this is what they saw in the garage. What appeared to be a large, heavy woman hanging from a light fitting, her face obscured by long black hair hanging down over it.

'Well, they figured they had probable cause, and they called for the paramedics and broke in. They discovered two things very quickly. The first that the woman was dead, the second that she wasn't a woman. That she was, in fact, their friend and colleague, Jack Thomas Doobey, a three-times decorated police officer with more than twenty-five years service.'

A tiny snigger rippled around the lecture room. Margaret invariably found that her lectures on auto-erotic deaths both amused and fascinated her students. Something to do with the human condition, perhaps tapping into the latent fear that most people have of the dark side of their own sexuality.

'He'd done a pretty good job of turning himself into a woman,' Margaret said. 'As you can see. Good enough to fool his fellow officers, at least until they got right up close.' She segued through several other transparencies as she spoke, including close-ups of Officer Doobey's carefully made-up face, his black wig, the glued-on fuschia-pink fingernails that adorned hairy fingers, the dress, the layers of padding beneath it to give him hips and breasts.

'He had gagged himself.' Red silk over pink lips. 'And tied his hands behind his back.'

'How'd he do that?' a black girl on the front row asked.

'Stand up,' Margaret said.

The girl glanced at her fellow students self-consciously and got reluctantly to her feet.

'Step out in front of the class and clasp your hands in front of you,' Margaret ordered. The girl did as she was told. 'Now bend forward, reaching for the floor, and without unclasping your hands, step through them.' The girl struggled a little to follow the instructions while her classmates laughed. But with only a little difficulty, she managed to do what she had been asked and stood up with her hands now clasped behind her back.

'You see? Easy.'

Another series of transparencies flashed on-screen to reveal how Officer Doobey had rigged up a pulley mechanism to raise and lower the hanging noose through a large hook sunk into the roof.

Margaret elucidated. 'He controlled the pulley with a remote control unit he had adapted from a basic stereo system. So that made-up, dressed up, gagged and tied, he stood on a chair with the noose around his neck and the remote control in his hands behind him. That way he could raise the noose until it was tight around his neck and taking most of his weight, literally choking him. And then at the last moment lower himself back on to the chair.'

The class looked back at her in awed silence, clearly visualising the scenario. Then the face of a dark-haired young man from The Woodlands popped up on the monitor and his voice came across the speaker system. 'But why, Doctor Campbell? I mean, why would he do that?'

Margaret said, 'Good question.' She paused, considering how to phrase her response. 'We are led to understand that by starving oneself of oxygen, one is able to heighten the sexual experience.' She registered the consternation on the faces of her students as they tried to imagine what was remotely sexual about dressing up as a member of the opposite sex and hanging yourself. Margaret smiled. 'But I don't recommend that you try it at home.' Which brought the relief of laughter to the room.

'When I got there,' she went on, 'I was able to determine pretty quickly that Officer Doobey had managed inadvertently to turn the remote control the wrong way around in his hands after setting the pulley in motion, and was unable to lower it again. You can picture the scene. There he is, hanging by the neck, choking on his own weight. The binding on his wrists that is loose when in front of him, is twisted and tight behind him. He has no flexibility of movement with his hands. He is fumbling desperately to turn the remote around to lower himself to safety. And then it slips from his fingers and smashes on the floor and he knows he is going to die. He struggles for a few moments, feet kicking, then gives up and succumbs to the screaming in his ears and the blackness that descends over him bringing, in the end, a very long silence.'

A silence filled the lecture room as these green freshmen conjured with images of death they could never have imagined. Images, Margaret knew, with which they would become only too familiar when they graduated into the real and unpleasant world beyond this cloistered academic environment. The hum of the sound system seemed inordinately loud in the silence. Margaret caught a glimpse of herself on the monitor. Pale and freckled, fair hair tumbling carelessly over her shoulders. The CCTV cameras did her no favours. God, she looked old, she thought. Much older than her thirty-four years. Perhaps all those images of death she had had to deal with herself over the years had etched themselves into her face. What was it they called it . . . character?

A young man with close-cropped blond hair at the back of the room asked, 'How could you know that for sure? Couldn't someone have set it up just to look that way, and really it was murder?'

'Yes, Mark, that's possible,' Margaret said. 'But I was able to rule that out pretty much straight off.'

'How?'

'Because Officer Doobey not only liked hanging himself, he also liked watching himself do it. He had set up a camera, and the whole drama was there on video tape. *Death By Hanging* – at a cinema near you.' Margaret grinned ruefully. 'It would make life a lot easier if all my cases were available on video.' She closed the folder on her desk. 'That's all for today, guys.'

In the corridor outside, the babble of excited student voices had already receded as they headed out for coffee, and no doubt a few cigarettes. Margaret never ceased to be amazed at how many young people were smoking now. A whole generation had given up, but the kids apparently didn't care about the health issues. It made Margaret think of her time in China where everyone, it seemed, smoked. Everywhere. But even the most fleeting thought of the Middle Kingdom, even after a year, touched raw nerves, and she immediately turned away from it. She pulled her leather jacket on under the turned-up collar of her blouse and stooped to take a mouthful of water from a stainless steel drinking fountain below a wall-mounted display case filled with the badges and stars of innumerable law agencies.

'Ma'am? Can I have a word?'

She looked up and saw the boy with the cropped head of fair hair from the back of her class. He was grinning shyly, clutching his satchel to his chest, and her heart sank. He always managed to find something he could ask her about after class.

She stood up and thrust both hands in the pockets of her jeans. 'Mark, I've told you before – it's Doctor, or Margaret. Ma'am makes me sound like a . . . well, like a schoolmarm.' And she immediately saw the irony in that. Because here she was, a teacher being cornered after class by a pupil with a crush on her. She smiled. 'Just call me Margaret.'

But Mark clearly wasn't comfortable with that. 'I've been thinking a lot, Doctor Campbell, you know, after your classes and all, about what it is I really want to do.'

Margaret grinned and set off along the corridor. He loped after her. 'And today you finally figured it out,' she said.

He frowned. 'What?'

'Auto-eroticism. Cross-dressing and oxygen starvation.'

He blushed to the roots of his hair. 'No . . . I . . . I . . . didn't mean . . .' he stuttered. 'I mean, what I meant was . . . I think I'd like to be a pathologist.' And he added, unnecessarily, 'You know, like you.'

They had reached the entrance hall, lights reflecting off red tile floors, flags representing all the foreign students at the college hanging limply above the stairwell. Margaret was losing patience. She turned on the young man, white sneakers squeaking on the glazed tiles. 'If you want to be a pathologist, Mark, you should be at med school. But, frankly, I'm not sure you'd have what it takes.' His face fell. But Margaret was unrelenting. 'And, Mark . . . go chase someone your own age.' She turned and hurried out past a photo portrait of the kindly looking silver-haired man after whom the college had been named. In the car park she paused for a moment, filled with regret. George J. Beto, she was sure, would not have spoken to a student like that. But Margaret had a propensity for harsh words. It was only too easy to hurt others when you were still hurting yourself.

Margaret's house was on Avenue O at the top of the hill, a spit away from the university campus. It was built of red brick, like the college, and had a grey tile roof. Sprawling on one level, it was set in a lush green garden, screened from the road by trees. It had made sense at the time to take on the rental. The plan had been to settle for a quiet life of academic seclusion. Then, after only three months, the job in Harris County had fallen vacant. Chief Medical Examiner of the third largest county in the United States, taking in Houston, the fourth largest city. She had thought long and hard about it, and the Dean had been very supportive, even encouraged her. She could always, he said, guest-lecture one morning a week.

He had grinned and in his clipped New York accent told her it would be quite a feather in his cap to have the CME of Harris County lecturing at his college. She never knew how much influence the Dean had had with the appointees, but one of them had told her later that the job had been hers from the moment she applied.

Margaret checked her watch as she drove up Seventeenth Street. There was just enough time to shower and change before heading back to her office in Houston, a good fifty minutes' drive if the traffic on the freeway was moving smoothly. But her spirits dipped as she drew her Chevy in behind a bright red pick-up with oversized wheels parked outside her house. Her landlord was standing on the porch with his arms folded across his chest. A young man in overalls and a baseball cap crouched at the open front door, a bag of tools on the stoop beside him.

Margaret slammed the door of her car and strode up the path. 'What do you think you're doing, McKinley?'

The young man looked alarmed and got quickly to his feet. But McKinley stood his ground defiantly. He was a redneck with money. Owned several of the houses on the hill. 'That ain't ver' ladylike kinda language now,' he drawled unpleasantly.

Margaret glared at him. He was a walking, talking cliché. Wrangler jeans, cowboy boots, a checked shirt and a scuffed white Stetson pushed back on his head. 'You didn't answer my question,' she said.

The younger man glanced from one to the other. 'Maybe I should go.' He stooped to pick up his bag. Chisels and screwdrivers rattled inside it.

McKinley put out a hand to stop him. 'You stay where you are, sonny.' And to Margaret, 'You changed the goddamn locks, lady.'

Margaret turned to the carpenter. 'You want to know why?' He looked like he'd rather eat his baseball cap. But she was going to tell him anyway. 'Because when I was out he was going into my house and going through my stuff. Left his big oily fingermarks on the bras and panties in my underwear drawer.'

McKinley's face reddened. 'Now that ain't true. You got no cause goin' sayin' stuff like that.'

The carpenter was examining his feet now with great interest.

'You want to see the proof?' Margaret asked McKinley. 'Two hours of video footage from the camera I hid in the closet?'

It was a bluff, but it proved to be a winning hand. McKinley paled. Then his mouth tightened. 'You changed the goddamn locks, lady. And that's a contravention, plain and simple, of the terms of your lease. I want you outta here.'

Margaret's cellphone rang and she fumbled in her purse to find it. 'What,' she barked into it.

'Been trying to get you for the last hour.' It was Lucy, her secretary, a God-fearing middle-aged Presbyterian lady who disapproved of Margaret.

'I always turn off the cellphone when I'm lecturing, Lucy. You know that,' Margaret said. 'Why didn't you try the college?'

'I did. And missed you.' She heard Lucy sigh at the other end. 'Doctor Campbell, we got a call from the sheriff's office in Walker County up there. They need your help out at a Tex-Mex eatery on Highway 45. Seems they got a truck full of ninety-some dead people.'

'Jesus,' Margaret said, and she could almost feel Lucy's disapproval all the way down the line from Houston. 'I'm on my way.' She hung up and pushed past McKinley into the house. She always kept an emergency flight case at home packed with all the tools and accoutrements of her profession.

'I mean it,' McKinley shouted after her. 'I want you outta here.'

'Tell it to my lawyer,' Margaret said and shut the door in his face.

IV

Margaret drove north-west on Interstate 45, past the Wynne and Holliday Units of the Huntsville prison complex, the tiny municipal airport that sat up on the right, the spur that took off west to Harper Cemetery. She passed several billboards advertising positions as Correctional Officers for the Texas Department of Criminal Justice. In Huntsville you either worked for the prison or the university. The warm October sun bleached all colour out of the sky and she could see the cluster of blue and red flashing lights in the distance identifying where the truck had been found. Strictly speaking, this was out of Margaret's jurisdiction. But the Walker County Coroner simply wasn't equipped to cope with something like this. Which was why the sheriff had called her office.

She turned on to the 190 and took a left on the access road to the Mexican diner. Three crows stood on a white picket fence gazing curiously across the scrub towards the parking lot where police officers moved, antlike, around its taped-off perimeter. More than a dozen vehicles choked the entrance to the lot and Margaret recognised a Pontiac driven by one of her investigators, and a couple of white forensics trucks. The centre of all the activity was a huge refrigerated container, the door on the driver's side of its tractor unit still lying open, just as Jayjay had found it. The Walker County Sheriff crossed the crumbling asphalt to greet her. He was a big man in his late fifties, with a grey suit and a white Stetson. His badge was pinned to a breast pocket from which poked a red and yellow re-election flyer. His big hand enveloped hers and crushed it.

'Ma'am, thanks for coming,' he said, and Margaret remembered her cruel words to her young student. The sheriff looked grim. 'We got a shit load of trouble here.'

Another man had followed him over. A year or two younger, perhaps. In his middle fifties. He had grey receding hair, neatly cut and thinning on top, and a world-weary face. He was medium height and chunkily built, spreading at the waist. 'Thank you, Sheriff,' he said. Clearly a dismissal. 'You guys are doing a great job here.' The sheriff nodded to Margaret and moved away, and the other man turned to her. 'You the ME?'

Margaret held out her hand and said coolly, 'Doctor Margaret Campbell.'

'Agent Michael Hrycyk.' He pronounced it *Rychick*. His palm was clammy hot. He flipped open a leather wallet to reveal his badge. 'INS.'

Margaret frowned. 'What interest does Immigration have in this?'

'You mean apart from the fact there's ninety-eight dead Chinese in there?' He flicked his thumb over his shoulder in the direction of the truck.

Margaret's stomach flipped over. 'Chinese?'

'Well, Asian. But probably Chinese. Almost certainly illegal. Which'll make 'em ours.'

'It won't make them anybody's, except mine, if they're dead.'

'You know what I mean.' He took out a pack of cigarettes.

'Don't light that here,' Margaret said. 'This is a crime scene.'

'I doubt it,' he said.

In the distance Margaret saw the first of the TV trucks arriving. It hadn't taken long. Ninety-eight dead Chinese in the back of a truck — the local stations would make a killing selling it to the networks. 'Why?' she asked.

He took her arm and started walking her towards the truck. 'There are anything up to a hundred thousand Chinese EWIs arriving in the States every year,' he said. 'Most of them nowadays coming across the border from Mexico.'

'EWI?' She removed her arm from his grip.

'Entry Without Inspection. An EWI's what we call an illegal immigrant. And in this case, an OTM as well.' He grinned a humourless grin. 'That's Other Than Mexican.'

'You have some interesting terminology,' Margaret observed dryly.

'Oh, it gets a whole lot more interesting than that, Doc. We used to call the Mexicans *Wetbacks* 'cos they always came dripping out the Rio Grande. But that ain't politically correct no more. Except it's what the Mexicans call themselves. *Mojados*. And I don't see no reason to call them anything they don't call themselves. Except maybe *spics*.'

Margaret glanced at him with dislike. 'And your point is?'

Hrycyk didn't like her tone and bristled. 'My point is, Doctor Campbell, these illegal Chinese are worth big money. Up to sixty grand a head these days. Which by my crude reckoning means that there's nearly six million dollars worth of dead meat in that container. And no one in their right mind is going to waste six million bucks.'

At the back of the truck a bunch of police officers was standing about watching two forensic investigators moving around inside the container. The investigators were wearing protective white, zippered, Tivek suits with built-in booties and hoods. Their faces were covered with surgical masks and they wore latex gloves. A photographer, similarly clad, was photographing the horror with a business-like detachment, alternating between video and stills. His lights illuminated a ghastly scene, and as the heat increased so the smell grew riper.

Hrycyk was unaffected. He said, 'Way I see it? The truck probably came up the 77 from Brownsville, or maybe the 281, or even the 59 from Laredo. They're the standard routes.'

'Headed where?'

'Houston.'

Margaret frowned. 'But we're sixty miles north of Houston here.'

Hrycyk shrugged. 'So they took a detour to avoid spot checks on the highway. But Houston's where they were headed.'

'Why? What is there in Houston for illegal Chinese immigrants?'

'A population of three hundred thousand Chinese for a start. The fourth biggest Chinatown in the country.'

'I had no idea,' Margaret said.

'Most people don't. The Chinese like to keep themselves to themselves. They built a new Chinatown down in the south-west of the city, and hardly ever leave it.' He began to take out his cigarettes again, then caught Margaret's eye and slipped them back in his pocket. 'Houston also has the third largest community of consuls in the US. Seventy at the last count. And that means papers – proof of identity, country of origin. You got papers you're halfway to becoming a legal resident. There's big business in papers.' He scratched his chin thoughtfully. 'Course, most of 'em don't stay. New York's the final destination. The *Jinshan*, the Mountain of Gold they're all looking for. But in the meantime, they'll hide out in safe houses and work sixteen, seventeen hours a day in sweatshops and restaurants and whorehouses to pay off the money they owe the *shetou*.'

'Shir-toe?' Margaret repeated the Mandarin word with the familiarity of someone who has spent time in Beijing.

'Snakeheads. People smugglers. The fixers who arrange everything: transport, safe houses, papers. Usually Chinese. Mean bastards.'

'So if these people in the truck really are illegal immigrants they would still have owed their smuggling fees to their snakeheads?'

'Hey, now you're catching on, Doc.' Hrycyk's smile was patronising. 'Their families back home in China will have paid a small deposit. Once they're here, they have to pay off the rest themselves. A precious cargo. So there ain't no motive for killing 'em.' He flicked his head towards the truck. 'Way I see it? Someone shut the air vent in the refrigerated unit by accident, or maybe forgot to open it. The driver stops here in the middle of the night to let them out for a piss and finds them all dead. Suffocated. He panics, takes off.' He chuckled. 'Saving the INS a whole lot of trouble in the process.'

'I'm sure their families will be gratified to hear that,' Margaret said coldly. The prospect of having to process ninety-eight bodies was bad enough without having to deal with a racist immigration officer as well.

Hrycyk bridled. 'Hey! Don't go feeling sorry for these little runts. They bring a lot of crime into this country. Carry in drugs to help pay off their fees, get involved in illegal gambling and prostitution. When they get caught they claim political asylum, get given C-8 immigration cards so they can be legally employed, then disappear again when the court throws out their case.' He stopped for just a moment to draw breath. 'Far as I'm concerned, the only good Chinese is a dead Chinese.'

'Well, as far as I am concerned, Agent Hrycyk,' Margaret said firmly, 'these poor people are entitled, like anyone else, to my full and undivided professional attention in determining how and why they died — regardless of race, creed, colour or nationality.'

There were now three TV trucks queuing up on the 190 at the end of the access road, and at least half a dozen other press vehicles drawn in behind. A group of journalists was standing debating rights of access with two of the sheriff's men where the crows had earlier sat on the white picket fence. The crows were gone. The vultures had arrived.

'Margaret . . .' One of the forensic investigators was standing in the doorway of the container. 'Stuff up here you might want to take a look at.'

'Give me two minutes,' Margaret said. She ran back to her car, opened the trunk, slipped off her jacket and shoes and pulled on a Tivek body suit, zipping it up and dragging the hood over her head before snapping on her face mask and gloves. Then she walked back to the truck, clumsy in her booties, carrying a small bag of tools. The investigator gave her a hand up and she stood unsteadily for a moment surveying the scene in front of her. A monstrous heap of arms and legs and bleak, dead faces crammed into the back half of the container. There was something infinitely sad in those pale, frail Chinese figures whose American dream had come to such an abrupt end. The investigator handed her what looked like a small notebook in a plastic evidence bag. Margaret took it out and thumbed carefully through it. Its pages were covered with a frantic scrawl of indecipherable Chinese characters.

'Found it lying on the chest of one of the bodies,' the investigator said. 'Pencil was still in his hand.'

'What is it?' Hrycyk called from below, craning to see what she was holding. He was clearly frustrated not to be closer to the action.

'It's a notebook.'

'Anything in it?'

'Sure.'

'Well, what? What does it say?' His patience was wearing thin.

'I don't know about you,' Margaret said caustically, 'but my Chinese isn't that good.'

Hrycyk cursed. 'Well, at least the Chinese guy they're gonna send from Washington might come in useful for something, then.'

'What Chinese guy?' Margaret asked, a sudden thickening in her throat.

'The Criminal Justice Liaison at the Chinese Embassy. This whole thing's already going political.'

She turned away, anxious that Hrycyk should have no sense of her distress. To him the Criminal Justice Liaison at the Chinese Embassy in Washington was just another Chinese. She knew him better as Li Yan, Deputy Section Chief, Section One of the Criminal Investigation Department of Beijing Municipal Police. A man whose intimate touch she knew only too well. A touch that pained her now to remember. She moved into the back of the truck, more ready to face the horrors it contained than the feelings she had spent a year trying to sublimate, feelings of love and betrayal turning slowly to anger and maybe more. 'Where's the body you took this from?' she asked the investigator brittlely.

They picked their way through two dozen corpses, men and women who had clawed in despair at the walls of the container, even at their own clothing. It was a pitiful sight. A man in jeans and sneakers was half propped against the left side wall. He had shreds of thinning hair brushed back from an unusually dark face, a sparse moustache barely covering his upper lip. Margaret noticed the nicotine stains on the fingers that still held the pencil with which he had scrawled his last desperate words.

V

Wang's Diary
I first saw Cheng that night in Fujian when they took us offshore in the small boat to board the cargo ship waiting in international waters. She sat at the back of the boat clutching a brown bag, looking very small and vulnerable. She made me feel like such a fraud. This was real for her. This was her life. Full of danger and uncertainty. I know that many of these people make this journey not for themselves, but for their families, for the money they can send home from the Mountain of Gold. I thought of her, even then, as my *yazi*, my little duck. I know it is the term they use for illegal immigrants, and never did it seem more appropriate than when I thought of poor little Cheng. I decided, then, that I would do my best to protect her on this long, hard trip. If I had known how powerless I would be to save her from the rapes and

the beatings I would have taken her off the boat that night and sacrificed this whole venture. All I have been able to offer her since is comfort. I do not know if she knows that I have fallen in love with her. She does not, I think, love me. I am twice her age. She likes and trusts me, perhaps like a daughter trusts a father. I know that when we reach *Meiguo* I will lose her. I wish I had never made this journey.

VI

Li Yan freewheeled down the hill past dark stone mansions lurking in dappled shadow behind gnarled old trees. They had strange, Scottish-sounding names like Dumbarton House and Anderson House, painted placards on wrought-iron gates. He left Georgetown's grid of tree-lined narrow streets behind him and swung his bicycle towards the bridge over Rock Creek. Sheridan Circle was thick with traffic, and he turned uphill into a maze of residental streets that took him over the rise and down again towards Connecticut Avenue.

The Embassy had taken over the old Windsor Hotel, two seven-storey blocks set at right-angles, backing on to another loop in the erratic meanderings of the slick that was Rock Creek, almost due north from where its mean little mouth oozed into the slow-moving body of the Potomac. Only a ten-minute cycle from the White House.

They had offered him a car, and he had declined it. He had spent all his adult life cycling between the offices of Section

One in the Dongzhimen district of Beijing and the police apartment he had shared with his uncle in the old embassy quarter,
not far from Tiananmen. An hour's cycle. By comparison, the
twenty minutes from his townhouse in Georgetown was easy,
although it had taken him time to get used to the gradients.
Besides, he knew he needed that regular daily exercise to get
the blood flowing through his veins, carrying oxygen to his
brain, sharpening his senses — and to counter the effects of
the thirty cigarettes a day he had been smoking until very
recently.

His neighbours had got used to seeing him this past year,
pedal-pushing up O Street in all weathers, turning north and
disappearing towards the cemeteries at the top of the hill,
sweat streaming in rivulets down his strong-boned face in
the summer heat, dragon breath billowing about his head in
the winter frost. Today, as he drifted down to Connecticut off
Kalorama Heights, he was in shirt sleeves and slacks, the warm
fall air flowing past his cheeks like soft silk, gently raking the
fine, square-cut bristle of black hair that covered his scalp.
There was the threat of rain in a changing sky, and he carried
a waterproof cape in his satchel. It had been, nominally, his
day off, and he had made plans for that afternoon. Until the
call on his cellphone, and the crisp summons to the Embassy.
A matter not to be discussed on the telephone.

He took long, loping strides across the red-carpeted expanse
of what had once been the lobby of the Windsor, and climbed
the staircase two at a time. The First Secretary was waiting
for him in a spacious office on the second floor, windows

opening out on to the small circle of tree-shaded green below. He dropped an airline ticket on his desk, slanting sunlight burning out across its polished surface, and said, 'You haven't been to Houston before, have you, Li?'

Li felt a stab of apprehension. 'No, First Secretary.'

'Your flight is first thing tomorrow. The Ambassador himself will brief you this evening.'

'What's happened?'

'Nearly one hundred *renshe* found dead in the back of a truck by the local police. Given all our promises to try and stamp out the flow of illegals from China, Beijing is acutely embarrassed. A severe loss of *mianzi*. Yours will be an exercise in damage limitation.'

For a moment, all that Li could think of was that there was a chance he might have to face Margaret. And he had a distinct sense of foreboding.

From the stand-alone redbrick block of the Joseph A. Jachimczyk Forensic Center for Harris County, on the corner of William C. Harvin Boulevard and Old Spanish Trail, Margaret gazed out of her office window towards medicine city and tried to push thoughts of Li from her mind. She focused instead on the spectacular skyline of shining glass tower blocks and skyscrapers in the heart of Houston, a city within a city. The Texas Medical Center. Forty-two medical institutions serving five million patients a year in a hundred buildings spread over seven hundred acres and twelve miles of road. With an annual operating budget of more than four billion dollars and research grants of more than two billion, medicine city employed fifty thousand people, attracted ten thousand volunteers and one hundred thousand students. Like everything else in Texas it had ambitions to be the biggest and the best. And probably was. Although not quite big enough to displace Li entirely from her mind.

Margaret's little empire was on the southern fringes of this medical metropolis, in parking lot territory. On quiet days she could gaze from her window at the shuttle buses that took employees back into the heart of the city from the acres of parking lot that surrounded her building. But this was not a quiet day. And it was not about to get any quieter. Lucy buzzed through from the outer office. 'That's them now, Doctor Campbell.'

'Thank you, Lucy, show them in.'

FBI Agent Sam Fuller was younger than she had expected, about her own age. He was quite good-looking in a bland, inoffensive sort of way. Well-defined features, a good strong jaw, soft brown eyes that met hers very directly, a fine, full head of hair. His handshake was firm and dry.

'This is Major Steve Cardiff,' he said, turning to the young man in the dark blue uniform who stood beside him, peaked hat lodged firmly under his left arm. Margaret looked at him for the first time. He was younger than she was. Thirty, perhaps. He was broad-built with a square head, dark hair cropped to air force regulation length, and he had a slightly pockmarked complexion, as if he might have suffered acne as a teenager. She realised with a tiny stab that he looked very much like Li Yan, or at least a Western version of him. It brought a lot of conflicting emotions bubbling to the surface, and she had to work hard to keep them from showing.

'How do you do?' She shook his hand. It was cool and strong.

He grinned, and his orange-flecked green eyes sparkled. 'Just call me Steve,' he said. 'Even my ex-wife does. Though she usually prefaces it with *you bastard.*' And in spite of all her tension, Margaret found herself smiling.

But Agent Fuller wasn't playing the game. He remained studiously serious. 'You probably know, Doctor Campbell, that the Bureau has a Memorandum of Understanding with the Armed Forces Institute of Pathology. Effectively, they are our pathologists. We call them in when we need expert advice. Major Cardiff here is from the Office of the Armed Forces Medical Examiner, part of the AFIP set-up. He'll be leading the pathology team on this case.'

Margaret's smile faded. Nobody liked the FBI. They took everything and gave nothing. Besides which, they were the organisation that investigated irregularities in all the other agencies. So they were born to be unpopular. 'Well,' she said, more calmly than she felt, 'I appreciate the offer of help, gentlemen, but we are quite able to cope on our own, thank you.' Which was a lie. She had just spent the two hours after lunch phoning around the pathology departments in medicine city trying to round up a team capable of coping with ninety-eight autopsies. But she wasn't going to have the FBI walk in and trample all over her.

'I don't think you understand, Doctor Campbell,' Fuller

said evenly. 'Washington is anxious that we deal with this as quickly and efficiently as possible.' He paused. 'We're not offering you our help. We're taking over the case.'

'Well, I have news for you, Agent Fuller.' Margaret placed her fingertips at full stretch on the desk in front of her to keep herself steady. 'This is not Washington DC. This is the Lone Star State. And in Harris County I have absolute jurisdiction over the bodies in my care.'

'The bodies were found in Walker County. You have no jurisdiction there.'

'The bodies are now in Harris County, at Ellington Air Force Base, where I had them moved just over an hour ago. They're mine.'

Steve raised a finger, like a schoolboy in class. 'Excuse me.' They both turned to look at him. 'I don't mean to get involved in the argument, but these are people we're talking about here, right? They don't belong to anyone – except maybe the relatives who might want to give them a half-decent burial.'

Margaret blushed immediately. Of course, he was right. They were fighting over these bodies like vultures at a feeding frenzy. But the FBI man was not about to be deflected.

'How the hell did you manage to move ninety-eight bodies in . . .' he checked his watch, '. . . just over four hours?'

Margaret said, 'Quite easily, actually. I figured it was going to take most of the day to get a fleet of refrigerated semi-trailers kitted out and sent up there. Never mind the time it would take to then label and bag the bodies. So I got the local police to rent a single tractor unit. We hooked the trailer up to that and took it straight down to Ellington Field with the bodies still on board.'

Steve waved his finger at her now and grinned. 'Hey, that was smart thinking, Doctor.' Fuller glared at him.

Margaret said, 'My office has an MOU with NASA, for the rental of one of their hangars down there in the event of a major disaster, like an aircrash. It was my view that this fell into that category. And we have a company here in Houston, Kenyon International, that specialises in providing sophisti- cated facilities for conducting mass autopsies anywhere in the world. I have already engaged their services. They are setting up in the NASA hangar as we speak.'

'Fine,' Fuller said tightly. 'You've done a good job, Doctor Campbell. But we'll take it from here.'

'I don't think so,' Margaret said. And with an apologetic glance at Steve, 'You want to challenge my jurisdiction in the courts, that's okay by me. But by the time you get a ruling it's going to be a whole helluva lot harder for us to tell how these poor folk died.'

'Hey listen, folks,' Steve said. 'Jurisdiction's a big word, right? I always had trouble with big words. That's why I got a Webster's Encyclopaedic Dictionary. But since I don't happen to have it on me — it won't exactly fit in my coat pocket — why don't we agree to put our interpretation on hold until we have a chance to consult it. I mean, how can we worry about whose jurisdiction it is when we don't even know what it means?' Margaret and Fuller looked at him as though he were insane. He grinned. 'That way we just pool our resources and get on with the job.' He raised his eyebrows, still smiling. 'What do you say?'

Margaret realised Steve was offering a compromise — a way out of the impasse that saved face on both sides. *Mianzi.* How very Chinese of him, she thought. She glanced at Fuller and could see that he was still undecided.

Steve said, 'Sam, you wheel in your fingerprint go-team. I'll fly down a couple of investigators and some of my pathologists and put them at Margaret's disposal — you don't mind if I call you Margaret, do you?' Margaret thought, how could she mind? But he didn't give her the chance to respond. 'Now, you can't tell me you haven't been having problems getting enough knife-jockeys for the job?'

She couldn't resist his smile. 'I'll be happy to accept your offer of help, Major.'

'Steve.' He beamed, and turned to Fuller. 'Sam?'

Fuller nodded reluctantly.

'Good.' Steve pulled on his hat, then pulled it off again quickly. 'Aw shit, sorry. Not supposed to put it on till I get outside.' He waggled his eyebrows again. 'Regulations. Always forget. You got a phone I can use?'

CHAPTER TWO

I

Ellington Field was a vast expanse of grass and tarmac south-east of Houston, on the road to Galveston. It was where Air Force One would land the President when he came to the city, and where the Governor would fly in and out on official trips to Washington. The National Aeronautics and Space Administration also maintained a substantial presence on the base with a huge white hangar near one of the main runways. It had three enormous air-conditioning units supported on scaffolding along either side, and vast doors that slid shut, to make it an ideal staging area for handling mass casualties and multiple autopsies. It was 8 a.m., and a dozen pathologists were about to start post-mortem examinations of the bodies of the ninety-eight Chinese immigrants just over twenty-four hours after Deputy J. J. Jackson had found them on Highway 45.

Six refrigerated semi-trailer rentals stood in a row on the tarmac outside the hangar doors. Four of them had sixteen bodies stacked inside on a double tier of makeshift plywood staging. The other two contained seventeen. Two teams of two from the Office of the Armed Forces Medical Examiner had worked late into the night removing the bodies from the container that had been brought down from Huntsville. Each body had been assigned a number, marked in black on a six-inch yellow plastic placard placed next to it, then individually and collectively photographed. They had been examined for gross injuries or blood and assessed for rigor mortis. Core body temperatures had been taken by making tiny incisions in the upper right abdomen and inserting a chef's type thermometer into the livers. Finally, each foot had been tagged with the same number as the yellow placard, then zippered into a white body bag, with the corresponding number tied on to the zipper's pull tag. Stacked in rows in the refrigerated semi-trailers, they now awaited the full process of US autopsy procedure. It was not the America these Chinese migrants had dreamed of.

Margaret walked briskly through the hangar, blinking in the fierce glare of the 500-watt halogen floodlamps that illuminated the nearly twenty stations that had been set up along one side. Plastic sheeting stretched across tubular frames formed partitions between them. Twelve of the stations were purely for autopsy. Mobile tables had been wheeled into each, plastic buckets hanging below drainers to catch body fluids. Other stations were dedicated to ancillary procedures like the collection and review of personal effects, fingerprinting, dental examination, total body x-ray. Opposite the stations, tables had been set up with computers for recording their findings. Each table was manned by at least three assistants, two of whom were earmarked to help with the work in the station. The sounds of voices and the hum of computers echoed around the vast corrugated space.

It always struck Margaret as ironic that it took so much time, money and effort simply to record the passing of life. The human obsession with death. Perhaps, she thought, we imagined that by examining it in all its guises we might one day find a way of defeating it.

'Doctor Campbell, good morning.' Steve stepped across to greet her from the station he had been allocated. 'Fine day for wielding the knife.' He waved an arm around the hangar. 'Spectacular set-up you have here.'

'I think I gave you permission to call me Margaret,' Margaret said.

Steve's eyebrows, behind the anonymity of his surgical mask, were still animated. 'So you did. I was just being polite – in case you'd forgotten.'

They cut bizarre figures in this NASA hangar in their green surgical gowns and plastic aprons, shower caps, masks and goggles.

'Are we about ready yet?' he asked.

'First bodies are coming through the line now.'

Steve's grin stretched his mask across his face. 'See you at lunch, then.' And he headed back to his autopsy station.

In spite of the face she had put on for Steve, Margaret was filled with apprehension. There was an encounter today she could not avoid, a confrontation with the man she wished she could hate, but knew she still loved. She turned towards autopsy station number one and felt her hackles rise at the sight of Hrycyk standing by the table waiting for her. He wore a surgical gown over tee-shirt, jeans and trainers, and looked ridiculous with a green plastic shower cap pulled down on his head.

He glanced at his gown. 'Came prepared,' he said. A body bag was wheeled past on a gurney destined for autopsy further down the line. He grinned. 'I guess that's what you'd call a Chinese take-out.'

Margaret walked briskly into her station. 'You're a very sick man, Agent Hrycyk.'

He was quite unabashed. 'So I've been told.'

Margaret spread out a cloth of gleaming knives on a stainless steel side table, and lifted the French chef's knife that she used as her main cutting tool. 'I'll look forward to opening you up one day to find out why,' she said.

II

Li was met by Fuller at Houston Hobby airport. It was the first time he had met the FBI agent, although they had spoken on the telephone. And it was his first time in Texas, although he had been in the United States for almost a year. They shook hands warmly on the concourse and Fuller took him out to the short-term car park where he had left his Chrysler Jeep.

'Li Yan,' he said, as if trying out the name for size. 'I hear you guys have your family name come first.'

'That's right,' Li said.

'So that would make you, uh, Mr Li, or Agent Li, or whatever?'

'Just plain "Li" is fine.'

'Uh, okay. But if I was to call you by your first name it would be Yan, right?'

'If you wished to be familiar,' Li said, 'you would call me Li Yan.'

'Oh. Right.' Fuller glanced at him. 'Your English is pretty good.'

Li had lost count of the number of times he had been told this, as if it was an extraordinary thing that a Chinese could speak English as well as an American. But it was his job to foster good relations between US and Chinese law enforcement agencies, and so he was always polite. 'I was taught by my uncle from an early age,' he said. 'And then I spent time in Hong Kong with the British police before the handover. I also spent some time in Chicago where I learned some interesting new vocabulary.'

'Like what?' Fuller asked.

'Like "motherfucker", and "shithead".'

'Hey!' Fuller laughed. 'You almost sound like a native.'

Li had learned long ago that it amused people when you could swear in their language.

Fuller negotiated a network of roads leading through a forest of advertising hoardings out on to Highway 45, where they turned south for the short trip to Ellington Field. 'So . . .' he said. 'Criminal justice liaison. What kind of job is that exactly?'

'Just what it sounds like,' Li said. 'I provide a bridge between the criminal justice organisations of both our countries. And I make myself available to help in any investigations that your people have on-going that may have Chinese involvement. Drugs, people-smuggling, computer fraud, that sort of thing.'

'I guess,' Fuller said, 'you probably have your hands full just trying to keep track of the number of law enforcement agencies we have here in the US.'

Li allowed himself a tiny smile. 'When I bring senior Chinese police officers to the United States to meet with senior American police officers, the Chinese are outnumbered around ten to one. My people cannot understand why you need so many agencies: the Justice Department, the FBI, the INS, the DEA, the Secret Service, the NSA . . . When your people come to my country it is a one-stop shop.'

Fuller laughed. 'I like your sense of humour, Li.'

Li said, straight-faced, 'I did not know I was being funny.' Although he did. But now Fuller wasn't quite sure. So he changed the subject.

'You know about what's going down here in Houston?'

'Ninety-eight dead Chinese found in a truck. Almost certainly *renshe*, illegal immigrants. Autopsies begin today.'

'Ren . . . what? What d'you call them?'

'*Renshe*. Human snakes. It is the name we give to smuggled Chinese, because of their ability to wriggle past tight border controls.'

The FBI man nodded. 'Right.' He paused. 'The thing is, Li, this is starting to get embarrassing.' Fuller flicked a wary glance in Li's direction. 'Now it's not my job to get into the politics of all this, but folks in Washington are unhappy at the number of incidents where Chinese illegals — *renshe* — are turning up dead on boats in American waters and trucks on American soil. It's been on the increase since all those people died when the Golden Venture ran aground off New York nearly ten years ago. Your people were supposed to be doing something about it. But the numbers just keep going up and up.'

'There has been a huge campaign against illegal immigration in China,' Li said, without any hint of defensiveness. 'As soon as we arrest the little snakeheads, others take their place. It is the big snakeheads, the ones who finance the traffic, that we need to catch. Like Big Sister Ping in New York. You cannot kill the snake without first cutting off its head.'

'And how do you propose we do that?'

'Most of the Chinese immigrants now come in from Mexico,' Li said. 'Houston is the hub. From here they fan out all over the rest of the country. Since we cut off the supply of money from New York, it might be fair to assume that the operation is now being financed out of here.'

'That's quite an assumption.'

'It is somewhere to start,' Li said.

The roads on either side of the freeway were thick with hoardings raised on single stalks advertising everything from adult movies and massage parlours to used cars and ice-cream. Tiny flags fluttered in great profusion over sprawling used car lots, and enterprising people sold hardware out of what looked like wooden shacks. They turned east off the freeway and the rising sun shone straight in their eyes. Fuller flicked down his visor and snapped on a pair of sleek wraparound sun-glasses that gave him a slightly sinister air. He turned and grinned at Li. 'Almost mandatory now for any self-respecting FBI agent. Kind of inscrutable, huh?' And then he remembered that's how they always described the Chinese. 'Uh, no offence,' he added quickly.

Li smiled to himself. 'None taken.'

'Just about there,' Fuller said. The road took them through small clusters of single-storey housing, past green watered lawns and stands of shady trees. On their left Pete's BBQ House advertised boiled crawfish as its speciality. 'You'll meet INS Agent Hrycyk. He's an ass, but unfortunately we're going to have to work with him. He, uh . . .' Fuller glanced nervously again in Li's direction, '. . . he doesn't much like Chinese.'

Li shrugged, 'I have been here long enough, Agent Fuller, to know that a lot of people don't much like Chinese.'

Fuller nodded, embarrassed, glad that he could hide behind the shades. 'You'll also meet the Chief Medical Examiner. Attractive enough, but I don't figure any of us are going to like her much. She's a real hard case. Doctor Margaret Campbell.'

Li felt as if he had just left his insides somewhere back on the road, and his heart was beating so hard he was sure Fuller must be able to hear it. But apart from a slight colouring of his high, wide cheekbones, not a trace of it showed on his face.

III

In spite of the air-con, Margaret was perspiring under the heat of the halogen lamps. The body lying face down on the table in front of her was a pale jaundice colour, almost hairless. She was working her way through the external examination, shouting out brief sporadic observations for the assistant at the table to tap into the computer. She would write a full report later and fill out the avalanche of paperwork that would have to go with it.

The knuckles of the subject were severely bruised where, she assumed, frantic attempts had been made to break out of the container. Several of the fingernails were torn and had bled. Dried blood was clotted around the nail beds, and there were smears of blood on the notebook and pencil that had been found with the body. She had identified petechial haemorrhaging around the eyes and in the mouth. She expected to find the same on the surfaces of some of the chest organs. Fingertips, toes and lips were tinged with blue.

'So what does it all mean?' Hrycyk asked. He had been watching the process carefully and listening to every word. 'Petechial haemorrhaging . . . what is that?'

'Pinpoint haemorrhages where tiny blood vessels have burst,' Margaret said. She sighed. 'On the face of it, it looks like you might have been right, Agent. The haemorrhaging, along with the blue tinging on the fingers, toes and lips, are all consistent with suffocation. But I'm not about to commit myself just yet.'

'You don't have to,' Hrycyk said. 'I already examined the air intake on the container.'

'So did I.'

He looked faintly surprised. 'So you'll know it was closed?'

'I know it was closed when I examined it.'

'Jesus, you people *never* want to commit, do you?'

'Oh, I'll commit alright,' Margaret snapped. 'Murder, if you don't get out of my face.'

Margaret then turned her attention to a tiny bruise and pinprick in the semi-lunar fold of the left buttock, on the medial aspect, almost at the point where the left met the right.

Hrycyk's eagle eye was on to it immediately. 'What is it?'

'Looks like an injection site.'

Hrycyk frowned. 'You mean he was taking drugs or something? Injecting himself?'

Margaret tutted her irritation. 'Have you ever tried injecting yourself in the buttock?'

Hrycyk made an effort to picture it. But his imagination came up with a blank. 'Can't say I have.'

'And it's a single puncture mark, so clearly not a regular occurrence. And very recent. Probably within the last twenty-four hours.'

'So what was he injected with?'

'I have no idea. But tox might tell us when we get the results back.'

'How long?'

'Ask Major Cardiff. His people are doing all the toxicology.'

'Doctor Campbell . . .' Fuller's voice separated itself out

from the racket beyond Margaret's autopsy station. Someone, somewhere, was playing rock music very loudly. Some pathologists Margaret knew could only work with music playing, as if somehow the music could drown out the heightened sense of mortality that always seemed to accompany a body on a slab. She turned. Fuller said, 'This is the criminal justice liaison at the Chinese Embassy in Washington.'

Margaret found herself staring at an oddly alien figure standing awkwardly at the entrance to her station, next to a wary-looking Agent Fuller. She had forgotten how Chinese Li looked after a separation. When she had been with him, she never noticed. He was just Li Yan. The man she made love to. The man she talked and laughed and cried with. Now he was a stranger. A tall, strongly built Chinese man with a square-topped crewcut, and big ugly features that she had once grown to love. She had traced every contour of them with her fingers. He wore a simple white cotton shirt that fitted loosely across his broad chest and shoulders, and was tucked into the narrow waistband of dark, pleated slacks. She had forgotten how beautifully clothes hung on the Chinese frame.

They stood, simply staring at each other, for a prodigious amount of time. 'Hello, Li Yan,' she said finally.

'You know each other?' Fuller asked, amazed. Li had given no indication of it.

'Yes,' Li said. And he knew that Fuller was wondering if he had spoken out of turn about her in the car. But he didn't take his eyes off Margaret for a minute. The icy sensation in his chest was almost painful. How often had he seen her like this? Hidden behind the mask and the goggles, almost every inch of her covered by cotton or plastic. Except for the gap between the tops of her gloves and the short-sleeved gown. And he saw the freckles there on pale skin, the down of soft, fair hair. He wanted to touch her so much it hurt.

The momentary spell was broken by the almost brutal way that Margaret turned over the body on the table. 'Mr Li and I met when I assisted the Beijing police during a couple of murder enquiries. He was deputy head of their Serious Crime Squad.' Her voice was cold and controlled. 'I'm glad you're here,' she said. 'Since none of us read Chinese, maybe you can tell us what it was this man was writing in his diary.'

Li looked at the body in front of him for the first time, and it felt for a moment as if the world had stopped turning. He put a hand on the end of the table to steady himself. 'Wang,' he said, his voice almost a whisper.

'You know this guy?' Hrycyk asked, incredulous.

'Wang.' Li's voice cracked as he said the name again. 'Detective Wang Wei Pao. Senior Supervisor, Class Three, Tianjin Municipal Police.' He paused. 'I didn't really know him. I briefed him.'

Margaret saw that Li was affected by this man's death and immediately regretted her callousness. She had spent her life regretting the things she did and said, and the hurt she inflicted on the people she loved.

'So what the hell was a Tianjin cop doing on that truck?' Hrycyk demanded to know, untouched by the moment.

'He was working undercover,' Li said, regaining some degree

of composure. He saw Fuller and Hrycyk exchange glances. 'An operation we mounted more than six months ago. He volunteered for the job, and he was ideal for it. He was born in Fujian Province which is the departure point for most of the illegal immigrants. He spoke the dialect. It was easy for him to make contact with a local snakehead and get the next boat out.' He remembered Wang's enthusiasm. He was fed up with the routine in Tianjin, his marriage had broken down and he'd been looking for something else to fill his life. 'He phoned us whenever he could, under the pretence of phoning home. And he posted several reports, so we were able to follow his progress. But we never knew that it would take so long.' He paused for a moment. 'Or that it would end like this.'

'Wait a minute,' Fuller said. 'Are you telling me you people mounted a unilateral operation here, without keeping us informed?' He looked at Hrycyk. 'Did the INS know about this?'

'We sure as hell did not.' Hrycyk glared at Li as if he was the embodiment of everything he hated about the Chinese.

Fuller's face was flushed with anger. He turned on Li. 'So what kind of liaison are you, that sends an undercover Chinese cop on to US soil without telling us?'

Li remained calm. 'We took a clear policy decision on this. We decided to do nothing that might put the life of our operative at risk.'

'And keeping American law enforcement in the loop would be putting your man's life at risk?' Fuller was incredulous.

'It is a matter of trust,' Li said evenly.

'What, *you* don't trust *us*?' Hrycyk threw his hands in the air as if it was the most absurd thing he had ever heard.

Li said, 'The history of co-operation between US and Chinese law enforcement is not exactly an illustrious one. You might remember the Goldfish Case.'

Fuller sighed his impatience. 'That's ancient history!'

Margaret asked, 'What is the Goldfish Case?'

Li spoke to her directly for the first time. 'A gang operating out of Shanghai in the late eighties was filling condoms with heroin and sewing them into the bellies of large goldfish that were then shipped out with live fish to San Francisco. It is normal for a number of fish to die in transit, but officials in San Francisco became suspicious when they saw stitching in the bellies of some of the fish.'

'This is completely irrelevant,' Fuller insisted, but he was on the defensive now.

'Is it?' Li asked. He said to Margaret, 'When gang members at the American end of the operation were brought to court, the prosecution here asked the Chinese to release one of the gang members from Shanghai to give evidence in court. The Chinese agreed. It was the first co-operative US–Chinese drug prosecution. But when the guy got on the stand he changed his testimony and claimed political asylum. That was more than ten years ago. He is currently walking around a free man in the United States.'

'He said he was tortured by the Chinese police. Beaten and blindfolded and stuck with an electric cattle prod,' Hrycyk said.

Li's laugh was without humour. 'Well, he would say that, wouldn't he? And in a country where people are prepared to believe the worst that anyone wants to claim about the People's Republic of China, the odds were pretty much stacked in his favour.'

Hrycyk stabbed an accusing finger at Li across the prone form of the dead detective. 'You telling me stuff like that never happens in China?'

'No,' Li said simply, taking the wind out of Hrycyk's sails. 'But it's never happened on my shift. And if you could put your hand on your heart and tell me a prisoner's never had a confession beaten out of him in the United States, then I'd call you a liar.'

Hrycyk looked as if he might be about to leap across the table and take Li by the throat.

Margaret said caustically, 'I don't think Detective Wang gave his life just so that China and America could go to war.' She brushed past them and lifted a plastic evidence bag containing Wang's bloodstained notebook from the computer table and held it up to Li. 'His diary,' she said.

IV

Wang's Diary

April 10
The ship that is taking us across the Pacific was waiting in the darkness for our flotilla of small boats several miles off the coast. It is a rusty old Korean freighter with

three holds. About one hundred of us are packed into the rear hold. Another sixty or so in the next. The third is stacked with food and water for our trip. There are no windows, and only one fan in the roof. It is freezing cold all the time, and the air in here stinks. We sleep on the floor, cheek by jowl. Our toilet facilities consist of a bucket for the men and a bucket for the women. Hygiene is impossible, and I have picked up some kind of eye infection. My eyes are red and sore, and agony if I rub them, which I do when I sleep and wake up with tears running down my cheeks. To be red eyed, they say, is to be envious. The people I envy are those who are not aboard this ship.

The food is appalling. Water, rice, peanuts, some vegetables. But they never give us meat, or fish. My wife always nagged me to lose some weight. Now she has her wish.

They let us up on deck once a week to wash in salt water. My hair is crusted with it, my skin white, as if I had rolled in rice flour. There are always *ma zhai* making sure we do what we are told. Sometimes they beat us, and they know we will not retaliate because there are three Cambodians on board with machine guns. *Khmer Rouge* mercenaries. We know that such people have no compunction about taking lives, although of course the *shetou* want us delivered to America in one piece. Our hides are worth sixty thousand dollars apiece, but only if we are alive inside them.

April 25

Three *ma zhai* came down into our hold last night. They had been drinking, and they did not care who they damaged. They dragged three of the young women away, and none of us did anything to stop them. Although I know that standing up to them is futile, I still feel guilty about doing nothing. I wish that I had my gun and my badge, and that I could just arrest these scum and have them thrown in prison.

When they brought them back the women's faces were streaked with tears and they hid their eyes. No one said anything. We all knew what had happened. And I know that my *yazi*, my little duck in the next hold, must be going through the same thing. It makes me sick and angry to think about it, but there is nothing to be done. Nothing. Nothing. Nothing.

Li read through the account of Wang's appalling journey with an increasing sense of bleakness. He sat in a small office on a gantry overlooking the interior of the hangar below. Twelve pathologists cutting open the dead flesh of his countrymen. Wang, and men and women just like him. People who, for whatever reason, had submitted themselves to the pain and indignity and humiliation of an endless journey to the promised land, in the hands of ruthless individuals who raped and beat them for pleasure and dollars. Only to end up here. Laid out on a succession of stainless steel tables. The tears that blurred the pages in front of him were their tears.

June 15

It has been two months since we set sail. It seems like five years. Nine thousand miles of Pacific Ocean and, mercifully, the weather has been kind. Until last night. We encountered a terrible storm. The freighter rolled from side to side for fifteen hours, tipping into giant waves, water pouring into the holds. We felt certain we were going to die. Many people were sick and today the air is sour because they will not let us clean up down here. One man, I think, died. He had a wife and young child. He had not been well for several days, and after the storm he was unconscious for many hours. They came this afternoon and took him away. His wife begged them to let her go with him, but the *ma zhai* refused. Someone said they had thrown him overboard.

June 17

Disaster. Last night we reached the coast of Guatemala. The weather was poor, and the freighter could not come in close to shore. They made us stand in the dark on a shallow reef, up to our thighs in water, half a mile offshore, waiting for the small boats to come and get us. Seven boats came in the end, with Taiwanese on board, to take us ashore. Then they made us walk through fields in the dark for hours until we reached a road where there were vans waiting. Only half of us had been brought ashore, and we were crammed in those vans all day in the suffocating heat, waiting until tonight, when they were to get the rest. But just half an hour ago, a man came running up to the vans to tell us that this time the police were waiting and the others had all been arrested. He said that some peasants had seen us come ashore last night and tipped off the police. Now, someone told me, they are taking us to Guatemala City.

August 2

We have been here for six weeks now, on the ranch of a Taiwanese not far from Guatemala City. We sleep in barns and outbuildings. It is cramped and uncomfortable. But at least it is warm and dry. The food, as always, is terrible. They say we must wait until it is safe to move. The Guatemalan police, they say, are still trying to find us.

We have been shocked to see how the Guatemalan peasants live. Whatever reason people may have for leaving China, they have better lives than this. The poverty is desperate, medical facilities are almost non-existent. And yet we also see big cars, and houses owned by wealthy people. The Taiwanese who owns this ranch is rich. Wealth accumulated, no doubt, from the trade in illegal immigrants like us.

Cheng sleeps curled into my back most nights, with her arms around me. She is pale and lovely and very fragile. She has been raped and abused, but her spirit is still strong. Stronger than mine. Sometimes I think it is only Cheng that has kept me going.

It is strange. I no longer think of myself as Detective Wang, of the Tianjin Municipal Police. I am one of these people now. An illegal immigrant. Homeless and helpless and desperate to reach America. The Beautiful Country, the Mountain of Gold. After all this, you have to believe it is true.

Li read, with an increasingly heavy heart, of the detective's growing relationship with Cheng, and of the further moves to which they had then been subjected. Several trucks had arrived at the Taiwanese ranch. Wang and his companions had had to crawl into a narrow space beneath false floors in the back of the trucks, which had then been loaded with grapefruit and driven north into Mexico. Forty hours without food or water or the chance to move. They had had to soil themselves where they lay, squeezed together like sardines, lying in their own filth.

In a forest, they had been released from the trucks and taken to a collection of huts in a clearing where they joined more Chinese awaiting passage into the United States. There they had stayed for several more weeks, and then been moved twice more on foot, at night, walking long hours through rough, uncompromising country.

October 10
Tonight we will cross into the United States. Someone told me that the border is only a few hours from this place. At last, at long last, the prospect of freedom from

this hell. We are on some kind of ranch in open scrub country. They keep cattle here. We have been given fresh clothes. It does not matter that they do not fit. I have been able to wash properly for the first time in weeks. It feels like heaven.

One of the *coyotes* came and handed out cigarettes. They are the ones who are arranging the final leg of our journey. Mexicans, I think. Someone said they were drug smugglers who have turned to smuggling people because it is safer and there is more money. I tried to speak with one of them, but the language was impossible. His English was even worse than mine. So I must rely on what I hear from others. The cigarettes are good. It is so long since I had a smoke.

A short time ago a man came to the ranch-house. He wore a suit and carried a black bag. One of the *ma zhai* said he was a doctor, and that we must be vaccinated against something called West Nile Encephalitis. He said it was everywhere in the southern states of America, and that we must be protected against it. The *ah kung* had ordered it. I asked him who this grandfather was, and he told me it was none of my business. No one knew who Kat was. But if he wanted it done, it would be done. It seemed a strange nickname to me. Kat. The Cantonese word for 'tangerine', a symbol of good luck. I felt anything but lucky.

When it was my turn to go into the room, the doctor told me to drop my pants and bend over a chair. He wore rubber gloves and a white mask. He kneeled down behind me and stuck a needle in my ass, nearly into my balls. It hurt like hell.

Now we are fit to be American citizens.

A very large refrigerated truck has arrived in the yard. They say we will cross the border in the back of it, hidden behind boxes of fruit and vegetables. Tomorrow, they say, we will be in Houston, Texas. We will be in America.

Li could barely bring himself to read Wang's final erratic scrawl in the blood-smeared book. *Tell my little girl that she was my last thought. Tell her —* And there was a line running down to the foot of the page, as if he had not had the strength to hold pencil to paper any longer.

Li would carry the message himself to Wang's daughter if he could. It was the very least he could do. She would know always that her father had loved her. And yet, how could he tell her that her father had not died in vain? That he had not been sent on a fool's errand? Wang's real job would not even have begun until after his arrival. The journey had been simply to establish his credentials, to raise him above suspicion in order that he might insinuate himself into the very heart of the people-smuggling operation and maybe, just maybe, get himself a glimpse of the dragon's lair — and within touching distance of the *ah kung* they now knew was called Kat.

And Li stood accused, in his own eyes, of being the fool who sent him on that errand. Guilty as charged. Guilty for life. Just plain guilty.

He buried his face in his hands and wept.

V

Margaret looked up as Steve sauntered into her station. She was on her second autopsy, nerves stretched by the ordeal of performing a post-mortem examination of Detective Wang, concentration shattered by the arrival of Li. Fuller and Hrycyk had been in a huddle at the computer desk for a long time now, each making several lengthy calls on their cellphones. So she was relieved to see Steve's friendly smile.

'Hi,' he said. He had pulled down his face mask. He nodded towards the body on the table, a young woman in her early twenties, chest gaping, ribs exposed like a carcass in a butcher's shop. 'Your second?'

'Yes,' She heard the strain in her own voice.

'Notice anything you might say they both had in common?' His question was so casually asked, it made her stop and look at him very directly for a moment.

'Are we talking injection sites in the buttock here?' she asked.

'Hey,' he smiled, 'nothing gets past you, does it?'

She pulled a face. 'I take it they're not unique.'

'One hundred per cent to date. That's more than twenty. I got one of my investigators checking the rest of the bodies out in the trailers.'

'It's a strange place to choose to inject anything.'

'Certainly is. And it would take a professional to do it.'

'So what do you think they were injected with?'

'I have no idea. But I'm wondering if maybe we shouldn't

be taking extra precautions here. We don't know what these people might be carrying, or why someone felt the need to inject them at all.' He paused, still the smile playing around his lips. 'I did a little reading up on illegal immigrants before I came down. Apparently thirty-four per cent of illegal Chinese taken into custody have been found to be chronic carriers of Hepatitis B.'

'Wow,' Margaret said. 'That's a high percentage.' Then she shrugged. 'But we have perfectly adequate protection against Hep B, or any other nasties in the blood. As long as we're careful.' She paused again, looking at him very carefully, 'What makes you think we might need extra protection?'

For the first time, Margaret saw his mobile brows furrow in a frown. 'I don't know, Margaret. I get kinda spooked sometimes, you know, when I don't know what I'm dealing with. I was paranoid about my first AIDS case. I even wore boots with steel toe-caps in case I dropped a knife or something . . .' He laughed uneasily at his own vulnerability. 'It's just strange, that's all.'

'What's strange?' Fuller, with Hrycyk in tow, had come back into Margaret's station.

'Injection sites on the underside of the buttock,' Margaret said. 'It's not a place you would normally choose to stick a needle.'

'You mean there's more than one of them?' Hrycyk asked.

'It looks like they might all have been injected,' Steve said.

Fuller scratched his head. 'So why *would* someone pick the underside of the buttock?'

Margaret shrugged and glanced at Steve. 'Maybe so it wouldn't be spotted on a cursory examination. I mean, I don't figure anyone expected them to be laid out on an autopsy table being subjected to this kind of scrutiny.'

'So, do you have any idea what they were injected with?' Fuller persisted.

'A vaccine against West Nile Encephalitis.' Li's voice startled them, and they turned to find him standing in the entrance to the autopsy station.

'How do you know that?' Margaret asked, and she saw immediately that he had been crying. There were telltale red dots around the corners of his eyes that she had seen before. And in that moment she wanted just to hold him, and would have forgiven him anything. But she gave no outward sign of it. Not even the hint of a crack in her cold façade.

Li said simply, 'Wang's diary.' Whatever demons he had had to wrestle with had been banished for the moment. 'Wang describes how a doctor came and vaccinated them all the night before they crossed the border.' He dropped the diary, back in its evidence bag, on to the table and peeled off his gloves. 'They were told it was against West Nile Encephalitis.'

'Bullshit!' Hrycyk said. 'Snakeheads aren't going to spend money vaccinating illegals against anything.'

'Well, not against West Nile Encephalitis, anyway,' Margaret added. 'The only cases of West Nile I've heard about in the last six months involved a couple of crows.' She looked to Steve for confirmation.

He shrugged. 'It's not a serious problem. I mean, I doubt if any of us round this table have been vaccinated against West Nile. And it's not a requirement for visitors to the US.'

Li frowned. 'So what were they injected with? Is it possible they were murdered?'

Hrycyk was scathing. 'Of course they weren't murdered. Why would anyone murder them? These people were worth six million bucks — alive.'

VI

A line of stainless-steel sinks had been set up at one end of the hangar, supplied with hot and cold running water and dispensers of anti-bacterial liquid soap to allow the pathologists to scrub down at the end of the day. They had each completed four autopsies and were now halfway through the task of examining all ninety-eight bodies. Conversation along the line of sinks was animated, revolving around important questions like where they were going to get a drink that night, and the best place to get something to eat. Everyone had been booked into the Holiday Inn on West Holcombe Boulevard on the edge of medicine city, including Margaret.

She stood next to Steve soaping her hands and arms. She had already dispensed with her surgical gown and apron and changed back into her jeans and tee-shirt. Her hair was scraped back from her face and held in a band at the back of her head. She was hot, and tired, and distracted.

Li had left some hours earlier, and she was not sure when, or even if, she would see him again. Their encounter had been unsettling, blowing away the protective fabrications she had built up around herself over the last fifteen months, since she had returned from China determined to put him behind her. The little half lies she had tried to convince herself were absolute truths: that the differences between them of language and culture were too great to overcome; that she would be happier here in the US without him; that he would be happier in China with a woman of his own race.

And now he was in America. Had been here, she knew, for nearly a year, making no attempt to get in touch with her. It wasn't as if he didn't know that she had taken up a lecturing position at the college of criminal justice in Huntsville, because she had told him that was where she was going. But from his reaction to meeting her across the autopsy table here in Houston, it was clear he had been unaware that she was now the Chief Medical Examiner for Harris County. At least until today.

'So . . .' Steve's voice sounded beside her, '. . . suffocation?'

'That's how it appears,' she said. 'Although they'd probably been in the truck for about twenty-four hours — right through the heat of the previous day.'

'Ah,' said Steve. 'Core liver temperature.'

'Mine were all a hundred and seven degrees Fahrenheit or higher.'

'Mine, too.'

'They'd also eaten, and all of my bladders were pretty much empty, so it would seem they had been allowed out at some point to relieve themselves.'

'Which means that the air vent was open when they set out . . .'

'. . . and closed, either accidentally or on purpose, when they stopped somewhere en route.'

'And they died either of suffocation or hyperthermia.'

'Or a combination of the two.'

A thoughtful silence hung between them, then, for a moment, and Margaret noticed a trace of blood in the water in Steve's sink. She looked at him, immediately concerned. 'Where's the blood coming from?' And she saw for the first time how pale he looked. His smile was almost convincing.

'Ah, it's nothing.'

'You cut yourself?'

He took a long time to compose his reply. Finally he said, 'Usually I leave the organs piled at one end of the table before I section them. When I went back after coming through to talk to you about the injection sites, they had slid down the cutting board, and when I went to lift them I felt this little jag in my finger. I had left my knife lying on the cutting board and the organs had slipped over the top of it. My left hand is well protected. I wear chain mail under the glove in case of a slip. But on my cutting hand, my right, I usually only wear the latex. That's the hand I lifted the organs with. The tip of my knife made a tiny puncture about halfway down the middle finger.' He held his open right hand out for her to see, and she saw a tiny fleck of blood oozing from an almost imperceptible nick. 'At the time I didn't think I had cut the skin.' He grimaced. 'Guess I was wrong.'

'Jesus, Steve,' Margaret said. They both knew that this smallest of accidents would have made him vulnerable to contracting any viral or bacterial infection carried in the blood of the victim. 'What have you done about it?'

He shrugged. 'What could I do? I've taken a lot of samples from the guy and asked the AFIP people at Walter Reed to do a complete blood screen. I've drawn some of my own, for a baseline, and I guess I'll be checking it every six weeks for the next year for HIV and Hep B and C.'

Margaret felt sick. She looked at him with the heartfelt concern of someone who is only ever a split second's carelessness from exactly the same predicament. 'You said you thought you hadn't cut the skin.'

He grinned ruefully. 'Hey, you're talking to paranoid Steve, here. I never take chances.'

But Margaret didn't smile. 'What about whatever it was these people were injected with?'

'I've asked the lab to do several specific panel tests to cover as wide a spectrum as possible. Between PCR and the virus panel we should find out what it was pretty fast.' He smiled bravely. 'If it was West Nile, then with luck I get free immunity.' He dried his hands and stretched a flesh-coloured Band-aid over the cut. He looked up at Margaret. 'I was going to ask you out to dinner tonight. You know how the line goes: I know this great little place . . . Only, I don't. At least, not in Houston.'

All thoughts of Li now banished, Margaret said, 'You know, funny you should say that. 'Cos I know this great little place . . .'

VII

Li gazed from the rear passenger window in wonder as Consul-General Xi's driver took them west on Bellaire, under Sam Houston Parkway, and into the heart of Houston's Chinatown. Li did not know what he had expected, but it was not this. In Washington, Chinatown consisted of a couple of blocks of old tenements, with a few restaurants and Chinese foodstores. Here, one modern plaza followed another, set back off the boulevard. Walkways under green-tiled roofs over shops which advertised their wares and services in Chinese and English. Peggy's Skin Care. China Fast Food. Asian Pacific Travel. Sweet Country Café. A brick apartment block with a neon Kung Fu sign next to a notice announcing the E-W Cultural Exchange Association. A hoarding advertising 'Immigration Passport Photos and Greencard Citizenship', next to an acupuncture centre.

'You see? Wherever we go, we create little China.' Consul-General Xi grinned at him, and Li saw that his bad teeth had been patched up to give him an American smile. There were, he had noticed, dental practices everywhere in Chinatown. Perhaps it was what you did when you got a little money, fixed up your teeth so that you felt a little more like an American citizen. Bad teeth were endemic in China.

There were also, he had observed, a proliferation of psychics. Perhaps they offered the hope of future citizenship. And a large number of vasectomy reversal clinics appeared to be trying to make up for decades of the One Child Policy, a chance to procreate without punishment – or fear of your children starving.

But Li did not see China in any of it. He saw America plastered with Chinese characters, like graffiti.

'In terms of area, Houston has the third largest Chinatown in the United States,' the Consul-General said, stubbing out his cigarette. He opened a window to let out some of the smoke, then closed it again to preserve the air-conditioning. 'On the surface, perhaps, it looks like a quiet city suburb. But beneath the surface, there is a lot of crime. Gambling, prostitution, protection rackets. For the most part, the local police stay out. So crime flourishes. And, of course, the Americans estimate that the illegal smuggling of Chinese generates revenues of more than three billion dollars a year.'

They passed a large shopping area off to their right, called Diho Square. The parking lot was nearly full, and Li could see only Chinese faces. An old man wearing a white cotton jacket and pants, with open sandals and a white Stetson, turned his ramshackle bicycle on to the road. 'So who runs the criminal syndicates?' Li asked.

'Most of the major businesses, legitimate and otherwise, are run by organisations known here as tongs. The tongs employ street gangs as enforcers to guard the massage parlours and gambling dens. The gangs finance themselves by collecting protection money from small traders with shops and restaurants. It is a very rigid structure, with a very clear hierarchy, all the way from the *ma zhai*, the little horses, or ordinary gang members, through their leaders, the big brothers, or *dai lo*, to the *shuk foo*, the uncles who are their liaison with the tongs.'

'Who is the *ah kung*, Consul-General Xi? Do you know?'

The Consul-General looked at him, surprised, and a little annoyed. 'I am wasting my time telling you all this, Li, since obviously you are already well informed.'

Li inclined his head slightly. 'It is always useful to gather intelligence based on local knowledge, Consul-General.'

The Consul-General raised an eyebrow. 'They were right when they said that you were like your uncle.'

Li glanced at him. 'You knew him?'

'Only by reputation.'

Li sighed inwardly. Even here in America he was still haunted by the ghost of his uncle. Since his first day at the University of Public Security in Beijing, he had had to bear the burden of his uncle's reputation as one of the finest police officers ever to grace the Beijing municipal force. He had either had to live up to, or live down that reputation. Never judged on his own merits, always against the yardstick of his Uncle Yifu – a man he had loved dearly. 'I am not really like him at all,' Li said. 'But I try to honour his memory by following his teachings.'

He remembered the dreadful vision of the old man lying murdered in the bloody bath, skewered by his own ceremonial sword. It was as vivid now as it had been then, and the pain of it never diminished.

'Each of the tongs has an *ah kung*,' the Consul-General was saying in answer to his question. Li forced the image of his uncle from his mind. 'But it is generally recognised that one of them is supreme. He is *the* grandfather. But outside of a very small inner circle, no one knows who he is.'

'His name, or at least his nickname, is Kat,' Li said, and he felt the Consul-General's eyes turn towards him.

'How do you know this?' the Consul-General asked.

'Because one of those who died in the truck at Huntsville was an undercover Chinese police officer.'

The Consul-General was clearly shocked. 'You are sure?'

Li nodded. 'I briefed him for the job. He was to come to America as an illegal immigrant, and infiltrate the gangs at this end, hoping to pick up clues to the identity of the *ah kung*.' Li paused. 'I have read his diary. At least he was able to give us a name.'

'Kat,' the Consul-General said thoughtfully. 'My wife always presents me with a tangerine plant for luck at Spring Festival.' He took out his cigarettes and offered one to Li, who declined. Since coming to America he had made a determined effort to give them up. Only when he was with other Chinese was he tempted to fall back into his old ways. The Consul-General lit up. 'I will open the door and look at the mountain with you, Li.' And Li smiled to himself. Whenever anyone told you they were going to be straight with you, it usually meant the opposite. 'There are no flowers dropping from the sky in Beijing over the matter of these illegal immigrants.'

'Nor in Washington,' Li said.

'I have spoken today with the Minister of Public Security.

The government is embarrassed by the high profile nature of this case.'

'Particularly since they are in the process of trying to negotiate a more favourable agreement with the World Trade Organisation.' Li couldn't keep the cynicism out of his voice.

The Consul-General looked at him sharply. And then he smiled. 'I see you have also accumulated a little political acumen on your journeys.' Then his smile faded just as quickly. 'The Minister would like to put an end to this business, once and for all. There is to be a major crackdown in Fujian and Canton. He wants you to put a stop to it at this end. The Americans have been told that you will be entirely at their disposal. But one way or another, the authorities in Beijing want you to cut off the head of the American snake with, or without, their help.'

CHAPTER THREE

I

From the twin torches that marked the angle in the stairs leading up the outside of the building to the restaurant, flames danced and dipped in the warm evening breeze. A terrace ran around the semi-circular frontage of the Canyon Café and was open to the night, looking out over a panoply of lights on Westheimer towards the sparkling finger of the Transco Tower rising into a black sky.

Margaret felt the night air like silk on her face and was glad that they had managed to get a table on the terrace, away from the noisy crowds in the dark interior and the Mexican band music that blared out over the speaker system. She sipped on her Coyote Margarita and enjoyed the sweetness of it passing over the savoury salt crust around the rim of her glass.

But she had mixed feelings. She had still heard nothing further from Li, and was wondering if perhaps he had already returned to Washington. She was flattered by Steve's unmistakable interest in her — it was a long time since a man had asked her out — but their night was overshadowed by the apprehension that hung over him following his accident in the hangar. She had watched him closely, and he was doing a good job of hiding his anxiety. But occasionally she caught him succumbing to a momentary lapse, and she would have a fleeting glimpse into the deep, dark chasm of his uncertainty.

Their shared starter arrived. Grilled turkey skewers basted in a rich, smoky barbecue sauce, served with papaya fruit salsa and cucumber-mint dipping sauce over a tossed salad. Steve waggled his eyebrows at her. 'This is good stuff. I don't get to eat much Mexican in Maryland.'

'Is that where you live? Maryland?'

'The Office of the Armed Forces Medical Examiner is just outside of DC in Maryland, so I rent up in a little town called Gaithersburg.'

'On your own?'

'Only since my wife took my little girl and ran off to live with a banker down in Alexandria.' He scratched his head thoughtfully. 'Did I say banker? Usually I get it wrong. Easy mistake to make.' Margaret grinned. 'Anyway, she told me he wore nice aftershave and didn't come home each night smelling of dead people. Did I mention that he also makes ten times as much money as I do?'

'No competition.' Margaret smiled.

'None at all.' Then Steve's grin faded. 'Only thing I regret's my little girl. Don't get to see much of her these days.' But he wasn't about to dwell on it. 'So how about you?' he asked quickly.

'What you see is what you get,' Margaret said.

'Oh, I doubt that. Chief Medical Examiner of the third largest county in the United States? That's no mean achievement for a thirty-four-year-old woman. Not to mention two and a half years living in China, working with the Chinese police on some pretty hair-raising stuff.'

Margaret cocked an eyebrow at him. 'You've been doing your homework.'

'The internet's a wonderful thing.' He waved a finger at her. 'And I'm sorry about that.'

'About what?' she asked, taken aback.

'Oh, the eyebrow thing. It's catching, you know. I never realised I did it myself until I saw an interview I did on TV once.' He waggled his eyebrows around his forehead. 'Like two demented hairy caterpillars every time I opened my mouth. After that I took them to eyebrow training, but they still won't lie down when I tell them.'

Margaret laughed, and felt a marvellous release of tension in the laughter. She liked Steve a lot. And in the twinkling of his orange-green eyes she could see that he was pleased he had made her laugh.

'So tell me about you and Li Yan.' He killed her laughter as effectively as he had created it.

'What makes you think there's anything to tell?' She was on the defensive now.

'Anyone who's done their homework would know that you and he had some kind of relationship in China.' He paused, gauging her reaction carefully. 'Was it just professional, or . . .' He let the 'or' hang.

Margaret hesitated only briefly. It was not something she had discussed with anyone, and there was a whole dam inside her waiting to burst. 'We were lovers,' she said and wondered if it was disappointment or disapproval she detected in Steve's eyes. She knew that in China it was considered a cachet for a Chinese man to have an American lover, but that a Chinese woman who had a relationship with a white man was thought to be a whore. She suspected that Americans might view her in the same light.

Steve said, 'But it's over.' He didn't couch it as a question, but that's what it was.

'Yes.'

He sat back, watching her carefully. 'Why don't I believe you?'

She smiled. 'Maybe because it's only over in my head, and not in my heart.'

'I don't think I understand.'

She said, 'You have to realise that life in China is very different, Steve. While they like to say that women hold up half the sky, it is still a society dominated by men. Women are second-class citizens. Even professionals like me.' She paused. 'Li Yan never treated me that way, but he was a senior police officer. He was having a relationship with a foreigner. It was frowned on by his superiors. We could not even live together officially without being married. Life was not easy.' She flicked her hair back over her shoulders, a little, self-conscious mannerism. 'And then there were all the linguistic and cultural differences. Every time a Chinese woman even glanced at

Li Yan I would feel vulnerable. How could I compete? There was so much that he couldn't share with me that he could with a Chinese lover. And then there was the question of commitment. Was I really prepared to spend the rest of my life in China?' She gave a tiny, sad shrug. 'I couldn't. I knew I couldn't. Just as I knew I couldn't ask him to give up his country and come to America with me. Whichever way it went, one of us would be a fish out of water.' She drained her Margarita. 'So I told him it was over, and I came home.'

The waiter came to take away their starter. With all their talking, they had eaten less than half of it. A waitress brought their entrees. In front of Margaret she placed a plate of flame-grilled shrimp rubbed with chilli spices and skewered with vegetables. Steve was having fresh chilli tuna topped with an avocado fan and smooth chipotle sauce. The food smelled great, but somehow neither of them had any appetite. The waiter filled their wine glasses. 'Enjoy,' he said.

They picked in silence at their food for a few minutes before Steve took a mouthful of wine and asked, 'Any regrets?'

She met his eye. 'Every minute of every day,' she said, and his disappointment this time was clear, almost tangible.

'So now he's in America, you'll get back together?'

'Not a chance.' Her voice was strained by hurt and anger.

Steve looked perplexed, but also relieved. 'Why not?'

'Because he's been in Washington for nearly a year, Steve. Because he's never once tried to contact me. I read about his appointment in January, and I spent every night for weeks sitting by the phone waiting for him to call. He never did.

Obviously he no longer feels about me the way I feel about him. He got a hell of a shock today. I don't think for a minute he expected to see me in that hangar at Ellington Field.'

It seemed extraordinary to her that she was saying these things out loud. Things she had been keeping bottled up inside all this time. And here she was unburdening herself to a man she had only just met. But there was something in his eyes, an empathy there that was drawing her out of herself, allowing her to release the mental toxins that had been poisoning her for so long. She felt better, even as she spoke.

'I've been wondering about that ring on your wedding finger,' he said.

'Jesus!' She laughed out loud. 'You like picking at sores, Steve, don't you?'

'Oh, yeah, especially when you pick off that itching scab and make it sore all over again. The good bit is that it stops being itchy for a while.'

'The point being that the raw pain is better than the itch?'

'Exactly.'

She drained her wine glass and held it out for him to refill. 'Okay,' she said. 'Here's the raw pain. I married a guy when I was too young to know any better. A lecturer in genetics at Chicago. Good-looking, smart as hell, great future. He hanged himself after being convicted of raping and murdering one of his students.' She took a large mouthful from her refilled glass.

Steve was stunned to silence and took a moment or two to recover. 'Jees, Margaret, that's one scab maybe I should have left unpicked.'

'But you're right,' Margaret said, hanging on to control by the merest thread, 'the raw pain is better than the itch.' She turned the gold band around the base of her wedding finger. 'Actually, I only started wearing this again to keep guys like you at a distance – and to keep them from asking awkward questions.'

He reached out and took her hand in his. It was firm and cool and held her gently. His eyes looked into hers with an almost unbearable directness. 'No more questions,' he said. 'I promise.'

She laughed. 'Bit late now.'

But he didn't laugh with her. 'Never too late,' he said very seriously. 'For any of us.'

They walked side by side in the dark towards the three arches of the Waterwall. Through them, illuminated by concealed lighting, water poured in a constant stream down a high wall shaped like a horseshoe around an artificial pool. They could see the silhouettes of people against the water, moving between the arches, lovers hand in hand, a woman with a long shawl dancing in the fine spray, a slow elegant dance of the night. Behind them, two tree-lined pedestrian walkways ran along either side of a long, manicured lawn, towards the rising shadow of the Transco Tower, lights still shining in every window.

Couples sat on benches under the trees, locked in embrace, kissing in the darkness. Shadowy figures moved about on the lawn below. As they neared the wall, Margaret felt the cool spray in the warm air. They had walked this way in silence since leaving the restaurant, and now, finally, Margaret put her arm through Steve's. She felt his warmth and his strength through his shirt. But she was also aware at once of his uncertainty when at length he said, 'I was told this afternoon that Li Yan was being officially attached to this investigation.'

She tensed, and then immediately forced herself to relax again. 'So?' she asked.

He said, 'I didn't want to say anything during the meal. I figured I'd inflicted enough damage already.'

'So you saved this one till you knew my guard was down, huh?' He looked at her quickly, and saw in the reflected light of the streetlamps in the road, that she was smiling. He was relieved.

'I didn't know how you'd cope with it, that's all,' he said. Then added quickly, 'Being in close contact with him again, you know, while this thing's on-going.'

She shrugged. 'I'll just have to, won't I?' She thought for a moment. 'I'll avoid him when I can, and ignore him when I can't.'

They were right up at the Waterwall now, the spray falling on them like a light drizzle. The arches were formed in a freestanding wall which reached an apex centrally above them. Beyond was a cobbled area leading to the pool below the curve of the Waterwall itself. The woman with the shawl was still dancing, drifting light-footed over the cobbles, arms stretching her shawl out to either side like the wings of a butterfly.

Steve took Margaret's hand and led her through one of the arches. 'Hey, it's wet,' she protested.

'Does it matter?' he asked.

'I guess not.'

Her hair always separated into curling strands when it was wet. She brushed it out of her face, and almost before she knew it, Steve had stooped to kiss her lightly on the lips. She drew back.

'Hey, I gave you permission to call me Margaret, not to kiss me.'

'Who's asking?' he said, and he pulled her towards him and kissed her again. This time she didn't draw away, and she felt his arms slip around her waist, and she draped her arms over his shoulders and raised herself on tiptoe to kiss him back.

Their cab drew in past a Pizza Hut to the car park of the Holiday Inn. Across South Main, the floodlit heart of the Texas Medical Center filled the night sky. Margaret and Steve walked into the hotel foyer. As always it was busy. People in wheelchairs, others hobbling on crutches. Pale-looking Arab men whose wives were robed from head to toe leaving only the narrowest strip across the eyes. Eastern European children with large, dark-ringed eyes and a dreadful pallor. Sick people. Wealthy foreigners come to America to buy the best medical care available. A bunch of Steve's pathologists and investigators was drinking at the bar of the Bristol Room restaurant. 'Hey Steve,' one of them called. 'Where you been, man? Come and get a beer.'

Someone else shouted, 'And bring the Medical Examiner with you. It's not fair keeping her all to yourself.'

Steve grinned, embarrassed. 'I'm having an early night,

guys.' There was a low murmur of suggestive 'ooohs'. 'And you should, too,' he added. 'Heavy day tomorrow.'

'Yes, *sir*,' someone else hollered, and they all saluted.

'Down boys,' Steve shouted. 'Or I'll set my eyebrows on you.'

They could still hear the laughter as the doors of the elevator slid shut, and then the silence between them was broken only by the hum of the motor.

'I enjoyed tonight,' Margaret said.

'Me, too. We must do it again sometime.' Steve paused for just a moment. 'Like tomorrow.'

'Before you leave, you mean?' She didn't really intend it, but there was a slight sting in her tone.

He looked at her seriously. 'I get out of the air force in six months, Margaret. That was the deal. They pay me through med school, I give them three years of my life. I was doing great working out of the ME's office in San Diego when they called in my contract. But I'm a free man in April.'

'A lot can happen in six months.' She knew it was way too early to make any kind of commitment.

'A lot can happen in twenty-four hours,' he said. 'Live for the moment. We could be dead tomorrow.'

'Yeah, or still alive and full of regrets.'

They got out on the fifth floor and started down the long hallway, walking slowly so as to delay the moment when they would stop at Margaret's door. When eventually they got there, they stood for a long time not knowing what to say. Finally Margaret reached up and kissed him lightly on the cheek. 'See you tomorrow, then.'

'Margaret . . .'

But she put a finger up to his lips to stop him. 'We can't run before we can walk, Steve. And I'm still learning how to walk again.'

He nodded solemnly. 'I could lend you a bicycle.'

Which made her smile, and she kissed him again. On the lips this time. Then, 'Good night,' she said firmly, and she unlocked her door and stepped into the darkness of her room.

She knew immediately he was there. She could feel his presence almost as clearly as if she could see him. But her eyes had not yet adjusted, and all she could see, through net curtains, were the illuminated twin peaks of St Luke's Medical Tower across the road in medicine city. She fumbled for the light switch without finding it, and then the bedside lamp flickered on, and she saw Li perched on the edge of her bed, the strain of apprehension etched clearly on his face.

'You bastard,' she said, almost in a whisper. 'Do you have any idea what you put me through these last ten months?'

He looked surprised. 'You knew I was in Washington?'

'Of course I knew you were there, for Chrissake! It was in all the papers. This isn't China, Li Yan. It's not a state secret when someone gets appointed to a new job.'

He appeared crestfallen. Unable to meet her eye. 'You're the only reason I took the job,' he said.

It was both what she wanted and didn't want to hear. 'So it took you all this time not to find my phone number?'

Li stood up. He was like a giant in the room, both his size

and his presence filling it. But it was in a small voice that he said, 'I lost my nerve.'

Margaret had no patience with him. 'Oh, gimme a break! You're a big boy now, Li Yan.' And then she remembered the red spots around his eyes earlier in the day. That he had wept over Wang. Big boys weren't supposed to cry either.

'It was you who walked out on me, remember,' Li said.

'You *know* why.'

But Li pressed on. 'We hadn't spoken in nearly six months. When I was still in China it all seemed like it would be easy. I would come to America, and I would pick up a phone and we would be together again.'

'So why didn't you?'

'Because you were still half a continent away, Margaret. Because I had no idea whether you would want to be with me again.'

'Oh, Jesus!' She bit her lip and looked away from him. 'How could you ever doubt it?'

'Very easily,' he said. 'I loved you, Margaret. But whatever you say, *you* left *me*. Got on an airplane and flew back home. I couldn't know that there was any way back for us. And I got scared to ask in case there was not.' He held out his hands in front of him, a gesture of despair. 'When I got here, the job just took over. It is twenty-four hours a day, seven days a week. Time passes. And it is easier to live in ignorance than with an unpalatable truth.'

But she wasn't about to forgive him so easily. 'Is that one of your Chinese proverbs, Li Yan? One of those little pieces of wisdom that just roll so easily off the tongue? Because, you know, there's been nothing easy for me, any single day in fifteen months. We had no future in China, you know that. But I've spent every waking minute since I left wondering if I made a mistake, knowing that I was just as unhappy here on my own.'

She glared at him, hating him for making her love him. Hating herself for being so weak.

'Margaret . . .' Li took a step towards her.

She turned her back on him, moving off towards the window, looking sightlessly out on a semi-derelict car lot and the lights of the traffic on South Main. 'I don't want to hear it, Li Yan,' she said. 'Just go away.'

Li stood helplessly looking at her. It was the rejection he had always feared. They had encountered each other by chance, but he had had to steel himself to come up here, to face her hostility, to try to explain himself. He wasn't about to turn back now. He stepped up behind her and put a hand lightly on her shoulder. He was not expecting the speed with which she turned around and took her open palm across the side of his face. His cheek stung, and he stood smarting, waiting for the next blow. It came this time from the other side and he turned his face with the slap to take some of the force out of it. But still it hurt. She had strength in her hands and her arms. But now he caught them, and their strength was no match for his.

'Are you done hurting me now?' he asked her.

She made a vain attempt to free herself. 'Not by a long way,' she whispered. And his mouth was on hers, soft and moist and sweet, and she felt a strange falling sensation that travelled all the way through her to her loins.

He let go of her arms and lifted her in his, as if she weighed nothing at all, carrying her to the bed and dropping her on the bedspread. As she struggled to wriggle out of her jeans and pull off her tee-shirt, she saw the light from the window fall obliquely across his pectorals, his white shirt dropping to the floor. She felt guilty now, that she had been kissing another man only an hour before. Li fell on top of her, his smooth skin seeming to envelop her, his hands running over all her softness. His mouth pressed hard to hers. She had not been aware of him removing his pants, but she felt his nakedness hard against her like a rock. So much, she thought, for ignoring him when she couldn't avoid him. His mouth slid down to her nipples and pulled them in, each in turn, and she moaned when eventually she felt him slip inside her, and all thoughts of Steve were finally banished.

'Jesus! Sweet Jesus,' she whispered. It had never been like this with anyone else.

CHAPTER FOUR

I

Margaret stood outside the NASA hangar, still in her gown and apron. The clear evening sky was turning pink as the dipping sun promised a spectacular sunset. Bombers, jets and Second World War fighters had been taking off and landing all day, swooping overhead, to the cheers of the crowds gathered along the edges of the tarmac. Drinks tents and hamburger stalls had kept them fed and watered as they watched displays by Russian Polikarpovs, British Hurricanes and American Wildcats, oblivious to the conveyer belt of bodies being processed in the large white hangar just a few hundred yards away. The car parks were full. The Wings Over Houston Airshow had been a great success.

The last of the refrigerated semi-trailers was gone, autopsies completed, the bodies now in the hands of the morticians who would prepare them for shipping back to their families in China once identities had been established. As yet, more than two-thirds of them remained John and Jane Does. Fifty-two men and fourteen women. All of them in their twenties. None had carried official papers of any kind, even forgeries. Their clothes were not their own. There had been clues in Wang's diary as to several of the names, and others had carried personal items – letters, photographs, engraved jewellery – that would eventually identify them. A sad collection of anonymous young men and women whose dreams had turned to death on a hot day in Texas.

'Going to be another scorcher tomorrow.' She turned to find Steve standing beside her, almost as if he had read her mind. And she was flooded with a sudden guilt at the memory of what had happened the night before. He deserved better.

'You look tired,' she said. There were deep shadows under his eyes, and some of the sparkle had gone out of them.

'Didn't sleep too good,' he said. Margaret glanced instinctively at the plaster on his finger. He caught the look. 'That,' he said, 'among other things.' And she felt a fresh prickle of guilt.

'I take it there's been no word back from Washington on the lab results.' She knew there hadn't, but she was desperate to deflect the conversation away from the subject of her and Steve. It was ironic, she thought, that just as she had met, for the first time in years, a man who might have interested her, Li Yan appeared back in her life, as if determined somehow to keep her trapped in her cycle of unhappiness. And then she remembered, with a slight tremor, how it felt when Li made love to her and she thought how she could take any amount of that kind of unhappiness.

'I figure it'll be tomorrow at the earliest before we get

anything definitive,' Steve said. 'By which time,' he added, 'I'll be back in DC.'

'And I'll be headed back to Huntsville to try and sort out the mess with my landlord.'

'What mess is that?'

'Oh, he's trying to evict me because I changed the locks.'

'Why d'you do that?'

'Because the guy's a real sleazeball. He's been harassing me with suggestive comments ever since I signed a lease on the place. And then I caught him sneaking in and going through my underwear.'

'So why don't you just find somewhere else?'

'Oh, because there's still six months of the lease to run, and I paid up front. And I didn't want to be bothered right now with trying to find a new place.'

He looked at her for a long time. Then finally he said, 'Why do I get the feeling, Margaret, that you're happy to talk about anything but us?'

'Because there is no us!' she snapped, angry that he was forcing her to confront this. And she turned and walked briskly back into the hangar, feeling like she had just inflicted hurt on some poor vulnerable animal who had trusted her. She pulled off her apron and gown, hopping briefly at her table to rip off plastic shoe covers, and headed for the row of sinks at the far end.

She scrubbed her hands and forearms vigorously with antibacterial soap as if she thought there might be blood on them, and that it might not come off. After a few moments she turned and saw Steve at the next sink calmly washing his hands.

'Does this mean I don't get to take you out to dinner tonight?' he asked with a wry, resigned smile on his face.

'Sir!' The urgency in the call made both of them turn. One of the AFIP investigators was running down the hangar towards them. 'Sir.' He stopped in front of them, slightly breathless. 'We're outta here.'

Steve frowned. 'What do you mean?'

'Just got called back to Washington, sir. Urgent. There's a flight from Hobby in just under an hour.'

Steve turned to Margaret. 'Guess that answers my question.'

'Your presence is required, too, ma'am,' the investigator said.

Margaret was taken aback. 'Me? Why?'

'No idea, ma'am. Guess it's a need-to-know basis.'

Steve turned to her again, grinning this time. 'Hey, I know this great little place in Washington . . .'

II

Li stood in the car park of the Houston District Office of the Immigration and Naturalisation Service of the United States watching groups of immigrants, mainly Hispanics, gathered under the trees outside the door of the two-storey building on the corner of Greenspoint and Northpoint. Traffic on the Interstate, a couple of blocks away, was a distant rumble. A black, uniformed officer approached him.

'Sir, do you speak English?' Li nodded. 'Sir, you cannot hang around this area. Either get in line or move out to the street.'

Li sighed and took out his ID. 'I'm waiting for Agent Hrycyk,' he said.

The officer examined his plastic photocard with its US and PRC emblems. 'Sorry, sir,' he said, tipping his hat, 'thought you was an immigrant.' And he moved off, embarrassed, towards the groups by the door.

Li glanced up at the verdigrised miniature of the Statue of Liberty that stood on a plinth overlooking the car park. Many of the original immigrants who had come to populate this vast country had had to pass beneath the eagle eye of this lady on their approach to Ellis Island. More than two hundred years later, in Texas, they were still having to do the same thing.

Hrycyk came hurrying through the crowds of would-be Americans at the main entrance and flicked Li a look. 'Let's get one thing straight,' he said. 'You are an observer here. You are not an active participant. If and when I want your help, I will ask.' And he carried on across the car park to his battered old Volkswagen Santana. He had the driver's door open before he realised that Li had not followed him. 'Are you coming or not?' he called. ''Cos if not, I'm quite happy to leave you here.'

Li sighed and walked over to the car and got in the passenger side. Hrycyk started the motor and lit up a cigarette. Li lowered the window on his side.

'Did I tell you you could open the window?' Hrycyk growled. 'I did not tell you you could open the window. It fucks with the air-con. Please close it.'

'I will if you put out your cigarette,' Li said evenly.

Hrycyk glared at him, and then stubbed out his cigarette viciously in an overflowing ashtray. 'I don't know what gives you people the idea you can come over here and start telling us what to do, but if you think you're gonna have me dancing to your tune, you got another thing coming.' He jammed the shift into Drive, and they lurched forward at speed towards the exit where an irritated Hrycyk then had to stand on the brakes and wait until there was a gap in the traffic.

On the opposite side of the street rows of single-storey brick buildings advertised passport photos in five minutes. They were doing brisk business, even at this hour of the day. Hrycyk glanced at Li, and then followed his gaze. He snorted. 'Fast food immigration. It's a goddamned boom industry around here.'

He drove them south in heavy traffic on Interstate 45, turning west on to the 610, connecting eventually with Westheimer and heading into the setting sun towards the jewel in Houston's shopping crown, The Galleria. They were going, he explained grudgingly, to meet an INS agent who had been working deep undercover in the Chinese community for nearly eighteen months.

'He's Chinese, I assume,' Li said facetiously.

'Of course he's fucking Chinese!' Hrycyk didn't see the joke. 'You don't think we'd send a Caucasian in there with Yul Brynner make-up, do you?' Li didn't want to inflame him further by asking who Yul Brynner was. 'When I say deep cover, I mean deep cover. We haven't even had contact with this guy for more than three months. It wouldn't surprise me if he'd gone native on us, switched sides. I wouldn't trust any of you people as far as I could throw you.'

Li let all of Hrycyk's aggressive anti-Chinese prejudice slip by him. One day, perhaps, there would be a reckoning. But right now it was not politic. 'So why are you making contact now?'

'Why do you think? Ninety-eight dead Chinese in a truck, and the brass in Washington crawling all over the Justice Department demanding results. We don't want to blow this guy's cover if we can avoid it. But it's time for us to know what he knows. And if we have to, we'll pull him.'

The Galleria was a shopping mall of typically Texan proportions, on three levels and with tentacles spreading out, it seemed, in all directions. It was still jam-packed with early evening shoppers, and Li hurried after Hrycyk past a bewildering display of shops and fast food outlets. They stopped at an open-plan Starbucks coffee shop overlooking a huge ice-rink. Hrycyk looked around as if he expected to see someone there. Then he approached the counter and ordered a cappuccino. He turned to Li and said brusquely, 'Sorry, they don't do tea?'

'I'll have a white mocha,' Li said and drew a look of surprise from the INS man. He shrugged. 'I've developed a taste for the stuff.'

'First Chinese I ever knew that didn't have his face stuffed in a jar of green tea,' Hrycyk growled. 'I suppose you think I'm paying?'

'Good of you to offer,' Li said.

They sat at a table by the rail looking down on the ice-rink. A dozen or so kids, watched by proud parents, careened across the ice performing triple salchows with the fearless ease of the young. Their yells of glee echoed up into the arched glass roof fifty feet above them, punctuated by occasional sprinklings of applause.

Hrycyk stuffed his shirt back into his pants where the stretch of his belly had pulled it free, and took out a pack of cigarettes. 'Any objections?'

Li shook his head.

Hrycyk lit up. 'By the way, we found out who owned the truck. It was bought five days ago by a company which was only registered in Mexico City the week before. The names on the registration are phony, of course. No way of tracing them.' He took a long slug of his cappuccino and a deep draw on his cigarette, then glanced at his watch.

'So what are we doing here?' Li asked, sipping at the hot sweet chocolate-coffee mixture.

'You ever seen a Chinese in a Starbucks?' Hrycyk asked.

'You're looking at one,' Li said.

'Jesus Christ, apart from you!' Hrycyk's patience with Li was wearing thin.

Li thought about it. He regularly drank at a Starbucks in Georgetown, but the only Asians he had ever seen in there were second or third generation Americans. Chinese, as a rule, did not drink coffee. 'Guess not,' he said.

'You see?' Hrycyk pointed an accusing finger at him.

'That's the thing about you people. You think you're so fucking superior. You come to America, make no attempt to integrate. You take over a corner of whatever city you end up in, call it Chinatown and turn it into the place you just came from. That's why it's safe to meet our man here. Because the Chinese hardly ever leave Chinatown, and they don't drink coffee. Oh, sure, you'll try it sometime, but you always turn up your noses. 'Cos it's not Chinese. It's too goddamned American!'

Li looked at Hrycyk with an intense dislike. Conveniently the INS agent appeared to have forgotten he was sitting drinking coffee with a Chinese who liked the stuff. 'It's funny,' he said, 'how everything "American" seems to come from somewhere else.'

Hrycyk glared at him. 'What do you mean?'

'Well, that cappuccino you're drinking . . . isn't that Italian? And isn't the coffee itself probably Colombian?' He paused to let Hrycyk stew on this for a moment, then added, 'And isn't Hrycyk a Polish name?'

'Ukrainian,' Hrycyk growled.

'*Very* American,' Li said.

Hrycyk thought about a comeback. But it was either too strong or not clever enough, and he clearly decided against it. He looked at his watch again. 'Bastard's late,' he said. 'He should have been here waiting for us.' The air fibrillated with the distant sound of Hrycyk's cellphone and he fumbled in his pocket to retrieve it. He snapped it open and barked, 'Hrycyk,' into the mouthpiece. He listened intently for several moments, then said, 'Shit,' and flipped the phone shut. He looked at Li. 'Our undercover man is late in more ways than one.'

Yu Lin lived in a terraced pink brick condominium on Ranchester, in the heart of suburban Chinatown. Living accommodation was on the second level, up green-painted metal stairs. Several squad cars, a paramedic van, a forensics vehicle and other, unmarked cars, were crammed into the small parking area out front. A large crowd of Asian onlookers had gathered in the street, demonstrating that indefatigable Chinese quality of curiosity. Flashing police lights cut through the twilight, illuminating dark eyes and patient faces.

Hrycyk drew his Santana in under a dusty tree and Li followed him as he brandished his badge and pushed his way through the crowd of police officers at the foot of the stairs. They clattered up the steps, turning left on the balcony and along to the open door of what had been Yu's apartment. It comprised a small open-plan kitchen-living area and one tiny bedroom. Yu was in the bedroom, sprawled on his back across a bed coloured dark red by his blood. He had been hacked almost to pieces. Hrycyk looked at him dispassionately. 'That was careless,' he said softly.

The apartment was full of police officers and medics. Li had half-expected to find Margaret there, but of course she was otherwise occupied. A pathologist from the Medical Examiner's office was examining the body, the flash of his photographer's camera throwing the scene into bleak relief. The lead homicide officer shook Hrycyk's hand and said, 'Doc thinks it was a machete. Maybe several. He's counted thirty-six wounds so far.'

'Who reported it?' Hrycyk asked, and Li realised that racist though he might be, Hrycyk was nobody's fool. He had gone straight to the key question.

'His girlfriend found him.' The homicide man nodded towards the living room. 'She's out there. Doesn't speak a word of English. She was hysterical, apparently. It was a neighbour who called it in.'

Li leaned into Hrycyk and said quietly, 'Does she know who he was?'

Hrycyk shook his head. 'I doubt it.'

'Do you want me to speak to her?'

Hrycyk hesitated. It probably stuck in his craw, but he didn't have much choice. 'Go ahead,' he said curtly.

Li made his way back into the living room where a slight, long-haired girl sat on the sofa. She could only have been eighteen or nineteen and there was very little flesh on her bones. A female police officer sat beside her holding her hand. Li nodded to the officer who stood aside to let him sit next to the girl.

'Do you want to tell me what happened?' he said in Mandarin.

The girl looked at him for the first time, startled. Fear was written all over her face. She drew back. 'Who are you?'

'I'm a police officer,' Li said. He took her hand gently in both of his. 'No one's going to hurt you. No one's going to make you do or say anything you don't want to. Okay?'

She nodded, reassured by his tone and his manner. 'Okay.'

'Have you known Yu Lin for long?'

'Couple of months,' she said.

'And you don't speak any English.'

'No.'

'How long have you been in America?' Li asked. She cast him a look of concern. 'It's alright,' he said. 'I won't tell *them*. It doesn't matter a damn to me if you're illegal or not.'

'Eight months,' she said. 'I came with my brother. My uncle is with one of the tongs here in Houston. He paid our *shetou*, and now we work for him. Already my brother is a *dai lo*, you know, a gang leader.'

Li nodded. 'And Yu Lin?'

'I met him at the club where I work. But my brother doesn't like me seeing him. We are Fujian. He is Taiwanese. My brother says he is not a real Chinese.'

Li flicked his head towards the bedroom. He said, 'Do you think your brother did this?'

Her bottom lip quivered for a moment, like jelly on a spoon, and then her face crumpled and she burst into tears. 'I don't know,' she said. 'I don't know.'

'Hey,' he said. 'Take it easy.' And he put both his arms around her and she pressed her face into his chest, and he felt the sobs shake her fragile frame. There was nothing, he knew, that he could do for her. Her lover had been hacked to death. Her brother was shaping up as a suspect. It would not be long before the authorities discovered that she was an illegal alien, and she would be hauled up before the immigration court and threatened with repatriation. Her American Dream was very quickly turning into a nightmare.

He nodded to the female officer who came to offer comfort in his place as he gently disentangled himself. He found Hrycyk outside on the balcony, leaning on the rail smoking a cigarette. Hrycyk turned a pensive gaze on him. 'Well?'

'Looks like Yu got himself into conflict with the girl's brother,' Li said. 'Could be that simple.'

'Or it could be that he'd been rumbled and they decided that he knew too much.'

'That's possible, too,' Li said. 'In which case you've got a leak in the agency.'

Hrycyk straightened up, bridling. 'What the hell d'you mean?'

'It's a bit of a coincidence that they should decide to take him out the very day he's scheduled to break cover and meet up with you. I mean, how would they know that?'

Hrycyk glared at him, but the implications of what Li was saying were not lost on him. Hrycyk's cellphone rang again. He threw his cigarette butt down into the street and answered it. He listened in silence, flicked Li a glance, then said, simply, 'Sure,' and hung up. He thought for a moment, then looked at Li again. 'We got fifty minutes to get across town to Hobby and catch the next flight to Washington.'

III

The rain was driving horizontally across the tarmac at Dulles. The temperature had tumbled to just a few degrees above freezing. Their airport security vehicle ploughed through the darkness on the apron, the lights of the main terminal receding behind them, the rain caught in their headlights like stars at warp speed. Li peered through the windshield trying to see where they were going. Hrycyk had been less than illuminating, and Li suspected that was because he had no idea where they were going, or why.

There were lights up ahead now, and the roar of an engine. As they drew close, an army-camouflaged helicopter took shape in the dark, buffeted by the wind, lights blazing, rotors turning. It was waiting for them. Their driver drew up alongside it, and Hrycyk cursed when he realised he was going to have to get out in the wet. He pulled up his collar, hunching himself against the downdraught and the rain, and slipped out into the night. Li ran across the tarmac in his wake. Uniformed arms extended from an open doorway and drew them up into the belly of the chopper. In the faint yellow electric light of the interior, he saw colourless faces looking up at him. Margaret, Fuller, Major Cardiff in his air force blue. Someone handed him a helmet with a built-in headset, and strong hands pushed him down into a canvas seat. The door was pulled shut as he slipped on his helmet and heard Hrycyk's voice. 'What's all this about, Sam?' They lurched to one side as the helicopter lifted off into the night.

Fuller shouted above the roar of the engine, 'They're flying us up to a little town in Maryland called Frederick. The army base at Fort Detrick.'

'What the hell's there?' Hrycyk demanded to know.

'USAMRIID,' Fuller said, and when Hrycyk looked blank, spelled it out for him. 'The United States Army Medical Research Institute for Infectious Diseases.'

'Jesus!' It was the first time Li had seen Hrycyk overawed by anything. 'That's the biowarfare defence place.' He thought about it for a moment, glanced at Li, then turned back to Fuller. 'Christ, and they're going to let a foreign national in there? A *Chinese*?' Fuller just shrugged. Hrycyk was completely nonplussed. 'For God's sake, Sam, what is going on here?'

'You'll find out when we get there, Mike,' Fuller shouted.

Li looked to Margaret for some kind of elucidation. She gave the merest shrug of her shoulders. And he saw that Steve Cardiff, sitting next to her, was pale as a ghost.

By the time their chopper touched down on the landing pad at Fort Detrick, the rain had stopped. Stars, twinkling in a very black sky, were periodically obliterated by occasional scurrying clouds. An almost full moon cast its silver light across the landscape, and in the distance you could see the outline of the Catoctin mountains of Western Maryland traced against the sky. They were driven across the base in two army jeeps, and Li saw the flashing orange lights at the security gates, before they turned into the car park outside the USAMRIID building. It was a collection of ugly, windowless, concrete blocks, designed to contain the most dangerous organisms on earth. It wouldn't win any prizes for its architecture.

In the front reception area they had to fill out forms, and were in turn handed guest security passes by a silver-headed security man. A young, uniformed woman with hair neatly pleated up the back led them along a wood-panelled corridor. Portraits of past USAMRIID commanders followed their progress to the Joel M. Dalrymple conference room where a large oblong table had been set up with more than twenty seats around it. There were already a dozen other people standing about in groups talking, several of them in uniform. Li took the opportunity of whispering to Margaret, 'What are we doing here?'

'I don't know,' she said grimly. 'But I have a real bad feeling about it.'

Steve brought over an older man in a dark suit to meet Margaret. Li drifted away.

'Margaret, this is Doctor Jack Ward,' Steve said. 'Doctor Ward is *the* Armed Forces Medical Examiner.'

Doctor Ward shook Margaret's hand solemnly. 'It's a pleasure to meet you, Doctor Campbell. I've heard a very great deal about you.'

Margaret glanced at Steve then back to Doctor Ward. 'Have you?'

'Yes,' said the doctor. 'You have . . .' he chose his words carefully, '. . . something of a reputation.'

'Really?' said Margaret. 'Reputations can be good or bad. I hope it's not the latter.'

'I'm far too much of a gentleman to say,' the doctor said, and allowed himself the most distant of smiles.

Margaret looked to Steve to see if he had shared in this obscure joke. But he was standing with a glazed look in his eyes, staring into the middle distance. He became aware of her looking at him and quickly refocused. 'What?'

'I didn't say anything,' she said.

'Oh.' He seemed flustered. 'Sorry. Stuff on my mind.'

A commanding voice cut above the hubbub in the conference room. 'Ladies and gentlemen, would everyone like to take a seat around the table?' It took a few minutes for the assembled to settle and for the possessor of the voice, in full army uniform, to introduce himself as Colonel Robert Zeiss, Commander of the USAMRIID facility which was hosting this hastily arranged meeting. He, apparently, was going to chair it, and he began by introducing everyone at the table. There were a couple of doctors from the Armed Forces Institute of Pathology; several senior USAMRIID officers; two representatives of the FBI in addition to Fuller; three representatives of an organisation which Zeiss referred to as FEMA, but without explanation; a middle-aged man in a grey suit from the CIA; and a secretary seconded from the Commander's office to take notes. Curious eyes fell on Li and Margaret as they were introduced. Hrycyk sat at the far end of the table with his arms folded, watching and listening, and not saying much.

'We're also expecting someone from the CDC very shortly,' Zeiss said. He looked at Li. 'For the uninitiated, that's the Centers for Disease Control in Atlanta.'

Steve's attempted smile at Margaret across the table lacked conviction, and the sense of impending doom that had been descending on her over the last couple of hours started to become acute. Why *were* they here? And why the need for all these high-ranking military medical people?

She had her back to the door and did not turn until Zeiss said, 'Oh, and this is Felipe Mendez, emeritus professor of genetics, formerly of the Baylor College of Medicine in Houston.'

Margaret felt a sudden restriction across her chest. She turned to see Professor Mendez shuffle into the conference room with what he probably imagined was haste. He was just as dishevelled as she remembered him, his overcoat hanging open, buttons missing from his jacket, trousers two sizes too big, belted at the waist and gathered in folds around his loafers. His hair was whiter than when she had last seen him, thinner, but just as unruly. The only thing about him that reflected any measure of care and attention were his neatly trimmed white goatee beard and moustache.

His watery brown eyes smiled at the faces around the table. 'Apologies,' he muttered. 'So sorry to be late.' He found an empty seat opposite Margaret, put his battered old leather briefcase on the table and sat down. For a moment she thought he hadn't seen her, until he looked up and smiled beatifically. 'Hello, Margaret my dear,' he said. 'It's been a long time.'

She had no opportunity to respond. Colonel Zeiss was anxious to get the meeting underway. 'Ladies and gentlemen, just so that none of you are labouring under any illusions, the reason you are all here tonight is that in our view we are facing a full-scale national emergency.' He had everyone's attention now. 'As some of you already know, blood and tissue samples taken from the bodies found in the truck at Huntsville have revealed that the victims appear to have been injected with the virus which caused the Spanish Flu pandemic of 1918.' His announcement prompted a mixed reaction around the table.

'Flu?' Hrycyk said dismissively. 'Is that all? I get a shot against the flu every year.'

Doctor Ward spoke for the first time. 'The Spanish Flu was the most pathogenic flu virus in history,' he said. 'It killed more people in three months than the Great Plague in three hundred years. And there is no "shot" that will protect you against it, Agent Hrycyk.' He leaned forward. 'Your own figures for illegal immigration should tell you that the ninety-eight Chinese we found in that truck are probably just the tip of the iceberg. They died by accident. We have no idea how many others successfully crossed into the United States bringing the virus with them.'

Margaret was puzzled. 'I don't understand,' she said. 'How do you know it's the Spanish Flu virus? I don't remember being off the day they did virology, and my understanding was that we didn't even know about the existence of viruses in 1918. So you've nothing to compare it with.'

Doctor Ward responded coolly, 'Perhaps, Doctor Campbell, you were too busy helping out the Chinese police to keep up with the news. A research team at AFIP managed to partially sequence the Spanish Flu virus at the end of the last decade.'

Margaret felt her face colour. 'Then perhaps you'd like to enlighten me, Doctor,' she said, trying to retain as much dignity as possible.

'There are others around the table besides yourself, Ms Campbell, who require enlightenment,' Doctor Ward said. By now Margaret had the very firm impression that she didn't like the good doctor very much. He took a moment to compose himself. 'Back in the nineties,' he said, 'a team of researchers at AFIP HQ in Washington, led by Doctor Jeffrey Taubenberger, discovered that tissue from seventy Spanish Flu victims had been stored at AFIP's National Tissue Repository. They were able to recover fragments of viral RNA from the lung tissue of a twenty-one-year-old private who died from the flu at Fort Jackson, Carolina, in 1918. Along with other samples, and soft tissue recovered from an Eskimo grave in Alaska, they were able to sequence enough of the recovered fragments to establish for the first time that the 1918 pandemic was caused by an H1N1-type virus, and that it was completely unlike any other human flu virus identified during the past seventy years.' The doctor paused to let his words sink in. There were others around the table to whom this was also news.

He went on, 'The closest match they could find was with a strain known as Swine Iowa 30, a pig flu isolated in 1930 and kept alive at various culture repositories ever since. It lent some credence to those who had always believed that the virus mutated from a strain found in birds, was passed on to pigs and then ultimately to humans – a unique sequence of mutations giving the virus its unparalleled pathogenic qualities.' He sat back. 'And of course, it was by a unique sequence of good, or bad, fortune that we actually identified the virus in these Chinese immigrants. The viral panel requested by Doctor Cardiff included a routine test for flu virus. But it was sheer chance that one of Doctor Taubenberger's team got to cast an eye over the results. She immediately recognised part of the sequence, and initiated further, specific tests that proved positive.' He leaned forward, elbows on the table, fingers interlocked. This was his moment and he was making the most of it. 'Ladies and gentlemen, we are ninety-nine per cent certain that what we are dealing with here is the original Spanish Flu virus. Last time around it killed anything up to forty million people. This time, it could be a whole helluva lot more.'

'I'm sorry to be a nuisance,' Margaret said, cutting short Doctor Ward's moment, 'but I'm beginning to wonder now if I *was* off the day they did virology. I mean, if all of these people were injected with this virus, how come none of them showed any flu-like symptoms?'

'Because they weren't suffering from the flu, my dear.' Mendez's interjection took Margaret by surprise. She turned towards him, blinking.

'What do you mean?'

'They were only carrying it,' he said. 'In a non-infectious form. They weren't affected by it at all.' He now had the attention of everyone around the table. He ran nicotine-stained fingers through his pure white whiskers. 'The virus with which they were injected was genetically manipulated so that the DNA in their genomes would be transformed to contain its code.'

Margaret was struggling to keep up with this. 'I thought that RNA viruses couldn't get into the human genome.'

Mendez smiled. 'My dear, if you want to be technical about it, then you are absolutely right. But by using standard gene therapy methods, it's not too difficult.' He leaned forward and looked around the faces at the table, intoxicated by his own knowledge. 'All you have to do is to take a retrovirus called Moloney Leukemia virus and use it to nest the code for the RNA flu virus along with a few genes required to make the nested virus into an active transcript.'

'Woah . . . Hey, hold on there!' It was Hrycyk. 'This is going wa-ay over my head.'

Mendez looked at him appraisingly. 'I'll try to make it simple, then.' And Hrycyk shifted uncomfortably, as if in having to make it simple, Mendez was passing comment on the perceived level of Hrycyk's intelligence. The professor said, 'Viruses are made either of DNA or RNA. In this instance, our flu virus is made of RNA. Simply put, what you do is splice the code for the RNA flu virus into the Moloney Leukemia virus, which is going to act as your vector, or carrier. Then you coat that virus to make it into a retrovirus which can convert its RNA into DNA and integrate into the DNA of its host.'

'Hang on.' Hrycyk cut in again, at the risk of looking even more ignorant. 'Doc, you said you were going to make this simple.'

Mendez smiled patiently. He had always had a good way

with his students, and for him this was just like any other class. There was always one obstinately ignorant student. 'In the simplest terms, for the gentleman at the end of the table,' he said, 'these Chinese hopefuls had their DNA transformed to make them, effectively, into walking-talking flu viruses.' He raised an eyebrow in Hrycyk's direction inviting a further question. When it did not come, he added, 'However, the flu would not have become active until their DNA got converted back into its infectious RNA form.'

'And how would that happen?' This from one of the AFIP doctors.

'Good question.' Mendez leaned back in his chair, still smiling. 'I don't know. At least, I know how the change would be triggered, but not what would trigger it.' He placed his hands, palm down, on the table in front of him. 'That's what I've been brought out of retirement to find out.' There was an odd tone to this, and he leaned forward and looked along the table towards Zeiss. 'That's the party line, isn't it, Colonel?'

Zeiss looked uncomfortable. 'The Department of Defence considers you to be the foremost expert in this field, Professor,' he said.

Mendez nodded. 'Yes, when it suits them.'

Hrycyk said, 'Hey, I'm sorry to butt in on this mutual admiration society. I mean, call me stupid, but I still don't quite get this.'

Margaret said, 'Agent Hrycyk prefers his English in words of one syllable.'

'What exactly is it you don't understand, Agent Hrycyk?' Mendez asked, still with his patient smile.

'All this stuff about triggers and nests . . .' He glared at Margaret. 'I don't know about words of one syllable, but just plain English would help.'

'Okay,' Mendez said. He thought for a moment. 'The Moloney Leukemia virus has been used to disguise our flu virus to get it into the genome. It has also been genetically manipulated – there is no point in me trying to explain the process to you because you simply wouldn't understand it. But it has been manipulated to contain certain genes required to make the disguised flu virus active by transcribing it back to its infectious RNA form.' He put a hand up to stop Hrycyk's protests. 'Let me finish, Agent. These genes have been pro-grammed to be activated by some kind of protein encountered in the environment – most likely some sort of taste or smell found in a particular food or drink.'

Hrycyk said, 'What, you mean they eat a pork chop and suddenly they get the flu?'

'Crudely put, but broadly accurate,' Mendez said. 'The trouble is that we don't know what will trigger that response.' He waved his hand towards the ceiling. 'And finding it is going to be like searching for . . .' he searched himself for an appro-priate simile, '. . . a speck of dust in the Milky Way.'

A long silence settled on the table as everyone around it fully digested the substance of what they had just heard. Margaret, the tension in her chest making her feel almost physically sick, was the first to break it. She avoided looking at Steve and directed her question to Professor Mendez. 'Professor, you're telling us that these people have been injected with a form of Spanish Flu that will only become active when they eat, or drink, or smell some specific thing.' She paused. 'Why? I mean, why would anybody do that?'

It was Zeiss who responded. 'I think we have to take the view that what we are dealing with here is a bioterrorist attack on the United States. A very clever, very subtle, attack with a lethally effective potential.'

Margaret shook her head in disbelief. 'But that's insane! Something like the Spanish Flu doesn't recognise national boundaries. It's not just Americans who'll die. A virus like that will kill people all over the world.'

Zeiss said, 'We are not necessarily dealing with a rational enemy, Doctor Campbell. We could be looking at fanatical extremists who just don't care about the consequences. Anyone from Islamic fundamentalists to extreme right-wing militia groups intent on discrediting the Chinese.'

Hrycyk cut in from the end of the table. 'Or maybe the Chinese themselves, trying to bring America to its knees.' He glared at Li. Li returned the look with an implacable sense of what Fuller would probably have called inscrutability.

Margaret was scathing. 'By killing their own people?' she asked.

'The Japs used kamikaze pilots, didn't they?' Hrycyk said, with what he clearly imagined was reason on his side.

'Jesus . . .' Margaret's exasperation escaped in an oath. She pushed her chair back. 'I'm not sitting here to listen to this.'

'Sit down, Doctor Campbell!' Zeiss's voice cut sharply across the table. And then he quickly turned his focus on Hrycyk. 'And shut up, Agent Hrycyk. We're not hear to listen to your anti-Chinese ramblings.' Hrycyk's face reddened, more from anger than embarrassment. He turned his glare from Li to Margaret.

Zeiss continued, 'The whole purpose of this meeting tonight is to put together the basis of a task force to deal with this emergency in its initial stages. We require to hunt down these people smugglers and take their organisation apart. We need to know who injected the illegal aliens and why. And we need to know how many of them are walking around out there carrying the virus into the population, and how it is going to be triggered.' He nodded towards the professor. 'Which is why Professor Mendez has been brought on board.'

'Without any guarantee of success, I would hasten to add,' Mendez said. 'Even if I can identify the trigger, we may still be too late. It may be that the genie is already out of the bottle, and we just don't know it yet.'

'Until we have information to the contrary,' Zeiss said firmly, 'we must proceed on the basis that we are still in the preventative stage of this operation.' He glanced at his watch and sighed. 'Unfortunately we are still waiting for Doctor Anatoly Markin from the CDC. Doctor Markin is an expert on viral bioterrorism. He was among the top echelon of scientists who ran the Soviet biowarfare programme, Biopreparat, right up until the mid-nineties. Now he works for us.' He stood up. 'I suggest we take a break until he gets here. Then he can brief us on exactly what kind of pandemonium we can expect if this virus gets activated.'

There was a shocked sense of anti-climax as the meeting broke up, albeit temporarily. The implications of the information that had been disseminated around the table were terrifying, and hard to take on board. Li stood up slowly. It had been a difficult meeting for him. No matter how good his English, he had struggled to keep up with the technical jargon. But its meaning, in the end, had become all too painfully clear to him. Illegal immigrants from his country were being injected with a lethal flu virus which they were unwittingly carrying into the United States. The ease with which such a situation could blow up into full-scale confrontation between the US and China was clear to him. Hrycyk's attitude was likely to be shared by many millions of Americans. The decision to involve Li in the investigation, even if only at ground level, was almost certainly a political one, designed to maintain some kind of equilibrium between the two countries. If, and when, it ever became public, however, there was no telling how popular reaction might shape political responses. Li felt as if he were being asked to perform a balancing act on the razor-sharp blade of a knife. If he didn't fall to one side or the other, he was in danger of being cut in two. It was not something, he realised, that he could afford to think about. All he could do was keep his head down and focus as narrowly as possible on the investigation. He would ignore everything else and do what he was good at. He turned to see where Margaret was, but only in time to catch sight of her hurrying out into the corridor.

Steve was halfway along it before Margaret caught up with him. 'Steve . . . ?' He stopped, and she thought she saw death in those eyes that only twenty-four hours earlier had been sparkling and so alive. 'Have they tested your blood samples for the virus?' He nodded. She could barely bring herself to ask. 'And?'

He said bleakly, 'I don't know yet. I haven't had the results.'

'Oh, Steve . . .' Margaret took his hand. 'Until you know otherwise, you've got to believe you're okay.'

'I can't,' he said simply. 'Margaret, I'm frightened to eat or drink anything. If I have got the virus, who knows what might trigger it?'

Margaret said, 'Then you've got to eat Chinese.'

He looked at her with incredulity. 'Even I don't think that's funny, Margaret.'

'I'm not being funny,' she insisted. 'Think about it. If Chinese food triggered the virus it would have happened by now. It has to be something else.'

'Steve?' Doctor Ward walked briskly up to them. He looked grim. 'They tell me the results have come through. We'd better go along and find out the worst.' He cast a sideways glance at Margaret that made her feel like an intruder on someone else's private grief.

Steve nodded, oblivious. 'See you later,' he told Margaret. And she watched him walk stiffly along the corridor with the Armed Forces Medical Examiner, and she could not imagine what kind of hell he must be going through right now. An arm slipped through hers and she found herself being steered towards the door. Professor Mendez smiled at her affectionately.

'So much catching up to do, my dear, and so little time to do it,' he said. And her heart sank, for the catching up could only mean a confrontation with a past she would rather forget.

Li watched from the door of the conference room as Margaret disappeared with Professor Mendez. His sense of loneliness and alienation was immense. Hrycyk pushed past him. 'Where are you going?' Li called after him, feeling that he knew what the answer would be.

Hrycyk turned his now familiar glare on Li. 'What's it to you?'

'If you are going for a smoke, I will join you.'

Hrycyk frowned. 'I thought you didn't.'

Li confessed, 'I have been trying to stop. But I could do with one right now.'

Hrycyk snorted his derision. 'And I suppose you'll be wanting to bum one of mine?'

'Good of you to offer.'

Hrycyk glared again. 'That's the second time today you've got me with that,' he growled. He paused, then, 'I figure I can spare one,' he said, 'but we'll have to go outside.'

The camaraderie of the smoker, even between two men who disliked each other so intensely, was irresistible − and increased by the sense of exclusion created by the need to stand out in the cold and wet to share their habit.

*

PETER MAY | 113

The break room was quiet. Margaret recognised a handful of
faces from around the table in the conference room. There
were one or two others, mostly women wearing camouflage
fatigues, on a break from the night shift. She hit several buttons on the drinks dispenser and got her coffee black and
sweet. 'How do you take yours?' she asked Mendez.

'I don't,' he said. 'Never have. Got an allergy to the damn
stuff. Plain water'll do me.'

She got him a cup of cold water and they wandered over
to a free table. There was a bleak desolation about the place.
The smell of stale carry-in food hung in the air, the harsh
glare of fluorescent light reflecting back off hard melamine
surfaces.

'This place has one of the few Level Four laboratories in the
world,' Mendez said. 'They can deal with the most virulent and
nasty bacteria and viruses known to man. In fact, they nurture
and feed them in little glass petri dishes. Have you been here
before?' Margaret shook her head. 'I have,' he said. 'Several
times. And I always spend the next day and a half washing. Not
that washing is going to stop the Ebola virus from turning my
organs to mush, or anthrax from filling my lungs with fluid.
But I always feel . . .' he chose his word carefully, '. . . contaminated.' He smiled. 'The windows that look into the Level Four
labs are very small, and the glass is several inches thick. They
have a notice on the windows that says "No Photographs". Not
because you could photograph anything particularly secret or
incriminating. They're just scared the flash on your camera
might startle the guy in the space suit working inside, and he

might just drop one of those little glass dishes. Then the shit would really hit the fan.'

'How in God's name *do* they keep that stuff contained?' Margaret asked.

Mendez shrugged. 'You want to see the huge decontamination showers they have just for the monkey cages. Poor little things get pumped full of every disease they figure Saddam is preparing to use against us. And then all the water and waste from Levels Three and Four go into a separate sewage outlet for decontamination before rejoining the main sewage supply. The air is taken in through a high efficiency particulate air filter, and passed out through another two. In fact, when you go out you'll see a row of chimneys at the back. That's effectively the exhaust system for the labs.' He chuckled. 'But you know, no matter what they say, I wouldn't like to live in Frederick. If anything ever goes wrong here, that nice little German town with its antique shops and church spires is going to be the first to know about it.' He leaned forward and lowered his voice. 'And, you know, they say this place is used for defence only. But the Government lies to us about so much else . . .' He sat back and let Margaret draw her own conclusions. He shrugged again. 'Who really knows?' he said, and sipped at his water. Then without warning he changed the subject. 'I read about your appointment in the Houston papers. Kept meaning to look you up.'

Margaret said, 'I had no idea you were at Baylor. Last time I heard you were still in Chicago.'

'Oh, it's quite a few years since I moved, my dear. But, then, you'd have known that if we'd kept in touch.' There was the faintest hint of an accusation in this. 'How *is* Michael?'

'Dead.' She hadn't meant to be quite so brutal. But that faintest hint of an accusation had stung her. Mendez had been her late husband's mentor at the University of Chicago before Michael had graduated and taken, against Mendez's advice, an unfashionable post lecturing in genetics at the Roosevelt. Margaret never knew exactly what had happened between them — Michael had never confided — but there had been some kind of falling out.

The colour drained from Mendez's face, and he appeared to be genuinely distressed. 'Poor Michael,' he said. 'I had no idea. You hear nothing in Texas about what's going on in the rest of the union. I have often thought they still believe themselves to be a separate country down there.' He paused. 'What happened?'

Margaret shook her head. 'Honestly, Felipe, I'd rather not talk about it. At least, not now. Some other time, maybe.'

He put a hand over hers. It was warm and comforting. 'I am sorry, my dear. I have no wish to resurrect painful memories. I am just so . . . shocked. Such a brilliant mind, such a bright future.'

Yes, Margaret thought bitterly, and a libido he could not control. She said, 'You took early retirement?'

A little colour returned to his face, and an edge to his voice. 'I'm afraid my retirement was forced rather than voluntary. I had a good few years left in me, I think.'

Margaret was taken aback. 'What on earth happened?'

For a long time he seemed lost in his own thoughts, before becoming aware of her watching him. He must quickly have replayed her question, because a sad smile crept over his face. 'I was based at the Michael E. DeBakey Center for Biomedical Education and Research at the Texas Medical Center. It was a wonderful position. We were working at the cutting edge of gene therapy, on the verge of some extraordinary break-throughs.' He paused to draw a deep breath and steady himself for his revelation. 'And then a couple of my patients died during the course of clinical trials.'

Margaret put her hand to her mouth. 'Oh, my God,' she whispered.

Resentment now crept into the voice of the old genetics professor. 'I, or at least my department, had failed to obtain adequate informed consent. There was a major scandal. A lawsuit. It was suggested to me, as a remedy, that I take early retirement. The alternative was the humiliation of dismissal. Not being particularly drawn to the prospect of humiliation, I opted for the former.' He sat back, forcing himself to smile. 'A premature end to a promising career.' Then he leaned for-ward again, in confidential mode. 'Of course, the Government conveniently choose to forget all that every time they want my help.'

Margaret knew how hard it must have been for a brilliant mind just to switch itself off, for a man like Mendez to find suddenly that his talents were no longer required. He had never been the easiest of men to like, but she felt genuinely sorry for him now. 'That must have been a nightmare, Felipe,' she said.

But he recognised the look in her eyes. 'Good God, my dear, I don't want your pity. I'd rather have your company. A little of that acerbic wordplay we used to indulge in when you so disapproved of Michael being a disciple.'

'I didn't disapprove of *you*,' Margaret countered quickly. 'I just thought Michael was too easily led. He needed to develop a mind of his own.'

'Are you telling me it was his idea and not yours to go to the Roosevelt?'

'It was a joint decision.'

'Ah. And that was Michael developing a mind of his own, was it?'

Margaret took a deep breath. 'I don't want to fight with you, Felipe. That was all way in the past. And I'd rather it stayed there.'

Mendez appeared to relax, and his smile became beatific once again. 'Of course,' he said. 'I'm sorry, I don't mean to drag up old, painful memories. Believe me, they are just as painful for me.' He took both of her hands, now, in his. 'But I would like to hear, someday, when you feel up to it, what happened to Michael. I understand you have a place up at Huntsville.'

She felt uncomfortable, her hands trapped in his. 'That's right,' she said.

'And I have a place just thirty miles down the road at Conroe. An old ranch house on the lake. I can get pretty lonely rattling about in that old place all on my own sometimes.' He squeezed her hands. 'I'd appreciate a visit. I really would.'

She said, 'I'll stop by sometime.' But knew that she wouldn't.

Li shivered in the cold wind that blew, almost uninterrupted, across the wide open spaces of the two-hundred-acre Fort Detrick. In the moonlight, you could see the rows of new, young trees that lined the sprawling parking lots, and hear the wind in their leaves. Lights still twinkled in low, huddled, buildings, and white water towers on stilts stalked the perimeter. The first cigarette had felt rough in his throat, and not as pleasurable as he had anticipated. The second, with which Hrycyk had parted very grudgingly, was altogether more satisfying.

The two men haunted the front of the building, walking in slow silence together along the tree-lined main drag of Porter Street and back again. They had decided on a second cigarette after there appeared to be no activity inside. Eventually Hrycyk said, 'So you people still wear those blue Mao suit things over there?'

'Not for a long time,' Li said.

Hrycyk looked at him as if he suspected him of lying. 'I've seen pictures on TV.'

'Probably stock footage from the days of the Cultural Revolution. And some of the old folk still wear them. They were cheap and hard-wearing.'

'But you still go around on bikes, right?'

'Most people own a bicycle,' Li conceded. 'But a lot of people now own a car as well. In fact, there are so many cars in Beijing that the traffic just grinds to a halt at rush hour. It's one of the most polluted cities in the world.'

'No kidding!' Apparently Hrycyk approved. As if pollution somehow meant civilisation.

Li said, 'The average young Beijinger today works for a private company, might even be self-employed. He smokes the same brand of cigarettes as you, carries the same make of cellphone and drives the same kind of car.'

Hrycyk looked sceptical. 'A Santana? Gimme a break.'

'Actually, we build them in China,' Li said. 'Millions of them, in a factory near Shanghai.' He smiled, 'Who knows, Agent Hrycyk, you might even be driving a Chinese-built car, contributing in your own small way to the growth of the Chinese economy.'

'My worst fucking nightmare,' Hrycyk said, and flicked his cigarette butt into the night. 'Next time I'll make sure I buy something totally American, like . . .' He thought about it for a moment. 'Like a Chrysler Jeep.'

'Oh, we build those in China, too,' Li said. 'In a factory on the outskirts of Beijing. We call them Beijing Jeeps.'

Hrycyk scowled at him, for once at a loss for words. He thrust his hands in his pockets, and they walked in silence back towards the main entrance. Finally he muttered, 'Can't believe we're here in the middle of the night talking about a fucking flu epidemic. I mean, the flu! Jesus! It can't be that serious, can it?'

The lights of a car raked the line of trees and swung past

them on the road. It pulled up outside the USAMRIID building, and a small man hunched in a big coat hurried inside.

Li said, 'Looks like the man who's about to tell us just got here.'

CHAPTER FIVE

I

Anatoly Markin was a short man. No more than five five. Margaret put him at about fifty. His skin was pasty white, flesh hanging loosely on a round face, dirty fair hair oiled and scraped back over a flaking scalp. Around his eyes and nose and mouth, his skin was crusting and red, and had shed itself down the front of his crumpled suit. Margaret noticed, too, what looked like psoriasis around the knuckles on his fingers. His eyes, beneath strangely blond eyebrows, were an odd, pale blue and had a disconcerting quality when turned in your direction. He looked like a reptile which had been out of water for too long.

Markin sat at the head of the table and blinked at all the faces assembled around it. Doctor Ward was sitting further along from Margaret. But he had returned without Steve. She felt sick, fearing the worst, but had not had the chance to ask. Incongruously, Li and Hrycyk were sitting together near the far end.

Colonel Zeiss made the introductions and sat back,

effectively handing the meeting over to Markin, who sat in silence for a long time, just looking at them, breathing in short, shallow bursts that crackled in his chest. At length, in a cartoon Russian accent, he said, 'My hair, ladies and gentlemen, used to be jet black.' He ran a scaly finger along one of his thick, blond eyebrows. 'My eyebrows, too.' He had their full attention now, and his breath wheezed and gurgled in the silence of the conference room. 'I have not gone prematurely grey. My hair never regained its colour after it was bleached blond by the hydrogen peroxide disinfectant we sprayed into the air in Zone One of Building 107 at Omutninsk. That is where we first developed tularemia for the purposes of biological warfare. We put it into little bomblets, and managed to kill a lot of monkeys with it on Rebirth Island. That was in the early eighties. Ten years after we signed the 1972 Biological Weapons Convention.' He smiled. 'We lied a lot.'

He placed his hands on the table in front of him, as if to draw their attention to the dry, cracked skin and red, flaking knuckles. 'Over the years,' he said, 'I have been vaccinated against almost everything you can imagine, from anthrax to plague. Many, many times over.' He paused for effect. 'You see the result before you. A man whose immune system has been shot to hell.' A bitter laugh turned into a cough, and phlegm rattled in his throat. 'I have more allergies than you people can count. I have lost my sense of smell, my sense of taste. My skin falls off me in drifts. If I did not spend an hour rubbing moisturisers and oils into my hands and face and scalp each morning, I would be red raw.'

His eyes grew suddenly very intense and he leaned forward on his elbows. 'And you people thought that smallpox was dead! That there were only two remaining repositories in the world — one here in America, and the other at the Ivanovsky Institute of Virology in Moscow.' A momentary silence, then, 'Hah!' he shouted and slapped his palms on the table and sat back. 'We developed a weapons-grade variety of it at a secret laboratory at Zagorsk and were producing a hundred tons a year of the stuff at Koltsovo.' He shrugged, as if in apology. 'Okay, so mortality rate is low — only fifty per cent. But morbidity is excellent. Up to ninety per cent of unvaccinated people exposed to the virus will contract it.' He seemed to be enjoying himself now.

'Then there is anthrax. Wonderful mortality rate. Up to ninety per cent if untreated in the first two days. Horrible way to die. The bacteria takes over your lymphatic system before entering the blood and producing toxins that attack your organs. Your skin turns blue and your lungs fill with fluid and you drown. We knew just how effective it was when we had our own little biological Chernobyl at Sverdlosk. Spores were released accidentally from our plant there and killed most of the night shift at a ceramics factory across the road. Given the right atmospheric conditions, the release of a hundred kilos of spores in any big US city would kill around three million people. We were developing a strain of anthrax that could be deployed in an SS-18 missile. A single one of which would have wiped out the population of New York City. At Stepnogorsk, we were producing two tons of anthrax a day.'

Some of those around the table had undoubtedly heard this before. But it was news to Margaret. She sat in stunned and horrified silence as Markin continued to catalogue the monstrous affront to civilised behaviour that had been perpetrated by the former Soviet Union with its hugely funded biowarfare programme. He appeared to draw succour from their disapproval.

'Of course, smallpox and anthrax were not the only concoctions we were preparing for the arming of the SS-18s. There was plague, the bubonic variety of which killed a quarter of the population of Europe in the Middle Ages. And then there was Marburg, a rare filovirus that acts in much the same way as Ebola. And all that,' he added, 'when you Americans were hailing Mikhail Gorbachev as the great reformer, the man who would draw the world back from the brink of Super Power confrontation. Well, I'll let you into a little secret. In terms of biowarfare, there *was* only one Super Power. And that was the Soviet Union.' He grinned, the whole superiority of his tone condensed in his next words. 'And you know what? You people didn't even know it.'

He stood up, as if his seat had suddenly become very hot. 'I'm telling you this because you need to know that we knew what we were doing. We spent billions on research, built massive plants capable of bacterial and viral weapons production on the grand scale. We had thousands of scientists and researchers working full-time on ways to destroy the population of the West with infective agents.' He took his time looking around the table, meeting the eyes that were all turned towards him. 'And then suddenly it was over. The Soviet Union was no more. The money stopped, the programme was pulled, weapons stocks destroyed.' He shrugged extravagantly. 'They have a limited life anyway. A use-by date, just like you'd find in the supermarket.' He drew a deep crackling breath. 'But the know-how didn't go away. What do you think happened to all these thousands of scientists when the government stopped paying them?' He stabbed a finger into his own chest. 'Like me, they went to work for the highest bidder.' His eyes were alight now. 'But unlike me, they didn't all go to work for the good guys.' And he sat down again just as suddenly.

'My friends, we have scattered the seeds of our own destruction to the four corners of the earth. Many of my former colleagues, I believe, now work for the new republics. Others are in the employ of the Russian Mafia. Yet more went abroad. To Iraq — Saddam pays well — and to other Arab countries. To India and Pakistan. Some are working for multinationals, others for entrepreneurs. I have heard that Arab terrorists would pay handsomely for some of that know-how. And who knows who else is out there itching to spend money on killing Americans with the superbugs we created.'

'Jesus Christ!' Hrycyk muttered under his breath. 'Jesus fucking Christ!'

Margaret looked at her hands. They were trembling. The picture Markin was painting of a world filled with abominable viral and bacterial creations, and a whole community of educated and intelligent people only too happy to unleash them, was as grotesque as he was himself.

Markin knew very well the effect he was having. A slow grin spread itself across his face as he took in their expressions.

The same question Margaret had asked earlier occurred to her again. 'Why?' she said.

Markin looked at her, perplexed. 'Why what?'

'Why did you do it? Break the Convention? Spend all those billions on creating biological weapons of mass destruction?'

Markin held out his hands, palms up, as if it were the most obvious thing in the world. 'Because we thought you were doing it, too,' he said.

'And we weren't?' Hrycyk asked.

Markin sighed. 'Apparently not.' He smiled. 'I know — difficult to believe, isn't it? We thought so, too.' He shrugged again. 'Although I doubt, as you people would claim, that it had anything to do with your moral superiority. More likely the fact that it would have been impossible for your government to spend the billions of dollars required without anyone knowing about it. The difference, I suppose, between democracy and totalitarianism. We could get away with it, you couldn't. But I digress.' And he leaned forward, tightly focused now. 'The point is that the kind of gene technology that was employed on these Chinese immigrants is not the preserve of a handful of scientists at the cutting edge of their discipline. Any number of my former colleagues would have been capable of performing the kind of manipulation required. But not all of them would have been smart enough. Because make no mistake, what we are looking at here is a very clever piece of work. This has not been cobbled together by some half-baked terrorist. It is the work of a polished professional employing the kind of perverse logic we can only stand back and admire.'

Fuller spoke for the first time. 'I can't say I find much to admire in it, Mr Markin.' Margaret glanced at him. He looked grim.

'Ah, but you must always respect your enemy,' Markin said. 'Admire him, even. *Never* underestimate him. In this particular instance, we are dealing with a mind of great ingenuity. Even the use of the Spanish Flu virus is ingenious. Because there is no vaccine against it.'

'So how did these people manage to get hold of the virus,' Margaret asked, 'if there were never any preserved live cultures?'

Markin was dismissive. 'Oh, there have been several attempts to recover soft tissue and culture the live virus. There was one expedition to dig a bunch of miners out of the permafrost in Norway. Soft tissue was also recovered from the crew of a submarine trapped under the Arctic ice pack during the pandemic in 1918.' He nodded towards the AFIP contingent. 'Yet more found in an Eskimo grave in Alaska.' He rubbed his jaw, and skin showered on to the table like snowfall. 'Of course, none of them was able to culture live virus.'

'Why would they want to?' This from Hrycyk.

'You have to understand, sir,' Markin said, 'that we know virtually nothing about why the 1918 flu was so virulent and so deadly. And many doctors believe that it is only a matter of time before a similar pandemic strikes again, that we are in fact merely in an inter-pandemic period. For medical science to be able to study the Spanish Flu virus and to know what made it such a killer would go a long way to enabling us to protect ourselves against a future attack.'

'But you haven't answered the question,' Margaret persisted. 'If no one has been able to culture the live virus, where did it come from?'

Markin waved his hand dismissively. 'Easy,' he said. 'You don't need live virus. If you can retrieve a reasonably intact sample of the viral RNA from soft tissue, you can transcribe it to DNA. Amplify the DNA by adding it to genes in a bacteria called plasmids, then inject the plasmids into human or monkey cell cultures and bingo, you produce live virus. Effectively, you have cloned an identical replica of the original.'

'Just like that,' Hrycyk muttered, and had the situation not been so grave, Margaret would have laughed.

Markin was oblivious. 'The Spanish Flu was a particularly good choice,' he said gleefully. 'Usually a flu will attack the weakest in a community. The very young and the elderly. But the Spanish Flu, for some reason, went for the fittest and strongest. Usually in the fourteen to forty age group. And it acted with extraordinary speed. It could reduce a strong, vigorous adult to a quivering wreck in a matter of hours, completely overwhelming the body's natural defences. There are many, many accounts of how people were affected by it.

'Usually influenza victims die of a secondary infection. Pneumonia. Which nowadays is treatable with antibiotics. But the Spanish Flu acted so fast it killed its victims even before pneumonia set in. The virus caused an uncontrollable haemorrhaging that filled the lungs, and victims drowned in their own blood. It swept across the United States in little over seven days, in the process killing more Americans than would later die in the whole of the Second World War. In three months, worldwide, it is estimated that it killed between thirty and forty million people. Only nine million died during the four years of World War One.'

Markin took a long pause to let his facts and figures sink in. He held his audience absolutely in his thrall, and he knew it. He went on, 'The Spanish Flu was incredibly infectious. In 1918 American people stopped going out of their homes. If they did, they wore face masks. Shops were shut, public meetings were cancelled, funerals were banned. Some more isolated communities put armed guards on the roads into their towns and villages and shot anyone who approached. Today, with modern travel, increased communications, increased populations, the death toll would be devastating. We could be talking about hundreds of millions of people. Hospitals and public health services simply couldn't cope. They would quickly break down. No one would be immune. Soldiers, police officers, health workers. They would all be as vulnerable as anyone else. A complete breakdown of law and order would almost certainly follow. Believe me, I know. We did a lot of research into the effects of a full-scale biological attack.'

He reached for a glass, and filled it with water from a jug, and drank while everyone sat in silence watching him. They knew there was more to come.

When he had emptied his glass, he ran a tongue over

cracked lips and said, 'One of the problems we had in the Soviet Union in developing efficient biological weapons was finding an effective method of delivery. Most organisms are obliterated in the blast generated by a warhead on impact. Creating some kind of aerosol spray fine enough to carry the bacterium or virus and be delivered by air was next to impossible. I have often heard promulgated a scenario whereby a small private plane flies over Washington DC releasing anthrax spores in an aerosol spray, like a fine crop duster. In this scenario, no one even knows it has happened, and millions inhale the spores and die. In truth that would be almost impossible to achieve. So fine would be the spray required that any remotely adverse weather conditions would disperse it and destroy its efficacy. There would be only a handful of victims. On the other hand, mankind has, built-in, the most efficient aerosol spray in existence – human breath. And in close contact with other human beings it is extraordinarily efficient at passing on infectious diseases. Coughing, sneezing, even just breathing in a confined space, will fill the air around you with your invisible, contaminated spray. You cough into your hand and you have coated it with the virus. You shake hands with someone else, or they handle a sheet of paper that you have touched, and then rub their eyes, or eat a sandwich. They are now infected. Almost nothing else in nature is as efficient at passing on disease as human beings themselves. Which, of course, makes people the perfect delivery system for a biological attack. And the illegal Chinese immigrants in our midst, ideal unwitting carriers. Trojan Horses awaiting activation.' He paused momentarily before delivering his *coup de grace*. 'And when their disease becomes active,' he said, 'it will be apocalyptic.'

As the meeting broke up, Margaret saw that Li had been cornered by Colonel Zeiss and they were in a huddle with Fuller and Hrycyk. Doctor Ward was making a hurried exit with the Commander's secretary. As she turned to go after him, Mendez caught her arm. 'Margaret . . .'

But she said, 'I'm sorry Felipe, I'll catch up with you later.' And she hastened after the Armed Forces Medical Examiner. She called to him and caught up with him at the end of the corridor as the Commander's secretary flashed an electronic ID at a reader on the wall and the double fire doors ahead of them opened. Ward seemed irritated by Margaret's pursuit. 'What is it, Doctor?' he asked irritably.

'Where's Steve?'

Ward's face darkened. 'We have received confirmation that Major Cardiff has been infected with the flu virus,' he said grimly. 'He's been confined to the isolation ward here on the base until further notice.'

II

A young female orderly in green camouflage fatigues led her through a maze of corridors, fluorescent ceiling lights set at regular intervals reflecting off a shiny white floor. Hessian-lined walls were pasted with notices and posters. Electronic doors opened ahead of them as the orderly waved her magnetic ID. And then Margaret could hear the hubbub of voices, and at the end of the corridor they turned into an open area with an L-shaped desk, like the admitting desk in any hospital. Except that all the staff wore army camouflage. On her left, a door stood open to a room where pale blue protective biosuits hung in rows from hooks on the wall. On her right, the door to the isolation ward was firmly shut. It had a window at eye-level, and beneath it a secure hatch where foodstuffs and other items were fed into the ward via a chamber which bathed everything in ultra-violet light. To the right of it, a two-way autoclave was built into the wall for the retrieval of potentially infected material. On the left, there was a door into the changing area which led to the decontamination showers, providing a germ-free airlock for staff entering and leaving the ward.

Margaret was trembling. She felt as if she might throw up at any moment. And she remembered the words Mendez had used to describe how he felt after each visit to this place. *I always feel contaminated*, he had said. She was an experienced doctor, but in that moment she knew how he felt, and she was almost overcome by an enormous sense of vulnerability.

She became aware of the orderly talking to her. 'This is Ward 200,' she was saying. 'Originally it was a part of the Walter Reed Military Hospital in Washington. In theory it'll take four beds, but we have it set up with just one in each room. We haven't had anyone in here for more than fifteen years.' She indicated a unit mounted on the wall to the right of the door. 'You can use this intercom to communicate with the patient.' She pressed a buzzer and said, 'Doctor, you got your first visitor.'

Margaret peered apprehensively through the window. There was an ante-room with white painted brick walls. To the left was the stainless steel door to the main decontamination shower. Through the back wall were doors leading to the two single-bed care rooms. Thick, corkscrewed yellow cables hung from the walls at regular intervals. Nursing and medical staff who entered the ward in their protective bio-suits could plug into them, and move around with independently supplied air. Steve was sitting on the edge of the bed in the room on the left. He was wearing white cotton pyjamas and what looked like paper slippers. Beyond him, Margaret could see banks of life-support equipment, monitors and cables. A cartoon was playing on a wall-mounted TV. He jumped off the bed and wandered through with a broad grin on his face. When he reached the intercom on his side of the glass, Margaret heard his voice crackle across the speaker. 'What a relief, huh?'

Margaret frowned. 'What do you mean?'

'Well, now that I know I have it, I can stop worrying about whether I'm going to get it. Which means I can do all my worrying about what's going to trigger it.'

She felt tears pricking her eyes. 'Oh, Steve . . .'

'Hey,' he said. 'Don't get all soppy on me. If I'm going to get sick, this is probably the best place in the whole world to be. And it's only the flu, after all. Did they tell you this is really part of Walter Reed?' She nodded, afraid even to try to speak. He spread out his arms to either side. 'So welcome to Wally World.' Then he lowered his voice. 'You know, they call this ward "The Slammer". I'm beginning to think maybe I'm only here for failing to pay my parking tickets.' And, as an afterthought, 'Didn't George Dubya make that a capital offence when he was Texas Governor? Good thing we're in Maryland, or I could be on Death Row.'

There was something manic about his relentless attempts to be funny, as if perhaps in stopping for a moment reality might encroach. Margaret could only raise a pale smile. 'Is there anything I can get you?' she asked.

'Books,' he said. 'Something to read. I've spent my life avoiding watching television, and that's all they've got here. I've passed the last hour reading the instruction labels on every bit of equipment in the place. Not particularly edifying, but a cut above South Park.' He flicked his head over his shoulder towards the TV set. 'I had no idea that American humour had descended to the level of schoolboy vulgarity. Do you think we caught it off the British?'

Margaret couldn't even bring a smile to her lips this time. 'Anything else?'

'Yeah, my personal stereo. It's in my desk in the office. My tapes are on the bookshelf.'

'They'll not let me go rifling through things in your office, Steve,' she said. 'Can't one of the guys get that stuff for you?'

He looked suddenly embarrassed. 'Well ... there *was*

something else. I kind of don't like to ask the guys, you know?'

Margaret couldn't hide her surprise. 'What could you ask me to get that you couldn't ask the guys?'

He shrugged, and to her horror she saw tears filling his eyes. 'I keep a picture on my desk. In one of those little silver frames. It's my kid, you know? Little Danni.' He tried to grin. 'They'd probably think I was just being soft.'

Margaret looked at him, surprised that he would be embarrassed by a thing like that. Sometimes men could be strange about sharing their emotions with other men. As if it was somehow a sign of weakness. She would not have put Steve in that category. But, then, she realised, she had only known him a matter of days. In truth she didn't really know him at all. All that she knew for certain was that he was vulnerable and scared and desperately trying to hide it – particularly from himself. 'Sure,' she said. 'I'll do that for you – if your boss'll let me.'

It was Steve's turn to be surprised. 'Why wouldn't he?'

'I don't think he likes me much, Steve.'

'Nah, he's just a grumpy old bastard,' Steve said. 'He's like that with everyone.'

But Margaret was not convinced. 'So why doesn't he wear a uniform? Or does he consider himself above all that?'

'Oh, no. He doesn't wear one because he's not in the services.'

Margaret frowned. 'How come? I mean, *you* are. And all the other pathologists.'

'Yeah, but we're all from different services. *The* Armed Forces Medical Examiner is a civilian; not answerable to any one service. So there's no risk of bias.'

'Well, he's biased against me, I don't care what you say.' She knew that by just keeping him talking she was making him take his mind off himself.

'Well, if he is, I'm going to have to sort him out,' Steve said. 'Boss or no boss. And, I can hardly get in any worse trouble than I am already. Can I?'

Margaret grinned. 'I guess not.' And for a moment neither of them knew what else to say. Small talk had been exhausted. Then Margaret said, 'Well, you're just going to have to hurry up and get out of there. I don't much care for men who break their promises.'

He half smiled, half frowned. 'What do you mean?'

'You promised to take me to this little place you knew in Washington.'

His smile faded. 'And I suppose the only reason you'd go now is because you felt sorry for me.'

It was a strange, unexpected slap in the face. But she supposed she deserved it. After all, it was only a matter of hours since she had turned him down for dinner that night. 'I'd go,' she said, 'because I enjoy your company.'

He looked at her long and hard through the window, and she saw him bite his lower lip. He put his hand up on the glass, and she placed her hand on the other side of it, a mirror image, palm to palm. But there was no warmth or comfort in it. Just the cold hard surface of the glass.

'I'm sorry, Steve,' she said. 'I'm so sorry.'

His eyes filled again. He said, 'You've no idea how lonely it is in here.' He swallowed, fighting to control himself. 'I'm scared, Margaret.'

Margaret found Doctor Ward in the reception area of the main entrance, in discussion with a number of Steve's colleagues, and several of the USAMRIID officers who had attended the meeting.

'Could I have a word, Doctor Ward?' she asked.

Ward turned and glared at her. 'I'm busy right now.' And he turned back to the others.

Margaret stood smarting for a moment at his rebuff. Then she said, 'So one of your people is dying in an isolation ward and you're "too busy" to talk to me about it.'

She saw the back of his neck flush deep red. A hush fell over the group. 'Excuse me, gentlemen,' he said, and he turned to lay a dark look on her. 'I don't care to be spoken to like that, Doctor,' he said tightly.

'Well, at last you and I have found something in common,' Margaret said, meeting his eye with an unwavering stare. She saw red spots appear high on his cheeks. Contained anger.

'What do you want?' he asked evenly.

'Steve asked me to get some stuff for him from his office. I wondered if I could drop by tomorrow.'

'I'll get one of the secretaries to have it sent up to him,' Ward said.

'No. Steve asked me to get it,' Margaret said. 'Some of it's personal.'

'Personal?' Ward tried out the word, and from his expression did not appear to like the taste of it. 'Why would he ask you to get something *personal* for him?'

'With the greatest respect,' Margaret said, showing no respect at all, 'that's none of your fucking business, Doctor.'

Ward blanched. He gave her a long, hard look. 'You're a very hostile young woman,' he said.

'Actually, I'm not,' she said. 'But when people make it clear they don't like me, as far as I'm concerned they lose all right to my civility.' She thrust her jaw out defiantly. 'So what is it you don't like about me, Doctor Ward? I'm not aware of having done anything to offend you — at least, before tonight.'

Ward took a long time considering his response, or perhaps deciding whether or not to make one at all. Finally he said, 'My father was a medic in Korea in the fifties, when I was just a teenager. He died at the hands of the Chinese. Rather horribly, I'm led to believe.'

Margaret stared at him. 'And your point is?'

'I would have thought that was obvious,' he said.

And Margaret knew then that her relationship with Li was likely to prove just as difficult in the United States as it had in China. She looked at Ward with contempt. 'I used to think, Doctor Ward, that intelligence and reason were one and the same thing. Clearly I was wrong.' She took a deep breath. 'I'll come by and pick up Steve's things tomorrow.' She turned towards the door, but stopped and, half turning back, added,

'By the way, I think you'll find there are a lot of men and women in China who lost their fathers in Korea, too.' She tossed her guest security pass on the desk and walked out.

The chill air stung her hot cheeks, and she felt the wind cut through her like a cold steel blade. There was a line of cars sitting at the kerbside, engines running. Uniformed drivers sat waiting patiently for their passengers, and it suddenly occurred to Margaret that she was a long way from home with no way of getting back. The rear passenger door of the car second from front opened and Li leaned out. 'Are you coming?' he called.

She didn't need a second invitation. As she slid into the rear seat beside him she said, 'Where are we going?'

'Washington,' he said. 'The military have laid on transport.'

'But I'll not get a flight back to Houston at this time of night.' Even as she said it, she realised that she had not the faintest idea what time it was. She looked at her watch. 'Jesus!' It was nearly 1 a.m. 'Are the military going to put us up in a hotel as well?'

'I was thinking,' Li said, 'that you could stay over with me. I live in Washington, remember? Or, more accurately, in Georgetown.'

It came as something of a shock for Margaret to realise that although she was back in America, the country of her birth, she was still on Li's home patch. 'Well, that would be cheaper,' she said, 'and in keeping with the Bush budget cuts.' She smiled. 'Provided, of course, you have a spare room.'

'I didn't think we'd need that,' Li said. And Margaret was

immediately self-conscious. Their conversation was certainly being overheard by their driver. Then she thought of Doctor Ward and his disapproval and immediately felt guilty at her self-consciousness. And guilty about Steve, and the images that flooded her mind of the face behind the glass in the isolation ward telling her how scared he was.

'Sure,' she said. And leaning forward, 'Georgetown, please, driver.' But when she sat back again, her mind was filled with confusion and uncertainty. Last night it had been so easy making love to Li. Tonight she knew that the world was never going to let it be an easy relationship.

III

There was very little traffic on Wisconsin Avenue. The occasional restaurant or club was tipping its last customers out into the early morning. The odd group of university students on their way home from some party wandered by, engaged in still animated chatter, as if they had not had enough of the night already for talking. Margaret smiled, remembering her own student days. How the most trivial things had been of such crucial importance, how she and her group were going to change the world. She guessed it was the same for each successive generation. What disappointments lay ahead with the realisation that it was they who changed, and not the world.

Li told the driver to let them off on the corner of Wisconsin and O. Peter's Flower Stand was all closed up. A few forlorn stalks and crushed flower heads lay scattered across the redbrick sidewalk. Margaret reflected on the strange coincidence that she and Li both rented houses in streets called 'O'. The shadow of the trees lay darkly along the street in the strong moonlight. The first few leaves of fall were gathered in the gutters, wet and sad after the earlier rain.

As they walked silently along the sidewalk, side by side but not touching, Margaret looked at the two- and three-storey brick townhouses painted green and red and white, the Georgian windows, the wrought ironwork, the expensive cars parked at the kerb. She glanced at Li. 'How can you afford to live here?' she asked. The two-bedroomed police apartment he had shared with his uncle in Beijing had been extravagant by Chinese standards, modest by American. But this was millionaire territory. Rich people lived here. She knew that the Kennedys had owned a house somewhere close by, in one of the streets off Wisconsin, while he was a Senator. Their last home before his final move to the White House.

'The Embassy pays for it,' Li said. 'Before I took the job, I had a long conversation with the man I would replace. Like most of the rest of the staff he had a tiny apartment in the Embassy building over on Connecticut. He said you could never escape from the job. When it was night-time here, it was daytime in China, and vice versa. And because he was in the building he was on call twenty-four hours a day. So I made it a condition of accepting the post that they got me an outside apartment.'

'And they agreed?' Just like that?'

He shrugged. 'Apparently they have owned the house here on O Street for many years. I don't know who used it before, or what for, but I had another, very good reason for needing a bigger place.'

'What was that?'

'I was not alone.'

Margaret stopped and looked at him with a mixture of consternation and anger. 'Are you telling me you've brought a woman here with you?'

He nodded solemnly. 'I've been meaning to tell you. But somehow the moment just never seemed right.'

Margaret stared at him in disbelief. 'And do I know her?' she asked facetiously.

Li nodded again. Then he said, 'She really misses those cold winter days when you used to take her kite-flying in Tiananmen Square.'

Margaret felt like a big, soft gloved hand had swung out of the night and knocked her over. She caught her breath. 'Xinxin?' Her incredulity almost robbed her of speech. 'Xinxin is here in America?' It had been almost as hard to leave the child as it had been to leave Li.

'I've adopted her now, officially,' Li said. 'Her father is having a child with another woman. He did not want her back. And no one has heard anything from my sister since she went south to have her baby boy.' He shrugged. 'So I needed a room for her, and another for her nanny.'

The house was set back behind a small garden. It had blue-painted shutters at the windows and was smothered in ivy. Red-tiled steps and a path led through lush green shrubbery to the front door. A security lamp clicked on as they approached it, flooding the garden and the street with a bright, cold light. Li unlocked the door and turned on a sidelamp in a long, narrow hallway. There was a staircase on the right leading steeply up to the second floor. Margaret squeezed in past a bicycle leaning against the wall. Li smiled. 'I still like to cycle to my work.'

Almost immediately, a young Chinese woman appeared, blinking, at the top of the stairs. She wore a long nightshirt and was in her bare feet. She had short, dark, club-cut hair above a round, flat, almost Mongolian face. She put her hand up to her eyes. 'Is that you, Mister Li?'

'Yes, Meiping. I have a guest with me. Doctor Campbell. She will be staying the night.' He paused. 'Is Xinxin sleeping?'

'Yes, Mister Li.'

'We'll maybe look in on her before we go to bed.'

'Sure, Mister Li. Anything you want?'

'No, it's alright, Meiping. You can go back to bed.'

'Thank you, Mister Li. Goodnight, Mister Li.' And she padded off back to her bedroom.

'She has been a remarkable find,' Li told Margaret. 'The Embassy got her for me. Xinxin adores her.'

He took her into a front room that overlooked the street through Georgian windows. The furniture was lacquered Chinese antique, formal and not very comfortable. Li shrugged. 'It came with the house.' She followed him into a fitted kitchen with a small, round table at its centre. A pull-down lamp lit the circle of it very brightly, leaving the rest of the room in darkness. Li threw a switch and concealed lights beneath the wall units flickered briefly and lit the perimeter of the room. He opened a tall refrigerator. 'Drink?'

Margaret said, 'I'd rather see Xinxin first. I promise I won't wake her.'

The house was tall and very narrow, but extended a long way back from the street. At the top of the stairs a hallway ran to a room at the front of the house, and another ran crookedly towards the back, down three steps, past a small bathroom, and up another two to where doors led off to the back bedrooms. Meiping's room was on the left. Li gingerly turned the handle on Xinxin's door and they crept into the darkness of her room. The reflected light from the hall cast itself faintly across Xinxin's face where her head lay on the pillow, tilted to one side, her mouth slightly open. The room was filled with the slow, heavy sound of her breathing. Margaret perched herself gently on the edge of the bed and looked at the little face, marvelling both at its familiarity, and at the way it had changed in not even a year and a half. It was a long time in the life of a seven-year-old child. Her face had become a little thinner, her features more well defined. Her hair, which Margaret had always tied in pigtails high up on each side of her head, was longer and fanned out across the pillow. A single strand of it fell across her cheek and into her mouth. Very carefully, Margaret drew it away from her lips, and the child's eyes flickered open. They were bleary and sleepily distant and looked up at Margaret, unblinking, for a very long, silent moment. Then a little hand clutched Margaret's. 'You gonna read me story tonight, Magret?' she asked in a tiny voice thick with sleep.

'Tomorrow, little one,' Margaret whispered, and she tried very hard to stop her eyes filling with tears.

'We gonna make dumplings tomorrow?'

'Sure we are, sweetheart.'

A little smile flickered across Xinxin's lips. 'I love you, Magret.' And her eyes closed, and the slow heavy sound of her breathing filled the room again.

Margaret stood up quickly, the light from the hall blurring in her eyes, and she hurried out past Li, wiping them quickly dry as he pulled the door shut behind him. It was as if she had never left. But one thing at least had changed. She turned to Li. 'You know what?' she said hoarsely. 'That's the first time I ever had a conversation with her in English.'

Back in the kitchen, she sat watching as Li poured her a vodka tonic in a glass filled with ice and fresh cut lemon. He remembered how to make it just the way she liked it. The fizz of the bubbles tickled her lip and nose as she took a long pull at the drink, and she felt the alcohol hit her bloodstream almost immediately. With it came a wave of fatigue, and she remembered it was a long time since she had slept – there had been precious little of it the night before.

Li sat astride a chair opposite her, leaning into the ring of light with a bottle of cold beer in his hand. He had pulled on a tee-shirt and kicked off his shoes, moving barefoot around the cold kitchen tiles. Now, as he took a long suck at the neck of his bottle, she looked at his fine, strong arms, and saw the contours of his muscles below the stretch of his tee-shirt. She felt that same falling sensation inside again.

She took another drink of her vodka and forced her mind to focus on other things. And as she did, the events of the day flooded back into it, along with a big wedge of depression. She thought about the bodies she had autopsied, the injection sites in the the semi-lunar fold of the buttock, the revelations about the Spanish Flu, and the box of horrors that the vile Anatoly Markin had opened up at Fort Detrick. And she thought about poor Steve through the glass in the isolation ward there, and wondered how many more poor souls were lying sleeping tonight with the virus nested away in their DNA, awaiting some unknown trigger to unleash it upon an unsuspecting world.

She said, 'I don't understand why they want me on this task force. They have the entire resources of the Armed Forces Institute of Pathology at their disposal.'

Li said, 'You are the medical examiner in Houston. That is where the investigation will be focused. It is essential that you are on board.'

She looked at him. 'And you?'

'I am a political inclusion,' he said, his voice laden with irony. 'But my people want me involved, too. They want an end to this just as much as the Americans. Contacts have already been set up between FEMA and my Embassy.'

'FEMA,' Margaret said, and she remembered the three unexplained FEMA representatives who had sat at the table at Fort Detrick. 'I know I should probably know, but what the hell is FEMA?'

'The Federal Emergency Management Agency,' Li said.

'Since this is a multi-agency task force, FEMA will finance and administer it.'

She looked at him in wonder. 'How do you know all this, Li Yan?'

He smiled. 'It is my job, Margaret. I have spent ten months in Washington familiarising myself with every law-enforcement agency they're prepared to tell me about, and some they aren't.' He shook his head. 'There has been a great deal of empire building here over a great many years, and now a huge number of vested interests are jealously guarding their budgets and their turf. US law enforcement is the most labyrinthine and arcane field of study I have ever undertaken. I was never quite sure if there was any real point to it, until now.'

She drained her glass. 'I've got to get some sleep.'

He rounded the table as she stood up, taking her by the wrist and turning her into him almost before she knew it, his body hard and strong, pressed against hers, his arms enveloping her. She felt his breath on her face, and smelled the sweet fresh alcohol on it. He kissed her softly, and she looked up into his eyes. She sighed. 'I don't think this is a good idea, Li Yan,' she said. And she felt his hold on her slacken and he moved very slightly away from her.

'What do you mean?' She heard both the disappointment and the hurt in his voice.

She struggled to give form to her thoughts. 'I think maybe we should, you know, keep things between us on a professional basis for a while. When we start getting personal, you and I . . .' she gasped, exasperated by her own inability to find the right words, '. . . we only ever seem to generate pain.'

'I don't remember there being much pain between us last night.'

And he was right. There had been only pleasure. But how could she tell him that the pleasure never made up for the pain that followed. Seeing Xinxin tonight had brought it all flooding back. She needed time and space to find her perspective again. 'Things are always just too complicated with us, Li Yan,' she said feebly. And she wondered if she wasn't simply taking the coward's way out. Afraid to confront the contradictions of a cross-cultural relationship in her own country, afraid to face the disapproval of her peers. Or maybe she was just afraid to grasp the thing she wanted most in the world in case it all slipped away from her again.

The telephone shattered the tension between them, its long, single ring spiking the dark like electricity. Li moved catlike across the kitchen to answer it before it woke Xinxin.

'*Wei*?' He spoke automatically in Chinese, then quickly corrected himself. 'Hello.'

A voice heavy with sleazy innuendo said, 'Didn't get you out of your bed, did I?' It took Li a moment to realise it was Hrycyk.

'No,' he said.

'She's there, though, huh?'

'What do you want, Hrycyk?'

'I want you both on the 7 a.m. flight to Houston. My people have set up a series of raids in Chinatown. We're going to start pulling in as many illegals as we can find. And I want my agents properly protected in case any of them have got the flu. So we need the little lady along.' He paused. 'Is she there, or do I need to track her down somewhere else?'

Li said reluctantly, 'She's here.'

There was an almost imperceptible chuckle at the other end of the line. 'Thought so. Sweet dreams, Chinaman.' And he hung up.

Li stood for a moment, anger and humiliation smouldering inside him. Slowly he replaced the receiver and turned to tell Margaret what Hrycyk had told him.

She listened in silence, and then nodded. 'We'd better get some sleep then.'

And when he had taken her upstairs and left her in his room to go off and sleep on an unmade bed somewhere else, she stood by the window bathed in the moonlight that slanted in through the trees, and wished she had told him to stay. She was lonely and confused, and then with a sudden sickening start remembered her promise to take Steve the photograph of his little girl tomorrow. Impossible now. Another failure. Her great talent, it seemed, was for inflicting hurt on the people she cared about most.

CHAPTER SIX

I

There were fifteen INS agents, including Hrycyk, in two unmarked white vans parked in the shopping plaza opposite the two-storey Dong'an apartment block. Margaret had spent most of the day securing supplies to ensure that the raiding party was properly equipped. They were all crouched uncomfortably in their white Tivek tear-resistant suits, hoods pulled tightly over their heads. Each wore a flimsy plastic face mask, filtered air blowing down over their faces from portable, battery-powered HEPA filter systems held in the small of their backs by a belt around the waist.

'Just don't fart,' she had warned them, and their laughter had broken the tension in the build-up to the raid. Both Li and herself were similarly equipped, and they all knew that they would present a bizarre spectacle as they stormed the building.

Police back-up had been requested to deal with any traffic and crowd control problems that might arise in the street outside. They were going to have to stop the early evening traffic on Bellaire to let the INS vans cross its six lanes and into the pot-holed parking area alongside the crumbling apartment block. There were two minutes to go.

Outside, the sinking sun was burning the sky red and the heat of the day was starting to fade. It had been a stark contrast to the icy temperatures they had left behind them in Washington. The parking lot was quiet. There were a few cars scattered across its undulating tarmac. In Susie's nail salon, a group of Chinese women sat in the window waiting for a manicure. In the café next door a couple of old men sat sipping at mugs of green tea and eating hot, sweet dim sum straight from the steamer.

Hrycyk was crouched on Margaret's left. He leaned in very close. 'You get a buzz out of it, or something?' he asked.

She frowned. 'What are you talking about?'

He lowered his voice. 'Sleeping with Chinamen.'

If there had been space she would have swung a clenched fist into his face. Her anger boiled inside of her, and she turned to hiss in his face, 'Yeah, and I'd sleep with every last one of them before I ever slept with you.'

She heard the radio crackle from the front of the van and a voice screamed, 'Go, go, go!' They heard a screech of tyres out on the boulevard, and their engines which had been ticking over on low rev suddenly fired up and they lurched forwards, the underside of their vehicle scraping on the road as they bumped down off the sidewalk and slewed across the boulevard into the parking lot. The back doors flew open, and they were spilling out into the fading light, running left and right, securing the exits.

Margaret was last out, just behind Li. They were the only members of the group not carrying a weapon. They followed the main body of agents along the cracked and uneven paving stones that marked the front of the building. Margaret glanced up at rusted wrought-iron balconies on windows with neglected-looking ornamental shutters. In a tree opposite the arched entrance to the main courtyard, a red squirrel sat frozen in terror as these bizarre-looking creatures in white rushed past.

In the courtyard, a metal staircase ran up to a mesh walkway running left and right into open corridors leading to the upper apartments. At the far end, a man carrying a bucket emerged from a cellar door. For just a moment he was like a rabbit caught in the headlamps of a car. Then he dropped his bucket and a foul cocktail of urine and human excrement spilled across the cobbles. He turned and ran, jumping up to try and catch a handhold on the top of the back wall. Two agents caught his legs and pulled him on to the ground, turning him face down in the shit and handcuffing him almost before he could scream. Several other agents clattered up the metal stairs to secure the corridors. The rest funnelled through the door from which the man with the bucket had emerged.

At the briefing, they had been given hand-drawn plans of the block, with key areas marked in red. They knew from intelligence previously received from Yu Lin that the illegals were kept in a large cellar area below the main apartments. So far the drawings had been completely accurate.

Nothing, however, had prepared them for what they would find in the basement. The stink of human waste, hot and fetid, rose to meet them as they ran down cold stone steps. Their HEPA filters did not protect them from the foul stench of captive humanity. It was dark, and the walls ran with condensation and dampness. As Margaret stumbled to the foot of the stairs, grabbing Li's arm to steady herself, someone flicked a light switch, and they found themselves looking down a long, narrow room with a concrete floor, double tiers of rough, wooden bunk beds lining the walls on each side. Dozens of pairs of dark, frightened eyes peered at them in the harsh yellow light. Somewhere towards the back of the room a woman screamed, and a child started crying.

'Jesus,' Margaret whispered. 'There are children in here.' She had not been expecting that.

A young man wearing jeans and a leather jacket tried to make a break for the stairs. A chorus of INS voices called on him to stop, and he found himself staring down the barrels of several guns pointing directly at his head. He stopped, resigned, and raised his hands, a sick smile on his face. Margaret heard Hrycyk's voice. 'He'll be one of the *ma zhai*. Get him outta here!' An agent stepped up to pull his arms down and cuff his hands behind his back. 'Bring the vans in now.' Hrycyk's voice again, barking into a handset. He turned to the other agents. 'Let's get these people up the stairs before I throw up.' He turned to Li. 'Tell them no one's going to hurt them. If they come peaceful they'll be fed and watered, and get the chance to clean up.'

Li spoke rapidly in Mandarin to the frightened faces that peered back at him out of the gloom, depressed and resigned, knowing that their dreams of the Golden Mountain were over. Reluctantly they began gathering together what few miserable belongings they had and filing out towards the stairs under the watchful eyes of the men in white.

One woman sat on her bunk, making no effort to move. Silent tears made tracks through the dirt on her face. Li made his way towards her and crouched at her knees. He took her hand. 'Are you alright?' he asked her.

She shook her head. 'My husband died on the journey,' she said. 'I lost my baby. I have no family to go back to. Only his family. And they don't want to know. They wouldn't pay my snakehead.'

Li said, 'Anything must be better than this. Surely?'

She looked at him bleakly and said, 'Death, perhaps.'

Li lifted her pillow. Beneath it were a few items of clothing neatly laid out, a broken wrist watch, a faded colour photograph, the glaze cracked where it had been folded. A couple smiled for the camera, standing erect, arm in arm before the Gate of Heavenly Peace in Tiananmen Square. Li realised, with a shock, that it was the woman who sat on the bed. 'Your husband?' he asked. She nodded. He slipped the pillow out of its stained and filthy cover to make a bag and put her clothes and her watch and her photograph inside. 'You can't stay here,' he said. He took her arm to help her to her feet, and she flinched away in pain. He looked round and saw Margaret standing there.

'Let me have a look at her,' she said, and she leaned over to draw the skimpy cotton dress off the woman's shoulder.

It was striped with dark bruising. 'My God,' she said. 'This woman's been beaten.'

'Who beat you?' Li asked her.

'The *ma zhai*,' she said simply. 'Because I couldn't pay. They said I would have to give massage, and when I said no they beat me. They said, then I have to work in clothing factory to pay my debt, and live here for many years until it is all cleared. They said I have to pay for my husband, too, even though he is dead.'

Li was sickened. Could life possibly have been so bad for these people in China that it was worth enduring this? He knew that virtually none of them was fleeing political persecution. They were what the United Nations would call 'economic migrants'. The idea that in America they would find the fabled Golden Mountain was an illusion. And yet the myth persisted.

Margaret said, 'Ask her if she was vaccinated before they brought her across the border.'

The woman nodded to confirm that she was.

'How long ago was that?' Li asked.

She shrugged. 'Five weeks, maybe six.'

Li told Margaret, and they were silent for a moment. The implications were not lost on them. At the briefing, Hrycyk had told them that the INS estimated around eight thousand illegals crossed the border into the US every month. If these people were being injected with the flu virus as long as six weeks ago, then already there could be up to ten thousand carriers in the country. It was a terrifying prospect, and raised the scale of the whole thing beyond anything any of them might have imagined.

Margaret said, 'I'm calling in the Department of Health. We can't just lock these people up. They're going to have to be held in isolation and individually examined.'

Hrycyk came hurrying down the narrow passage between the rows of bunk beds. 'Jesus fucking Christ,' he said. 'There's no toilets or running water in this place. They've been shitting all over the floor.' He paused and looked at Margaret. She could see his concern through his visor. 'There's another room through the back there,' he said. 'And there's a guy sneezing and coughing his lungs up. I think he might have the flu.'

Margaret pushed past him to hurry back towards the other room. Hrycyk grabbed her arm. 'This mask's gonna protect me, right? I'm not gonna get the flu as long as I got this on?'

'I wouldn't worry about that,' she said. 'You've already caught something a whole lot worse.'

She saw the alarm on his face. 'What do you mean? What have I got?'

'It's a nasty disease of the intellect called Racism,' she said. 'And I'm not sure if there's any cure for it.'

He let go of her and sneered, 'Yeah, very fucking funny.' Then, 'Hey,' he called after her as she headed down the aisle. 'Better not stick around for the next port of call. Little whorehouse down the road. You might get squeamish about picking up your own kind.'

Li came at him out of left field, catching him totally unawares. The two men crashed backwards, demolishing one of the flimsy beds and tumbling to the floor. Hrycyk was overweight and seriously unfit. He was no match for Li who grabbed a handful of Tivek at the American's neck and raised a fist to smash down into Hrycyk's face.

'Yeah, go on, do it!' the INS agent urged him. 'Fucking do it, and your feet won't touch the ground till you hit Tiananmen.'

Li felt Margaret pulling his arm. 'For Christ's sake, Li Yan, grow up! Didn't your uncle ever tell you that violence was the first resort of the moron? Don't get down there in the gutter with animals like him.'

Li shook his arm free of her and stood up. Hrycyk scrambled to his feet, trying to recover at least a little of his dignity. He stabbed a finger through the air towards Li. 'Gonna have you, Chinaman,' he said, spluttering all over the inside of his visor. 'Gonna fucking have you.'

II

Hrycyk's Santana cruised slowly across the parking lot before drawing gently to a stop, engine ticking over quietly. The row of shops below the green-tiled roof at the far side looked innocuous enough. There was a video store, a grocery shop, a hairdresser's, a restaurant. Yellow light fell in slabs across the tarmac, loud music playing somewhere nearby drifted across the warm night air. If it wasn't for the Chinese characters on the shopfronts, you could have mistaken this for any suburban shopping plaza in America.

The raid on the Dong'an apartments had netted more than

fifty men, women and children. None of them had papers. They were all, almost certainly, illegal. Margaret had determined that the man Hrycyk feared might have the flu was suffering from a bad head cold. They had also picked up half a dozen *ma zhai*, and were holding them in company with the same people they had once held prisoner themselves. Under Department of Health supervision, the INS had already dispatched the immigrants on buses north to Huntsville, where FEMA had rented an entire unit from the State prison to keep them in secure isolation until they could be brought in front of the immigration court.

Li sat in the front seat beside Hrycyk, Margaret in back. The tension in the car was tangible. They still wore their Tivek suits and HEPA filters, each aware of how ridiculous they appeared to the other. There might have been something faintly comic about their situation were it not so grave. They were waiting for the vans to go in first.

Finally, Margaret could contain her curiosity no longer. 'Which one's the whorehouse?'

Hrycyk was clearly striving to come back at her with some caustic comment. But nothing came to him. He said lamely, 'The hairdresser's.'

She looked at the hairdressing salon. A brightly lit picture window gave on to the interior of the salon. They could see what looked like a group of women sitting waiting to take their turn in the chair. 'Looks like they're waiting for a perm,' she said.

Hrycyk sneered. 'Those aren't women in there,' he said.

'That's men waiting their turn in one of the back rooms.
Massage, they like to call it. But anything goes, depending on
how much you're prepared to pay. Still takes a lot of blow-jobs
to pay off your snakehead, though.'

They heard the squeal of tyres, and two white INS vans
and three black and whites careened across the lot, brakes
burning rubber as they drew up in front of the salon. They
saw the silhouettes in the window jump to their feet, alarmed.
White-suited figures poured from the back of the vans and
into the salon. Uniformed police officers got out of their vehicles and stood around outside, hands on hips, daring anyone
to interfere.

'Time to go,' Hrycyk said. And he got out of the car. Li and
Margaret followed him across to the hairdresser's. By the time
they got inside, the half-dozen male customers were sitting
down again sheepishly on the bench. Hrycyk grinned at them.
'In for a haircut, boys?'

One of his agents emerged from a corridor leading to the
back shop. 'Three rooms in back, chief,' he said. 'Two of them
occupied. Just giving them time to make themselves decent.
Apparently the girls live in. There's an apartment up the
stairs.'

'Let's take a look,' Hrycyk said.

They went down the corridor past two shut doors on the
left. A third, on the right, stood open to reveal a small room
almost filled by a makeshift massage table covered with white
towels. There was a single chair against the back wall, below
a cracked mirror. The other walls were scarred and dirty and

pasted with old posters from Chinese movies. The air was heavy with the unpleasant smell of human body odour. And there was something else in the air, Margaret thought, high-pitched and disagreeable. The stink of sexual slavery.

A narrow staircase at the end of the corridor dog-legged up to the second floor. Another corridor with two bedrooms off it, a bathroom, and a sitting room at the far end. A couple of INS men were escorting one of the girls down the hall. She was wearing an obscenely short sleeveless blue cotton dress and white, high-heeled shoes. There were bruises on her arms and legs. Her face was hidden by the long black hair that flowed across it from her bowed head. As they approached, she threw her head back defiantly, flinging the hair out of her face. She was a pretty girl, late twenties, but her face was thin and haunted. Her eyes met Li's, and she stopped in her tracks, and for a very long time they stood staring at each other.

Hrycyk looked from one to the other. 'What?' he said. 'What's going on?'

Suddenly the girl bolted, breaking free from the grasp of the INS agents. She threw herself into the bathroom, slamming the door shut in their faces. They heard the key turn in the lock.

'Hey!' One of the INS men rattled the door handle.

Li pulled him roughly aside and threw his right shoulder squarely against the door. There was the sound of splintering wood, but the door remained intact.

'For Christ's sake, Li, what are you doing?' Hrycyk screamed.

Li ignored him and threw himself at the door again. This

time it burst open, in time for them to see the girl climbing out of the bathroom window. Li shouted at her, but none of them knew what it was he said.

The girl dropped from view, and they heard her land on a tin roof below. Li was across the bathroom in two strides. He put his foot through the glass, smashing the frame and started climbing out after her.

'Li, if you don't stop, I'll fucking shoot you,' Hrycyk bawled after him. 'You're just an observer here.'

But like the girl before him, Li dropped from view and clattered on to the tin roof below. Hrycyk ran across the bathroom and peered out after him. Margaret followed and craned to see over his shoulder. The tin roof covered a small outbuilding that housed the bins. The girl had jumped down into the alleyway at the rear, kicked off her shoes, and was running barefoot towards high mesh gates at the end, caught in the full glare of security lights which had snapped on. Li was going after her like a man demented.

Hrycyk turned to Margaret. 'What the hell's he doing?' he hissed.

Margaret was at a loss. 'Damned if I know.'

'Jees . . .!' He turned and ran back down the stairs, breathing heavily, Margaret following in his wake.

Out back they saw that the girl had reached the gates. But they were locked. She turned, her back pressed against the mesh, and watched Li approach. He had slowed to a strange, almost loping gait. Hrycyk, his breath coming now in stertorous gasps, ran after them.

As Li finally approached the girl, she seemed to cower below him. He stood for a long moment, then lifted his open hand as if about to strike her.

'Li!' Margaret screamed. She overtook Hrycyk and drew level with Li. 'What are you doing?' She looked at the strange, almost twisted expression on his face. She had never seen him look that way before. He stood breathing hard, unable to take his eyes off the girl. Margaret turned her gaze towards her and for the first time thought that there was something vaguely familiar about her.

Hrycyk caught up with them, several INS men running up behind him. His gun was in his hand, but hanging loosely at his side. Years of smoking, and the strain of being a hundred pounds overweight, had taken their toll. Gasping for breath, he said, 'For fuck's sake, what is going on . . . ?'

Li still had his eyes fixed on the girl, something like hatred burning in them now. He said, 'She is Xiao Ling. My sister.'

Margaret looked quickly from one to the other in astonishment. She had met Xiao Ling only once, in a tearoom in Beijing two years ago. She doubted if she would have recognised her.

Hrycyk was unmoved. He nodded to his men. 'Take her away.'

Li stepped in front of them. 'I don't think you understand,' he said with a dangerous intensity. 'She is my *sister*.'

'I don't care if she's your sex-change uncle,' Hrycyk told him happily. 'She's an illegal-fucking-Chinese-alien-prostitute, and she's going to jail!'

III

The lights of Huntsville were spread out below like clusters of fireflies dancing in the warm Texas night. Margaret could follow the line of the Interstate snaking north by the headlights of the cars. But at this time it was not busy and there was little traffic. She saw the landing lights of the tiny Huntsville airfield, and on the other side of the highway the blaze of light around the perimeter of the Holliday Unit, where the Texas Department of Criminal Justice processed criminals also suspected of being illegal aliens. Some comedian had nicknamed it the Holliday Inn, and the name had stuck. Now the facility had been turned over exclusively for the use of the task force.

The small army helicopter touched down gently on the tarmac. A journey which would normally have taken an hour had been accomplished in less than fifteen minutes. Ducking under the downdraught, Margaret ran towards the lights of the terminal building, little more than a shed with windows. She crossed through the headlights of the car that was waiting for her and climbed in the back. The army driver turned and nodded. 'Ma'am,' he said, 'you wanna go straight there?'

'Please.'

He engaged the shift and as he turned the car, its lights raked across the runway, illuminating rows of tiny single-engined aircraft lined up along either side. They drove slowly over a pitted road past playing fields, rows of bleachers erected to accommodate the faithful who came to watch the Huntsville Hornets on a Saturday.

They turned right past a filling station and the lights of the Hitchin' Post restaurant, before making a left and passing under Interstate 45. In less than two minutes they were on the access road to the Holliday Inn, which shimmered silver under the floodlights raised around its perimeter, light glinting on miles of shiny razor wire curled around the top of high mesh fencing. As they pulled into the brightly lit car park but front, Margaret could see the guard in the watchtower above the main gate following their progress. She stepped out into the glare of lights that bathed the prison in what felt like permanent day, and walked towards the gate.

The guard called from the tower. 'Stand below.' Margaret did as she was told, and watched as he lowered a red plastic bucket on the end of a rope. 'Put your ID in the bucket,' he shouted. She dropped in her plastic photocard from the Medical Examiner's Office, and he drew the bucket back up the tower. He took several moments to examine the ID before making a phone call. 'You'll get it back on the way out,' he called. 'Stand by the gate.'

As she reached the gate, she saw a black female officer approaching it through a corridor of fencing that led from the administration offices in H block. She unlocked an inner gate, before opening the outer gate to let Margaret in. They shook hands.

'I'm Deputy Warden Macleod,' the officer said. 'You gonna have to get in one of these white suits to go in back. But I guess there ain't much I have to tell you about that.' She locked the gates behind them, and as they walked towards H block she said, 'You people don't hang around. They tell me they're going to have the first hearings tomorrow morning. Usually it's a week before we're processing people over to Goree.'

Margaret said, 'They're not going to Goree. The Immigration Court there's too small, and we can't exactly evacuate a whole prison unit to keep these prisoners isolated.'

Deputy Warden Macleod looked surprised. 'Where you taking them then?'

Margaret said, 'The Dean at the College of Criminal Justice has agreed to let us use their courtroom. It's bigger, and they're just going to shut down the college for the day.'

The deputy warden raised an eyebrow. 'Well, that's a new one on me.'

Margaret said, 'They used it once for a real life capital murder trial. Some guy from Conroe with financial problems. Kidnapped his neighbours' kid for ransom, but ended up killing the child. They found him guilty and gave him the death penalty.'

The deputy warden whistled softly. 'You know, I ain't never been too sure that we got the right to take a man's life, no matter what he's done. I figure the Big Man's the only one with the right to make that judgment.'

'Then you're in the wrong job, in the wrong town,' Margaret said. 'They say it's going to be a record year for executions over at the Walls Unit.'

Deputy Warden Macleod pressed her lips together in an expression of silent disapproval.

In the main hall of H block, the floor was polished to such a shine Margaret could see her reflection in it. A large notice read: HARD WORK APPLIED WITH INTELLIGENCE AND RIGHT THINKING WILL LEAD TO SUCCESS. The deputy warden followed Margaret's eyes. 'Warden's a religious man,' she said. 'We believe in encouraging all our prisoners to take the right path.' Clearly a shiny one, Margaret thought. The deputy warden opened a door to their left. 'You can get changed in here.'

After she had passed through the security 'airlock' gates leading to the rest of the prison, Margaret was met by another female officer in a Tivek suit and face mask. 'All of the staff beyond this point are suited up,' the officer said. 'We got Department of Health people advising us on everything we do.'

They walked down a long, broad, tarmacked area between low prison buildings on either side, passing through locked gates in fences that cut the main drag into sections. 'They call this Main Street,' the officer said. 'This is where the prisoners get their exercise.'

Almost on cue, a group of immigrants emerged from a building away to their left, led by a single officer in a protective suit. There were, perhaps, a dozen of them. They were sorry figures in their white prison-issue jackets and trousers, several sizes too big for their slight, Chinese frames. At least, Margaret, noticed, they looked cleaner.

The officer said, 'We're feeding them in batches. Never

seen such a compliant bunch of prisoners. They just do what they're told. No questions.'

They passed through another gate. This one had a sign attached to it. THE USE OF PROFANITY IS A DECLARATION OF STUPIDITY. And below it, in Spanish and English, NO HABLAN; NO TALKING. They were going to have to start thinking about getting Chinese translations, Margaret thought grimly. They had three hundred beds here. But it was never going to be enough. This place was going to start filling rapidly.

In the processing block, at the top right-hand side of main street, sad Chinese faces sat in a caged area waiting to be interviewed, fingerprinted, photographed and documented. They displayed no curiosity about the white-suited figures with their plastic face masks. That uniquely Chinese sense of fatalism, that had served them through five thousand years of turbulent history, and most recently the insanity of the Cultural Revolution, had descended on them like a soporific cloud.

Li sat in an office on his own through the back. Margaret closed the door behind her and sat opposite him at a scarred desk. Somewhere, in the hours since she had last seen him, he had acquired a pack of cigarettes. The air was laden with his smoke, an ashtray overflowing in front of him.

'I thought you gave up,' she said.

'So did I.' His eyes met hers only for a moment before flickering away again.

They sat in silence for a long time before she said, 'The news isn't good, Li Yan. INS have been pulling in illegal

Chinese immigrants all over — in New York, Los Angeles, San Francisco . . . Seems most of them crossed the border from Mexico. Houston's just a staging post for moving on.' She paused. 'Early intelligence from interviews suggests they've been getting "vaccinated" as they crossed the border for nearly three months now. That could mean as many as twenty-five thousand illegal Chinese infected with the virus.'

Li looked at her. He heard the despair in her voice. He knew what it meant. These were numbers that it would be almost impossible to deal with. But right now he found it hard to care. He tried to focus on what she was saying. '. . . and because they're illegal, they're not going to come forward, no matter what kind of appeal we make. Even when they get sick. Jesus. . .!' She stood up, unable to contain her frustration. 'These poor bastards really are the ideal delivery system for a bioterrorist attack. I mean, how are we supposed to deal with these numbers? We're going to have to *build* a quarantine facility, never mind the legal implications of trying to keep them all locked up. And your government's not going to want them back. Christ, can you imagine what's going to happen when this all gets out? As it will. There's going to be panic. There's going to be vigilante groups hunting down and murdering Chinese — whether they're illegal immigrants or not.'

She stopped and looked at Li. And she knew that no matter the scale of the nightmare, Li was battling his own demons. She sat down again and took one of his hands in hers.

'Have they let you see her yet?' He shook his head. 'But do

you know? Have they told you?' she asked. 'Was she one of the ones that got vaccinated?'

He looked at her, and she saw the pain in his eyes. All he could bring himself to do was nod. And she knew that for him, the nightmare had just got very personal.

CHAPTER SEVEN

I

It was nearly 1 a.m. when her driver turned into Avenue O to drop her off at the house, the lights of Huntsville twinkling in the valley below. She had left Li, finally, waiting to talk to Xiao Ling. And now, almost overcome by fatigue, all she wanted was to sink into her own bed and shut out the world for a few hours of precious respite. Tomorrow the waking nightmare was set to continue. Nothing in her most terrifying dreams could possibly compete.

But the night was not yet done with her.

As the car turned the corner, she saw half a dozen large cardboard boxes and several bulging suitcases piled out on the sidewalk at the front of the house. A Ford Bronco sat at the kerbside, a figure slumped in the driver's seat.

'Jesus,' she whispered under her breath. 'What now?' She opened the door and told the driver, 'Wait here a minute.'

In the moonlight she saw that the boxes were filled with all her personal bits and pieces, clothes swept out of her closet and half stuffed in suitcases taken from under her bed. Since she had been there, she had not spent enough time at the house to accumulate much. Most of the detritus she had acquired on her journey through life was still in Chicago, at her mother's home. Which was just as well. No doubt if the Huntsville house had not been a furnished rental, all the furniture would have been out on the sidewalk as well.

She stormed angrily over to the Bronco and pulled open the driver's door. Professor Mendez almost fell out into the street. He awoke with a start, clutching at the steering wheel and blinking in confusion.

'Felipe!' Margaret grabbed him to stop him sliding out of the seat. 'What in heaven's name are you doing here?'

He seemed disorientated. He squinted out at the headlights of the car which had brought Margaret home. Then he looked at Margaret as if seeing her for the first time. 'Margaret?' And suddenly some mist lifted from his mind. 'Margaret. I was waiting for you to get back. I must have fallen asleep.'

'Why?' she asked, somewhat disorientated herself. 'I mean, why were you waiting for me?'

He said, 'I knew, when you told me the other night that you would stop by, that you would not.' He smiled ruefully. 'So I thought I would be the one to do the stopping by.' He snorted. 'But, then, when I got here, there was an appalling man dragging all your things out of the house on to the side-walk. I asked him where you were, and he said he didn't know and he didn't care.'

'Bastard!' Margaret hissed.

'So I asked him what the hell he thought he was doing

with all your stuff, and he told me it was none of my god-damned business. He was your landlord, he said, and he was evicting you. When I remonstrated, he gave me a mouthful of abuse and left.' He paused. 'Looks to me like he changed the locks.'

'Oh, no . . .' Margaret turned and ran up the path to the door, fishing the keys out of her pocket. Mendez got stiffly out of his Bronco and followed her. By the time he reached the door she was cursing. 'He has!' she said. 'The bastard's changed the goddamned lock.'

'That's what I thought,' Mendez said. 'So I figured I'd better hang around until you got back – not least to make sure that no one stole your belongings.' He smiled his apology. 'Guess I wasn't much of a guard dog, falling asleep on the job.'

Margaret stood with her hands on her hips, mind reeling, not the faintest idea what she was going to do. She could have wept. 'I'm going to sue him,' she said, frustration bubbling to the surface. 'He had no right.' And, absurdly, 'What if it had been raining?'

'It still might,' Mendez said. Then quickly added, 'Look, why don't we get it all into the back of the Bronco, and you can stay the night at my place. In fact, you can stay as long as it takes you to get things sorted out. As long as you like.'

'Oh, Felipe,' she said, and she threw her arms around his neck, almost overcome by gratitude. It was one less decision she had to make. One fewer burden to carry into tomorrow. 'What on earth would I have done if you hadn't been here?'

'Probably have worked your charms on the military man in

the car,' Mendez smiled. 'In fact, you still could. He can help us load up before he goes.'

II

Li's chair scraped across the floor as he stood up, the sound of it reverberating dully around the naked white walls. Xiao Ling was led in by a heavy-set Hispanic guard holding her by the arm. He let go of her and said, 'She's all yours.' And he left, closing the door behind him.

Under the glare of the fluorescent light, everything about her looked burned out. She was drowned by her white prison clothes, her face pale and colourless with all its earlier make-up washed away. Her eyes were dull and lifeless. Only her hair appeared to have retained its colour and vitality. Li pulled back the hood of his Tivek suit and removed his visor, in defiance of the regulations. He knew that although she carried the virus, she was neither infected nor infectious. She was his sister, and he was not going to talk to her through a piece of plastic.

'Why?' he asked. A single word, a single question, conveying a whole world of misunderstanding.

She gave an almost imperceptible shrug, and without meeting his eyes said, 'Can I have one of your cigarettes?'

He nodded and lifted the pack from the table and held it out. She took one and he lit it, watching her closely all the time. She pulled up the chair opposite him and sat down. 'Why won't you look at me?' he said.

'Why, why, why,' she said listlessly. 'Is that all it's going to be? Questions? Recriminations?' She blew a jet of smoke into the air, and then turned defiant eyes on him for the first time. 'I don't have any answers, except ... I don't know. I don't know, Li Yan. I don't know why any of it happened. It did, that's all. And even if I *could* tell you why, you probably wouldn't be happy with the answer.' She took another desperate pull at her cigarette, and he saw that her hands were shaking. 'I thought you might have asked me how I was. But maybe you don't care.'

He stared at her, trying to sort out the cocktail of conflicting emotions in his head. 'How are you?' he said, finally.

'Like shit,' she said. 'In my head, in my heart, in my body. Satisfied?'

He sank slowly back into his chair, placed his hands on the table in front of him and looked at them for a long time. His memory of the last time they had been together, at his apartment in Beijing, was still very clear in his head. Pregnant, and with Xinxin in tow, she had arrived in the city for an ultra-sound scan. If it was a boy, she had told Li, she was going to have it, in defiance of the government's One Child Policy. If it was a girl, she would abort. She had left to go for her scan, and he had never seen her again. When he arrived home that night, he found Xinxin alone in the apartment, crying hysterically; a five-year-old girl left on her own. Her mother had gone, leaving a note saying she was headed south, to the home of a friend in Annhui Province, to have her baby boy. She knew, she had written, that Li would see Xinxin was taken care of.

It had changed Li's life. The child's father, a farmer in Sichuan, refused to take her back, saying she was her mother's responsibility. Li had become, in effect, a surrogate father, and for almost a year Margaret her surrogate mother. He had never married, never felt the urge to father children, and yet here he was, the sole adult responsible for a young child. His blood. His life. And he loved her with every last part of himself.

Her mother had just abandoned her. Her own mother! In selfish pursuit of some outmoded superstitious Chinese need for a son. He felt his anger rising again as he thought about it. 'Why' seemed like the most reasonable question in the world. A question he had every right to ask. And then he replayed Xiao Ling's answer. *Even if I could tell you why, you probably wouldn't be happy with the answer.* And he knew that, in truth, it wasn't an answer he sought. It was an outlet for his anger. A focus for his rage. Two slow-burning years of it.

And then, when he had seen her in the massage parlour, painted and pouting, a common prostitute, his anger and astonishment had been quickly eclipsed by shame and humiliation. Now they all simmered together in his head and in his heart, and she sat before him defiant and, apparently, quite unrepentant.

He turned his hands palm down in an attempt to control his feelings. 'Okay,' he said. 'Never mind the why's. Just tell me what happened. You owe me that much.'

She flicked him a look. 'It's a long story. I wouldn't know where to begin.'

'How about the night you abandoned your child.' He had

tried very hard to keep the bitterness out of his voice, but it hung in the air, like the smoke from her cigarette.

If she was aware of it, she gave no indication. She sat, concentrating on her tube of tobacco, squinting her eyes against the smoke. 'You probably think it was easy for me,' she said, 'leaving my little girl.' She paused. 'It was the hardest thing I ever did in my life.'

The 'why' question immediately pushed its way back into Li's mind, but he forced himself to stay silent. He lit another cigarette.

Almost as if she had read his mind, she said, 'When I look back, I don't really know what drove me. But that's what I was. Driven. By hormones maybe, or by the weight of five thousand years of Chinese culture. You know that the orphanages in China are full of little girls who've been abandoned. I wasn't the only one, Li Yan.' There was almost an appeal for understanding in this. Li stayed stony-faced. She stubbed out her cigarette and helped herself to another.

'You remember my friend from school?' she said. 'Chen Lan? She gave herself an English name, Christina, and made us all call her by it. She married a man from Annhui Province, and went to teach there at a school in a remote hill community. I went to stay with them to have my baby. I told them my husband and my little girl were killed in a road accident in Sichuan. Everyone was very supportive. The chairman of the local committee even arranged to have a car on standby to rush me to the hospital when the time came. The nearest town was nearly an hour's drive away. My contractions started during a rainstorm, and the car skidded off the road on the way to the hospital. No one was badly hurt. But when they finally got me to the maternity unit, my baby was born dead.'

She relayed her story, with an apparent lack of emotion, as if something more than her baby had died inside her. She had sacrificed everything. Her husband, her child, her brother, only to see the reason for it all washed away in a rainstorm.

She turned glazed eyes on her brother. 'I stayed with Christina and her husband for nearly six months after that, but I could not rely on their charity forever. I knew I could not go back home. And I did not have the courage to face you. Or Xinxin. So I went to Fuzhou in Fujian Province. I had heard it was part of the new economic miracle and that there were jobs to be had. I thought maybe if I had a little money I could get to Taiwan and start a new life there.

'Christina gave me the address of a friend so I had somewhere to stay when I arrived. They were a young couple. Very friendly. They took me under their wing. He had several market stalls and gave me a job running one of them. I told them it was my plan to try to get to Taiwan when I had enough money. I worked there for nearly a year.

'Then one day he came to my stall and told me they had a chance to go to America. He had made contact with a snake-head who could arrange it all for a small deposit. He said I could use the money I was saving for Taiwan to pay my deposit, and I could earn enough money in America to pay off the rest when I got there. It was fifty-eight thousand dollars.' Her eyes still shone with awe at the recollection of the figure.

'It seemed to me like the biggest fortune I could ever imagine. I did not know how I could possibly pay it off. But he said in America you could earn that kind of money very quickly. It was like a dream. In my head I could really see myself in the Beautiful Country. I wanted it to be true. So I said yes.

'We met with the *shetou* one night and handed over our money. He told us to be ready to go at a moment's notice. But it was a month before we had word to meet the next night outside a fishing village north of Xiamen. There were nearly twenty of us. They gave us false papers and put us on a fishing boat that took us across the Straits of Taiwan. We landed somewhere near Tainan. Then they took us in vans to Taipei and we stayed there in an apartment for about three weeks before they put us on a flight to Bangkok. We stayed there in a filthy place for another ten days, and then I was split up from my friends. I pleaded with the local *shetou* to let us stay together, but she said it was not possible. I was put on an airplane with some other people I did not know, and we flew to Panama City. We were given new papers there, and they put us on a farm where the *ma zhai* came every night for sex. If you refused they beat you and forced themselves on you anyway.'

Still there was no emotion. The words came from her mechanically, as if it were someone else's story. Oddly, it made it all the more vivid for Li. He felt the skin on his face prickle with shock and anger. This was his sister that these *ma zhai* had beaten and raped. He remembered her as a child, forever laughing, full of mischief, a pretty little girl for whom his friends had always had a fancy. Days of innocence. Innocence long since gone. To be replaced by a hard, unrelenting cynicism, reflected in the granite set of her features.

'Eventually they took us north in the backs of trucks,' she said. 'Twelve, fifteen hours at a time. Through countries I can hardly remember. Nicaragua, Costa Rica, El Salvador, Guatemala . . . Finally into Mexico. So close now. You could smell the Golden Mountain, see it gleaming in the sunshine across the border. If you closed your eyes you could imagine touching it.' She curled her mouth, and blew out the last of her smoke in disgust. 'Only there *was* no Golden Mountain. Just a filthy basement in Houston, and more *ma zhai* telling me I owed the *shetou*, and that if I didn't pay they would beat me until I did.'

Li stood up and walked across the windowless room, trying to contain his anger and frustration. It was almost more than he could bear to hear. The story was so familiar to him, he could tell her what would happen next.

'They wanted me to work in a massage parlour. They said it was the only way I could make enough money to pay off the *shetou*. At first I refused.' She shrugged listlessly. 'But you can only resist for so long. There comes a time when you must accept the inevitable. In a way I was lucky. One of the boys thought I was pretty. Too good for massage, he said. So I started work at a club in Chinatown. The Golden Mountain Club.' A jet of air escaped her lips and she shook her head. The irony was still not lost on her. 'They called me a "hostess", which meant that anyone with enough money could have sex with me. All the big *shetou* came to the Golden Mountain Club, and the *shuk foo* from the tongs. There were gambling rooms in back, and private rooms upstairs where they took the girls for sex. The other girls said I was lucky because I was prettier than them, and all the really important people wanted to sleep with me – the ones who paid the most money. I didn't care. They were all the same to me. But sometimes they would give me five hundred dollars, more if they had won at the card table. And I was able to start paying off my debt.'

She shook her head, lost in some world of her own. And in a small voice she said, 'I don't know what happened. Maybe I offended someone, maybe the other girls were jealous and had it in for me. I don't know. But one day my *ma zhai* told me I was fired from the Golden Mountain Club. He said he'd got me another job in a massage parlour, with an apartment up the stairs. I would only have to share with two other girls.' She screwed up her face in disgust at some memory she was not about to share. 'It was the worst thing ever,' she said. 'Even worse than the beatings. I'd been there for a month when you came with the INS.'

Her story ended as bluntly as it had begun. Li stood with his back to her, trying to make his mind as blank as the wall he was staring at. And when he could stand the silence no longer he turned and saw big wet tears streaming silently down her face.

She said, 'When I saw you there, Li Yan, none of it mattered any more. Losing the baby, the beatings, the sex in squalid little rooms. All I felt was shame. That my own brother should know me for what I had become. And I could see myself through your eyes and know it, too.' Her sobs came in short, rapid explosions from her chest, uncontrolled, uncontrollable. She buried her face in her hands, doubling over and letting her grief for the person she had once been completely overcome her. A long, deep, low moan escaped her lips, and Li felt it like a blade in his heart. He moved around the table and took her by the shoulders, lifting her to her feet, and drawing her into his chest, holding her tightly there to smother her sobs and never let her go again.

III

The still waters of Lake Conroe shimmered in the moonlight, caught in glimpses between the trees as Mendez drove them east on Lakeside. Exclusive residences sat darkly behind trees and hedges and high security gates. Mendez took a right and they turned into a long dirt track that headed away from the water towards where a big old ranch house had its red-tile roof peppered with the shadow of a great oak tree shading the front porch. The house had been extended several times over the years, at the side and back, and rooms had been built up in the roof. To their left a couple of chestnut mares grazed in the moonlight behind a white painted fence, paying scant attention to the arrival of the Bronco.

Their headlights swept across the front of the house and Margaret saw the freshly painted pillars that supported the roof over the stoop, a red door set in the blue-painted clapboard siding. Bay windows overlooked the porch from the main front rooms. Fleshy shrubs grew in strategically placed pots. An old wooden rocking chair sat looking out over the pasture towards the lake. For some reason Margaret thought it looked as if it was a long time since anybody had sat in it.

Mendez swung his recreational vehicle into a dusty parking area opposite a double garage built on to the side of the house. A security light came on, and Margaret saw that the garage was open to the elements, the door retracted into the roof. It was filled with all manner of junk accumulated there over many years. Shelves piled with tools and offcuts of wood, extension ladders, step-ladders, an old exercise bike, a lawnmower, the bench seat out of an old Chevy, a shopping cart.

She followed Mendez into the garage. 'Sorry about the mess,' he said. 'Always meant to clean this out some day. Just never got around to it.' A dog started barking somewhere in the house. He punched an entry code into a numeric pad on the wall beside an interior door and it swung open into a small bootroom. A rack of shotguns stood against the back wall, an antique gun cabinet with glass fronted drawers filled with cartridges. The barking got louder. 'Don't mind Clara,' Mendez said. 'She can be a bit excitable. But she's a great retriever.' And as he opened the door into the kitchen, a large, shiny-coated Red Setter danced all around him in excitement, oblivious to Margaret. Mendez made a great fuss of her. He flicked on a batch of light switches and said to Margaret, 'Go on through to the sitting room. Put your feet up. I'll feed the dog and fix us a nightcap.'

Margaret wandered through a big square kitchen with dark-wood cabinets and a large central island with a built-in hob and an extractor overhead. Dirty dishes, caked with the leftovers of solitary meals were piled on every available surface. A short panelled corridor led past a well-stocked bar into an extensive sitting room with a wood-burning stove and the kind of huge television screen you find in bars where sports fans congregate to watch matches. Tall windows gave out on to a glassed-in porch at the rear filled with soft furniture and another TV.

She kicked off her shoes, sinking into the deep-piled carpet, and let herself drop into a big soft leather recliner to stare up at a fan turning lazily in the ceiling. For a moment, she closed her eyes and just drifted, wishing that sleep would take her and keep her until she could wake up when all this was over. Was it really only twenty-four hours since the briefing at USAMRIID? And she remembered again, with a start, that she hadn't been able to get any of the things that Steve had asked her for. The books. His personal stereo, the photograph of his little girl. She remembered her hand and Steve's separated by the glass of the isolation unit, and how she had felt his fear pass right through it. She felt guilty that she had barely given him a second thought all day.

'Scotch?'

She opened her eyes, heart pounding, and realised that she had drifted off to sleep, although it could only have been for a few seconds. She swivelled in the chair and saw Mendez through the large hatch between the bar and the sitting room. 'Vodka tonic, if you have it. With ice and lemon.'

'No problem.' He lifted a remote control from the counter and pointed it at the TV. The red standby light turned green, the receiver issued a brief, high-pitched whine, and the giant screen flickered to life. The CNN news desk came into sharp focus. Twenty-four hour news. Margaret recalled many lonely nights in hotel rooms in China with only CNN for company, a tenuous link with home. 'I'm a news junkie,' Mendez said. 'Only time this thing's not on is when I'm out or sleeping. And sometimes even then I forget to turn it off.'

'Well, you won't miss much with a screen that size,' Margaret said.

Mendez grinned. 'Like it? I got it for the World Series. That's my other vice. Sports. That and smoking.' His grin turned sheepish. 'Cigars.' He nodded towards the back porch. 'That's my smoking room out there. Catherine wouldn't let me smoke in the house. Hated the smell of it. Said it clung to the carpets and the furniture. Nearly five years since she died, and I still can't bring myself to smoke in the house.'

He came out with their drinks, handed Margaret her vodka, and sank into the settee with a large Scotch on the rocks, and Clara trotting after him to settle at his feet. He lifted his glass. 'Here's to unexpected reunions,' he said.

Margaret raised her glass. 'I'll drink to that. You saved my life tonight, Felipe.' She took a long drink and felt the bubbles carry the alcohol into her bloodstream, and she sank deeper into the recliner. She closed her eyes and felt as if she were falling backwards through space. She opened them again quickly, afraid she would fall asleep and spill her drink.

'Goddamn!' she heard Mendez say. 'They're *still* at it.'

She looked at him, surprised, and saw that he was watching the TV. She glanced towards the screen and saw pictures of soldiers on the ground, carrying M16 automatic rifles. They were looking up as a US Army helicopter passed overhead, the downdraught from its rotors making waves through a tall green crop growing on the hillside. 'What is it?' she asked.

'CNN are running a feature on this crop-spraying the US Army's got involved in down in Colombia.' He fumbled with the remote to turn up the volume.

A spokesman for the Colombian government said it had always been his country's policy to co operate with the United States in the war against drugs, but that the spraying of coca crops in the north of the country with the biological agent fusarium oxysporum *did not come within the terms of joint operations agreed by the two countries.*

Political rhetoric on both sides of this controversial debate seems more designed to obscure than to clarify. For the Colombian govern-ment to admit that the United States has been taking unilateral action would be to play into the hands of its political enemies who claim that they are no more than puppets of the Americans.

'It's absolutely intolerable,' Mendez said. He reduced the volume and turned to Margaret. 'Do you know anything about this?'

Margaret waved a vague hand in the air. 'I think maybe I saw something about it in *Time* magazine a few weeks ago. I didn't read it, though. What's the deal?'

'The US government's been spraying this *fusarium oxysporum* all over parts of Colombia which have been identified as coca growing areas. The idea is to kill the plants where they grow and cut off the cocaine trade at source. It's pretty much been recognised that we've been taking unilateral action without the active consent of the Colombian government. But the Colombians are scared to admit it, because it would mean admitting that they'd effectively lost control of their own country to a foreign power – no matter how friendly.'

Margaret shrugged. It didn't seem like something she could get worked up about. 'But if it's killing off the coca crop, isn't that a good thing?'

'If that's all it was doing, perhaps.' Mendez took a stiff drink of his Scotch and sat forward, his face a mask of intensity. 'But the fact is, not only are we spraying this stuff over another sovereign state, we're doing it without any regard to what this phytopathogenic fungus is doing to the people who live in those areas. It's insane!'

Margaret repeated the name of the fungus thoughtfully. '*Fusarium oxysporum*. I don't think I know anything about it, Felipe.'

Mendez shook his head, wrestling to constrain his anger. 'The government claims that its advisers were told by the scientists that they could develop a safe strain of *fusarium*, resistant to mutation and sexual gene exchange. Crap! *Fusarium oxysporum* is well known to have very active genetic recombination. It is highly susceptible to mutation and chromosome rearrangement, with horizontal gene flow contributing to its variability.'

Margaret laughed. 'Felipe. I'm not a student of genetics. I have no idea what you're talking about.'

But Mendez didn't respond to her amusement. He was too intensely focused. 'The point is, Margaret,' he said, 'There is no way to control gene flow in *fusarium*, and that's what makes it such a successful pathogen. If you drench a geographical area with the stuff, which is what we're doing, you're not just going to kill the coca plant, you're going to infect large numbers of people and animals with some pretty horrific diseases.'

'God.' Margaret sat up and took a sip of her vodka. 'And does the government know about this?'

'They damn well ought to,' Mendez said. 'There's more than enough evidence out there.'

'What sort of diseases are we talking about?'

'Well, in humans with normal immune systems, you can expect widespread skin and nail infections, a pretty nasty respiratory disease, and fungal infection of the liver.' Mendez took a gulp of his Scotch. 'In people with underdeveloped or ageing immune systems, i.e. the young and the elderly, it's known to cause an early ageing disease called Kaschin-Beck. It particularly affects children. But it'll also affect chickens, rats, monkeys . . .' He stood up and went to refill his glass. 'For Christ's sake, Margaret, it's tantamount to waging biological warfare on the people of Colombia. Is it any goddamn wonder that others want to do the same to us?'

He took another large gulp of Scotch, forcing himself to take a deep breath, and then smiled. 'I'm sorry,' he said. 'It's late. You've got problems enough of your own. And you're not interested in all this stuff.' He shrugged apologetically. 'It's just one of my hobby-horses. When you've got time on your hands, sometimes you let things stew a little too much.' He pointed the remote at the TV and switched it off again. 'So,' he said, returning to his seat and nudging Clara aside with his toe, 'maybe we should change the subject, and you could tell me about you and your Chinese policeman.'

Margaret looked at him cautiously. 'You tell me what you already know.'

'Well,' he said, 'I did a little inquiring in the last twenty-four hours . . .'

She sighed wearily. 'Don't tell me you're another of those who disapproves of cross-cultural relationships?'

There was sympathy in Mendez's smile. 'Hardly, my dear. As a Mexican who married a white, Anglo-Saxon American girl, I lived in one for more than thirty years. So I know what it's like to have to deal with the unspoken disapproval of both your families, to be aware of the whisperings of colleagues.' He shook his head sadly. 'It was worse for Catherine, of course. Married to a *spic*, even one who was now an American citizen. She had to deal with a whole mountain of disapproval.'

Margaret nodded. 'Yes, the man's always a lucky dog, the woman a whore.'

'Ouch,' Mendez said. 'I detect some pain in there.'

'A little bruising, that's all,' Margaret said. 'Li and I . . . well, let's just say there was always some impediment to our having a settled relationship.' She smiled a little bitterly. 'Usually me.'

And she drained her glass. 'I met him when I first went to China after Michael . . . well, after Michael's death.'

'I know how Michael died,' Mendez said quietly after a pause. He was staring into his glass, and then his eyes flickered up to meet hers. 'I made a point of finding out after we spoke yesterday. I was shocked. Couldn't believe it at first. It just didn't seem like the Michael I knew.'

'I lived with him for seven years,' Margaret said. 'Thought I knew everything about him. When I obviously knew nothing about him at all. It makes you feel like such a complete idiot.'

Mendez said, 'That's really why I came to see you tonight, my dear. To tell you how sorry I was. About Michael. You must have gone through hell.'

Margaret nodded sadly, memories flooding back, her defences against them always so easily breached. 'It's why I went to China in the first place,' she said. 'A kind of escape. And Li Yan was just so . . . different from anything or anyone I'd known before. He helped me get a perspective, rebuild my life.' She gave a small, despairing shake of her head.

Mendez did not miss it. 'What?' he asked quickly.

She said, 'He needs me right now, probably more than I ever needed him, and there's not a damned thing I can do to help him.'

'What do you mean?'

'It's a long story, Felipe.'

Mendez grinned ruefully. 'I'm awake now,' he said.

She nodded. 'Me, too.' Her eyes were gritty, and her limbs felt like lead, but that overwhelming sense of sleep that had threatened to engulf her when they first got in had somehow passed. So she told him about Li and his sister. The whole sad tale of Xinxin, and how fate had somehow contrived to bring Li Yan and Xiao Ling together again in the most bizarre of circumstances – Xiao Ling, an illegal immigrant, paying off her debt by working as a prostitute, infected by the virus. 'She'll be detained with all the rest,' Margaret said. 'Locked up for God knows how long. I don't know how Li Yan's going to deal with that.'

'She can apply for bail at the immigration court,' Mendez said.

'She's infected, Felipe! They're not going to let her, or anyone else, back into circulation. They're going to be kept in isolation. Quarantined. We don't know what triggers the flu yet. I mean, you know that better than anyone.'

'It's true,' Mendez nodded solemnly. 'We don't know what triggers it. But we're already building up extensive intelligence about what doesn't.'

'How do you mean?'

He said, 'Department of Health and INS interviewers have been instructed to question people already taken into custody on what they've been eating and drinking since they arrived in America. That way we should be able to establish very quickly a list of "safe" foods. A diet that we know will not trigger the virus.' And Margaret remembered her almost prophetic words to Steve. *If Chinese food triggered the virus it would have happened by now.* Of course, it made sense. Mendez went on, 'Under proper supervision, there's no reason why someone like Xiao

Ling couldn't be released into the protective custody of her brother. And I don't see any reason why she shouldn't be able to claim political asylum either. On the basis of what you've told me, she could easily argue that she was persecuted in China under the One Child Policy.'

He stood up. 'I know a very good lawyer in Houston,' he said. 'Owes me a favour or two. I'll call him.'

'What? Now?' Margaret had been caught by surprise at how quickly this had all turned around.

'Sure.'

'Felipe, it's the middle of the night!'

Mendez grinned. 'If I'm not in my bed, I don't see why anyone else should be.'

CHAPTER EIGHT

I

They drove past dilapidated wooden huts and old trailers set back among the trees on University Avenue. Battered pick-up trucks looked abandoned in dirt drives cluttered with rusted car wrecks and accumulations of trash. The occasional, shiny new satellite dish stood pointing incongruously towards a leaden sky, the first red light of dawn creeping into it from the east.

As they went up the hill towards Main, they passed, on the left, the unimpressive offices of the District Attorney. Across the street the old county jailhouse was now home to a law firm.

Mendez chuckled. 'Most folks would say that all lawyers should be put in the local jailhouse.' Which was ironic, because they were on their way to meet the lawyer they hoped was going to get Xiao Ling freed from custody. He and Margaret had driven straight up to the Holliday Unit, while it was still dark, to collect Li. Li had spent a sleepless night there wrestling with the conflicting options that confronted him.

Margaret's phone call had come like a bright light shining into a very dark place. Now she sat up front, beside Mendez. Li sat in the back staring gloomily from the window. His initial hopes had since faded with news that the INS was almost certain to oppose Xiao Ling's release.

They passed a mural on a side wall depicting the 1836 Battle of San Jacinto at which Sam Houston had led his Texan army to victory over Santa Anna and freedom from Mexico. They took a right into Main and drove past the impressive square of the Walker County Courthouse dominating the centre of Huntsville, then left into Sam Houston, drawing in beside a colourful display of birds of paradise set behind a low brick wall. The morning air was still cold as they stepped out on to the sidewalk, and laced with the smell of fresh coffee drifting down from the Café Texan. They walked past Scotties antique store, a window cluttered with bits of pottery and old furniture, shelves piled high with cheap bric-a-brac which the owner liked to call 'memorabilia'. The non-smoking section of the café was empty. A sign in the window read, NORMA'S SKIN AND NAILS UPSTAIRS. Margaret had seen the sign often, and always wondered where the rest of Norma was kept.

The Café Texan was an old-fashioned southern breakfast-diner. Low stools lined up along a red counter. Pots of Cona coffee sat on hotplates behind it. A large-breasted girl in hotpants served eggs over easy, and grits, and pancakes with maple syrup, to customers in Wranglers and Stetsons. Country music played over the sound system. On execution days, and for several days beforehand, the Café Texan played host to the country's media who would cram the place in the early hours speculating on whether or not there would be a last-minute reprieve. In recent years, those had been few and far between, and they were drawn now only by the crowds of protesters that gathered outside the Walls Unit in the run-up to controversial executions.

Li attracted some curious looks as an older woman with steel-grey hair came up to them and said, 'How y'all doin?' and took them to a table at the back where a pasty-faced middle-aged man in a crumpled suit stood up to greet them. He had cut himself shaving, and his thinning grey hair was a little dishevelled. 'Jesus, Felipe,' he said. 'You any idea what time I had to get outta my bed to get here?'

Felipe grinned and shook his hand. 'No rest for the wicked, Dan.' He turned and introduced Margaret and Li, then told them, 'This is Daniel L. Stern, attorney at law, smartest lawyer this side of the Mississippi, and just as crooked.'

'You only ever gotta be as crooked as the law itself,' Stern said, grinning back at Mendez. He sat down again. 'Damn, this is good grub. What you folks having?'

But none of them was hungry. Li and Margaret ordered coffee, and Mendez an iced tea. They watched Stern devour a double helping of grits smothered in maple syrup.

'Don't get a chance to eat like this too often,' he said. 'Wife says I gotta watch my waistline.' And almost without pausing to draw breath, he added, 'So this is some case you're throwing at me, Felipe. Scary stuff. Jesus, if this ever gets out, there'll be rioting in the streets.' He looked at Li. 'And you people had better run for cover.'

'Then you know how important it is to keep this under your hat,' Mendez said.

'Hey,' Stern chided him. 'I think I know a little bit about client confidentiality, Felipe.' A serving of French toast arrived, and he poured on more maple syrup. 'So the way I see it, we have here a young woman who was forced to leave home in order to have her baby. Could the authorities have forced her to have an abortion?' He raised a hand to preempt any reply. 'Never mind, we'll say they could.'

Margaret studied Stern with distaste as he shovelled French toast into his face. He was a fast-mouthed conveyer of ersatz justice, delivered on tap to the man with the most dollars in his hand. She glanced at Li and knew that he did not like him any better than she did. But with his sister's freedom at stake, he was keeping his feelings to himself.

'After the Tiananmen Square massacre in eighty-nine, the One Child Policy became grounds on which lots of Chinese were granted asylum in American courts.' Stern winked at Felipe. 'See? I didn't really go back to bed after your call. Been doing my homework.' And he turned back to Li and Margaret. 'But after the *Golden Venture* went aground off of New York, the US reversed its policy on that, until President Clinton announced in ninety-seven that the One Child Policy should be considered political persecution. So your sister,' he said to Li, 'was driven from her home, but lost her baby and knew the only way she was gonna have the freedom to fulfil her human rights to have children was by escaping the country of her birth.' He shrugged. 'It's irresistible stuff. No judge in an American court's gonna send her back.' He stabbed a finger at Li. 'And you'll testify if needs be? How she's been separated from her daughter for two years? And how you've had the sole responsibility of looking after the child in her absence?'

Li had no idea what kind of trouble this might get him in with his Embassy, but he nodded. It was all true. 'Sure,' he said.

'Good.' Stern seemed very pleased with himself. 'And if Professor Mendez and Doctor Campbell approve a diet that you promise to see she sticks to, then I figure we're home free.' He finished off his French toast, drained a mug of coffee and wiped his face with a paper napkin. 'Okay,' he said, and stood up. 'Let's go get her outta there.'

Armed correctional officers of the TDCJ controlled the front and rear entries to the College of Criminal Justice at the top of the hill. There was also a substantial police presence cordoning off the college from the rest of the campus.

The prisoners had been brought over from the Holliday Unit on two buses an hour earlier and were being held in the Eliasberg Room, a brick-walled conference room at the back of the court. Its conference table had been removed and replaced by rows of plastic chairs. Judge McKinley, a laconic black man in his forties, who presided over the immigration court at Goree, had been given chambers in a library room through the wall from the prisoners.

The officers handling the prisoners were still wearing

their Tivek suits and HEPA face masks, but the judge, on assurances from Department of Health officials that none of the prisoners was infectious, had refused to take any precautions, and entered the court as usual wearing his black gown over a charcoal-grey suit. On a bench, flanked by the Stars and Stripes on one side and the Lone Star of Texas on the other, and set high above the court officer and a Chinese translator, he looked out over the rising tiers of an almost empty courtroom. There were three tables set out front, one in the middle for the prisoner, and one on either side. The INS lawyer, a young, anxious-looking woman in her early thirties, sat at one of them, the other was for representatives of the accused. But of the sixty-seven people due to appear before the court that day, only Xiao Ling had any legal representation.

Stern sat looking bored, leaning back chewing reflectively on the end of his pencil as the first immigrants were brought before the judge. Margaret sat at the back of the courtroom watching proceedings with a detached sense of horrified curiosity. Illegal immigrants had few, if any rights. The court was required to allow them to make contact with their consulates, and they had the right to legal representation. But virtually none of them had access to a lawyer, never mind the means to pay for one. An anonymous Chinese in a crisp, dark suit sat very erect about three seats away from Margaret, watching proceedings and scribbling occasionally in a notebook on his knee. Margaret guessed he was from the Chinese Consulate. Li had gone earlier to speak with his sister, and was now waiting outside the court until she was called. Margaret wondered if he was trying to avoid the consular official.

The court was sitting, Margaret knew, on a constitutional knife edge. The media would not normally be interested in the proceedings of an immigration court in Huntsville, but would have rights of access if they so desired. She was certain that it would not be long before some local newshound would figure out that there was something a little out of the ordinary going on up at the college, and put in an appearance. She had no idea how the authorities would deal with that. She was just glad that it was not her responsibility.

A procession of pathetic figures in white prison uniform was brought before the judge by a burly sergeant wearing a face mask and gloves. Virtually none of them spoke English, and Judge McKinley had to resort to using the interpreter, a process with which he was clearly quite familiar. They all faced the same questions. Name. Nationality. Did they understand the charge against them? Why should the court not deport them back to China? Would they like time to prepare a defence and seek representation? Case continued for seven days. Each took five minutes or less to process.

They were about seven or eight cases in when Margaret turned to see Agent Fuller entering the court. He made his way quietly down the steps and sat several rows from the front, watching the proceedings impassively.

It was nearly an hour before Xiao Ling was brought in. Margaret guessed her case was imminent when Agent Hrycyk wandered into the back of the court, gave her a wink, and sauntered past Fuller, down to the front where he took a seat on the public benches behind the INS lawyer. He was pale-faced and puffy-eyed, and looked as if he had had about as much sleep as Margaret. A few moments later, Mendez slipped into the back of the courtroom. He saw Margaret and waved a slip of paper at her, smiling, before taking an aisle seat.

Li followed Xiao Ling into the back of the court and sat beside Margaret. She was aware of the Chinese consular official looking curiously along the row in their direction. But Li kept his eyes facing front. If he had to give evidence, Margaret thought, it might not be too long before he was appearing before an immigration court himself asking for political asylum.

They watched as Xiao Ling was led to the table at the front and told to sit. Stern rose to his feet. 'If it please Your Honour, my name is Daniel Stern, attorney at law in the State of Texas, and I'm appearing for the accused.'

The judge scratched his chin thoughtfully. 'Thank you, Mister Stern, how does your client respond to the charges?'

'Judge, my client intends to claim political asylum on the grounds of persecution in her native China under that government's One Child Policy. I don't know if you are familiar –'

Judge McKinley cut him off. 'I know all about the One Child Policy, Mister Stern,' he said sharply.

'Of course, Your Honour. Then I would like to apply for bail for my client in order to give us time to prepare a case.'

The INS lawyer was on her feet immediately. 'We object, Your Honour. Given the special circumstances surrounding all the accused in these cases, we think it would be unsafe for the court to grant bail in any of them.'

The judge said, 'Thank you, Miss Carter.' He looked at Stern. 'Mister Stern?'

'Judge, taking account of these . . . special circumstances . . .' he put particular emphasis on the words, and smiled across at the INS bench '. . . I'm proposing that the court attach special conditions to the terms of the bail granted to Miss Xiao Ling.' He pronounced her name, 'Shaolin'. 'We have in court today the brother of the accused.'

Margaret was aware of Li shifting uncomfortably, and she saw Hrycyk glaring back at them from the front of the court.

Stern went on, 'Mister Li Yan is a senior law enforcement officer with the Chinese police, and a special criminal justice liaison here in the United States, based at the Chinese Embassy in Washington. If the court is prepared to release the accused into his protective custody, then he will guarantee her reappearance in this court on the date Your Honour fixes for the hearing.'

Miss Carter was on her feet again. 'If it please Your Honour, we don't believe that this meets the special needs of the case, and that Miss Xiao Ling, along with all the other accused here today, should be held in quarantined custody until such time as the court determines a proper resolution.'

'Judge, I hadn't finished,' Stern said.

The judge nodded. 'Go ahead, Mister Stern.'

'Your Honour, we also have in court today two senior members of the federal task force assembled to deal with the special circumstances alluded to. That is Doctor Margaret Campbell, Chief Medical Examiner of Harris County, and Felipe Mendez, emeritus professor of genetics at Baylor College of Medicine. They are prepared to approve a diet for Miss Xiao Ling that will guarantee her status as a non-infectious person during the period of her bail.'

'Objection, Your Honour. We don't believe that anyone can make that guarantee.'

Judge McKinley sighed, as if he were starting to lose interest. 'Mister Stern? Do you have this list?'

Stern looked to the back of the court and received a nod from Mendez. 'We do, Your Honour.'

'Let me see it.' The judge held out his hand.

Mendez rose and made his way to the bench. Xiao Ling watched the proceedings from her table, bewildered in spite of a running commentary provided by the court translator. Stern said, 'Your Honour, this is Professor Mendez.' Mendez handed the list to the court officer who stood up and handed it up to the judge.

The judge considered it for a very long couple of minutes. Then he looked down at Mendez. 'This looks like a menu from a Chinese take-away, Professor,' he said, to a sprinkling of laughter from around the court. 'Making me damned hungry, too.' He looked at his watch. 'And we're still a couple of hours away from lunch.' More laughter. Then his smile quickly faded and he asked sharply, 'Professor, how can you guarantee this diet is safe?'

Mendez said, 'Your Honour, the list of foods you have there

has been prepared overnight by the Department of Health after extensive interviews with the prisoners appearing before you today. All these foods have been safely consumed without activating the flu virus. They form the basis of the diet to which all the prisoners will be subject, both for their own safety and for the safety of the officers in whose custody they will be placed.'

Hrycyk leaned forward to whisper urgently in Miss Carter's ear. She stood up quickly. 'Judge, is the Professor really saying he can *guarantee* that this diet is safe?'

McKinley looked at Mendez. 'Well, Professor? Are you?'

Mendez smiled easily. 'I'd stake my reputation on it, Your Honour.'

McKinley raised an eyebrow and looked at Miss Carter. 'Miss Carter?'

She glanced at Hrycyk who was tight-lipped with anger. But all he could do was give a frustrated little shrug. She turned back to Judge McKinley. 'Ummm . . .'

The judge said, 'Miss Carter, if all you're prepared to do is issue Buddhist chants, then I'm afraid I'm going to have to grant Mister Stern his request.' He glanced at his diary. 'I'll set the hearing for one week from today. Meantime, Miss Xiao Ling is released into the custody of her brother.'

Miss Carter said quickly, 'Your Honour, if you would be prepared to grant a recess in this case, that would give me time to prepare a proper rebuttal.'

McKinley swung an irritated look in her direction. 'Miss Carter, you can rebut all you like at the hearing next week.

I've made my decision.' He banged his wooden hammer on its gavel. 'Next!'

II

Li and Xiao Ling embraced in the entrance lobby outside the Hazel B. Kerper Courtroom. Her face was wet with tears. She was confused and emotional, but aware that somehow the court had released her into the custody of her brother. The sergeant took her gently by the arm and told them that she'd have to go back to the Holliday Unit first to change and pick up her things. He figured she'd be ready in about an hour. Stern had made a hasty departure, saying he had a case in Houston that afternoon, and that he would be in touch about preparing a brief for the hearing next week.

Hrycyk banged out of the court in a foul mood. He hissed at Margaret, 'You people are putting the whole goddamned country at risk!'

Margaret shook her head calmly. 'This country's in far greater danger from people like you, Agent Hrycyk. You're a dinosaur, did you know that? A relic from another age.'

'Yeah, sure,' he said sourly and moved off to engage in a whispered conference with Miss Carter.

Margaret turned to find Mendez standing looking at a flag mounted inside a glass case on the wall. It had green, white and red vertical stripes with the date 1824 crudely scrawled on the central white band. The bottom left of the band was defaced by a single bullet hole. 'You know what this is, my dear?' he said. 'It's the flag that was flying over the Alamo when John Wayne and Richard Widmark got killed.'

Margaret laughed. 'Don't you mean Davy Crockett and Jim Bowie?'

Mendez smiled and tugged at his white goatee. 'I can only ever see the actors,' he said. 'Hollywood spoils history for us, don't you think?' He turned twinkling eyes on her.

Her smile faded. She said, 'Felipe, you took a real risk in there. Putting your reputation on the line like that.'

He laughed out loud. 'My dear, my reputation is already in tatters. I have absolutely nothing to lose.'

Li approached them and held out his hand to Mendez. 'I don't know how to thank you, Professor.'

'Just take good care of her,' Mendez said. 'And make sure she sticks to that diet.'

Margaret had a sudden thought. 'Shouldn't we send a copy of the diet up to Fort Detrick for Steve Cardiff?'

Mendez said, 'I'm way ahead of you, my dear. It's already done.'

'Doctor Campbell ... Mr Li ...' They turned at the sound of Agent Fuller's voice. He was accompanied by Hrycyk and by a well-groomed Chinese man whom Margaret had seen hanging around outside the college when they first arrived. 'I'd like to introduce you to Mr Yi Fenghi. Mr Yi works for Councilman Soong, an elected member of Houston City Council, and the recognised spokesperson for the city's Chinese community.'

Yi bowed stiffly, and shook hands with them each in turn. He was a small man, no more that five-six, or -seven at the most. He had a clean-shaven, round face, and dark hair brushed straight back from his forehead and fixed there with gel. He wore an Armani suit, a white silk shirt and a plain blue tie. 'Pleasure to meet you, Doctor Campbell. Gentlemen.' His English was correct, but stilted.

'What do you say we go take a seat over there?' Fuller said, indicating a group of comfortable chairs by the window forming a square around a central table. And they moved away from the figures milling outside the courtroom and arranged themselves around the square. The window looked out on to a car park at the back, within the horseshoe shape of the college.

Fuller said, 'Apparently yesterday's raids have created a fair amount of panic in Chinatown.'

Yi cut in. 'Councilman Soong is very anxious that the community works with the police and the INS to sort out any problems that may exist. He has already been approached by many community leaders concerned that there has been no communication with the authorities over this new clamp-down. So he has called a meeting for this afternoon and hopes that representatives from your agencies will also attend. For information and advice.'

'I think we should go,' Fuller said. 'We're going to need the community on-side when this thing really breaks. What do you think, Li?'

Li looked at Yi speculatively. He said, 'I think if the messenger dresses in Armani suits and silk shirts, then his boss must be worth a few *kwai*.'

Yi was unruffled. 'Councilman Soong is chairman of the Houston-Hong Kong Bank,' he said. 'He is a ve-ery rich man. He has heard a great deal about you, Detective Li. He would very much like to meet you.'

'Would he?'

'He is from Canton. He began life in America as an illegal immigrant himself. He was granted amnesty by President Bush after Tiananmen. So now he is a real American.'

'The living embodiment of the American Dream,' Li said, his voice heavy with sarcasm. Margaret glanced at him, curious about his attitude. Then he said, 'Okay, let's meet with Councilman Soong.'

Yi stood up, smiling. 'At two o'clock this afternoon, then. At Enron Field.'

'A fucking baseball stadium?' This from Hrycyk. He could not hide his incredulity.

Yi said, 'Councilman Soong has a private suite at the stadium which he uses for confidential meetings.' Yi grinned. 'And Councilman Soong says, no soft soap, please. He likes to play hardball.' He nodded and headed towards the door.

Margaret said to Li, 'You didn't like him much, did you?'

Li said, 'He's a type. You come across them all the time in my job. Low life off the street. A hundred-dollar haircut and an Armani suit doesn't hide that.'

Hrycyk said, to no one in particular, 'I don't know how he can tell. They all look the same to me.'

Mendez ignored Hrycyk and said mischievously, 'Ah, but don't they say that it's clothes that maketh the man?'

Li said, 'They also say that a leopard never changes its spots.'

Margaret laughed. 'Never exchange proverbs with a Chinese, Felipe,' she said. 'You'll never win. They've got more of them than the rest of the world put together.'

III

There were storm clouds gathering in the sky. Great dark, rolling accumulations of rain filled with electricity and the promise of thunder. A hot wind had sprung up from the south-west and blew the dust of nearly six rainless weeks along the edges of the highway. Convicts in scuffed white prison outfits, trustees, raked the trash at the roadside, sweating freely in the hot humid midday.

The Holliday Unit was all the more oppressive, somehow, under the black sky. Margaret sat in the car park in Mendez's Bronco, the engine running to power the air-con. He had told her to leave it for him at her office car park. Baylor was only five minutes away in the Texas Medical Center and he would get the shuttle bus down to pick it up when he was finished there. He went off with Li, Hrycyk and Fuller to get a ride into Houston. Now Margaret sat waiting at the prison gate for Xiao Ling. She was going to take her to the Forensic Center on Old Spanish Trail and Li would pick her up after the meeting at Enron Field to take her to Washington.

Margaret was full of trepidation. Xiao Ling's English was limited, and she was expecting to be picked up by Li. Margaret tapped the wheel impatiently, aware of the guard watching her from the tower. She had called up to him twenty minutes ago that she was there to collect Xiao Ling. But there was still no sign of activity. Then she saw the main door of H block opening, and Deputy Warden Macleod emerged with Li's sister, dressed as she had been yesterday in her short blue dress and white high heels. It was a bizarre contrast to the prison uniform she had worn in court, a transformation from cowed illegal immigrant back to cheap prostitute. If clothes did not make the man, she thought, then they certainly made, or unmade, the woman.

She got out of the car and walked to the outer gate to meet them. As she did, the first heavy drops of rain started to fall from the sky. Margaret felt them big and cold on her bare arms and neck.

Deputy Warden Macleod said, 'She all yours, Doctor.'

Xiao Ling stood looking at her, and then glanced bewildered beyond her to the car park. 'Li Yan?' she asked.

Margaret shook her head. She pointed at Xiao Ling, then at herself. 'You come with me.'

Xiao Ling appeared confused. Frightened even. She shook her head. 'No.'

The deputy warden smiled. 'Well, I'll leave you good folks to it,' she said, and she locked the gate behind her, and started back along the corridor, leaving Margaret feeling very alone out there in the rain with this stranger who was her lover's sister.

She pointed to her wrist watch and made a circling motion

with her finger, hoping to indicate passing time. 'Li Yan. Houston. Later,' she said.

Xiao Ling looked at her blankly. Margaret was starting to lose patience, getting wet standing there as the rain got heavier. She took the girl by the wrist and started leading her towards the Bronco. But Xiao Ling resisted. 'No,' she said again, pulling her wrist away.

Margaret snapped, 'Well, have it your own fucking way. You can stay here in the rain if you want, but I'm going to Houston.' And she ran, sheltering her head with her purse, towards the Bronco. Something in her tone must have communicated more than her words – or maybe it was the rain – for when she reached the driver's door she turned to see Xiao Ling hurrying meekly after her. And then she regretted her anger and impatience, trying to remember just how frightened and disorientated the girl must be. But always getting in Margaret's way was an image of Xinxin, the daughter from whom Xiao Ling had simply walked away. Her own child, a child that Margaret had grown to love. Whatever else Xiao Ling might have done in her life, whatever pain and indignity she might have suffered, Margaret found it almost impossible to forgive her that.

Billboards on stalks grew like weeds along either side of the freeway, increasing in density the closer they got to Houston. Fast food joints jostled for space, shoulder to shoulder, like so many immigrants – Chinese, Mexican, Italian – fighting for custom against such well-established

American citizens as McDonald's and Cracker Barrel. A battle between burgers and Beijing duck, French fries and fajitas. Margaret and Xiao Ling drove in a silence broken only by the windshield wipers, a distinct tension between them. Traffic flow on the Interstate artery carrying them into the heart of the city was slowing down in the rain, like blood thick with cholesterol. Margaret was distracted by a car tailgating her, about two feet back from her rear fender. If she had to brake suddenly she knew its driver would have no time to slow down, especially in the wet. It would certainly plough into the back of her. She saw a gap on the inside lane, flicked on her indicator, and swung into it, leaving space for the car behind to pass. But when she checked her mirror, she saw that it had followed her and was still occupying the same space on her tail.

'For Christ's sake!' she muttered, drawing a look from Xiao Ling who immediately saw her preoccupation with the rear-view mirror and turned to look at the car behind. But she had no clear view of its driver through the rain-spattered rear windshield. Margaret indicated again and pulled out to the middle lane. The car behind followed. Margaret did not even have time to form an oath before Xiao Ling screamed, a shrill exhalation of fear that was almost deafening in the confined space.

Margaret looked at her. She was sitting rigid, staring straight ahead at nothing, all colour drained from her face. Beyond her, something caught Margaret's eye and she jumped focus to see a green Lincoln travelling level with them in the inside lane, its driver grinning at them through his window, a mouthful of bad teeth in an unpleasant Chinese face.

'Ma zhai,' Xiao Ling whispered. She was clutching her seat, rigid with terror, afraid to look out of the side window.

'What the hell's *ma zhai*?' Margaret said, and she had to make a fast steering correction to avoid crossing lanes. For a split second she almost lost control of the Bronco. 'Jesus!' Heart pounding, she glanced in the mirror and saw that the car behind had gone. And then almost immediately she was aware of it sitting level with them, at her side. A white Chevy. She flicked the passenger a quick glance. Another Chinese. But this one wasn't smiling. He drew a finger from left to right across his throat. Now Margaret shared Xiao Ling's fear. She clutched the wheel tightly. This was ridiculous. They were in the middle of a freeway driving at fifty miles an hour into the fourth largest city in America. What could these people possibly do to them? What did they *want* to do to them? And why? Xiao Ling seemed to know who they were, but Margaret wasn't going to get any sense out of her. As long as they didn't stop, she figured, they would be safe.

They covered the next mile flanked by the two cars, Xiao Ling whimpering in the passenger seat, frightened to look left or right. Finally, Margaret could stand it no longer. 'What the hell do these people want?' she shouted at no one in particular, and jammed on her brakes. She heard a squeal of tyres behind her, followed by the piercing blast of a horn. The Chevy and the Lincoln shot several car lengths ahead of them, and Margaret swung the Bronco violently across two lanes. More horns sounded as she squeezed into the exit lane, just in time to get on to the slip road that took them down on to the four-lane highway that ran parallel to the freeway.

Breathing hard, Margaret took them into the inside lane and slowed down to a sedate forty miles an hour. She checked both mirrors, and glanced over to the traffic speeding past on the 45. There was no sign, through the spray, of either of the cars whose presence had been so intimidating on the Interstate. Margaret glanced over at Xiao Ling and saw that she had relaxed a little, and she let a tiny jet of air escape through her pursed lips in relief.

They carried on parallel to the freeway for several more miles, through junctions and under flyovers. Eventually, when there was still no sign of the Lincoln and the Chevy, Margaret began to relax, too. As they approached the next junction, she indicated left and pulled across to the exit lane that would take them back on to the Interstate, and they picked up speed again, the cluster of glass tower blocks that was downtown Houston appearing now on the horizon. The sky overhead was so swollen and bruised, it had almost turned day into night. The headlamps of the traffic reflected off the wet surface of the road. Forked lightning lit the blue-black void beyond the skyscrapers. Fifteen minutes later, the road took them around the centre of the city, past Sam Houston Park and down to a huge intersection where they turned off on to the 59 and then the 288. Shortly after, they left the freeway altogether and drifted down on to North MacGregor Boulevard, overhung by the dripping trees of Hermann Park. They curved gently through lush, manicured lawns on to Braeswood and the stop lights at Holcombe. Rain drummed on the roof of the Bronco.

Margaret glanced at the car in the outside lane, and felt fear like a blade pass through her. It was the white Chevy, and the Chinese who had made the slash-throat gesture with his finger. She looked in her rear-view mirror and saw the green Lincoln on her tail. It flashed its lights, just to let her know it was there. Xiao Ling had not seen them yet. Margaret looked up at the traffic lights overhead. They were still at red. And then back at the Chevy. The passenger opened the left-hand side of his jacket and started drawing what looked like a gun out of a holster. Margaret jammed her foot on the accelerator, and the Bronco lurched forward, snaking through the red light, wheels spinning in the wet. Xiao Ling let out a yelp of surprise and clutched the edges of her seat. Horns blared as cars crossing the intersection swerved to avoid her. She heard more squealing tyres, all the time expecting someone either to hit her, or for a bullet to come crashing through the window. She cleared the lights and accelerated down Braeswood, looking in her mirror to see if anything had followed them, and when she saw that the road was empty, allowed herself to draw breath. Xiao Ling looked terrified.

'*Ma zhai*,' Margaret said, still with no idea what it meant. But Xiao Ling nodded.

Margaret took a left into William C. Harvin Boulevard. Flanked by trees and puddles in sprawling parking lots, she felt the almost overwhelming relief of getting on to home territory. At the end of the boulevard, in the middle of the road opposite the entrance to the Joseph A. Jachimczyk Forensic Center, she saw the glass security booth with the silhouettes of two armed officers inside it. She rounded it, cutting left across the central reservation and into the car park on the south side of her office building. There was a space there reserved for the Chief Medical Examiner. She drove into it and cut the engine. For a moment she just sat there, and then leaned forward to rest her forehead on the steering wheel. Her legs and hands were trembling. Xiao Ling was looking at her in a state of high anxiety. She had no idea that they were safe here. Margaret exhaled slowly, and then took a long, deep breath and sat up. As she opened the door and stepped out on to the wet tarmac, she saw the Lincoln and the Chevy pull up on the other side of the boulevard.

'Oh, my God!' she whispered, and was almost frozen to the spot by fear as the car doors opened, and four young Chinese in dark suits stepped out on to the road. She flicked a glance at Xiao Ling who had climbed out of the car and stood on the far side of the Bronco looking at them, a creature immobilised by fear, capable neither of action nor reaction. Her hair was streaked down her face by the rain, her dress soaked already and clinging to her slight frame.

The security guards in their glass booth were engaged in some private conversation involving much laughter. They were oblivious to what was going on outside.

The four Chinese simply stood there in the rain, their car doors wide open, looking across at Margaret and Xiao Ling. They gave no indication of wanting to do anything other than stare, and something in Margaret finally snapped.

'What the hell do you want?' she screamed through the rain. And she started across the car park towards them. Her first few hesitant steps turned into a brisk walk and then, as all four Chinese turned and got back into their cars, a positive run. Doors slammed shut as she sprinted through the downpour, and even as she made it to the boulevard the Lincoln pulled away from the far side, followed by the Chevy, and they headed off at speed towards the junction with Old Spanish Trail.

Margaret stood, dripping, on the sidewalk, tears of rage and fear streaming down her face. She felt almost as if she had been violated by their silent intimidation, and frustrated by her inability to confront them. She knew what she had done was crazy. What if they had simply pulled out guns and shot her? And yet, she also knew, that if you didn't confront your fears then they could crush you.

'You alright, ma'am?' It was one of the security guards calling over from the shelter of his booth.

'No thanks to you,' she shouted, and turned and strode back to where Xiao Ling stood waiting for her, marvelling either at her bravery or her stupidity.

CHAPTER NINE

I

Giant windows threw long arches of light across the marble floor. White pillars rose high into a vaulted ceiling lined with guastavino tile. Where once the smoke and steam and shrill whistle of freight and passenger trains had filled its vastness, only three solitary sets of footsteps now echoed across the concourse of what had been the elegant Union Station. The tracks beyond the terminal were long gone, replaced by a diamond of grass, the rumble of wheel on rail supplanted by the thwack of leather on wood and the roar of forty thousand baseball fans. Designed by the firm which built the Grand Central Station in New York City, and with a one-time reputation as the finest station in the south, this monument to the heyday of the American railroad was now home to the Houston Astros. Enron Field.

A uniformed security officer sat at a shiny mahogany desk right in the centre of the concourse. She turned a smile as bright as sunshine on Li, Fuller and Hrycyk. 'Can I help y'all?'

Fuller said, 'We have an appointment with Councilman Soong.'

Soong himself came down to take them up to his suite. He was a large man in every sense. He had an expansive personality, and an expanded waistline, a very round, smooth face and a thick head of neatly trimmed wavy black hair shot through with streaks of silver. Incongruously, he was wearing sneakers, a pair of Wrangler jeans and a red leather Astros baseball jacket. Solemnly he shook all their hands. 'Welcome, gentlemen. I am very pleased you can make it.' Then he grinned and waved his arm around the concourse. 'Impressive, yes? Restored to all its former glory.' He pushed open a tall glass door and took them into the stadium. To their left, a long corridor ran the length of the original terminal building, arches opening out on to the baseball field below. Before them, the field itself glistened in the rain beneath three tiers of seats rising into an angry-looking sky, puddles gathering in the red blaize that circled the mound. 'They gonna close the roof, I think,' Soong said. 'Too much rain no good for grass.'

'Jees,' Hrycyk whispered in awe. 'I've never seen them close the roof before.'

Soong beamed at him. 'You are baseball fan, Mistah Hrycyk?'

Hrycyk shrugged, suddenly self-conscious. 'Yeah, I go to the games sometimes. When I can.'

'Then you must be my guest next season,' Soong said. 'I can arrange seat for you in enclosure.' He pointed to a small enclosed area of seats immediately behind where the batsman faced the pitcher.

'Wow,' Hrycyk said, forgetting his reserve. He was like a kid with a candy bar. 'That's where all the celebs sit.'

Soong beamed. 'It cost twenty thousand dollar to buy seat there. And two hundred dollar a game. Roughly seventeen thousand a year. In thirty years you pay more than half a million dollar for one seat.' He paused for effect. 'I got three.'

Li looked at Hrycyk. The INS agent might dislike the Chinese, but when it came to baseball he had no problem accepting Chinese hospitality.

They heard the whine and hum of a motor, and the smooth sound of gears engaging through syncromesh.

'Yuh,' Soong said. 'They close the roof.'

They followed him out on to the near terracing, where they had a view across the field to the arched walkway they had just passed through. Above it, on eight hundred feet of track, stood a full-size replica vintage locomotive painted black and orange and red, the glass towers and skyscrapers of downtown Houston rising into the sky behind it, like the painted backdrop of a theatre set.

Soong laughed. 'Owner of team pay one and a quarter million dollar out of own pocket to install train,' he said. 'It run along track, blowing whistle and letting off steam every time Astros score home run. It's fun.'

Beyond it, set into the far side of the stadium, the roof was starting to close. It comprised two massive arced sections, one overlapping the other and supported along the open side on glass-panelled scaffolding more than two hundred feet high which ran on rails parallel to the train line. Through the windows of a small control cabin at the base of the scaffolding, they could see the engineer controlling the motors that closed the roof. The cabin moved along the rail with the scaffolding, overtaking the train as the first section stopped halfway and the overlap continued towards the near side of the stadium, above where they stood. Although the whole structure was designed with toughened glass panels to let in as much light as possible, the sky was almost black now, and the engineer switched on the floodlights from his little control room, washing the entire stadium with an unnaturally bright light.

Soong took great delight in displaying his knowledge of the facts and figures. He said, 'The roof weigh nine thousand ton and cover six-and-a-half acre. It generate its own electricity and take just twelve minutes to close. Pretty impressive, huh?' But he gave them no time to respond. 'You come with me, now. We got important stuff to talk about.'

They followed him under a bewildering array of hanging signs arranged to guide fans to their seats, and into a stairwell that led them up from the main concourse through club level to suite level. Soong arrived panting at the top of the stairs. 'I used to take lift,' he said, 'but now I take stair for health.' He grinned again. 'Only exercise I get, apart from sex.'

Fuller and Hrycyk gave small, dutiful laughs. Li did not. There was nothing amusing for him in the image of this fat man grunting and sweating over the delicate frame of some poor Chinese girl working to pay off her debt to a snakehead. Soong's wealth and confidence, his eccentricity – the sneakers and the baseball jacket — reminded Li of those corrupt petty officials back in China who lined their pockets at the expense of the people. Overweight, overbearing, over-confident.

A door led them into a long, curved and carpeted concourse. Large windows gave on to stunning views of the illuminated field below. After a lengthy walk around the curve of the stadium, they arrived at the elaborate wood-panelled entries to the row of private suites. Opposite, a panorama of windows looked out on to the freeway, the lights of the afternoon traffic a dazzle of reflections in the wet. Li could see rain caught in the headlamps, spray rising like mist. Soong opened the door to his suite and they found themselves entering a large room with a conference table at its centre and a hot buffet counter along one side. Facing the entrance, sliding glass doors gave on to a single row of seats with a spectacular aerial view of the field. Overhead they heard a soft thunk which vibrated gently through the building. Soong looked at his watch. 'We make good time,' he said. 'The roof just close.'

Eight sombre-looking middle-aged and elderly Chinese gentlemen, in uniformly dark suits and dark hair, white shirts open at the neck, sat around the conference table, noisily slurping green tea from tall glasses. A fog of smoke filled the room from their cigarettes. Ashtrays were full. They had been here for some time. Wary, hooded eyes fixed themselves on Li as Soong made the introductions. These were the leaders of the various business associations which represented Chinese commercial interests in Houston. The tongs. And they were clearly ill at ease sitting down with agents of the INS and FBI, and a police officer representing the country from which they had all, at one time or another, made illegal exits.

Soong, by contrast, had the appearance of a man supremely comfortable with his own status: as city councillor, director of the Houston-Hong Kong Bank, member of the Astros board. When Fuller, Hrycyk and Li were seated at the table, he offered them green tea from stainless steel flasks. Fuller and Hrycyk demurred. Li accepted. It was a long time since he had drunk green tea. There was a comfort in it. A taste of home. He lit a cigarette and, catching Hrycyk's eye, reluctantly tossed him one. Fuller coughed ostentatiously into his hand.

'Any chance we could open one of these windows?' he said. 'A guy could get lung cancer just breathing in this place.'

'Sure,' Soong said, nodding to one of the dark-suited gentlemen at the far end of the table who got up and slid open the door. As air rushed in, smoke got sucked out, drawn high up into the enclosed roof space of the stadium where it quickly dispersed.

Li said in Mandarin, 'Whereabouts in Canton are you from, Mr Soong?'

Soong scrutinised him quickly, searching for some ulterior motive in the question. 'I'm afraid my *putonghua* is not very good, Mr Li.'

'Neither is my Cantonese.'

'Then perhaps we should speak English,' Soong said in English.

'I'll drink to that,' Hrycyk said. 'Agent Fuller and myself can't speak Cantonese or Mandarin.'

And Li glanced at the INS agent, momentarily discomposed. Hrycyk clearly knew more Chinese than he was prepared to admit.

Ostentatiously avoiding Li's question, Soong folded his hands on the table in front of him and composed his brows into a frown of concern. 'I have to tell you, gentlemen, that the people of Houston Chinatown are not happy today, after yesterday's raids.'

'We picked up more than sixty illegal immigrants, Councilman Soong,' Fuller said evenly. 'These people had no papers, no right to be here. They were breaking the law.'

'Of course, Mistah Fullah,' Soong said. 'Chinese not above the law. We know this. But even illegal immigrants have rights in United States, yes?'

'Citizens of the United States have rights,' Fuller said. 'Illegal immigrants do not.'

Soong said, 'But many of these people escape from persecution in China. They have right to claim political asylum. They have right to bail, and legal representation.'

'In my experience,' Li said, fixing Soong with an unblinking gaze, 'illegal emigrants from China come to America for economic, not political, reasons. Except, of course, for those who have broken the law and are escaping prosecution.'

Soong was unruffled. A slightly puzzled, almost amused, frown settled around his eyes. 'Correct me if I am wrong, Mistah Li, but I understood that your own sister is seeking political asylum. From persecution under Chinese government's One Child Policy.'

Li felt a hot flush darken his cheeks and wondered how Soong knew about his sister and what had happened in court only a matter of hours before. But it made it almost impossible for him to argue his point. He caught Hrycyk smirking at him across the table.

Having dealt with Li, Soong turned his attentions back to Fuller. 'It is important,' he said, 'that Chinese people have confidence in American system. There are many illegal immigrant in America, Mistah Fullah, but if Chinese people feel they are being . . . singled out . . . then this is ve-ery dangerous for good relations in community.'

'What exactly do you mean by that?' Fuller asked sharply.

Soong was unruffled. 'I mean, Mistah Fullah, that Chinese people want to be good American citizen. We want to make money, pursue American Dream. Not break the law. But, if always there is fear of raid on business and home, then bad Chinese element they go underground. And that no good for you, or us.' He paused to let his point sink in. 'These people you arrest, you make gesture, you release them on bail, then people believe in American justice, people in community happy to help police again.'

Hrycyk blew a jet of smoke at the ceiling. 'And I don't suppose this anxiety to release all these illegals back on the street has anything to do with the money they owe their snakeheads? About three and a half million by my reckoning.'

'We are anxious like you, Mistah Hrycyk, to put snakehead out of business,' Soong said earnestly. 'All gentlemen round this table have legitimate business. Banking, import-export, retail sale, restaurant, entertainment.'

Li scrutinised the faces of the commercial interests around the table. They were all deeply reserved, eyes dark and impenetrable. Whatever was going on behind them was well masked. And none of them looked as if they might be about to give voice to their anxiety. They seemed more than happy to let Soong do it for them.

Soong continued, 'Illegal activity of snakehead bad for our business, scare people, depress economy. That why we wanna help. Stop street gangs, illegal gambling, protection racket. These things bad for everyone. But if people scared of police, then the gangs only have more power. You let people out on bail, like sister of Mistah Li, and people not so scared.'

'I'm afraid we can't do that, Mr Soong,' Fuller said. 'We opposed the release of Li's sister, but that was a court decision. We have no control over that.' He took a deep breath. 'The fact is, we're holding all the illegal immigrants arrested yesterday in protective quarantine – for their safety, and ours.'

There was a long silence around the table. Soong leaned forward. 'I do not understand, Mistah Fullah. Protective quarantine?'

Fuller said, 'What I'm about to tell you, Councilman, must not leave this room. I know I'm taking a risk here, but you people need to know what's happening. We're going to need your full co-operation, not least because the Chinese community will be the first to suffer.' The slurping of green tea had stopped. He had the full attention of everyone in the room. And he explained to them how for the last three months illegal Chinese immigrants crossing the border from Mexico had been injected with a flu virus which would be activated on consumption of a specific set of proteins, as yet unidentified. And that once activated, the virus was likely to spread like wildfire through the United States, leaving thousands of people dead in its wake. He said, 'This thing gets out, and every Asian face in the United States is going to be a target for vigilante groups, whether they're illegal immigrants, or third generation Vietnamese Americans.'

Outside, they heard the rain battering on the roof of the stadium. Sheet lightning flashed across the skyline of downtown Houston like bad stage lighting. The composure had left Soong's face, along with all the colour.

The grey-painted stonework of the Catholic Annunciation Church on the corner of Texas and Crawford was stained dark by the rain. The intermittent ratatat of a pneumatic drill echoed back at them off the walls of the buildings that crowded the intersection. Men in hard hats were digging up the road behind red and white striped drums, cutting through the remains of a railroad track that the City Fathers had simply tarmacked over during a previous era of short-termism.

Fuller, Li and Hrycyk hurried through the downpour to the sprawling empty car park behind the stadium where Fuller had parked his Chrysler. Hrycyk pulled up the collar of his jacket and shouted above the noise of the drill, 'American justice, my ass! Only two reasons those people in there want the immigrants back on the street. They want their pound of flesh.'

Li said, 'You almost sound as if you cared.'

'Sure I care,' Hrycyk shouted. 'I want to see the whole goddamned lot of them behind bars, or at the very least on a slow boat back to China. Community leaders! Those guys were all *shuk foo*, uncles in the tongs. You think they ain't involved someway in bringing in the illegals?' He snorted his derision. 'If they ain't, then you can bet your sweet life they're exploiting the cheap labour these people represent. Lot of restaurants without waiters last night, shops without assistants today, sweatshops without machinists, whorehouses without whores.' He gave Li a special leer.

Fuller said, 'And what's the other reason?'

Hrycyk said, 'They don't want us asking the immigrants a lot of questions. They might not know a lot, but I'm betting a good few of them have seen enough to incriminate more than one of the uncles in there in a whole range of illegal activities.'

'What about Soong?' Fuller asked.

'He represents the Chinese community,' Hrycyk said, no longer having to shout as the sound of the pneumatic drill receded. They splashed through the surface water gathered on the tarmac. 'These people *are* the Chinese community – or, at least, the commercial face of it. He's playing both sides, so that no matter what happens, he's going to come out looking good. Typical goddamned politician!'

They jumped into Fuller's car, shaking off the rain, and the windows quickly steamed up. Fuller turned to Li in the back seat. 'What did you make of them, Li?'

Li thought for a moment. 'I've seen them all before,' he said, and in his mind's eye he saw a parade of faces pass before him. Corrupt politicians and Party officials, businessmen on the take, civil servants with small salaries and big houses. 'I've seen them on village councils and street committees, at Party gatherings and on public platforms. I've arrested more than a few of them in my time, and I've seen them in football stadiums with a gun pressed in the back of their head and the piss running down their legs.' If not them, it was people just like them who had forced thousands of young men and women into prostitution and virtual slavery. The venom in his tone made Fuller and Hrycyk turn to look at him.

Hrycyk grinned. 'I take it you weren't impressed, then?' Li didn't think a response was required.

Fuller started up the engine of the Chrysler and said, 'Washington's diverting emergency funds to a massive operation along the Mexican border. They're going to quadruple the number of border patrol guards and enlist the help of the local police departments. Every vehicle coming into the country's going to be stopped, every truck searched with dogs and x-rays and carbon dioxide detectors.' The windshield wipers scraped rhythmically back and forth, the vents blew out hot air to demist the car.

Hrycyk was unimpressed. 'Now that's what I'd call shutting the stable door after the horse has bolted. We've been screaming for an increase in border patrol for years.' He hissed his frustration. 'Jesus, we been telling them long enough that people-smuggling was bigger than drugs. It's the goddamn drug runners who're bringing the people in, for Chrissake. They're experts at moving stuff in and out of the country. They've been doing it for decades.'

'Well, whoever's bringing them in,' Fuller said, 'that's who's injecting them. And I don't figure it's any of the people we just sat around the table with. Whatever else they're involved in, I don't think it's that. Did you see their faces when I told them what was going down?'

'Sure didn't look too happy,' Hrycyk conceded.

Li stared through the rain running down his window and somehow couldn't convince himself that the faces which had expressed such shock in Soong's suite were anything more than masks, like those he had seen on trips to the Peking opera with his uncle.

II

From her window, Margaret could see the sky breaking up, shredded by light and patches of pale blue. Dark, tumescent clouds edged by fine patterns of gold, sunlight bursting through the gaps, delineated like rods of platinum striking towards the earth. Even in her anger, she could not help but admire its magnificence.

'So I don't have a leg to stand on?' she barked into the phone. 'He can just throw me out on the street because I changed the locks without his permission?' She sucked in air through her teeth. 'I hope you're not thinking of charging me for that information.' She gasped her disbelief at the response. 'Well, thank you! Next time I need a lawyer, I'll know who not to call.' She slammed the receiver back in its cradle. 'Damn you!' she shouted at the ceiling, at the sunset, at the liquid gold reflections in every west-facing window in medicine city.

The phone rang and she snatched it back to her ear, surprised by the heat of her anger still retained in the plastic. It was Lucy. 'I think you should know, Doctor Campbell, that they can hear you at the end of the corridor.' And before Margaret had time to respond she added, 'And you should also know that hell and damnation are very real to some of us.'

'I know that, Lucy,' Margaret said. 'They're very real to me, too. Was there any other reason you called?'

'Mr Li is here.'

Margaret was at the door even before Lucy had time to hang up. The afternoon had felt interminable. She had been unable to concentrate on the mountain of paperwork which had piled up in her in-tray during the last few days. There were two bodies in the morgue awaiting autopsy – a murder and a suspect road accident – and she had spent an hour phoning the hospitals trying to enlist pathologists to do post-mortems out of hours. She held the door open for Li and waited until he was in and she could close it behind her before she threw her arms around him and pressed her face into his chest. 'My God, Li Yan, where have you been? Why are you never there when I need you?'

She felt his initial surprise, and then he held her at arm's length, concerned. 'Where's Xiao Ling?' he asked.

'I had them set up a cot bed for her in an office downstairs. She's sleeping.'

'What's wrong?'

And she felt her fear returning, and her hands started shaking as she took him step by step through the nightmare of their drive down from Huntsville. His face was carved from stone. Grim and thoughtful. 'What did they want, Li Yan?' she asked when she had finished. 'One of them had a gun, I'm sure. Only, when I tried to confront them they just drove away. Xiao Ling looked liked she'd seen a ghost. Like she knew them. She called them something . . .' She searched her memory for the words Xiao Ling had whispered. 'Ma ja . . . something like that.'

'Ma zhai?' Li said

'That's it. What does it mean?'

Li frowned. 'It means "little horses". It's what they call members of the Chinese street gangs here. We picked up a couple when we raided that cellar in Chinatown. They're the enforcers, the ones who beat and intimidate the illegal immigrants into coming up with the money for the snakeheads. And usually they are the ones sent to collect protection money from the shops and restaurants on the gang's turf.' He paused. 'Are you sure Xiao Ling recognised them?'

'She must have. How else would she have known what they were?'

He nodded.

'So what did they want?'

Li said, 'If they had wanted to hurt you, they would have.' He took a moment or two to think about it. 'So they must have wanted to scare you. Because that is what they did.'

'Yeah, and they were pretty good at it, too.' Her attempt at a smile fell short of its objective. Li drew her to him, brushing the hair from her face and softly kissing her forehead. She looked up into his face. 'But why would they *want* to scare me?'

Li's face coloured slightly. 'Not you, Margaret,' he said. 'Xiao Ling.' And he remembered Hrycyk's words as they left Enron Field just half an hour ago. *I'm betting a good few of them have seen enough to incriminate more than one of the uncles in there in a whole range of illegal activities.* She had worked in the Golden Mountain Club. She had been favoured by the bosses, she'd said. She must have seen things, heard things that someone was very anxious she did not convey to Li. 'She must know something,' he said, and he told Margaret about the club 'I'm going to take her to Washington tonight. She's not safe here.'

Margaret felt a depression wash over her at the thought of Li going. Everything in her life seemed to be in a state of flux. And the residue of fear from the encounter with the *ma zhai* was still powerful enough to leave her feeling vulnerable, even raw.

'When will you be back?' she asked.

He shrugged. 'I don't know. My first responsibility is to Xiao Ling. Once she is safe in Georgetown, with Meiping to look after her, then I will consider what my options are.' But he knew they were limited. He could either throw himself on the mercy of his Embassy and ask to be allowed to take her back to China with him, or he could let her take her chances through the American court system while he continued to play an active part in the investigation. Neither option left much room for Margaret. He knew she was afraid. He looked at her. Fear made her seem smaller, more defenceless. It was only the power of her personality that ever made her seem bigger, stronger than she really was. But then he hardened his mind to her. It was only two nights ago that she had told him she thought they should keep things between them on a professional basis. 'I must book a flight,' he said. 'Can I use your phone?'

She nodded, but before he could lift the receiver, it rang. Margaret answered it, and he saw immediately that something was wrong. The colour drained from her face leaving it chalk white, and her eyes were a pale, bloodless blue.

'Thank you,' she said, and hung up. He could see her hand trembling. She looked at him and he saw the cold, gold sunset reflected in her moist eyes. 'Looks like I'll be on that flight with you,' she said, almost in a whisper. 'That was a pathologist from AFIP. Steve's virus has gone active.'

III

The Office of the Armed Forces Medical Examiner sat up off the freeway in a low, anonymous brick building opposite a Best Western Hotel. It was surrounded by neatly trimmed lawns, and clusters of shrubs and trees circled by carefully tended flower beds. The pathologists there still called it the Gillette building, even though it was some years since Gillette had been forced by animal rights protesters to abandon it. The laboratories where the company had tested its products had been perfect for the purposes of the Armed Forces Medical Examiner, and the smoked, plexiglass windows and sophisticated electronic entry system had made it ideally secure.

It was dark when Margaret arrived. One of the pathologists from the team which had carried out the autopsies at Ellington Field led her up stairs to the second level and along anonymous hushed corridors to Steve's office. Overhead fluorescents flickered on and threw a man's life into sharp relief. 'I'll leave you to it,' the pathologist said. 'Anything you need, holler. I'm just down the hall.'

Margaret stood blinking in the harsh light, depressed and alone. This was Steve's space, where he spent so much of his life, and he was in every corner of it. But his physical absence was haunting.

Water sprinkled across a tiny arrangement of rocks on a desk pushed against the far wall, a soothing, peaceful sound in the stillness. Good *feng shui*, Margaret thought. Beside it, a favourite microscope, and a twelve-inch plastic model of the human body, torso and head, with removable internal organs brightly coloured. There were miniature cardboard drawers built one on the other, each carefully labelled. Tiny glass sample slides and piles of transparencies. On a shelf above, all his plaques and medals and framed certificates, a lemonade bottle with a DNA label on it. On the wall there was a painting of the astronauts who had achieved the first successful moon landing, smiling out stoically from their bulky NASA space suits. A bed pan in use as a flower pot made her smile. There were, she saw, a number of pot plants around the office, breathing fresh oxygen into the still air.

Above a cluttered bookshelf, a large sheet pinned to the wall was mounted with half a dozen photographs of plasticine heads that Steve had moulded from the skulls of Jane and John Does in an attempt to identify them. A hobby, he had told her. Pinned to the drawer of a metal filing cabinet were photographs of his little girl, Danni, taken on a beach somewhere. Just three years old. Plump and smiling in her little red bathing costume, she was grinning at the camera and splashing the cold sea water. Margaret could almost hear her screams of delight. And then, in the corner, Steve's computer, Danni's smile saving his screen from burnout. Her soft, brown hair was tied up in a ribbon and her mouth half-open in a smile breaking into laughter. Margaret reached out and touched the face, but felt only the cold glass of the screen. Tears formed in her eyes and she blinked furiously to stop them. And through the blur, she hunted around in the drawers of his desk until she found his personal stereo and headset, and looked up to see the rows of audio tapes on the bookshelf above.

There were around two dozen of them, and she had no idea which ones to take. As she fumbled through them, reading the labels which he had so clearly marked in blue felt tip pen, she was almost overcome by a sense of desperation and failure.

He should have had these two days ago, and now she wasn't sure if he would ever hear them again. Although they were before his time, he appeared to have all the Beatles albums. There were tapes of opera arias, Vivaldi's *Four Seasons*, Eric Clapton's *Pilgrim*, The Eagles, Handel's *Water Music*, Christina Aguilera. Like Steve himself, impossible to categorise. He was unique, and fleetingly she wondered if they might have had some kind of future together had they met some other time, some other place.

She decided to take all the tapes, and emptied a plastic carrier bag she found in one of the cupboards and swept the cassettes into it off the shelf.

She found the picture of Danni, in its little silver frame, tucked in beside the computer monitor where he could look at it any time he chose when he was working at the keyboard. It wasn't really silver. It was soft, polished pewter, with art nouveau patterns worked into the border. Danni looked out from it with her trademark smile.

'You're a little late, aren't you?' Margaret swung around, startled, to find Dr Ward standing in the doorway, his lips pinched and white, dark eyes filled with hostility. 'I was expecting you two days ago.'

She shook her head and found it hard to defend herself. 'I was called back to Houston.'

'And did it not occur to you to make other arrangements?'

There hadn't been time. She should have made time. She didn't know what to say.

'I'm going up there now.'

'Don't you want to know how he is?'

'I'll find out for myself.' But her defiance wavered with uncertainty. It was more than three hours since she had received the phone call. She hesitated. 'How is he?'

He said, 'From the onset of first symptoms – sore throat, swollen glands, rising temperature – they've been pumping him full of antibiotics and rimantadine.' Margaret had read about rimantadine, one of a new generation of anti-viral drugs, reputed to be up to seventy per cent effective in inhibiting secondary infection in cases of influenza A virus. 'So far he seems to have responded well. But the prognosis is uncertain.'

Margaret lifted the bag of cassettes and slipped the pewter frame into her purse. 'I'd better go, then.'

As she pushed past Ward in the doorway he said, 'For the first twenty-four hours he was asking for you all the time. But he hasn't mentioned you once today.'

Margaret stopped and looked into his face. Why did he want to hurt her? Because she knew about his human frailties, had touched his imperfection? Was it guilt, or anger, or just plain bigotry? 'I guess he must have other things on his mind right now,' she said, and hurried out.

Margaret pushed her rental car up to eighty on the freeway. It was a big car with soft suspension that rolled gently but too much on every bend in the road. She had passed Gaithersburg about twenty minutes earlier, and as she crested a rise, she could see the lights of Frederick spread out below her. Traffic was light, and another fifteen minutes took her on to the

Seventh Street exit, to skirt the north-western edge of the town to Fort Detrick.

During the forty minutes it had taken her to drive from the Office of the Armed Forces Medical Examiner to her destination, she had made a conscious effort to blank out the reason for her trip. Her mind had wandered, and at one point she had figured that the original German settlers must have named the fort *Dietrich* as in *Marlene*, and that time had corrupted it to Detrick, the soft German *ch* that came from the back of the throat hardened to a *ck* from much further forward on the tongue. And she had almost laughed at herself for allowing such trivia to fill her thoughts. Except that laughter was impossible, and now that she saw the orange flashing lights at the gates of Fort Detrick on the road ahead of her, she felt a constriction in her chest and found it hard to breathe.

The duty doctor was a young woman, dark hair scraped back into a pony tail. She wore army fatigues and carried the rank of major. Her complexion was sallow, and she had large sad eyes that conveyed something of the apprehension she was doing her best to mask. She led Margaret briskly through the labyrinth of corridors to Ward 200. The air at the receiving desk was bristling with tension. Several medical staff looked at Margaret with a mix of curiosity and concern.

'He's not good,' the doctor had said when she picked Margaret up at the front desk. 'Temperature's high, over a hundred and six, and there's fluid in his lungs, intermittent vomiting. He swings between fever and lucidity without warning. His symptoms have developed incredibly fast.'

Margaret reached the door to The Slammer and peered through the window. There were two medical staff in Steve's room, both wearing light blue protective suits, yellow cable corkscrewing behind them. She could barely see the figure lying on the bed. But she could see the IV feeding Lactated Ringer's solution into his arm to combat dehydration, and a forest of wires leading off to the equipment monitoring his condition.

'We've done everything we can to keep his temperature down, but it's a losing battle,' the doctor was saying. 'And it's impossible to tell at this stage if the rimantadine is having any effect. But he's strong, you know, he could ride it out.'

Margaret wondered how much homework the doctor had done on the symptoms and progress of the Spanish Flu. She remembered Markin's words: It could reduce a strong, vigorous adult to a quivering wreck in a matter of hours. And then it occurred to her, that when the prognosis is bleak and all hope gone, comfort is all that remains. It is the doctor's final crutch with which to face the patient's loved ones. Margaret searched the doctor's face for some sign that she knew something she wasn't telling. 'What do you really think?' she asked.

The doctor shrugged hopelessly. 'I have no idea. The next few hours will be critical.'

Margaret said, 'I have stuff for him. A picture of his little girl. Can I go in?'

The doctor closed the door behind her, and she found herself in a small changing room, shelves rising to the ceiling, cotton pants and shirts arranged in colours: white, khaki, blue, brown. Margaret laid her pale blue personal protective suit on the bench and undressed quickly. She slipped into a pair of white pants and shirt, fingers fumbling with the ties, before stepping into the protective suit and zipping herself in.

For a moment she was gripped by panic. Claustrophobia, fear. She turned and saw the plaque on the door, red lettering on white. EMERGENCY DOOR RELEASE. And almost gave in to an impulse to hit the release and get the hell out. She took a deep breath, and heard it quivering in the sealed confines of her suit, and then saw her world turn opaque as it misted her visor. She put a hand on the wall to steady herself, and then turned towards the outer shower. There was no need to decontaminate on the way in.

Clumsy in the suit, she stepped through a short, narrow corridor past the outer shower, closing the door behind her, and opened the heavy stainless steel door into the large chemical decontamination shower. On the inside of it, above a push-handle for opening, was a red warning sign: CLOSE OUTER SHOWER DOOR BEFORE OPENING INNER SHOWER DOOR. She pulled it closed behind her, and looked around the glistening walls of the stainless steel cubicle, pipes and shower heads, stop-cocks with knurled red turning handles. On the way out she would be bombarded in here by liquid chemicals designed to kill every living thing. Her breathing had become shallow and rapid, emphasised in her head by the loudness of it. She thumped the push-handle of the outer door with her open palms and it swung open into the ante-room with the white-painted brick walls that she had seen through the window from the outside. She swung the door shut again, and twisted awkwardly to find the nozzle at the back of her suit that fit the end of the yellow corkscrew cable that hung from the wall on her left, fumbling through her white latex gloves to make the connection. As it locked into place, the suit immediately began to fill with cool, filtered air, expanding around her, and she began to feel the panic diminishing. She could breathe again. The misting on her visor evaporated. She looked around, and saw on the shelf behind her the rows of short green booties that the doctor had told her to put on. Moving with the awkward, slow-motion gait of a spaceman, she reached up and pulled down a pair of boots, checking them for size and then slipping her inflated feet inside.

She saw the doctor, through the glass, waving her to the door. She disconnected from the yellow cable and waddled over to where she could open the hatch of the ultra-violet chamber to retrieve the photograph and cassettes, and handful of books she had bought at the airport. Then she turned back towards Steve's room. The nursing staff had spotted her by now, and one of them pointed to a yellow cable hanging free from the window wall on the far side of the bed. She hurried across the ante-room and into the special care room, rounding the bed, and connecting to the cable before she turned to look at Steve where he lay in the bed. The air rushed back into her suit and blew down over her head.

Steve's face was a strange, putty colour, with incongruously red patches high on his cheeks and forehead. His mouth was open and his breathing shallow, eyes shut, sweat beading across his brow. One of the nurses laid a cool wet towel across his forehead, and his eyes flickered open. He inclined his head a little to his right and the dull glaze left his eyes, a lustre returning to them as he recognised Margaret behind the visor. He smiled, and reached out a hand to take hers, wires trailing in its wake.

'Welcome back to Wally World,' he said. 'It's a fun place to spend forty-eight hours.' Phlegm caught in the back of his throat, throwing him into a convulsion of coughing that turned him scarlet and left him gasping for breath. When he had control again, he said, 'I knew I should have paid those goddamned parking fines.'

Margaret squeezed his hand tightly. 'I'm sorry I didn't make it yesterday.'

'Hey,' he said, 'what's twenty-four hours between friends? I knew if you couldn't make it there'd be a good reason.' He paused. 'So what the hell was it?' And then he broke into a grin. 'Only kidding.' He nodded towards the bag. 'What have you got for me?'

She held it open for him to see. 'Some books. Your personal stereo. And I didn't know which tapes you'd want, so I just brought them all.'

He flicked his head towards a blue and silver portable stereo on a shelf on the opposite wall. 'One of the nurses loaned me her ghetto-blaster. Jesus, she only had tapes of rap music. You know, that's *rap* with a silent C. Go figure.' He stopped to catch his breath. 'Put Clapton on for me.'

Margaret glanced up at the nearest nurse who gave an imperceptible nod of her head. 'Sure,' she said, and rummaged through the cassettes until she found the *Pilgrim* tape. She crossed to the stereo, slipped in the tape and pushed the Play button. The creamy sound of the Clapton guitar swooped and slid around the room, rising and falling in skin-tingling crescendos. And then his soft, tremulous voice praying for a healing rain to restore his soul again.

The tears ran hot and salty down Margaret's cheeks as she turned to see that Steve had closed his eyes, dried lips moving, almost as if he were miming the words. She moved back to his bedside and took out the little pewter frame. 'I brought Danni,' she said.

His eyes opened again and she saw that they, too, were filled with tears. He looked at the photograph in her hand and reached out to take it from her. For a long time he looked at the little girl smiling at him. Then he looked at Margaret. 'I wish I could have known her,' he said.

'You will,' Margaret said softly, urgently, and with more conviction than she felt. 'Be strong, Steve. You can make it through this.'

Steve clutched her hand again. 'I want to see her,' he said. 'Even through the glass. They've got the address and phone number out there. Martha's still down as my next of kin.' And he was racked by another fit of coughing. And when he caught his breath again, he said, 'Call her, Margaret. Please.'

IV

Li watched the traffic out on Connecticut Avenue drift past in the colourless sodium light, and felt the deep rumble of the Washington metro through the floor of Charlie Chiang's restaurant as a train pulled into the Van Ness metro station somewhere deep below them in the bowels of the city. His normal appetite for Charlie's excellent cuisine was on hold, and he picked at the shredded beef and noodles in the rice bowl before him. Sitting opposite, in some deep, dark world of her own, Xiao Ling ate in small, almost frenetic, bursts. Plain boiled rice. She seemed to have only the most tenuous grasp of why her diet was being restricted, but did not seem to mind that she faced a lifetime of dull and simple food. It had never been a priority.

Li had asked her several times about the *ma zhai*, and in small, teasing fragments, she had confirmed what Margaret had told him. Yes, she thought she recognised them. No, she didn't know their names. She was not sure if they worked at the Golden Mountain Club or not. Perhaps she had seen them at the massage parlour. She couldn't remember. Li was certain that her memory lapses were selective and inspired by fear. Whatever else they had done, the *ma zhai* had been successful in scaring her into silence.

Finally, he reached across the table, removing her chopsticks from between her fingers and taking one of her hands in both of his. 'Xiao Ling, we are in Washington now,' he said with as much reassurance as he could muster. 'You are safe here. Tell me about the Golden Mountain Club.'

She pulled her hand away and shook her head. 'I don't want to talk about it.' She took a long draught of Coke, one of a handful of soft drinks that had been identified as 'safe'. She met his eye. 'And if I told you, you wouldn't want to hear it. Believe me.'

He knew that her recent past was like an open wound. It would take time to heal, time before he could touch her again and she could revisit that place without pain. He did not want to force the issue, particularly since she was going to have to face yet more trauma in the next hour. He had not yet had the courage to tell her. Some instinct told him that if she knew, nothing would persuade her to come home with him. To come face to face with the daughter she had abandoned.

He felt sick. It was not only Xiao Ling who faced the trauma of reunion. He had no idea how little Xinxin would react to seeing her mother again after two years. At first he had told her that her mother was ill. That she had been taken off to a hospital for treatment, and then to a rest home in the country to recuperate. Initially, she had asked daily when her mother would be coming home. When would she be well again? Why couldn't she go and see her? It had broken Li's heart to lie to the child. It was such a breach of trust, and trust between child and adult was almost as important as love. Margaret's presence had been an invaluable diversion, a substitute mother-figure, a loving presence to fill the black hole left by the disappearance of her real mother.

Gradually, Xinxin had asked after her less and less, and in time not at all. There was a knowingness about her whenever the subject came up, as if somehow she had guessed. And she had become adept at side-stepping the issue when she was asked by children at school, or by their parents, or her teachers. She had never once asked after her father, and Li had been taken aback once, when collecting her from kindergarten, to discover that she had told her teachers that she lived with her uncle and that both her parents were dead.

Li paid the check and told Xiao Ling it was time to go. He asked Charlie to call them a cab, and the driver took them south on Connecticut, crossing Rock Creek at the Taft Bridge, guarded on either side by impressive carved stone lions couch-ant, and then turning right past the seven-storey hotel that was now home to the Chinese Embassy. From their cab, the only identifiably Chinese feature was the red and gold emblem of the People's Republic above blanked out glass doors. Xiao Ling did not even notice it. Li craned to see if there was anyone he knew coming or going. But the tree-lined street was empty, dark and deserted in the quiet mid-evening of a Washington fall.

They crossed Rock Creek again, just past Sheridan Circle, and found themselves passing into the precincts of Georgetown. The driver made his way down through quiet shady streets on to O and turned west, passing a towering red-brick church that dominated the east end of the street. When Li had paid the driver and they were left standing on the sidewalk, Xiao Ling looked around her in amazement. Painted townhouses with lacquered doors and Georgian windows, fresh-painted wrought-iron gates and chintzy shutters, crooked stairways and narrow alleys overhung by red-leafed ivy. Alarm systems everywhere, prominent on walls and in gardens. Expensive cars lining both sides of the street. She turned to Li. 'You *live* here?' All she had seen of America were filthy cellars, overcrowded apartments, night clubs and massage parlours in Chinatown. 'All on your own in a house this size?'

'Not on my own,' Li corrected her.

Xiao Ling frowned 'What do you mean?' Like Margaret before her, she was jumping to the wrong conclusion.

He took her by the arm and led her gently up the path to the front door. Through glass panels they could see that there was a light on in the downstairs hall. He unlocked the door, almost certain that she would be able to hear the banging of his heart against his ribs. 'I have someone living in,' he said. 'A nanny.' He closed the door behind them. 'I needed someone to look after Xinxin.'

Almost before she could react, Xinxin appeared from the kitchen calling his name. She was barefoot in her nightie, dressed for bed. Her hair, released from its bunches, was hanging in untidy clumps. She stopped abruptly, the smile frozen on her face. Mother and daughter faced each other for the first time in nearly a third of her life.

Li tried to react normally. 'Hi, little one,' he said. 'Guess who's here to see you?'

Xinxin took a couple of hesitant steps towards them, the expression on her face unreadable. Then she burst into a run, past Li's bike leaning against the bannister, and up the stairs stuffing her fist in her mouth to stop herself crying. They heard her footsteps on the polished floorboards, followed by the slamming of her bedroom door and a howl that was almost feral. Li felt as if someone had just driven six inches of cold steel into his chest. Then his face stung and burned white hot as Xiao Ling struck him with her open palm, a blow of such force that he stumbled and almost fell. Their eyes met for only a moment, and he felt their hatred sear his soul. A deep sob broke in her chest, and she ran down the hall, through the first door that she could find, passing a bewildered-looking Meiping. Meiping looked at Li, alarmed. 'Is everything alright, Mister Li?'

V

Margaret sat in someone's office staring at the shadows on the walls. A lamp on the desk burned a pool of light into a white blotter. Beyond it, only the shapes and shadows of the monsters that stalked her imagination moved in the darkness. Her body felt as if someone had been pounding at it with clenched fists. Her head ached and her eyes stung.

Tracking down Steve's ex-wife had not been as simple as she had expected. Martha and her new husband were out to dinner somewhere, leaving Danni in the care of a teenage babysitter who gave Margaret a cellphone number. But the cellphone was turned off, and Margaret had been forced to call the babysitter back for the name of the restaurant. The girl said she would have to call home and find out, and that she would call back. In spite of Margaret stressing the urgency of the situation, it was twenty minutes before the babysitter returned the call, saying that her home line had been engaged.

When, eventually, Margaret got through to the restaurant, it was the husband who came to the phone. The banker. He took some convincing that this was not one of Steve's practical jokes. Apparently there had been several. Margaret inwardly cursed Steve and his juvenile sense of humour, but still was unable to resist a tiny, sad smile. She assured the banker that this was no practical joke.

Then Martha had come to the phone, truculent and ready to be difficult. How serious could it be? Did Margaret know how long it would take her to get there from West Virginia? And it was far too late to be dragging a young child out of her bed.

Margaret, patience strained to the limit, had said simply, 'Martha, it might be the last time Danni gets to see her father. There's a very strong chance he could be dead by the time you get here.'

And the silence at the other end of the line had stretched out for an eternity. Finally, in a very small voice, Martha had said, 'I'll be there as soon as I can.'

There was a knock at the door, and a wedge of yellow light fell in from the corridor as it opened. Margaret looked up expectantly and saw the silhouette of Felipe Mendez standing in the open doorway. He looked almost like a caricature of himself, tousled hair, creased and rumpled overcoat, a battered briefcase hanging from the end of his arm. She heard, rather than saw, his smile. 'People who sit in the dark, my dear, are generally trying to hide from something,' he said.

'Life,' Margaret said. 'Or maybe it's death.'

'What's the news?'

'Temperature's still creeping up. Lot of fluid in the lungs now. He's very fevered. They're pinning everything on this rimantadine.'

'Ah, yes, the anti-viral stuff. Unproven.'

Margaret nodded. He stepped in and closed the door behind him, placing his case on her desk and drawing up a chair. As he sat down, his face fell into the circle of reflected light from the desk and she saw him clearly for the first time. He looked tired, older somehow. She could smell the cigar smoke clinging to his clothes. He said, 'I didn't get word until I was back in Conroe. This is the earliest I could make it.' He sighed. 'At the very least, we might learn more about what it is that has triggered the virus.'

Margaret glanced at him. It was such a cold and unfeeling thing to say. And yet, what else did she expect? Steve meant nothing to Mendez. His concern was to try to find out what had made the virus active, in order that they could prevent it happening to thousands of others. Live or die, Steve gave him a case study.

'The trouble is,' Mendez said, 'although we know exactly what he has eaten and drunk during his time in isolation, there were nearly forty-eight hours prior to that in which he could have consumed any number of things.'

'Didn't you ask him?'

'Of course. The night he was admitted.' He stroked his goatee thoughtfully. 'He was very helpful. Went through everything he could remember.' He exhaled deeply. 'Unfortunately, the memory is a very unreliable thing. Often faulty. And as you know, my dear, science is only too exact. However, the more data we have to work with the more we can narrow our search.' He laughed, but there was no humour in it. 'From a speck of dust in the Milky Way, perhaps to something the size of a pebble.' He smiled grimly. 'You look weary, my dear.'

'I could sleep for a week — if my nightmares would only give me peace.'

'Ah, yes, the waking kind. They're the worst. You can't just open your eyes and leave them behind.'

'Can't close your eyes and lose them either.'

A uniformed nurse knocked and opened the door. 'That's Major Cardiff's wife and daughter at front reception,' she said.

Margaret stood up immediately. 'I'll be right there.' She looked sadly at Mendez. 'He wanted to see his little girl, in case it would be for the last time.'

Margaret had been unaware of creating expectations in her mind, but Martha still took her by surprise. She was not what she had been expecting at all. A strikingly good-looking woman, tall and elegant, she had a thick mane of shiny, black hair. Her face was made-up for her night out, elaborate eye colour and a slash of red lipstick, although Margaret could see that she was pale now beneath the powder. She still wore her long, red evening dress beneath a man's overcoat that had been placed over her shoulders for warmth.

Danni, wrapped and swaddled in quilted anorak and scarf, stood clinging sleepily to her mother's legs, tired and bewildered. The banker stood behind them, at a discreet distance, in dinner jacket and silk scarf. He was shorter than Steve, heavier, and losing his hair. And there was no magic in his eyes. Margaret fleetingly wondered what it was about him that had made Martha choose him over Steve. Could it really have been as simple and as mercenary as his bank balance? Perhaps it was the smell of money he brought home on his clothes, instead of the smell of death.

'How is he?' Martha asked.

'Not good,' Margaret said. 'I'm not sure that you'll be able to see him now, even through the glass.'

Martha frowned. 'What do you mean, through the glass?'

'He's in isolation. Only properly protected medical staff are allowed any contact with him.'

Martha shook her head, as if this was something preposterous. 'Well, what on earth's wrong with him?'

'He cut himself during autopsy and contracted a viral infection.'

Danni's sleepy little voice interrupted the interrogation. 'Mommy, where's Daddy?'

'In a minute, honey.' There was irritation in Martha's voice. She said to Margaret, 'But you're treating him, right? I mean, if it's just a virus . . .'

'AIDS is caused by a virus, Mrs Muller.'

'Yeah, and so's the common cold. I'm not an idiot, Doctor Campbell. What kind of virus are we talking about here?'

An alarm sounded in the corridor, a repetitive monotone wail that sent shivers of chilling apprehension coursing through Margaret's veins. She turned towards the uniformed nurse who had been standing by. 'That's the emergency alarm in two hundred,' the nurse said in a hushed voice.

'Oh, God,' Margaret whispered. 'Let us through. Fast.'

Martha snatched Danni into her arms. 'I'll wait here,' the banker called after them, but no one was listening to him.

They followed the nurse through the maze of corridors, stopping only to let electronic doors swing open as the nurse waved her ID at the readers on the wall. The reception area was in a state of pandemonium. The alarm was louder here, almost deafening.

The doctor Margaret had spoken to earlier, and another two nurses, ran past them carrying blue suits into the changing room, making hurried preparations to enter the isolation ward.

Margaret ran to the window and peered through the glass. There were three space-suited nurses around Steve who was thrashing around on the bed like a man possessed, crashing into the protective rails on either side, wires and drip-feed ripped free and trailing on the floor. His eyes seemed to have sunk into the back recesses of his head, his lips cracked and bleeding. Blood-filled vomit coursed from his mouth. And when it stopped he began screaming and yelling before yet more vomit choked off his screams. And all the time the siren bore into their brains like some maniac with a drill.

And then suddenly, and without warning, Steve stopped fighting it, falling back limp on the bed, three or four shuddering convulsions racking his body, before he lay quite still, head turned towards the door, eyes wide and staring. Margaret knew his heart had simply stopped. His lungs had filled with fluid and blood, starving his brain of oxygen. The billions of replicated viral particles in his blood had finally infested and destroyed his essential organs. His nightmare was over. Theirs had just begun.

A scream exploded in Margaret's right ear, and she turned to see the terror on little Danni's face. Hoisted in her mother's arms she had seen it all through the glass. An unspeakable horror, and Margaret knew that it would live with her all her days. The tiny face which had smiled out from the pewter frame, from her father's computer screen, from the snapshots pinned to his filing cabinet, was distorted out of all recognition as she drew another deep, quivering breath and screamed again for her lost daddy.

VI

The lights of the capital reflected deeply in the dark, silently shifting mass of the Tidal Basin. Margaret stood on the steps of the Jefferson Memorial, beneath its towering marble, and looked directly north, beyond The Ellipse, and the South Lawn of the White House to the floodlit Truman Balcony with its distinctive arc of columns. She was not quite sure why she had come here. On a trip to Washington as a schoolgirl, she had been overawed by the scale and magnificence of the Jefferson Memorial. Even more than the commanding figure of Lincoln, gazing from his vast seat across the Reflecting Pool to the needle of the Washington Monument, Jefferson had seemed strong and eternal. Perhaps, she thought, she had returned all these years later in an attempt to rediscover her faith. Not in God, but in Man.

Officially, the memorial was closed. But she had simply abandoned her car in the park and walked across the lawns in the dark, climbing the fence and dropping into the well of the monument, circling it through the trees until she found herself standing on the front steps gazing across the water towards the home of the most powerful man on earth. Away to the right, light reflected off the white stone of the Bureau of Engraving and Printing where they printed the paper money that made the world go round. And then there was the Agricultural Department on Fourteenth Street, and other buildings that housed some of the primary Cabinet departments. Beyond them, although she could not see it from here, lay Capitol Hill; She was surrounded by all the great seats of government, of power and influence. All as defenceless as man himself against an organism so small it could not be seen with the naked eye. All their task forces and budgets and people, powerless to prevent a simple virus from destroying the life of one man and leaving a little girl fatherless. Bleakly, Margaret wondered how many more lives would be lost before this thing was over. How many more children would be left fatherless, motherless. Tens, perhaps hundreds, of millions. For the first time since the USAMRIID briefing she knew just what devastation they really faced. She had seen it first hand. And even greater than her grief was her fear.

She turned and walked slowly up the steps, through the pillars, into the vast circular hall at its heart. In the centre of it stood the massive bronze figure of Thomas Jefferson, a great shadow in the dark, reflected light from beyond casting his shadow in several directions at once across the polished marble floor. Pale light from streetlamps in the park slanted in between the pillars, lighting his words carved in the wall. *We hold these truths to be self evident: that all men are created equal, that they are endowed by their Creator with certain inalienable rights. Among them are life, liberty and the pursuit of happiness.* Margaret could almost hear them spoken. She wondered what had happened to poor Steve's inalienable rights. Life, liberty, happiness — all stolen away by a virus engineered by madmen. She took a deep breath, steeling herself for the fight against fear. Somehow these people had to be stopped.

CHAPTER TEN

I

There was a light on in the downstairs sitting room when she climbed the steps and walked the short path to the front door. A bell sounded somewhere deep inside the house when she pressed the bell-push. After a moment, the light snapped on in the hall, and she saw Li in jeans and tee-shirt shamble barefoot to the door. He had a bottle of beer in one hand. He frowned when he saw through the glass that it was Margaret. Something in the set of his face made her doubt her welcome. She could have stayed over in any number of hotels, and no doubt FEMA would have picked up the tab. But right now she needed human company and comfort. He opened the door and they stood staring at each other for a moment, and she knew immediately from his eyes that the beer in his hand was not his first.

She said simply, 'Steve's dead.'

Straight away his expression softened, and without a word he took her in his arms, almost squeezing the breath from her, and they stood in the open doorway for what must have been minutes. She clung to him and let the tears finally fall, silently, staining the front of his tee-shirt before she stepped back, wiping her face dry. 'Aren't you going to ask me in?'

He stood aside to let her into the hall and closed the door behind her, and then she followed him through to the kitchen where he prepared a vodka tonic in a tall glass filled with ice. She sat at the table, picking at a shred of skin which had peeled away from a cuticle. He drained his beer, opened another bottle and handed her the vodka. Still they had not spoken. Finally, when she had taken her first drink, he said, 'Was it bad?'

She nodded. 'Worse than you can imagine.'

He sat down opposite her. 'Then that is what waits for Xiao Ling.'

'Not if she sticks to the diet,' Margaret said, and for a moment was overwhelmed by the enormity of her ignorance. How could she know that for certain? How could she guarantee it for life? She looked around suddenly. 'Where is she?'

Li lifted his eyes towards the ceiling. 'Upstairs. Not speaking to me.'

Margaret frowned. 'Why?'

'Because I did not tell her that Xinxin was here. Because I made her face up to something she would probably have done almost anything in the world to avoid.'

Margaret was shocked. In all the angst about Steve, she had forgotten that Xinxin was here, and in her imagination she could picture the moment. 'What happened?' she asked.

He described to her the scene in the hall and her heart

ached for the little girl. She saw, now that she looked, the red, raised handprint on the side of his face, but could find no sympathy for Xiao Ling, and as she thought about it grew angry at him also for springing the mother on the child without warning.

'What in God's name did you *think* was going to happen?' she said, then immediately felt sorry for him when his head sank into his chest.

'What else could I do? If I had told Xiao Ling she would have refused to come. I did not ask for this, Margaret. Not for any of it.' He pleaded for her understanding and got it. She reached a hand across the table to grasp his. He squeezed it. If ever there was a moment, through their long and turbulent history, that each needed the other, this was it. A moment recognised by both of them.

He stood and led her upstairs to the room at the front where two days previously she had spent the night alone. Her choice. Her mistake. But not tonight. She had no idea where Xiao Ling was, and she didn't care. They undressed in the dark and fell together between the cool cotton sheets of his bed and found comfort in each other, simply touching and holding and letting time steal them off into sleep.

Li had no idea how long he had been sleeping, or what it was that woke him. But his heart was thumping, and he knew that his subconscious self was telling the barely conscious one that something was wrong. He sat up, listening intently. Margaret was still asleep, lying on one side, her arm flung across his pillow, hair tangled around her face and neck, breathing heavily. He heard nothing else and lay back down, staring up at the ceiling. The red glowing numerals of his digital clock on the bedside table told him it was 4.25. He remembered that Xiao Ling was in his house. And Xinxin. And that there was a threshold of pain still to be crossed. He closed his eyes and tried to shut out the thought. His heart rate was returning to normal. Perhaps it had been a dream.

And then there it was again. He sat bolt upright, aware this time of what he had heard. A loud creak, sharp and penetrating, like a nail being pulled from dense wood. Maybe it was just a floorboard. Xiao Ling or Xinxin or Meiping up to the toilet in the night. But he didn't think so. As he waited for it to come again, he heard the distant sound of breaking glass, so faint that he would not have heard it had he not been awake and listening. But of one thing he was certain; it had come from somewhere inside the house. Downstairs, he thought. Towards the back. He leapt out of bed and pulled on his jeans, and Margaret rolled over sleepily.

'What is it?' she asked, barely awake, and then was startled by his hand clamping itself over her mouth. Eyes wide, she stared at him in fright and tried to sit up. But he held her firmly in place and raised a finger to his lips.

'Intruders,' he whispered, his voice little more than a breath. And slowly he removed his hand from her mouth. 'Downstairs.' He looked around the room, searching for something he could use to defend himself. A weapon. And then he spotted in the corner the baseball bat and glove they had given him at the Embassy. Someone had come up with the bright idea that it would be good for international relations if they put together a baseball team to play in an inter-embassy league. There had been a few practice games. Li had made it to one of them and acquired the bat and glove in the process. But neither the team nor the league had come to anything. He lifted the bat and felt the comforting weight of it swing from his hand and was thankful for that bright idea. It had found its time.

Margaret had pulled on her tee-shirt and jeans and was slipping her feet into her sneakers. She was wide awake now and breathing rapidly. 'What about the others?' she whispered.

He nodded, and indicated that she should follow him. Very gingerly he opened the door and looked out along the upper landing. A night light glowed at the far end, casting deep shadows. But there was no movement, no sound. He moved quickly, cat-like along the landing, Margaret following in his slipstream, past the top of the stairs and along the hall. There were three doors at the far end. One, Margaret knew, was Xinxin's room, the other Meiping's. She assumed that Xiao Ling was in the third.

Li drifted past the doors to a window that looked out on to the flat roof of a terraced dining area that had been built out from the back of the house and into the yard years before. Moonlight cast the long shadow of a large lime tree across the bitumen, and Li caught the movement of a figure drifting across it to drop down into the narrow alleyway that ran between this house and its neighbour. He pulled back from the window and turned quickly into the third room. Xiao Ling was sitting up in her bed. She, too, had heard something. 'Get Xinxin,' he hissed at her. 'Take her into Meiping's room with Margaret.'

She was frightened and confused. 'What . . . ?'

'Just do it! Now. There are people in the house.' And he ran back into the hall where Margaret stood looking pale and scared. 'Get them all into Meiping's room,' he said, and he started back along the hall to the top of the stairs. There he hesitated, glancing back to see Xiao Ling and Margaret together in the hall. Margaret opened the door to Xinxin's room and hurried inside.

Li took a deep breath and took the bat in both hands, crooking his arms, ready to swing at a split-second's notice, and started down the stairs, one careful step at a time.

Nothing moved in the downstairs hall. He stiffened at the sound of a creaking floorboard. But it came from up the stairs, the girls moving into Meiping's room. He crept past his bicycle, laying each bare foot, one after the other, carefully on the polished floor, toes first, then heel, planting them flat and steady. At the end of the hall, the door to the dining terrace lay ajar, and the light of a distantly reflected moon fell silver and insubstantial through the gap. Very slowly, Li pushed the door inwards. He felt cool air on his face, as if from an open window, and saw shards of broken glass lying on the carpet. His breath came to him rapidly in shallow trembling gasps and seemed inordinately loud. He could hear nothing else above it. He backed up along the hall and, leaning across, pushed open the door to the living room. He had a very powerful urge to switch on as many lights as he could reach. But he knew that in order to make the intruders visible to him, he would make himself a very visible target to them. They would be more disorientated by the dark. After all, he knew the house and they didn't.

The light from the street lay across the living-room carpet in elongated squares, a distortion of the twelve-paned window. Li preferred the feeling of the carpet between his toes as he advanced into the front room. There was more comfort in it. His eyes lighted on a shadow in the kitchen doorway. It was a strange shadow, resembling nothing familiar to him. There was not the slightest movement in it, but Li could tell neither what it was nor how the light had created it. And then suddenly it grew large, expanding towards him, taking shape in the form of a man, hands raised above its head. A white Chinese face briefly caught the light from the window, and Li saw the reflection of polished metal pass quickly through it as a blade cleaved the air. He raised his bat and felt sharp metal slice into dense wood. And in a purely reflex action, he pulled back his leg, folding it into his chest and kicking out hard at the shadow. He felt ribs cracking beneath his heel, and heard a sharp cry of pain as his assailant staggered across the room and crashed into a wall unit laden with books and CDs and oriental knick-knacks that had come with the house.

His miniature stereo system bizarrely started playing at high volume. Li recognised the music immediately. A CD of opera arias that he had been listening to, trying to accustom

PETER MAY | 263

his eastern ear to the strange cadences of western music. Twin female voices swooped around the room singing Delibes' *Flower Duet* from *Lakmé*. Li wanted to scream at them to shut up, but another shape materialised out of the shadow. Another blade. This time he saw clearly that it was the kind of cleaver used by chefs in Chinese kitchens. A big square blade with a heavy wooden handle. He tried to skip out of the way, and tripped over the leg of his first attacker, landing heavily on his side. His baseball bat, a cleaver still buried in the striking end of the shaft, tumbled from his hand. He rolled over, trying to grasp it again, and found his fingers closing around the handle of the cleaver. He wrenched it free of the bat and rolled again as he heard the swish of a blade parting the air above him. Something flashed past his face, clearing it by no more than an inch, and he struck out blindly, swinging the cleaver in front of him, and felt it slice through something soft. A scream sought to find the pitch of the divas in their *Flower Duet*. But it failed to get there, making instead a ghastly discord. He realised that his face was wet, something warm, the temperature of blood. Something dark on his hand as he wiped it from his face. A body fell heavily on top of him, and he smelled five spice on its dying breath.

He pushed it aside and scrambled to his feet, the cleaver still in his hand, just in time to be smashed to the floor again by the assault of his first attacker throwing himself across the room. A deep groan of pain escaped the man's lips and Li knew that he had broken two, perhaps more, of his attacker's ribs with his initial kick. They fell awkwardly and Li lost his grip on the cleaver, his fingers sticky now and slippery with blood. In spite of his injury, his assailant was still strong, and a fist like balled steel crashed two, three times into Li's face. He could taste his own blood now filling his mouth. He swung his fist at the man's chest, connecting again with the damaged ribs. The man screamed and Li pulled himself free, scrabbling across the carpet for the cleaver or the bat. He found the bat, staggered to his feet and turned in time to see the man leaping at him again with grim, defiant determination. Li swung the bat with all his strength and heard the dreadful sound of splintering bone, his arm jarring with the force of the bat as it connected with the side of the man's skull. He made no other sound, dropping immediately to the floor in a heavy, huddled, lifeless bundle, like a sack of stones.

Li stood gasping for breath, almost paralysed by his own adrenalin. The divas had given way now to a deep, sonorous baritone, a grown man weeping as he sang the definitive aria from Leoncavallo's *I Pagliacci*. Li swung his head at the sound of a movement behind him, and he saw, clearly caught in the light from the street, a young Chinese dressed entirely in black, levelling a gun at his head. With a great yell of hopeless frustration, Li launched himself across the room in one last desperate adrenalin burn.

Margaret was both confounded and terrified by the sound of opera rising up through the house, like some ghastly funeral dirge accompanying the cries of battle that came from below. All three women were huddled on the floor beneath the window, a terrified and confused Xinxin crushed to Margaret's breast. And then, above the plaintive cries of Leoncavallo's baritone, came the sound of a single gun shot. Deadened by the confined space of the living room. A moment later, the mourning of the baritone was cut short, and a silence like death fell on the house.

They listened for a long time in that silence, hardly daring to breathe, before they heard the first creak of a footstep on the stairs. A sound like the whimper of an injured animal came from Xiao Ling's huddled form. Margaret turned angrily, her finger to her lips. 'Shhhh!' She needed her anger to over come her fear. She let go of Xinxin, who turned to clutch her mother instead, and stood up. She looked out of the window and saw that it was a fifteen-to-twenty-foot drop to the back yard. They could jump if they had to. She slid open the lower half of the sash and felt the cold night air raise goosebumps on her arms. That was the escape route, their last resort. But there had to be a first line of defence. She looked around the room, starting to panic, and saw a bedside lamp with a heavy ceramic base.

She reached over and ripped it from its socket, and darted across the room to stand on the far side of the door. She tore away the shade and raised the base of the lamp to shoulder level, clutching it with both hands, ready to swing and do as much damage as she could.

There was another creak from the top of the stairs, and they heard someone moving slowly down the hall, carpet over old floorboards creaking like footsteps in dry snow. The steps faltered, as if there had been a stumble. And then for a moment complete quiet. Only Li would know that it was this room they were in. An intruder would have a fifty-fifty choice between Meiping's room and Xinxin's.

The door swung open, and Margaret braced herself, ready to swing the base of the lamp. Then Xinxin's shrill shriek pierced the dark and she tore herself free from her mother and ran across the room to throw her arms around Li's legs. Margaret almost buckled at the knees, and stepped out from the shadow of the door to switch on the light. This time it was Xiao Ling who screamed as the figure of her brother stood swaying in the doorway, blood matting his hair. Shockingly red in the sudden light, it was spattered across his face, smeared on his chest and crusting on the fingers of his right hand like a pathologist's glove.

II

The night air was filled with the crackle of police radios and intermittent blue and red flashing lights. O Street was choked with police vehicles, ambulance, forensics, an unmarked truck from the morgue. Wealthy residents, wakened from their sleep, stood at windows wrapped in silk gowns watching with a mix of fear and curiosity, as three covered bodies strapped to litters were carried out to the vehicle from the morgue. It was nearly 6 a.m. Too late to go back to bed. Too early to go to work. All that any of them could do was watch.

Li watched, too, from the window of his bedroom. He found it hard to wipe from his mind's eye the blood running red against the white ceramic shower base as streams of comforting hot water washed it from his skin a little over an hour ago. His own blood had long since clotted in his nostrils and around the split in his upper lip. He had lost a tooth from his lower jaw and his face was swollen and bruised. His whole body ached. His mind was numb. Downstairs, forensics officers in hooded white Tivek suits were sifting through the debris of the battlefield. The photographer had already finished his work, staring dead eyes, open mouths, dark shadows on blood-stained carpet, all captured in the brief, dazzling illumination of his flash.

'Jesus, Li,' Fuller said. 'I wouldn't like to pick a fight with you.'

Li turned and looked at the FBI agent, and then beyond to where Hrycyk stood smoking in the doorway. He had seen them arrive a couple of minutes earlier. 'Just tell your INS buddy that,' he said, 'next time he wants to start getting personal.'

Hrycyk raised a hand of submission. 'Hey,' he said, 'I don't have to like you to respect you.' He pulled a pack of cigarettes from his coat pocket. 'Here, have a smoke. You look like you could do with one.' And he crossed the room to offer him the pack. Li drew one out and took a long, hard look at Hrycyk. Grey hair scraped back from his receding hairline, a face losing its shape, lined, and puffy from lack of sleep. Pale blue eyes with whites yellowed by nicotine. His shirt, stretched and pulled by his belly, in danger of dragging free of his trousers. 'What?' Hrycyk demanded. 'What are you looking at?'

'Just trying to figure out where the hell you come from,' Li said.

'I'll tell you where I come from,' Hrycyk said, bristling. 'I come from a time when people spoke their minds, said what they thought. Before all this political correctness crap. You may not like it, but I tell it like I see it – and, believe me, I seen a lot. I say what I think. And you get what you see.' He snapped open his lighter and lit Li's cigarette.

Li dragged on it through swollen lips and sucked the smoke gratefully into his lungs

'Yeah, and what you'll get is kicked out of the agency if you don't watch your mouth,' Fuller said. 'I happen to know there's a complaint file this thick on you.' He held up a hand, stretching thumb and forefinger apart to create a four-inch space. 'I know, 'cos I've seen it.'

Hrycyk turned a hostile eye on him. 'And wouldn't you people just love to see another INS man bite the dust.'

Fuller grinned. 'Take the early retirement, Hrycyk. Life could be tough without a pension.'

Hrycyk turned back to Li. 'See? That's what you get in this country now, smart-assed kids telling you what to say and what to think. Used to be a man had a right to freedom of speech. Next thing you know we'll be copying you people, declaring the People's Republic of America. Big brother just around the corner. Then we'll be Comrades, you and I.' He took another pull at his cigarette and blew smoke at the ceiling. 'What the fuck happened down there, Li?'

Li told them, in graphic detail, exactly what had happened,

just as he had told the homicide detective in his statement forty minutes earlier. They listened in awed silence, and Hrycyk let his cigarette burn down to the tip without taking another draw on it. 'Jees,' he said softly. 'You're a lucky man to still be alive.'

Fuller said, 'And you figure they were after your sister?'

Li nodded. He told them about the *ma zhai* harassing Margaret and Xiao Ling in Houston.

'Why the hell didn't you tell us this before?' Hrycyk wanted to know.

'I wanted to get her somewhere safe first.'

Hrycyk snorted. 'Yeah, real safe, wasn't it?'

'Why would they want to kill her?' Fuller persisted.

'Because she knows something,' Li said. 'She must. Something she saw, something she heard . . . She worked for a few months at the Golden Mountain Club.'

'High-class whorehouse and gambling den,' Hrycyk said.

Li said, 'Apparently all the tong leaders use it, all the top people in Houston's Chinese underworld.' He glanced at Hrycyk, reluctant to confess this in his presence. 'Seems my sister was one of their favourites.'

But Hrycyk was unaware of Li's discomfort. He was thinking hard. 'Then they find out she's your sister,' he said, 'and they start getting scared. Because she knows who these people are and they don't want her telling you.'

'You talked to her about it?' Fuller asked.

'Earlier,' Li said. 'Yesterday.' He shook his head. 'She wasn't very forthcoming.'

'Well, she's going to have to start coming forth pretty damn quick,' Hrycyk growled.

Fuller said, 'Let's go talk to her now.'

Li checked Xinxin's room first. Margaret sat against the headboard, Xinxin curled into her lap, fast asleep. She raised a finger to her lips. She looked tired and pallid, with dark rings beneath her eyes, but Xinxin needed the comfort and reassurance, and so she was prepared to sit with her for as long as it took. As he pulled the door shut, Li realised that Hrycyk had been peering over his shoulder. 'Cute kid,' he whispered.

'Cute Chinese kid,' Li said.

Hrycyk shrugged. 'Whatever.' He appeared to be faintly embarrassed, as if Li had discovered a hairline crack in the enamel of his racist image. 'Kids are kids. They're just cute.'

Xiao Ling was curled up on top of her bed, fully dressed, dried tears staining her cheeks. She sat up, alarmed, as the three men came into her room.

'It's okay,' Li said. 'They're sort of police officers. We need to talk to you about the Golden Mountain Club.'

She pressed her lips together and gave a tiny shake of her head.

'Oh, yes we are,' he insisted. 'Those men came here tonight to kill you because of something you know. We need to find out what that is, because the chances are they're going to try again.'

She glared sullenly at the three men. 'What can I tell you?'

'Just tell us about the club. What it was like. The people

you met. The other girls. Anything you can think of. Who ran it, how it worked.'

She drew her hands down her face, steeling herself to remember things she had buried, things she only ever wanted to forget. Her words came in bursts, as she dredged up the memories, and then spat them out fast to escape the nasty taste that came with them. Li translated as she spoke.

'The owner of the club was from Hong Kong. He was a small man, in his forties, I think. They called him Jo-Jo. I think his name was Zhou. He liked to touch the girls. You know, he never had sex with any of us. But he loved to sit at the bar and chat, and run his hands over a thigh, down an arm. Occasionally he would brush a breast with the back of a hand. He was a toucher. The other girls said he went off to masturbate in his office.'

Li was shocked at this from his sister, and embarrassed to translate it.

Hrycyk chuckled. 'Know the type,' he said.

Xiao Ling said, 'There were bouncers on the door, and young guys who kept order in the club. You know, sometimes people got drunk, maybe got violent with one of the girls, or there would be a fight. And the boys would throw them out. They were all members of the Silver Dragon gang.'

'Ma zhai,' Li said.

She darted a look in his direction. 'Yeah, ma zhai.'

'The ones who followed you in the car yesterday?'

'I don't know. Maybe.'

'Xiao Ling . . .' Li warned.

She lifted one surly shoulder and let it drop again. 'They looked familiar. Probably from the club. There were about twelve or fifteen of them that you would see regularly. And then there was the *dai lo . . .*'

'What the hell's a *dai lo*?' Fuller asked.

'The Big Brother,' Hrycyk said. 'The gang leader.' And both Fuller and Li looked at him, surprised. 'Hey,' he said, 'I been around this game a long time.'

Xiao Ling said, 'His nickname was Badger, because he had this strange white stripe running through his hair, on the right as you looked at him. He said it had been like that since he was a kid. I think he was proud of it.'

'Should be easy enough to find,' Hrycyk said. 'Unless he dyes his hair he's gonna stick out like a sore thumb.'

'There were lots of ordinary Chinese, and sometimes Vietnamese, who came to the club,' Xiao Ling went on. 'Mostly to drink and gamble. Occasionally, if one of them won a lot at cards, he would take one or two of us upstairs. But it was the snakeheads and the uncles, the *shuk foo*, who had the real money to spend. They usually dressed well and had big fat wallets. The girls always preferred a *shetou* or a *shuk foo* because they paid more and tipped well. But a few of them had some pretty unpleasant sexual preferences, and you would try to avoid them. There were some who liked you to hurt them, or wanted to hurt you. Some of them wanted you to piss on them while they jacked off.' She looked at Li with a sour expression on her face. 'Men are pretty disgusting, Li Yan,' she said.

Li's embarrassment in relaying this to Hrycyk and Fuller

was acute. But neither man seemed troubled or surprised by what they were hearing, or aware of his embarrassment.

'I told you before,' Xiao Ling said, 'that I was a favourite. All the important ones had me at one time or another. All the *shuk foo*, I think, and others. Guests. I would be given as a present, to show respect, or as a mark of subordination. Once to a man they called the *ah kung*, which I think is Cantonese for "grandfather".'

There was an immediate tension shared by all three men, but none of them wanted to interrupt her flow, or inhibit her by conveying this as significant. 'What was he like?' Li asked casually.

'The grandfather?' Xiao Ling pursed her lips and blew a jet of air through them to demonstrate her contempt. 'Like all the rest. Short and fat, with a big belly and bad breath. They get on top of you and hump for a couple of minutes and then they're all spent. It's hard to tell who you're with.'

'Anything else?' Li prompted. 'Anything else about him you can think of?'

She shook her head. 'The *shuk foo* who gave me to him as a gift told me that it was an honour for me to be taken by the *ah kung*. He said no one else knew that's who he was. And I was to tell no one or I would be in serious trouble. Then, when he introduced us, he called him something strange. A nickname. I remember thinking it was unusual. And the *ah kung* nearly struck him. He was very angry and told him never to call him that again.' She thought back for a moment, shuddering at some unpleasant recollection, and then she said, 'Yeah, that's right. He called him Kat. I asked one of the other girls what it meant, and she said it was Cantonese for "tangerine". You know, like for luck. I thought it was weird.'

'Who was the *shuk foo*?' Li asked.

Xiao Ling shook her head. 'I don't know his name. But he was always around the club. 'You'd need to ask the *dai lo*. He was Badger's uncle.'

CHAPTER ELEVEN

I

The Golden Mountain Club sat in a corner of Ximen Plaza, flanked on either side by rows of shops. Mona's Skin Care, Mountain Optical, Old China Fast Food. A billboard tacked to the exterior advertised, in Chinese characters, John P. Wu, Dentist – *Dentista*. Immediately next door was a Vietnamese restaurant boasting dancing and karaoke. The entrance to the Golden Mountain Club itself sat back in the shade of a covered walkway. A couple of felony notices in English and Spanish were pasted to the smoked glass of the door. A sign read: SMOKING PERMITTED WITHIN. Which brought a smile to Li's face. The idea of a non-smoking Chinese club was risible.

They had been watching the club from Hrycyk's beat-up old Santana on the far side of the plaza for nearly three hours. It had opened shortly after midday, and a steady flow of customers had followed the first staff – a dozen or so young to middle-aged men wearing suits and ties beneath overcoats that were superfluous in the midday heat of a Texas fall, several girls with short skirts and painted faces, miscellaneous youths in jeans and sneakers. You could tell the staff from the customers. The staff all had dead eyes and a reluctant gait. The customers had an air of anticipation about them, a sense of optimism.

Reluctantly, Li had left Xiao Ling at the house in Georgetown, protected by two armed police officers. She had refused to accompany them to the morgue where Margaret had made a positive identification of one of Li's attackers – the one who had made the slit-throat sign to her from the passenger seat of the white Chevy. He was the one Li had wrestled the gun from the previous night, blowing away one half of his face in the ensuing struggle.

Now he, Fuller and Hrycyk were going after the *dai lo* known as Badger. It was a straight line of connection from *dai lo* to *shuk foo* to *ah kung*. The problem, they knew, would be in persuading Badger to squeal. There were codes of honour and loyalty here that law enforcement officers had been unable to break in thousands of years.

It was nearly three when they saw the unmistakable white stripe through the dark hair of a young Chinese wearing a black leather jacket. He was walking across the plaza with the swagger of someone in possession of absolute self-confidence. His hands were pushed into the pockets of tight designer jeans, and he wore soft green suede shoes. His white tee-shirt was emblazoned with the logo of some American heavy metal band. The ubiquitous cigarette dangled from his lips. He swung open the door of the Golden Mountain Club and waltzed in like he owned the place.

Fuller was set to move there and then, but Hrycyk stopped him. The old immigration hand had been here many times before. 'Give him time to settle,' he said. 'Time to have a beer or two. Time to relax. We're not so likely to lose him that way. We go in now, he's still buzzing. Physically, mentally alert. And let me tell you, Agent Fuller, I've had it with chasing people up alleys. I'm too old for that kinda shit.'

So they waited another half-hour. Li and Hrycyk smoked more of Hrycyk's cigarettes. 'First stop, you're buying some of your own,' Hrycyk kept saying.

Fuller, full of impatience, and irritated by the constant smoking, kept the window wound down at his side. 'Next time,' he said, 'we bring along a HEPA mask so I can breathe.'

Li, sitting in the back, kept his own counsel and said nothing. Even if they were successful in pulling in the *dai lo*, he had grave doubts about how much, if anything, they would learn from him.

Hrycyk turned to him, and out of the blue said, 'You were kidding me, right? About this heap being built in China?'

Li shook his head solemnly. 'Rear off-side window winder always breaks off on them.'

Hrycyk looked at the broken window winder on the rear off-side window and narrowed his eyes. 'You already clocked that,' he said.

Li shrugged. 'Maybe. Maybe not.'

'Shit,' Hrycyk said. 'I'm trading this wreck in first chance I get.' He opened the driver's door. 'Time to go and get that little oriental bastard!'

Inside the main door there was a small reception area with a desk, and a gold 3D profile of the United States mounted on the wall behind it. It was gloomy here, subdued red lighting, smoked glass doors turning day outside into night. A flunky in a suit looked up, startled. 'Hey,' he said, 'this is private club. Members only.'

Hrycyk pushed a warrant in his face. 'Picked up my membership this morning,' he said. 'From a judge downtown.' And he flipped open his wallet to show him his badge. 'INS.'

Fuller waved his badge at him, too. And Li held up his maroon Public Security ID. 'Beijing Municipal Police,' he said. 'CID, Section One.' Which had a great deal more effect than either of the other two. The flunky paled. He reached forward under the desk, and Fuller grabbed his arm.

'Uh-uh,' he said. 'No warnings. Where's Badger?'

The flunky gulped. 'In the bar.'

'Show us.'

He pulled the little man out from behind the desk, and they followed him up dark, carpeted stairs and through a door into a large salon with tables set around an empty dance floor. There was a small stage at the far side, and a long bar set against the near wall. Subdued lighting around the perimeter of the salon revealed groups of two or three men, and the occasional girl, sitting drinking at tables. The light along the bar reflected in the faces of customers and girls perched on high bar stools, nursing drinks and smoking cigarettes. Badger and a couple of his *ma zhai* stood in a group at one end drinking beer by the neck. Some record from the singles charts was belting out across the sound system.

'Turn that shit off,' Fuller shouted at the flunky and pushed him towards the bar. The little man squeezed in past the barman and switched off the stereo. The sudden silence startled everyone in the salon, as much as if a gun had gone off. The hubbub of voices became instantly self-conscious and quickly died away. Eyes turned towards the three law enforcement officers. Hrycyk stepped up to Badger and pushed a gun in his face and flapped his badge at him. The *dai lo* grinned his passive defiance as Hrycyk frisked the pockets of his leather jacket and drew out his wallet, flipping it open to the ID window.

'Ko-Lin Qian,' Hrycyk said, reading off it. Then he grinned at the white stripe. 'Aka Badger. Aka Fuckhead. I have a warrant for your arrest. Turn around, put your hands on the bar.' The *dai lo* did as he was told, still the same defiant smirk on his face. Hrycyk kicked his feet apart and checked him for weapons. 'Okay,' he said, 'put your hands behind your back.' And he slipped his gun back in its holster and snapped on a pair of handcuffs.

The *dai lo* turned around to face him. 'So what you arrest me for?' he said. 'Breathing? I thought air was free in America.' A couple of his *ma zhai* sniggered.

'Free for Americans,' Hrycyk said. 'Not for illegal aliens.'

'I'm no illegal alien,' the *dai lo* said. 'I got papers.'

'Papers lie.'

'Truth is,' Li said suddenly, speaking in Mandarin, 'no

one gives a shit whether you're an illegal alien or not.'
Badger's smirk evaporated. There was an absolute hush in
the room.

'What the hell are you saying?' Hrycyk demanded.

But Li ignored him and continued in Mandarin. 'We want
information, kid. We need the name of your *shuk foo*. And
you're going to give us it.'

Li saw apprehension in the *dai lo*'s eyes. Badger glanced
quickly around the watching faces, then thrust out his jaw
defiantly at Li. 'You know I'm not going to do that.'

'Sure you will,' Li said quietly. 'Because I'm a nice guy, and
I'll ask you nicely.' He paused. 'Once.' And he sighed. 'After
that, who knows? Maybe I'm not such a nice guy any more.
You read the papers, you know how we do business in the
PRC.' He grinned.

Hrycyk was glaring at him. 'You gonna let us in on this
private conversation or not?'

Li shook his head. 'No.' He took Badger by the arm and
jerked him towards the door. 'Let's go.'

When they got to the car, they put Badger in the back and
Li slipped in beside him. Hrycyk turned and glared back at Li.
'What the hell was all that about in there?'

'Yeah, come on, Li,' Fuller said. 'We haven't been holding
anything back from you.'

'No, of course you haven't.' Li said. 'Let us just say at this
point you do not need to know.' He paused. 'Trust me.'

'About as far as I could kick you,' Hrycyk growled, and he
started the motor.

Badger snorted. 'Where'd you pick up this heap of shit?' he said sarcastically, making a poor attempt at bravado. 'The breaker's yard?'

'Shut the fuck up,' Hrycyk snarled angrily, and they jerked away across the tarmac with a squeal of tyres.

They drove in silence then along Bellaire until they turned on to the freeway at Sharpstown, heading east on the 59 before turning north on to the 45. Badger sat sullenly next to Li staring out of the window. As the skyline of downtown started growing on the horizon he asked in Mandarin, 'Where are you taking me?'

'INS lockdown,' Li said.

The *dai lo* shook his head bleakly. 'You know you've signed my death warrant.'

'Have I?' Li asked innocently.

'You know they're going to kill me. I'm not going to tell you what you want to know. But they'll make sure of it. One way or another.'

'So, if they're going to kill you,' Li said, 'why not tell us? What difference does it make?'

Badger looked at him scornfully. 'I'd rather die.'

'So die,' Li said, turning to the front again. 'Who gives a shit?'

Dark clouds were gathering again in the north-west, with the promise of more thunderstorms. They flashed beneath a couple of flyovers, the skyscrapers and tower blocks of downtown now directly ahead of them, late afternoon sunshine slanting through the clouds to reflect off acres of glass.

'Pull over,' Li said suddenly.

'What?' Hrycyk flicked a backward glance at him. 'What do you mean, pull over?'

'I mean stop the car,' Li said, almost shouting.

'Jesus Christ!' Hrycyk pulled across two lanes of traffic, to the accompaniment of a chorus of horns, and burned rubber to bring them to a halt on the hard shoulder.

'Wait here,' Li said, and he grabbed the *dai lo* by the collar and pulled him out on to a band of concrete littered with shredded tyre and fragments of glass. The barrier was scraped and scored, scarred by dozens of minor and several major accidents. He began walking him away from the car and glanced over the barrier to the slip road passing beneath them. It was a drop of about thirty feet. Beyond, he could see the distinctive building of the Texas Historical Museum, and in the distance the trees flanking Buffalo Bayou and the patch of green that was Sam Houston Park.

'What are you doing?' Badger was worried now.

'Maybe I'm going to throw you over,' Li said. 'Or push you in front of the next truck.'

'In the name of the sky,' the *dai lo* screamed at him. 'Are you mad?'

'Maybe,' Li said. They were having to shout above the roar of the traffic. He glanced back and saw the silhouettes of Hrycyk and Fuller leaning over the seats, watching them through the rear windshield. He turned back to the boy. 'You want to die or you want to live?'

'What do *you* think?'

'I think maybe we stopped here to let you have a pee, because we didn't want you soiling the car. And you got away before we could stop you. Jumping down on to that road and sprinting off towards the Bayou.'

Badger looked over the barrier. 'I'd get killed jumping down there.'

'So run until you get on to the ramp.'

The boy frowned at him. 'Why would you do that? Why would you let me go?'

'*Guanxi.*'

Badger looked at him as if he were insane. '*Guanxi?* What are you talking about? You don't owe me anything?'

'I will when you tell me the name of your *shuk foo*, then you'll have *guanxi* in the bank with me, big time. I'll let you go. You say you escaped. We don't have you in custody, they don't have to kill you. And they know you didn't even have time to tell me anything, even if you had been so inclined. Which, of course, you weren't.'

Badger stared at him hard for a very long time. A huge truck thundered past, throwing clouds of rubber dust and exhaust in their faces. Then, '*Guan Gong,*' he said. 'It's his nickname. That's all I know.'

Li said, 'If you're lying I'll put it about that we cut a deal, and you'll be a dead man anyway.'

'*Guan Gong,*' the *dai lo* said again, and met Li's eye directly.

Li shouted, 'Go!' And the *dai lo* ran, still handcuffed, his white stripe catching the sunlight as he went, feet hammering on the hard concrete.

Hrycyk and Fuller were out of the car in a second, weapons drawn, running towards Li.

'What the fuck's going on!' Hrycyk screamed.

'He got away,' Li said.

'You let him go?' It was Fuller this time, glaring at him, full of incomprehension.

Li shrugged. 'He gave us what we wanted.' And he started walking back towards the car.

Fuller and Hrycyk exchanged impotent glances, then Hrycyk looked along the hard shoulder to where the distant figure of the *dai lo* was heading down the slip road, almost out of sight. 'Fuck it,' he said, and headed back along the concrete to where Li was already waiting for them in the car.

II

The sunlit grey stone edifice of City Hall, a jumble of squares and rectangles carved into a black sky, looked out across what looked to Li like a large swimming pool. Lined with trees and picnic tables, the long turquoise blue rectangle of water stretched between the municipal building and Smith, where the curve of a blue glass tower reflected its neighbouring white skyscraper like a building toppling in an earthquake. Both dwarfed the City Hall.

Li and Hrycyk stood outside on the cobbled concourse, waiting for Fuller. Hrycyk was impatient and could barely stand still. 'Gimme a cigarette,' he said to Li. He had insisted they stop and that Li buy his own pack. Li handed him one and lit another himself. Hrycyk was shaking his head. 'I still can't believe you did that,' he said.

'What, gave you a cigarette?'

Hrycyk hissed his irritation. 'Let the kid go.'

Li shrugged. 'Seeing is believing.'

'I mean, is he stupid, or what? As soon as his people find out we're asking for *Guan Gong*, they're going to know he told us.'

Li let the smoke creep from the corners of his mouth. 'I guess he never stopped to think about that.'

Hrycyk gazed at him. 'You know you're a devious bastard, Li.' He meant it as a compliment.

'Thank you,' Li said. 'So are you.' He paused. 'Without the devious bit.'

Hrycyk laughed. 'You know, there are times, Li, when I think I might even get to like you.'

Li took another pull on his cigarette. 'Can't say I think I'll ever feel that way about you,' he said.

Fuller hurried down the steps to join them. 'Soong's not there. His office said we'd find him at the Houston Food Bank.'

'A food bank?' Li asked.

'It's a kind of charity thing,' Fuller said. 'Companies donate food to it. You know, stuff past its sell-by, or in damaged tins or packaging. Or just plain donations. The Food Bank distributes it to the poor of the State. Soong's bank donates manpower. All his employees put in one afternoon a week at the place. And so does he.'

*

The Houston Food Bank was in the Herstein Center warehouse between Jensen and Vintage on the Eastex Freeway, a bleak industrial landscape of gap sites and run down commercial properties. A couple of cops at the gates of the parking lot had pulled over a pick-up and were checking the treads. The driver was young and black, the cops were white, and Li thought it didn't take too much imagination to figure out why he'd been stopped. The parking lot was nearly full, and Hrycyk had to park a long way from the main entrance. As they crossed the lot, the first fat drops of rain began to fall. The sun had disappeared behind a brooding sky of battered-looking cloud. The air was full of electricity and the promise of storm.

Inside, they asked for Councilman Soong, and a young black man took them in back through the warehouse. They passed a line of Chinese volunteers packing foodstuffs into cardboard boxes on a conveyer belt. Through hanging straps of plastic, they entered an area of metal staging thirty feet high, piled on each level with plastic-wrapped boxes of food straight from the manufacturer. 'Being law enforcement people,' the young black man said, 'you folks'll probably be interested to know that we got prisoners down from Huntsville working here. Trustees working their way back into society. And a lot of the fresh food we get comes from the prison farms up there.' He grinned. 'So each time you put someone away, you're sort of doing us a favour.'

'I'll bear that in mind the next time I'm making an arrest,' Fuller said dryly.

Soong was driving a forklift truck between aisles at the far side of the warehouse, loading pallets on to staging. Movement detectors in the roof switched overhead lights off and on as he moved between rows. He was still wearing jeans and his red leather baseball jacket. Only now, he had completed the outfit with an Astros baseball cap. He grinned and waved when he saw them coming. 'Gimme minute,' he shouted. And they watched as he skilfully manoeuvred the forklift to slide a pallet on to the top level. He lowered the forks to the floor, cut the motor and climbed down, pulling off his gloves and stretching out a hand to shake theirs. 'Gentlemen,' he said. 'Pleasure to see you. To what do I owe honour?' But as usual he didn't wait for an answer, waving his arm around the warehouse instead. 'What you think of Food Bank? Good idea, yes? Good PR for Chinese help here. Good community relation.' He grinned mischievously. 'Besides, I always wanted to drive forklift.'

'We thought you might be able to help us identify someone, Councilman,' Fuller said.

'Of course,' Soong said. 'Anything I can do to help.' He looked at Li. 'You been in fight, Mistah Li?'

'A minor argument,' Li said.

'You not very good in argument, then.'

Hrycyk said, 'You should see the other guys.'

Fuller said impatiently, 'We're looking for an uncle with one of the tongs. A *shuk foo*.'

'You know his name?'

Hrycyk said, 'If we knew that we wouldn't be asking you. All we got's a nickname. *Guan Gong*.'

Soong looked startled. 'No!' he said. '*Guan Gong*? But you already know him. He was at meeting the other day. His name Lao Chao. He owns biggest restaurant in old Chinatown, not far from Enron Field. He sit at end of table near window.'

Li tried to picture him, and had a hazy memory of a thickset man with glasses and bushy hair swept back from a flat, broad face: an impression of someone who looked not unlike Chinese President, Jiang Zemin

'But Lao very respectable man,' Soong said. 'He no *shuk foo*.'

'You know what *Guan Gong* means?' Li asked.

'Sure,' Soong said.

Hrycyk turned to Li. 'What *does* it mean? You never told us it meant anything.'

'*Guan Gong* was a general in ancient China. A ferocious warrior. A hero of the Chinese underclass.' Li looked at Soong. 'An odd choice of nickname for a respectable citizen, don't you think?'

'*Guan Gong* symbolise values very precious to poor people,' Soong said indignantly. 'This is good name for upstanding member of community. Lao Chao, like many others at meeting, give generously to Food Bank and other charity.' He looked at Fuller. 'What you want him for?'

Fuller said, 'We believe he knows the identity of the *ah kung* we are looking for.'

Soong gathered his brows in consternation. 'There are many *ah kung* in Houston tong,' he said.

'Only one of them called Kat,' Li said, watching Soong closely. He was certain he saw a brief flicker of light in the dark, secret pools of his eyes. And then nothing. Just an outward appearance of surprise. His eyebrows pushed up on his forehead.

'Tangerine?' And he laughed. 'This is ve-ery strange name.'

'You never heard of him, then?' Hrycyk asked.

Soong pursed fat lips and shook his head. 'Sorry. Kat associated with good luck at Spring Festival. I never heard of anyone with name like this. What he do?'

Fuller said, 'We believe he's been funding and organising the trade in illegal Chinese immigrants across the Mexican border. The head of the snake.'

'And you think *Guan Gong* know who he is?'

'We know he knows,' Li said. 'And we have a witness who can identify them both.'

The dark, secret pools darted in Li's direction. 'Who?'

'A prostitute,' Hrycyk said. 'From the Golden Mountain Club. A gift from one to the other.'

Soong's gaze never left Li. 'Your sister,' he realised.

'That's right,' Li said. 'Someone tried to kill her last night. To shut her up. But they were too late.'

Soong shook his head and snorted noisily. For a moment, Li thought he was going to spit on the floor. But he had been in America long enough to sublimate the instinct and swallowed instead. 'I am sorry,' he said, 'that such things should happen in our community. You must find this snake and cut off its head.'

Hrycyk said, 'So where'll we find *Guan Gong?*'

'At his restaurant.' Soong checked his watch. 'For sure. He always there in the afternoon.'

Li reached out and caught his wrist. 'Nice ring,' he said in

Mandarin, turning Soong's hand over so that a large gold ring on the middle finger was facing up. It was set with a shaped oval of engraved amber.

Soong drew his hand away. 'It is my prize possession,' he said. 'A gift from my father. It once belonged to the Empress Dowager Cixi.'

'Worth a lot of money, then,' Li said.

'Priceless,' Soong responded. 'I raised the money for my journey to the United States on the strength of it.'

'You know,' Li said, 'that the smuggling of artifacts out of China is a capital offence.'

Soong smiled. 'Then it is lucky for me that we are no longer in China.'

Li smiled back. 'Lucky. Yes.' He paused. 'What's engraved on it?'

Soong ran a thumb over the stone. 'I've often wondered,' he said. 'Sadly time has all but worn it away.'

'May I?' Li held out his hand, and Soong reluctantly offered him his, so that he, too, could run a thumb over the engraving. Soong's hand was hot and damp. The amber, under Li's thumb, was cool, the engraver's work worn away almost to nothing. Li felt Soong's tension. He said, 'It is not often one gets to touch history.' He ran his thumb lightly over it again. 'Feels like it might have been a Chinese character. It is a pity we'll never know its meaning.'

Soong smiled and took his hand back. 'Indeed.'

'Are you people going to let us in on this conversation or not?' Hrycyk said, irritation clear in his voice.

'Just admiring Councilman Soong's ring,' Li said, smiling and holding the gaze of the Cantonese. And, then, as if snapping out of a trance, added, 'We had better go and talk to Lao Chao.'

Hrycyk drove them west along Elgin, through the black ghetto area of east central Houston. Rotting wooden shacks with crudely patched roofs sat behind lushly overgrown and untended gardens. All manner of flora reached for the sky through cracks in the sidewalk. The road was pitted and potholed, and each junction was punctuated by groups of disenchanted black youths, hands sunk deep in empty pockets, haunted eyes watching traffic. Ancient rusting cars limped across intersections, holed exhausts rasping fumes into the sticky afternoon, rap music belting from open windows. Li gazed thoughtfully from the back of the Santana. He was shocked by the poverty. They might have been in Africa, a shanty town on the edge of some third world city, instead of the fourth largest city of the richest country in the world. He lifted his eyes and saw the gleaming tower blocks of downtown Houston rising above the deprivation, almost taunting, a constant reminder to those who lived in the ghetto that the American Dream came true for some and not for others.

Lightning flashed in a bruised and brooding sky and moments later the air shook with the sound of thunder. And the rain came, suddenly and with such force that it raised a mist off the surface of the road. Worn wipers scraped

and smeared their way back and forth across Hrycyk's
windshield.

Li said, 'I guess the FBI will have a fat file on Councilman
Soong.'

Fuller glanced back at him. 'What's your interest in Soong?'
he asked noncommittally.

Li shrugged. 'I'd be interested to see the extent of his business dealings.'

'That's a matter of public record,' Fuller said.

'Yes, but it's what's not on the public record that interests
me,' Li said. 'You must have some kind of file on him.'

Fuller said, 'I'll check.'

Hrycyk laughed. 'Of course the FBI have got a file on him.
They're just not going to show it to *you*, that's all.' He glanced
at Fuller. 'Hell, they probably wouldn't even let me see it.'

Fuller said nothing.

They turned off Elgin on to Dowling and headed north
under the Interstate into the city's old Chinatown area,
block after block of low industrial units peppered with restaurants and the occasional Asian goods store. The Green
Dragon Restaurant sat on the corner of Dallas and Polk, an
ornately carved Chinese façade of intertwining dragons on
an otherwise featureless brick square. Hrycyk bumped the
Santana into an empty parking lot and they climbed the
front steps to glass double doors flanked by hanging red
lanterns. The lobby inside was in darkness except for lights
from fish tanks lining one wall. Air bubbled and glooped
through murky waters, and strange fish came nosing against

the glass to get a look at the newcomers. The restaurant beyond was filled with empty tables set for evening meals. The rattle of pans and the sound of raised voices came from unseen kitchens somewhere in the back. A girl in a gold lamé *qipao* drifted out of the gloom and looked at them curiously. 'We are not open yet,' she said.

Hrycyk showed her his ID. 'We're here to see Mister Lao Chao,' he said.

'One moment. I tell him.' And she crossed to the reception counter and lifted a phone. She dialled and listened, and then hung up. 'So sorry. He is speaking on telephone right now. You wait, okay?'

They stood around for a couple of minutes, Li and Hrycyk smoking, while the girl pretended to sort menus on the counter. 'You wanna try again?' Hrycyk growled at her eventually.

'Sure.' She lifted the phone and redialled and stood for a good half minute. She shrugged, pushing up painted eyebrows and wrinkling her forehead. 'Now he no answer.'

A single, dull crack sounded from somewhere in the building. The unmistakable report of a gun.

'Jesus!' Hrycyk stabbed his cigarette into an ashtray. 'Where's his office?'

The girl looked frightened. 'Upstairs.'

They ran up a double flight of carpeted stairs to a long corridor running over the restaurant. It was dark, and they couldn't find a light switch. But faint yellow light seeped out from beneath a doorway halfway along its length. Fuller got there first, gun in hand, and threw the door open. Li was on his shoulder as the door swung in to reveal a large office with flock wallpaper and a red patterned carpet which made it impossible to tell if there was blood on it. There was plenty on the big mahogany desk though, pooling around the head of *Guan Gong*, where he lay slumped across it, a gun in his hand, a hole in his face, and the back of his head blown away where the bullet had made its exit.

III

Margaret had arrived back in Houston a little after 1 p.m., depression following her like the stormclouds gathering in the western sky. She had not eaten for nearly twenty-four hours, but found that everywhere along Holcombe had already finished serving. Even after a year, she could not get used to the Texan habit of lunching before midday. Eventually she had found an all-day eatery in the Crowne Plaza and ordered a grilled chicken salad. It came piled high on the plate and the waitress said, 'I asked the chef why they build them salads so big, and he says to me, "People eatin' this late, they gotta be hungry".' It was 1.30 p.m., and Margaret marvelled at Texan sophistication.

She had eaten a little less than half the salad before going back to her office to face the mountain of paperwork piling up on her desk. Mail and telephone messages had accumulated in drifts, like snow, and she wished she could just plough them off to one side and let them melt away in the rain. As with her salad, she had no appetite for it, sitting gazing from the window unable to stop memories of Steve crowding her thoughts. And flickering images of Xinxin's tears as she had left that morning, mother and daughter still unable to come to terms with their unhappy reunion. That, in turn, had forced her back to the paperwork only to find a letter from the lawyer representing her landlord in Huntsville. It was official notification of her eviction — as if it hadn't already happened. She had thrown it on the pile, and opened an envelope with the official FEMA insignia on the bottom left corner. It was a list of all the contact telephone numbers of members of the task force, her own included, which had brought a bitter smile of irony to her face. Her home number was already out of date.

She had folded the list and slipped it into her purse, wondering what progress, if any, the task force had made. One of its number was dead. Li had only narrowly avoided being murdered by the assassins sent to silence his sister, and they were still no nearer, apparently, to identifying the *ah kung*. They had arrested hundreds of illegal immigrants all over the country and were already running out of holding facilities. There were thousands more out there, and probably thousands more still coming in, despite the clampdown on the border. And she knew that the task that faced Mendez in trying to identify the protein which triggered the virus was almost impossible. It had been only too clearly visible in the fatigue etched on his face the previous night. Margaret felt daunted, and frustrated by her inability to make any significant contribution.

Finally, she had slipped into a light, waterproof coat, and taken a fold-up umbrella from the bottom drawer of her desk. As she swept past Lucy in the outer office she had said, 'I'll be gone for the rest of the day,' and made her exit without giving Lucy a chance to respond.

Now, as she emerged from the car park into the rain on M. D. Anderson Boulevard, the thunder which had been threatening all afternoon cracked overhead, making her duck reflexively. The rain battered on the taut plastic of her tiny umbrella like peas on a drumskin. She splashed along the sidewalk under the dripping trees, past nurses and doctors in green and white surgical pyjamas hurrying between hospital buildings. Beyond the Women's University, at the very heart of the Texas Medical Center, the distinctive red roof of the Baylor College of Medicine, above tall windows like glass columns, was only just visible through the downpour. The ink ran on notices pinned to a pergola. Cars for sale, accommodation to let. Paper turning to mush in the rain. Margaret scampered across East Cullen Street and turned left towards the right-angled white facades of the Michael Debakey Center, with its tiered rows of windows cut like slashes in the stone.

A lab assistant took Margaret up in the elevator, and along endless corridors. She was young and bright, with sparkling eyes and conversation that bubbled out of her like water from a spring. Margaret barely heard her. She was shown into a tiny cluttered office that overlooked more parking garages to the rear, and sat miserably on the edge of a hard plastic seat clutching her dripping umbrella. Her sneakers, and her jeans from the knees down, were soaking. After several minutes the door opened, and she looked up as Mendez came in, a stained white lab coat hanging open over his shirt, a rumpled tie trailing loose at the neck. His face lit up. 'My dear, you're drenched. Can I get you a coffee? Water?'

'No, no.' Margaret stood up, embarrassed. 'I just called in to see if it would be okay for me to stay at the ranch tonight.'

Mendez's smile was at its most beatific. 'My dear, you don't have to ask.' He took her hands in his. 'My home is yours, for as long as you like. You know that.'

She shrugged awkwardly. 'It's just ... I don't have a key, Felipe,' she said.

Mendez laughed. 'But you don't need one. Just my entry code. I'll write it down for you.' He tore a sheet of paper from a pad, scribbled a four-digit number on it and handed it to her. 'If you want to hang on for half an hour, I'm almost finished here. I could give you a lift.'

'I've got my car,' Margaret said. 'Anyway, I'd like to get back and get showered and changed.'

'Of course.' He paused. 'You can spare a minute, though? I have something to show you.'

She followed him into a laboratory at the end of the hall, and slipped on a lab coat. 'You know why it was called the Spanish Flu?' he asked.

She shook her head. 'I've no idea. It originated here in the United States, didn't it?'

'So we believe. But we were still fighting a war then, and news of the pandemic was suppressed in most of the countries involved in World War One. It was first most widely reported in the Spanish press. Hence the Spanish Flu.' He waved her towards a monitor on a bench near the back of the lab, and she watched as he slipped a cassette into the built-in VCR. 'You're familiar with Viral Cytopathic Effect?' he said.

'Of course.'

The screen came to life in a seething mass of tiny organisms dividing, multiplying and ultimately destroying their host cells. Cell necrosis. She almost recoiled from the monitor. She knew without being told what she was looking at. 'It's what killed Steve,' she said. 'It's the Spanish Flu.'

'One stage advanced,' Mendez said. 'Another mutation down the line. It used its time in Doctor Cardiff to morph itself. To the virus, the good doctor was no more than a living laboratory, a human rat with which to experiment. I would suspect that, if anything, this new version of itself could be even more virulent.'

Margaret was repulsed. 'They recovered the virus at autopsy?'

'From the lungs, I believe.' Mendez looked at her sympathetically. 'I'm sorry, Margaret. You . . . were fond of Doctor Cardiff.' It was a statement, not a question.

She nodded mutely. In her head she had a clear, brutal and bloody image of Steve on the autopsy table.

'But you do understand, such steps must be taken in order to fight this thing.' She nodded again, and he said, 'Anatoly

Markin once told me about a Russian scientist called Ustinov who accidentally injected himself with Marburg while conducting experiments with guinea pigs. It was part of their biowarfare program. The poor man took three weeks to die, quite horribly. And when they recovered the virus from his organs they found that through the live incubator of a human being it had mutated into something altogether more stable and powerful. So they used the new strain as the basis of their further weapons research and called it "Variant U". Markin told me they thought Ustinov would have been amused by it.' He shrugged, a tiny sad smile stretching his full lips, and nodded towards the monitor. 'Perhaps we should call this "Variant C".'

Margaret looked at him coldly. 'You know what, Felipe? Chances are Steve would probably have have been amused by that, too. He had a pretty bizarre sense of humour. Personally, I just think it's sick.' She took a moment to collect herself. 'I'll see you back at the house.' And she swept out leaving Mendez to reflect on an error of judgment.

By the time she got to the ranch, the storm had passed. The air was hot and damp and hung in shifting strands of mist over the lake. The sky was torn along its western fringes, revealing ragged strips of blood red sunset behind the cloud. The chestnut mares stood glistening in the meadow, nostrils raised to the sky, sniffing as if they could smell the coming night.

Clara barked and danced around Margaret as she made her

way through the gun room and into the kitchen, but quickly returned to sulk in her basket when Margaret gave no indication that she was going to feed her. The dirty dishes piled on every available workspace were depressing, and Margaret wondered why Mendez didn't simply have someone come in for a couple of hours each day to keep the place clean. The smell of stale cigar smoke and alcohol hung sour in the living room. She switched on the ceiling fan, kicked off her shoes and went upstairs to her room to look out some clean underwear.

She stood for a long time under the shower, letting the hot water cascade over her upturned face and run in snaking rivulets between her breasts, pouring in a stream from the thatch of golden hair that covered her pubis. It felt so good she didn't want it to stop. Fatigue swept through her, deliciously warm, irresistibly enticing. She soaped herself with a soft sponge, smearing the lather in luxurious bubbling sweeps across her skin and then allowing the water simply to wash it away. She worked the shampoo through her hair and then rinsed it until it squeaked between her fingers, letting the water wash the soap from her eyes before she opened them to see the fleeting movement of a shadow beyond the bathroom door. A tiny, startled exclamation escaped her lips and she instinctively crossed her arms over her breasts.

'Who's there?' she called, but there was no response. The door was lying about six inches ajar, and she could see into her bedroom, clothes strewn across the bed where she had dropped them. She immediately turned off the shower, goosebumps standing up all over her body. Still there was no sound, and there was no further movement. She pushed open the door of the shower cubicle and grabbed a soft white towel from the rail, wrapping it around herself and stepping quickly out on to the mat. 'Hello,' she called again, and was answered by the same silence as before. Tentatively, she pulled the bathroom door open wide and saw that the bedroom was empty. Had she imagined it? And then she remembered that she was not alone in the house. Perhaps Clara had wandered in, curious about the strange perfumed smells. And she let out a deep breath for the first time in what felt like minutes.

Partly reassured, she rubbed herself quickly dry, slipped into her bra and panties and towelled her hair until it hung in curling clumps over her shoulders. She dragged a clean white tee-shirt over her head and pushed her legs into a pair of dark blue baggy cotton cargoes. A sense of security returned with the pulling on of clothes. She tugged a comb through her hair and padded barefoot down the stairs.

Mendez was sitting in the smoking porch puffing on a freshly lit cigar. CNN was playing on the big screen in the living room and on the small TV in the porch. Margaret glanced through the passage leading to the kitchen and saw Clara eating from her bowl. The reassurance that she had clung to briefly in her bedroom quickly evaporated, and was replaced by a sick feeling in her stomach. She slipped on her sneakers and opened the door into the porch. Mendez dragged his eyes from the screen and smiled. 'There you are, my dear. Good shower?'

'How long have you been here?' Margaret asked.

He frowned. 'I just got in.' Clara pushed past Margaret's legs in the doorway and dropped herself at her master's feet.

'And you haven't been upstairs?'

'No.' His frown deepened. 'Margaret, what's wrong?'

She shook her head, not sure whether to feel foolish or suspicious. Was it possible that he had been in her room, watching her in the shower? Clara had been busy eating, so it wasn't the dog she had seen. 'Nothing,' she said lamely. 'I just thought I heard someone up there, that's all.'

Mendez laid his cigar in the ashtray and stood up to cross the porch. He was strangely flushed, so that his white goatee appeared to stand out from his face. 'My dear, all this is getting to you. You need to relax. Let me get you a drink.'

'No, thanks.'

He put his hands on her shoulders and looked into her face. 'Are you sure you're all right?'

Her stomach was churning now. There was the oddest look in his eyes. 'I'm fine.'

His head was raised slightly, eyes half closed, as if he was breathing her in, the smell of her fresh and fragrant and warm. She tried to wriggle free of the hands on her shoulders, but they gripped her more tightly. And then suddenly she found herself pulled hard against him, and his face was pressed to hers. Wet lips, a clash of teeth, the smell of cigar smoke and the rasp of whiskers on her soft skin. She felt his erect penis pushing hard against her stomach, his tongue in her mouth. And for a moment thought she would be sick.

With a huge effort, she pulled herself free of him and stood back, gasping half in fear, half in anger. 'Jesus, Felipe, what the hell are you doing!'

He looked at her with something like panic in his eyes. 'Margaret, I'm sorry,' he blurted, and took a step towards her.

She stepped quickly back. 'Don't come near me!' She was breathing hard, fists clenched, trying to control an urge just to turn and run. She knew now that he had been in her bedroom watching her all that time.

'I'm so sorry,' he said again. 'Please don't leave. It won't happen again, I promise. You've no idea how lonely it gets here. How lonely I've been since Catherine . . .' His voice trailed away and he looked miserable, turning his gaze to the floor, unable to meet her eyes. 'I've always thought you were . . .' He lifted his eyes to look at her. '. . . desirable. I used to envy Michael. It's what I found hardest to forgive him. That he took you away. That when he broke with me I could no longer see you. I could hardly believe it when I saw you sitting at the conference table at Fort Detrick. It was as if fate had brought you back to me.'

Margaret stared at him in disbelief. 'You're sick, Felipe.'

He nodded. 'Yes. Sick with regret, Margaret. Sick that I allowed some base sexual instinct to spoil things between us. I promise . . .' His spaniel eyes pleaded with her. '. . . I promise it won't ever happen again.'

'No, it won't,' she said, and she turned and strode back into the living room, lifting her purse from the recliner. 'I'll come back and get my stuff in a day or two.'

'Margaret . . .' she heard him call after her as she went out through the kitchen. A sad, plaintive call of abject misery. She almost felt sorry for him.

CHAPTER TWELVE

I

It was after ten when she got back to Houston. The sky had cleared and the mercury fallen. The night air had a chill cutting edge to it as she crossed the car park and up the ramp into the lobby of the Holiday Inn. At reception they told her that Li was in room 735, and she rode the elevator up to the seventh floor. Her head felt full of fog. Nothing seemed clear to her any more. All the shapes and patterns of her life, which she had tried so hard these past twelve months to define with decision and clarity, were blurred and confused. She felt vulnerable and, worst of all, lonely. The safety and comfort she had hoped for at the Mendez ranch had vanished in a moment. And now there was only one avenue left open to her. But it was a road she had travelled before, and found it led nowhere safe.

Li opened the door of his room and stood against the light, naked except for a pair of boxer shorts. He loomed over her, taller than she ever remembered him. The television was on in the background, his room filled with the smoke of many cigarettes.

'Room service,' she said.

He said, 'I didn't order anything.'

'I read your mind.'

'And what did you see there?'

'Two people. A bed. Sex. Sleep.'

'In that order?'

'In any order you like.'

He pursed his lips and stood for a long time thinking. 'I don't have any change,' he said.

She frowned. 'What for?'

'A tip.'

'It's a complimentary service.'

'In that case you'd better come in. I've never been one to look a gift horse in the mouth.'

She pushed the door shut behind them. 'I'm not sure I like being called a horse.'

'But you have such lovely fetlocks.' He stooped to crook an arm behind her knees and lift her off her feet. She put her arms around his neck.

'As long as you don't feel the need to take a horsewhip to my hind quarters.'

He smiled. 'Some women quite like that.' He paused. 'I'm told.'

'Not by me. I'd be inclined to think it might spoil the ride.'

'Or spur you on to greater things.' He laid her on the bed and leaned over her, so that his breath brushed her face

She grinned and slipped a hand inside his boxers. 'That's all the spur I need.' And she closed her eyes and let a huge wave of sexual escape break over her. For a few minutes of exquisite pleasure she could be free of a life that was falling apart yet again. She felt his hands on her skin, his lips on her face, her breasts, and as he entered her, she flung her legs around his back and pulled him to her so tightly that she squeezed all of the air out of his lungs.

Afterwards, they lay for a long time in silence. The light of the television flickered in the darkness of the room, the canned laughter of a non-existent studio audience modulating in time to the regulation thirty-second gags of some mediocre sitcom. Eventually, Li raised himself on an elbow and saw that Margaret's face was wet with tears. He sat upright. 'What's wrong?'

She reached up and ran her fingers over his split lip, the bruising high on his cheek and around his left eye. 'It's just me,' she said smiling sadly. 'And life. I never seem to get the two things running in harmony.' And she told him about Mendez. His abortive sexual advances. A sad and lonely only man, she said. And she told him how she was homeless now, and unable to concentrate on her work, or on anything very much. She told him about the virus they had taken from Steve during autopsy. How it had used him to grow stronger, smarter. And she told him about her despair that there would ever be a way out of any of it.

He wiped the tears from her face with the flat of his hand. He had a great need to talk to someone, but she was too fragile right now to share his burden. So he held his peace and asked her about Xinxin and Xiao Ling.

Margaret shook her head. 'Xinxin won't speak to her, won't even acknowledge that she's there. And your sister isn't making much of an effort to change that.'

He heard the disapproval in her voice, and his own despair welled up inside him. He lay down again beside her and dragged the top sheet over them both, and they fell back into silence. After a time he reached for the remote and switched off the TV. Outside, the sound of late night traffic on Main drifted up to the open window. He heard Margaret's breathing slow and thicken and he turned over on to his side, pulling his legs up in the foetal position. He knew he wouldn't sleep. There was too much going on in his head. And then he felt Margaret shifting in the bed beside him, and the warmth of her body as she turned to fit herself into the curve of his back, pulling her legs up behind his. An arm slipped through his, and her hand cupped itself around the curve of his chest. He felt her breath hot on his neck. He wished he could lie like this forever.

Her eyes flickered open and she saw the red glow of the digital bedside clock. It was 2.30 a.m. The sheet was twisted around her waist. She reached over to find the reassuring warmth of Li and found the bed beside her empty and cold. She rolled over, immediately awake, and the shadow of his absence was dense and dark. She sat up and saw the silhouette of a man standing against the net curtain at the window. He seemed to be staring out into the streetlit night. 'Li Yan?'

The figure turned. 'I'm sorry. I didn't mean to wake you. I couldn't sleep.'

'Come back to bed. I know how to make you sleep.'

She heard his smile. And the regret in his voice. 'Too much on my mind. Do you mind if I smoke?'

'You've never asked me before.'

'We're in America now. I feel self-conscious about it.'

She laughed. 'Smoke, for God's sake!' He lit a cigarette and she said, 'So what's on your mind?'

'Fear.'

'What are you afraid of?'

'I'm afraid of what's going to happen to my sister when the *ah kung's* little horses get to her. Which they will.'

She pulled her knees up to her chin. 'She's under armed police guard, Li Yan.'

She saw the shake of his head. 'They'll still get to her. These people never give up.'

'But why?'

'Because she can identify the *ah kung*. She has seen him, and he knows it.'

'How does he know?'

'Because I told him.'

Margaret stared at him hard in the darkness. She saw the end of his cigarette glow red as he drew on it, and then the shadow of the smoke against the window. She felt herself tensing. 'You *know* who he is?'

He nodded. 'I wasn't certain. Until I made a phone call shortly before you showed up tonight.'

'Who is he?'

Li snorted in the dark. 'A man of impeccable reputation. Chairman of the Houston-Hong Kong Bank, board member of the Astros baseball team, elected member of Houston City Council.'

'Soong?' Margaret said, incredulous. 'The guy you met at the stadium yesterday?' She saw him nod his acknowledgement. 'How do you know?'

'Wang's diary spoke of the *ah kung*'s nickname. Kat. The Cantonese word for "tangerine", a Chinese symbol of good fortune. Soong wears a ring with the character for "tangerine" engraved in amber − amber the colour of tangerine. It is a very old ring, and the engraving is almost worn away. You can't see it with the naked eye. When I asked to run my thumb over it, he must have been gambling on my not being able to feel it either. But it was there, and I could read it with my skin as clearly as if I could see it. Kat.'

She watched him smoke in silence, running everything he had told her through her mind. Finally she said, 'If "tangerine" is a universal Chinese symbol for good fortune, then it could be coincidence. There could be hundreds, maybe thousands, even millions of people wearing jewellery engraved with that character.'

'That's what I told myself,' Li said. 'Then it occurred to me that it was such a big, ostentatious ring, that no woman he had slept with could have failed to notice it.' He moved towards the bed to stub his cigarette out in the ashtray, and sat down on the edge of the mattress. 'That's how Xiao Ling knows him. She was a gift to him while she was working as a hostess at the Golden Mountain Club. When I called her, she remembered the ring quite clearly.'

'Arrest him,' Margaret said.

Li laughed. 'And charge him with what? Wearing a ring? Your law enforcement people would laugh me out of the country.'

'At least you know where to start looking.'

He gasped his frustration. 'Margaret, a man like that will have been meticulous in covering his tracks. It could take months of investigation, and we might still find nothing. Meantime, all he has to do is get rid of my sister and we won't even have someone to say they heard him called Kat.'

'He's bound to make a mistake, Li Yan. Sometime. Somewhere.'

Li waggled his head. 'People like Soong don't make mistakes, Margaret. That's why they don't get caught.'

'Everyone makes mistakes,' Margaret said. 'Otherwise you and I would be out of a job.'

The long single ring of the telephone startled them. Li looked at the phone and it rang again, but he made no attempt to answer it.

'It's not for me,' Margaret said. 'No one knows I'm here.'

Li picked it up on the third ring. Soong's voice was barely a whisper, scratchy and tight with tension. His Mandarin, despite his previous protestations, was fluent. 'You know who this is?'

Li said, 'Yuh.'

'I know who the *ah kung* is,' he said.

Li heard the blood rushing in his ears. 'Who?'

'I can't tell you on the phone. And the minute I do we'll both be in danger.'

'What do you suggest?'

'A meeting.'

'When?'

'Now.'

Li glanced at Margaret. Her face reflected the pale light from the window. She was frowning. 'Where?' he said.

'My suite at the stadium. I'll leave the side door unlocked. Come straight up. And in the name of the sky, don't tell anyone.'

A click sounded in Li's ear and the line went dead. Slowly he replaced the receiver and sat lost in thought for more than a minute.

'Li Yan?' Margaret put a hand on his shoulder.

He turned. 'You were right,' he said. 'He just made a mistake.'

He relayed the conversation to her and she said, 'But you're not actually going?'

'Of course.'

'For God's sake, Li Yan, it's a trap. Surely you must see that? It would be madness to go on your own.'

He said, 'So I get the full weight of the task force behind me and we storm the stadium. Then what? There's still no proof against him. No evidence of anything. He's so careful, he didn't even say his name on the phone.' He stood up. 'The only way I'm going to get him is to let him play his hand. Compound the mistake.'

In a sullen silence, Margaret watched him dress. She knew there was no point in trying to make him change his mind. She had known him long enough to know what an exercise in futility that would be. When he stooped to brush her cheek with his lips, she whispered, 'Be careful.' And the moment he was out of the door, she snatched her purse and retrieved the list of telephone numbers sent to her by FEMA. She switched on the bedside light and ran her fingers down the names until she found the number of Fuller's cellphone. She snatched the phone and punched it in.

II

There was nothing moving along Texas when Li got there. The grounds of the Annunciation Catholic Church lay brooding in silent darkness on the south side of Enron Field. East on Texas, the lights of an occasional vehicle on the freeway raked across the flyover. On Crawford nothing stirred. No sound, no light, no movement. Houston was a city without a heart. No one lived at its centre. When the shops and offices closed for the day, and the last fan had left the stadium, it was a dead place. Empty. Even of muggers, for there was no one to mug.

Still, Li felt conspicuous as he drifted quickly under bleaching street lights, wondering if hidden eyes were watching his approach. The core of him was stiff with tension, but he forced his body to relax so that he could move freely. He hurried past the metered parking slots below the towering south wall of the stadium, under the ornamental canopies over the windows of the official Astros shop, to the double glass doors that opened on to the wide sweep of stairs that led from club level up to the private suites. He pushed each in turn. The left door opened and he slipped inside.

Light from the street fell in through tall windows on each level and lay in rectangles across the green-carpeted stairway. Li went up the steps two at a time to the suite level. On the landing he stopped and listened, straining to hear anything above the rasp of his own breath and the hammering of his heart. Three openings down, he saw a crack of light under the door to Soong's suite. There was no sound. He looked along the dark, carpeted curve of the concourse and decided to make his approach from another angle. He slipped past Soong's suite and fell into a long, loping jog through the food hall, past the Whistle Stop bar which sold libations to the wealthy, past the panorama of windows that looked out on to the night-cloaked field. There was very little light out there. The sky had cleared, and though studded with stars there was no moon. Through a swing door at the end, he found himself on the concrete staircase which Soong had brought them up the previous day. Arched windows on the landing threw light from the street across the stairs as he hurried down to ground level. Hanging signs pointed along the colonnaded walkway beneath the train to sections 100 – 104. Li plunged into its darkness and ran past the arched openings, beyond the Home Run Pump – a mock Conoco gas pump that lit up when the Astros struck gold – to the far concourse beneath giant hoardings advertising Coca-Cola, Miller

Lite, UPS. Behind floor-to-ceiling glass, the tables of Ruggles restaurant were pooled in darkness.

Li stopped and looked back across the field, and saw the solitary light shining in Soong's suite, like one gold tooth in a mouth of blackened stumps. Its light tumbled feebly across the seats below and lay in a faint slab on the grass. A light above the elevators at the far side of the concourse told him that they were still powered. He rode up to the next level and made his way beneath the giant scoreboard to the seating at the far side of the stadium. He jumped up and caught the rail dividing suite level from the one below and swung himself upwards, hooking a leg over the top rail and pulling himself up behind it. He was on a level again with the light from Soong's suite, but still had the length of the stadium to traverse. He broke into a jog again, following the concrete behind the seats, and vaulting the dividing rails that split the east side into sections at regular intervals.

Now just two suites away from the light spilling out into darkness, he stopped to catch his breath and listen again, his face shining with sweat. He caught the faint sound of a voice through glass, and very carefully approached the windows of Soong's suite. Below he could see, in the palest of lights, the geometry of the baseball field, the pitcher's mound like a moon orbiting the batsman's circle, the grass diamond delineated by red blaze that looked from here as black as tar. He listened hard. There was not even the faintest echo of bat on ball, or chanting fans. The stadium was only a handful of seasons old. If there were ghosts here, they would be the ghosts of trains, of porters and passengers, drivers and linesmen. But there was nothing. Just the muffled sound of Soong's voice. Li manoeuvred himself into a position that let him see in without being seen himself. Soong was talking animatedly on the telephone, but Li couldn't make out what he was saying. Soong hung up and lit a cigarette. The ashtray on the table was full to overflowing. The room was thick with smoke, like smog. Soong began pacing, and then suddenly he stopped and looked right at Li. Li froze, and for a moment felt trapped in the gaze of the *ah kung*. Then he realised that from the inside all Soong could see was a reflection of himself. He was looking at himself in the glass. Gone were the jeans and the baseball jacket. He wore a sombre blue suit, starched white shirt and red tie. This was serious business. Li wondered if he was impressed by what he saw. As Soong raised his cigarette to his mouth with his left hand, he saw his ring reflected in the window, and he paused, with his hand at his face, to run the fingers of his right hand over the faded etching in the fossilised resin that was the amber stone. A small vanity which had betrayed a larger vice.

Li stepped forward and slid the door open, taking some pleasure from the fear that blanched Soong's face and made him turn, startled, with a small cry.

Smoke swept past Li, drawn out by the chill night and sucked into the void. He raised his eyebrows in an expression of surprise. 'I thought you were expecting me.'

Soong recovered his composure quickly. 'Of course.' He smiled. 'But not by the tradesman's entrance.' It was a quick-thinking put-down, designed to re-establish his position of power. He turned to the table and lifted a black rectangular box about the size of a TV remote. It had a loop of chrome at one end, and looked like the kind of wand security men employ at airports to detect metal. 'You don't mind if I check you for wires.' It wasn't a question.

Li shrugged, and Soong quickly ran the wand over him from head to foot, front to back. Satisfied that he was clean, Soong dropped it back on the table and said, 'Smart man. Maybe we can get down to business now.'

Li said, 'You were going to tell me who the *ah kung* is. The one they call Kat.'

Soong smiled. 'I don't *really* need to do that, Mister Li, do I?' Li canted his head and shrugged his eyebrows and Soong added, 'But, you know, I'm not the monster you think I am.'

'You have no idea what I think, Soong.'

'Oh, I could have a pretty good guess. I'm sure you're thinking how you would love to get me in an interrogation room back in Beijing, stick me with a cattle prod, deprive me of sleep. And you're probably wondering how it was with me and your sister. When I fucked her. You know, that night at the Golden Mountain Club.' It was a deliberate and spiteful provocation, Soong testing his power, pushing Li to the limit, wondering perhaps just how far he could go. 'Well, she was just another whore.'

With a composure that he didn't feel, Li said, 'And you were just another trick.' He scratched his chin thoughtfully, trying to recall her exact words. 'What was it she said . . .? *Short and fat with a big belly and bad breath. They get on top of you and hump for a couple of minutes and then they're all spent. It's hard to tell who you're with.* Sound about right?'

Soong glared at him. He was vulnerable on vanity. 'I offer our people the chance of a better life,' he said in a voice that barely concealed his anger. 'Hope, not hardship, Mister Li. Dollars, not deprivation. In China they have no freedom. In America at least they can dream.'

'You're a real philanthropist,' Li said.

Soong bristled. 'No, I'm a businessman. Nothing in life is free. And, of course, there is a price to pay. But I enable them to pay it. I lend money to the families in China so they can make down payments to send their loved ones to *Meiguo* – to the Beautiful Country. When they get here, I find them jobs so that they can pay off the debts and pay up the balance. I make it possible for them to send money home to their families in Fujian. And I am much more efficient at it than the Bank of China.' He snorted his derision. 'They take three weeks to send cash. Their exchange rates are terrible, and they will only deal in yuan. My rates are as good as any you can find in America, I deliver the money in a matter of hours, and always in dollars.'

'What a hero,' Li said. 'If you were a Catholic they'd make you a saint.' He lit a cigarette. 'And I suppose the sixty thousand dollars you charge is just to cover expenses.'

'It is an expensive business transporting people halfway across the world, providing papers, accommodation, bribing officials. But, of course, I make a profit. It is the business I am in.'

'The exploitation business,' Li said. 'Charging poor people more money than they could dream of in a lifetime to come to America and be forced into slave labour. An only slightly more sophisticated version of what the British did to the Africans two hundred years ago.'

Soong was losing patience. 'There is no point in debating the issue with you, Li. You will never be convinced. But every single Chinese I bring into this country has the chance to work his way to freedom.'

'In brothels and gambling dens?' Li had a vivid picture in his head of his sister, tears streaming down her face, as she sat in the interview room at the Holliday Unit, and he took a long pull at his cigarette to try to keep his anger battened down.

Soong hissed his frustration. 'I never pretended it was easy,' he snapped. 'I travelled the same road myself, and look where I am now. I don't know many who would exchange their shot at the American Dream for life under the Communists.' He stabbed a finger in Li's direction. 'And as for your precious Chinese government, their attempts at stopping illegal immigration are a joke. Hah! I've seen the posters in Fujian myself. WE MUST INTENSIFY OUR EFFORTS IN STOPPING THE PATHOLOGIC SOCIAL TREND OF IRREGULAR IMMIGRATION. And . . . ATTACK THE SNAKEHEADS, DESTROY THE SNAKEPITS, PUNISH THE ILLEGAL IMMIGRANTS. It's pathetic!' Pinpoints of light burned deep in his black eyes. 'The truth is, Beijing wants them to go. There are too many people already in China, and too few jobs. And once they are here, all those illegal immigrants send money home. They inject millions into the local economy of Fujian. An economy that would probably collapse without them.' Tiny specks of spittle were gathering around the corners of his mouth. 'The snakeheads are the people's friends.'

'Shutting the air vents in that truck and murdering ninety-eight people wasn't very friendly,' Li said.

Soong's face coloured. 'That was an accident. The vent got closed by mistake. It was a terrible thing.'

'Yeah, it cost you six million dollars.'

'Actually,' Soong looked at him very directly and said levelly, 'it was more than that. I have already ordered that every penny paid to send these poor people to America be paid back to the bereaved families.'

'I'm sure that will more than compensate for their loss,' Li said.

Soong almost flinched from the acid in his tone. 'I didn't like you the first time I met you, Li,' he said. 'And you're not doing anything to change my first impressions.' He paused to take a deep breath and steady himself. 'It gave me nothing but pain to see my fellow countrymen die like that.'

Li leaned forward to stub out his cigarette. 'Is that why you're injecting them with a lethal virus?' He saw Soong's jaw clench, and the skin darken around his eyes.

'That,' Soong said, in a low, dangerous voice, 'was nothing to do with us.' He paused for a long time, then he said, 'About six months ago we sub-contracted the final leg of the journey — the border crossing — to a well-establish gang from Colombia. They had been bringing drugs into the United

States successfully for decades. They knew all the routes, every trick. And their success rate has been thirty per cent higher than ours.'

Li frowned. 'Why would Colombian drug smugglers want to bring in illegal Chinese?'

'Because the money's just as good, but the risks are a lot lower,' Soong said. 'The penalties handed out by courts in the US for people smuggling are much lighter than they are for drugs.'

'So why were they injecting them with the flu virus?'

Soong shook his head grimly. 'We have no idea. We made contact with them immediately after our meeting with you yesterday. Of course they denied it, but then they would, wouldn't they?' He walked towards the window and gazed at his own reflection for a moment. 'But we'll find out,' he said. 'We owe them around ten million dollars. As of today I have put a stop on all payments.' He turned and smiled at Li. 'We may be about to witness the first ever Chinese–Colombian war. One way or another we'll come up with answers and put a stop to it.'

Li said, 'And how are you going to stop me having you arrested?'

Soong laughed in his face. 'You can't have me arrested, Li. You have no evidence. Not a scrap. And I am a respectable citizen, a democratically elected member of the City Council.'

Li started to circle the table, Soong watching carefully his every step. 'Tell me how you managed to keep your identity a secret for so long, Soong,' Li said.

Soong shrugged. 'Quite simple. When you employ so many people in so many different countries, you never deal directly with any of them. Everything is delegated. So there are only a handful of people who know my real identity, and they are all making far too much money to betray me.'

'So what am I doing here?'

'You're here to be bribed, Mr Li. To put your tail between your legs and fuck off back to where you came from. And take your sister with you. That way you both get to live long and happy lives.'

'No one walking around with a killer virus in their genes is going to live a long and happy life,' Li said.

Soong waved his hand dismissively. 'Like I said, I'm not going to debate this with you. Name your price.'

Li said, 'You can't count that high.'

Soong let his double chin sink on to his chest, a smile on his thick lips. He gave a gentle shake of his head. 'Why did I just know you were going to be one of those?' he asked. Then he lifted his head and said brightly, 'I'll tell you why. Because my whole organisation operates on the basis that people everywhere are corruptible. And they are. From high and low-ranking officials in the Chinese bureaucracy, to immigration and law enforcement officials across the world. Almost everyone has his price. I say "almost", because there are always the exceptions. The ones who think they know better, or think they are better. Losers. People with a gift for dying young. You develop an instinct for them.'

'What a fine judge of character you are,' Li said.

Soong searched Li's face to find in it a reflection of the irony in his voice. But his expression was blank. There was something infuriatingly superior about him, and it was getting under Soong's skin. He said, 'It is for occasions just such as these that I took out my own insurance policy right here in the United States. In spite of what Congress might like to tell the world, officials in *Meiguo* are just as corruptible as they are in the People's Republic.'

His eyes lifted beyond Li towards the door, and Li cursed his lapse in concentration. He felt, more than heard, the movement behind him, and turned as the door swung open. His stomach lurched as he saw Margaret standing in the doorway, bloodless and scared. Perception followed a split second after incomprehension, but in that tiny fraction of time he felt as if the eight pints of blood coursing through his veins had turned to ice. And then he saw the gun at her head and, as she moved out of the shadow, the tense face of Fuller immediately behind her. 'Damn you, Li,' the FBI agent hissed. 'I knew you were going to be trouble.' He glanced nervously at Soong. 'Just as well the bitch called me, or she'd have been a witness to your phone call.'

Soong grinned. 'It was easy keeping him talking. He was eager listener.' And he turned smiling eyes on Li as if to try to underline his superiority while undermining Li's.

Fuller pushed Margaret into the room. He had her hair held in a tight bunch in his fist at the back of her head, his gun pressed to her skull just above the ear. 'What now?' His eyes were glassy and unfocused, a reflection of his uncertainty.

Li exhaled deeply, thoughts tumbling through his mind like a waterfall, but any clarity obscured by the spray. 'Change of circumstances,' he said, turning to Soong. 'We could discuss your offer now.'

'Too late,' Soong said. 'I couldn't trust you. You've already played your hand. And, like you said, I'm a fine judge of character.'

'For Christ's sake speak English,' Fuller said edgily. Li glanced at him and knew that his fear made him even more dangerous.

'We were discussing the terms of a bribe,' he said.

Fuller flicked darting eyes towards Soong who gave the slightest shake of his head.

Margaret was watching him closely. She said in as strong a voice as she could muster, 'You don't want to kill us in here, Mr Soong. You'd leave too many traces. Blood is very hard to get out of a carpet.'

Soong nodded. 'This true. Maybe more fun to shoot you in head down on field. Chinese-style execution.' He smiled at Li. 'That how you do it in PRC, yes?'

But Fuller wasn't playing. 'No games, Soong. Let's just take them somewhere safe and get this over with.'

'And if we refuse to go?' Margaret asked.

'Then I'll fucking shoot you where you stand,' Fuller said. 'I think Mister Soong can afford to replace the carpet.'

'I'm sure Mister Soong can afford lots of things.' The voice came out of left field, taking them all by surprise. Hrycyk stood in the shadow of the door, his gun pointing directly at Fuller. 'I'm sure he can afford to pay lawyers to keep him on Death Row for ten years. But this is Texas. We'll still juice him in the end.' He nodded towards the FBI agent. 'Why don't you just lay that gun on the table, Agent Fuller?' He let a tiny jet of air escape from between discoloured front teeth. 'Fucking FBI!'

Fuller swung towards Hrycyk, pulling Margaret in front of him, and fired towards the INS man. Hrycyk spun away against a panel of switches on the wall, a bullet spitting from his gun. Margaret saw blood running on varnished wood before the lights went out. But she had no time to think about it before all the air was knocked from her lungs as Li piled into both her and Fuller, smashing them against the wall. The three of them fell in a tangle to the floor. Margaret was trapped between the two of them, wriggling to get free. And then her head was filled with light and a crashing pain as Fuller's foot made contact with her skull. She gasped, and felt the power ebbing from her limbs. She went limp, a dead weight on top of Li, but still vaguely conscious. She was aware of Li pushing her aside and clambering to his feet. In a moment the light came on again, and Li was crouching beside her, helping her to sit up.

'I'm okay, I'm okay,' she heard herself saying, and she looked around the room which was burning out in her head in the sudden light. Soong was lying bleeding profusely on to his carpet from a wound high up in his thigh. He was clutching his leg and whimpering in fear and pain. Hrycyk was on his feet again, leaning against the door by the light switches, blood oozing through the fingers of a hand clutching his upper right arm.

'Sonofabitch, sonofabitch!' he kept saying.

There was no sign of Fuller. Fear stabbed jaggedly into Margaret's consciousness. She struggled to her knees. 'Where is he? Where's Fuller?'

Li jerked his head towards the sliding glass door. 'Out there somewhere.' And even as he said it, they heard him clattering across plastic seats in the dark.

Hrycyk held out his gun towards Li. 'Go get him.'

Li hesitated. He glanced at Margaret. 'I'm fine,' she said.

'Jesus Christ, go!' Hrycyk screamed.

Li stood up, took the gun from his outstretched hand, and then slipped out into the darkness of the stadium.

Margaret sat gasping on the floor. She had a hammering headache now. Hrycyk stood in the doorway, breathing stertorously. Soong was still whimpering and bleeding on the carpet. Margaret struggled to her feet and crossed to Hrycyk. Without a word she took his hand away from his arm and peeled off his jacket. He let her tear away the sleeve of his shirt without protest, keeping his eyes averted. He didn't even want to look at the wound. He heard Margaret gasp derisively.

'What a baby,' she said. 'It's just a scratch.' She pulled a handkerchief from the breast pocket of his jacket. 'Is this clean?' He nodded, and she used it to make a pad to place over the gouge that Fuller's bullet had taken out of the flesh of his upper arm. She tied it on with shreds of his shirt sleeve, ignoring his grunts of pain as she pulled the knots tight. 'That'll do until we can get you some proper treatment.'

The sound of a shot ringing around the stadium startled them. Hrycyk said, 'Li's going to need some light out there.' He switched off the lights in the suite and took her out on to the terrace. Silhouetted against the Houston skyline beyond, they could just see the outline of the replica locomotive sitting halfway along the tracks. 'Far end of those tracks,' Hrycyk said, 'there's a small control room where they turn on the floodlights. Guy did it when we were here yesterday and they was closing the roof.'

Margaret looked at him. 'Why are you telling me?'

'Because you're going to have to turn them on.'

Margaret shook her head, panic setting in. 'I don't know how to get down there.'

'Neither do I,' Hrycyk said. 'But you're in better shape to do it than me.'

Margaret glanced back at the shadow of Soong on the floor, a dark pool spreading in the carpet around him. 'What about him? He could bleed to death.'

'Like I give a damn,' Hrycyk said. 'Anyway, I know how to tie a tourniquet. So tight he'll squeal like a stuck fucking pig.'

She retraced Li's footsteps of less than thirty minutes before, running along the carpeted concourse on suite level, past the Whistle Stop bar and the food hall. She stopped briefly to press her face against the glass and peer out through the darkness of the stadium to try and get her bearings.

The locomotive track ran off at right angles from the left, at least one level down. A smeared impression of her features remained on the glass as she ran on to the end of the hall and out on to the landing. Another window, twice her height, gave out directly on to the track below. She found herself looking along its length, beyond the locomotive huddled darkly halfway down, to the tiny control booth at the foot of glazed scaffolding that rose two hundred feet up into the roof at the far side of the ground. She wondered why she could see it so clearly, and for a moment thought that someone somewhere must have turned on a light. Then she saw that the moon had risen over the east side of the stadium, full and clear, casting its silvered glow brightly across the field of play. By contrast, the seats along the east wing were thrown into deep, dark shadow.

As she ran down the concrete steps to the level below, she heard another gunshot. It cracked in the stillness like a dry twig underfoot. Margaret stopped and listened. But there was nothing else to hear.

Facing her, on the next level, was a door with a narrow glass panel. On the wall next to it was a sign which read: ROOF ACCESS. AUTHORIZED PERSONNEL ONLY. Margaret ran to the door and peered through its tiny window. It opened out on to the top of the colonnaded corridor that supported the superstructure upon which both the locomotive and the stadium roof supports ran on different lengths of rail. She pulled the handle, and to her surprise the door opened. The cold night air exploded in her lungs, and made her head ache even more. The pain came in pulses, with the pounding of her heart. She could hear the blood rushing in her ears.

To her left, several storeys of redbrick administration building rose above her. Straight ahead, the green-painted steel superstructure that bore the weight of the locomotive. She ran along the concrete beneath it, her head level with the rail line, and found herself suddenly bathed in moonlight, the stadium laid out below her on one side, the street thirty feet down on the other. The locomotive, which had appeared almost like a toy from a distance, loomed directly overhead, huge and forbidding.

She ducked under the rail line and scanned the seats around the ground. At first she saw nothing at all in the shadow. And then a movement caught her eye away to her right, high up near the far roof. She saw a figure running between rows of seats, but couldn't tell who it was. And then, perhaps forty feet below, on another level, another figure climbing up over the tiers, trying to reach the staircase that would lead him higher and on to the same level as the other man. He was clearly in pursuit. It had to be Li. In a moment, they would both come out of the shadow and into the full glare of the moon.

Margaret didn't wait to watch. She slipped back under the rail line and sprinted for the control capsule at the far end. It was shaped like a lozenge, standing on end, with windows curving round on each side. A short metal staircase on the right led up to a tiny, railed landing. The door gave way at the push of her hand, folding in the centre and opening in.

Inside, lit by the moon, was a bewildering array of levers and switches on a console built into the forward curve. Margaret stared at it, panic rising in her throat, half choking her. She gasped for breath, caught it, and then began throwing every lever and switch she could reach. She felt the deep vibration and growl of a motor springing to life somewhere beneath her, and the control capsule suddenly jerked forward. Margaret lost her balance and fell backwards, clutching at air. The back of her head hit something solid and very hard and was filled with a blinding light. And then blackness.

Li was still in the shadow of the east stand when he saw Fuller emerge into the moonlight. Somehow he had managed to get himself on to the top level, above the suites, where the seating rose up in breathtakingly steep tiers to the roof. Li would have to get back inside and up the internal staircase.

At first, Fuller had headed north, towards the huge elec-tronic scoreboard, scrambling loudly across the seats. Li had been able to follow the noise. And then almost on a level with the Miller Lite billboard, he had caught sight of him for the first time. Fuller had seen him, too, and fired on him, wildly wide of the mark. But it had forced Li to go more carefully. And then he lost sight of him again, and for several minutes heard nothing, fearing that somehow Fuller had found a way out of the stadium. That was when a single shot shattered the plastic seat to his right, and he had looked straight up to see the grim determination on Fuller's face as he leaned over the rail above him, gun poised for a second shot. Li threw himself into the

shadow of the overhang, landing awkwardly and winding himself in the process. He lay curled up for a good thirty seconds,
gasping for breath and thinking he was going to vomit. And
in those stricken moments, he heard Fuller moving away on
the upper level, crashing over seating and heading back for
the south end of the stadium. Even in his distress Li figured
that Fuller had probably parked out on Texas, and that that's
where he would want to exit the stadium.

Now he ran up stairs to a door that took him inside to club
level. He shook his head and wiped away the sweat that was
running into his eyes. He paused for a moment to recapture
the breath that rasped in his chest, and he cursed the day he
had been tempted to take up smoking again. Hrycyk's gun was
slippery in his hands as he reached the internal staircase. He
stopped to wipe his palms on the seat of his pants, and then
forced himself to climb the two flights two steps at a time.
When he reached the top landing, his whole body was shaking.
However much oxygen he sucked in it wasn't enough. His
legs were about ready to buckle under him. He pushed open
double doors and emerged into brilliant moonlight, teetering
momentarily on the edge of a staircase that dropped away in
front of him at an impossibly acute angle. The pitch was a
long way below, and he wondered, incongruously, what kind
of view you would get of the game from here. The players,
surely, would be absurdly small, the ball impossible to follow.
And yet there were at least another twenty rows of seats piled
up behind him.

He scanned the rows of empty seats above, stretching away

in a wide sweep to his left and into shadow. There was no sign of Fuller anywhere. And suddenly everything was plunged back into darkness. A large cloud, sailing on the back of the chill night breeze, had blotted out the moon. Li was aware of a strange, distant humming, but had no time to figure out what it was before he saw the dark shape of a man rising up on the edge of the roof forty feet above. He felt the bullet whistle past his ear, before he heard the crack of the gun. And then he saw Fuller fall, hitting the corrugated roof with a smack. The FBI agent grunted as the air was knocked from him, and then cried out in helpless fury as his gun went skidding from his hand and clattering off into oblivion. Li heard the scrape of metal on metal as it went sliding away across the roof and knew it was safe, for the first time, to move freely in the open.

He dragged weary legs up the final flight of steps to the point where mesh fencing stretched across tubular steel sealed off the top of the stand from the roof. He could see from the distortion of the mesh that this was where Fuller had climbed up before him. Tucking his gun in his belt, he pulled himself up, hand over hand, fingers slotting through mesh, until he was able to grasp the lip of the roof and swing himself on to the corrugated outer shell of it.

Slowly, he straightened up, careful to maintain his balance. It was breezy up here, and he felt the wind whipping around his legs. The roof rose in front of him at a steep angle, and fell away to his left. The pitch was more than two hundred feet below him now, the diamond tiny and insignificant. The towering skyline of downtown seemed just a touch away, and he was scared to look down towards the freeway in case he canted towards it and fell to his death.

At the apex of the roof, another fifteen feet above him, Fuller crouched on all fours, too terrified apparently to move.

'Give it up, Fuller,' Li shouted. 'Come down.'

Fuller shook his head mutely.

Li cursed inwardly and dropped on to all fours himself. He had never been good with heights. He crawled up the lip of the roof towards the FBI agent, not quite sure what he was going to do when he got there. He stopped about five feet short of him, and could hear his breathing, see the panic in his eyes. They were both drenched in sweat. For an eternity they stared at each other; hostility, fear, all wrapped up together along with a heightened sense of vulnerability. Li felt like he was clinging to the edge of the world.

Fuller sprang at him like a cat, with an almost animal growl. There was madness in his eyes. Li was completely unprepared, and felt himself slipping over the edge as he tried desperately to get out of the way. Fuller's elbow caught him in the face and he felt blood in his mouth. His fingers slid across the corrugated metal like fish on ice. He felt his nails tearing as he tried to dig in. But it was hopeless. There was no way he could stop himself. And then he felt himself tipping backwards into space and knew that his body would be shattered by the rows of seating that waited for him like so many teeth a hundred and fifty feet below.

But he fell no more than a handful of feet before hitting hard, riveted metal. Something unrelenting and sharp cut his cheek. He barely had time to realise that he had fallen into the cradle that held the floodlights, when he became aware of Fuller jumping in beside him, stooping quickly to pull the gun out of his belt. Li made a feeble attempt to stop him, a hand clutching at nothing. Fuller climbed on top of the gantry, straddling the struts immediately above Li's prone form and pointed the gun down at him. There was a strange, manic smile on his face. A man who had pushed himself so close to death, felt its breath in his face, that he knew now he was invincible.

Li accepted death then. Accepted its inevitability. And with that acceptance came the startling revelation that nothing in life really mattered much after all. All the pain and fear, the blood, sweat and tears, hopes and ambitions. They all came to this. Death. An end. How pointless it all had been. Margaret, Xiao Ling, Xinxin. And fleetingly he wondered if there really was life after death. If, perhaps, he would meet his uncle again, have one more chance to beat him at chess. Or, maybe, as many chances as exist in eternity. He almost laughed. Laughter close to tears.

A blinding light filled his world. An excruciating pain in his head. He had often wondered what it would feel like to die. But he had not expected the pain. He blinked fiercely and saw Fuller still standing over him, an arm shielding his eyes. He felt the heat of the lamps next to his head, and realised that someone had turned on the floodlights. But still he did not seem able to move. Fuller drew his arm away from his eyes and looked down at Li again, startled, discomposed.

And beyond him, Li saw a shadow passing over, huge and dark. Fuller sensed it, too, and looked round as nine thousand tons of retractable steel roof swept him off the gantry and locked into place, crushing him against the fixed girders of the south stand. Li felt warm blood wash across his face, and for a moment the floodlights turned crimson.

Margaret stood on the steps of the control cabin looking up through bullet-proof glass, green-painted beams and struts soaring into the sky above her, and understood that somehow she had managed to close the roof.

When pain and consciousness had seeped slowly back into her head, she had realised that the control capsule, at the base of the outer roof struts, had travelled along a hundred metres of track, back towards the south stand, and come to a standstill against a concrete buffer. The huge, supporting wall of steel and glass that held up the inner section of roof on her left was still gliding past. Disorientated, and fighting an urge simply to close her eyes and drift away again, she had dragged herself to her feet, without any real idea of how long she had been out. It was then she had seen, clearly marked, the panel of switches for operating the floodlights. She cursed herself for having allowed panic to blind her earlier. She threw the switches, and saw the stadium snap into sharp relief, the green of the field, the red of the blaize, vivid and unreal. For a moment she had been dazzled, and then the deep vibration that came up through the floor beneath her had stopped as the glass wall on her left shuddered to a halt.

She left the capsule, and hurried down the steps, running along the concrete to the door that would lead her back into the stairwell. Below her she saw uniformed and plain-clothes officers fanning out across the pitch, and became aware for the first time of the wailing sirens that filled the night. Each jarring step filled her mind with pain, and somewhere at the back of it, struggling for conscious space, was a large, prickly ball of fear. What had happened to Li?

On the stairs she heard the boots of police officers hammering up from the level below. She turned and ran up the next flight, past the suite level to the upper concourse, and out on to the terraces of seating where she had last seen Fuller heading. The whole stadium was laid out beneath her, brightly lit under the dazzle of floodlights, empty rows of dark green seats stretching away on all sides. A noise behind her made her turn, and she saw the bloody spectre of a man staggering down the steps towards her. It took a moment for her to realise that it was Li, and she let out a tiny gasp of horror. He reached the step above her and stopped, dark eyes staring out from his crimson mask. She could see no visible wound, and the blood was drying rust red on him already. His legs folded beneath him, and he sat down hard on the concrete steps, fumbling for his cigarettes. He pulled a crushed one from the pack and lit it.

'Where's Fuller?' she asked in a small voice.

He took several pulls on his cigarette before blowing the smoke from his lungs. He looked up at her and said grimly, 'He's dead.'

III

It was a perfect morning. The sky was a clear, pale blue. Dew lay white on the grass of Sam Houston Park. The long shadows of downtown skyscrapers reached across the tiny patch of parkland like dark protective fingers. The sun peeped between the glass and concrete structures, flashing off windows, lying in long yellow strips. A mist rose off the pond like smoke, sunlight playing in the water of the fountain. A chatter of early morning birds flew screeching playfully between the spars of the old red-roofed bandstand that stood dwarfed and incongruous in the centre of the meadow.

They walked beneath the wet, shiny leaves of dripping trees, and Margaret saw that they each left trailing footprints in the dew. The first few cars were turning off the freeway into the grid system of streets in the city's centre, the vanguard of the one hundred and thirty-seven thousand people who worked in downtown during the day. The early morning air was chill yet, but they were warmed by the coffee they had picked up from a Starbucks, minutes after it opened.

Hrycyk's face was a pasty, puffy white, and there were deep shadows under his eyes. He had refused to be taken to hospital for treatment, and the medics had cleaned and dressed his wound at the stadium and put his arm in a sling. He had found an overcoat in the trunk of his Santana and draped it now over his shoulders for warmth. The stadium manager had allowed Li access to the home team dressing room to shower, and got him pants, tee-shirt and a jacket from the Astros shop. He looked like a walking advert for the team. The long shadow of his peaked baseball hat hid the bruising on his face, and the newly acquired gash in his cheek.

Margaret rubbed the goosebumps on her arm. She shivered in the cold each time they moved out of the sunlight, and she was glad of the hot, sweet coffee burning its way down inside her.

It had been Hrycyk's idea to come here, a short fifteen-minute walk from the stadium. All hell was going to break loose in the hours ahead, he had said, and they were unlikely to have another chance like this to exchange information.

So far they had exchanged nothing. Soong had been taken, under armed police guard, for emergency treatment at a facility in medicine city. He would face hours and days of intensive interrogation when he was fit. None of them knew yet whether he would make it easy or hard. But Li suspected Soong would fight it all the way, although he had said nothing as they walked in silence through the deserted downtown streets. Now he accepted an offer of a cigarette from Hrycyk and struck a match to light them both.

Hrycyk sucked in a lungful of smoke and squinted at Li. 'Jesus,' he said, 'I hate you people.' He paused. 'But I hate the FBI more.' He rubbed his face with his left hand, cigarette pinched at the end of his index and middle fingers. 'Thing is, it was you that put me on to him. Way back at Yu Lin's house. When you said it was too big a coincidence that he got murdered the day we were going to pull him back in. That there had to be a leak in the agency.' He pulled up a gob of phlegm from his chest and spat on the grass. He glanced self-consciously at Margaret. 'Sorry, Doc.'

'That's alright,' she said. 'After two years in China I'm used to it.'

He gave her a look, as if he resented the implication that he might be guilty of behaving in some way like a Chinese. Then he turned back to Li. 'Thing is, I spent my life in the INS. No way could I believe any of the guys I worked with would be capable of betraying one of their own like that.'

'Even a Chinese?' Li asked.

Hrycyk grinned reluctantly. 'Even a Chinese.' He paused, and the smile faded. 'Only person outside the agency who knew we were bringing him in was Fuller.' Some bitter thought flitted through his mind and soured his expression. 'We had the bastard tailed. Tapped his phones, even his mobile. All strictly in-house, if you get my meaning.'

'In other words you didn't have the authority to do it,' Margaret said.

Hrycyk shrugged. 'I couldn't comment.'

They walked past the perfectly preserved homes of Houston's earliest worthies, saved from demolition and transplanted here by the visionaries of the Harris County Heritage Society. Pillars and balconies, white picket fences, shady terraces. An old log cabin, an ornate Victorian bungalow. They contrasted bizarrely against the downtown skyline.

Hrycyk said to Margaret, 'My people got me out my bed last night after your call to Fuller. He came right off the line and called Soong at the stadium. I alerted the cops and went straight there.' He looked at Li. 'Lucky for you guys I did, otherwise you'd both be dead meat by now.' He chuckled, amused by what he perceived as the irony of the situation. 'Jesus. I can't believe I actually saved the life of a Chinaman.'

'So now you are stuck with me forever,' Li said.

Hrycyk frowned. 'How come?'

Margaret said, 'There is an ancient custom in China, Agent Hrycyk, which says if you save a person's life, you become responsible for them for the rest of it.'

Hrycyk stared at her. 'You're shitting me?'

Margaret said, 'It is an obligation you cannot escape.' And Li said, 'So whenever I am in trouble you can expect a call.'

'Jesus Christ!' Hrycyk spluttered.

CHAPTER THIRTEEN

I

A gentle wind, warm now that the chill had been burned off it, blew across the parking lot as Li and Margaret walked from her car towards the terminal building. The dust it raised off the tarmac blew around their ankles. Li carried his overnight bag in his left hand, a cigarette in his right, and a silence laden with tension.

After Hrycyk left them, they had gone back to the hotel and eaten a light breakfast, before collecting Li's bag from his room and driving out to Hobby. There hadn't been much to say. Li's part in the investigation was effectively over. A message on his answering service had summoned him back to Washington to report to his Embassy. And then he had the whole mess of his family to deal with, to resolve somehow. Of course, he would have to return to Huntsville with Xiao Ling for the second hearing in front of the immigration court. Between now and then there was no reason for him to be in Houston, nor Margaret in Washington. They were still separated by half a continent, and neither of them appeared to know how to bridge the gap.

In the departures hall, Li collected his ticket, and Margaret walked with him to the gate. The first available flight went via Dallas and would take more than two hours. Li was not looking forward to it. They stood awkwardly before the entrance to the baggage check. Still neither of them knew what to say. Finally Li forced a smile and said, 'I'll e-mail you.'

'Will you?'

He shrugged. 'Sure.'

'Why?'

He was puzzled. 'What do you mean?'

She sighed. 'What would we have to say to each other in an e-mail, Li Yan? If we're not together, if we can't say the things we want to face to face, what's the point?'

He studied her features for a long time. 'Do you want us to be together?'

'More than anything in the world.'

'But?' He knew there was a 'but'. Somehow there always was with Margaret.

'I'm not sure it would work any better here than it did in China.'

'Why?'

'For all the same reasons. Because of what we are. An American and a Chinese. Oil and water. Because of where we are. Houston and Washington. Still a world apart.' People always said if you were in love nothing else mattered. She wanted to believe that, but couldn't. She wanted to tell him she loved him, but was scared that would only hurt them more. She said, 'Tell Xinxin I'm thinking of her.'

He nodded, not trusting himself to speak. Then he laid his bag at his feet and took her in his arms, almost crushing her. They stood that way for so long that people were beginning to stare. When, finally, he let her go, her face was wet with silent tears. She reached up on tiptoe and kissed him, and then turned and hurried out of the building without once looking back.

II

Lucy looked up from her desk in surprise and said, 'You look terrible, Doctor Campbell.'

'Thank you, Lucy,' Margaret said. 'That makes me feel a whole helluva lot better.' She stopped immediately and raised both her hands in instant apology. 'I'm sorry. I forgot. Hell is very real to some of us.'

'Particularly,' Lucy said dryly, 'those of us who have been left trying to keep the ship afloat with nobody at the helm.'

'Stormy waters, Lucy,' Margaret said. 'Forced me to abandon ship. But I'm back now, and I'll try to sail us into calmer seas.'

'Well, you're going to have to do a lot of calming at the Houston Police department. Homicide have been agitating for twenty-four hours now for reports on two autopsies that have not even been carried out yet.'

'I thought we arranged for Doctor Cullen . . .'

'Called back to say he couldn't make it.' Lucy smiled sweetly. 'Of course, that was after you'd, uh . . . disappeared . . .

yesterday afternoon.' She paused. 'Something wrong with your cellphone?'

Margaret ignored the jibe and sighed. 'You didn't tell them the autopsies hadn't been done, did you?'

'Now you know I wouldn't lie about a thing like that, Doctor.' She hesitated. 'I've been . . . stalling them.'

Margaret smiled. 'Thank you, Lucy. Ask Jack to wheel them out, would you? I'll do them now.'

She went wearily into her office and her heart sank when she saw her desk groaning under the weight of paperwork that had accumulated, even since yesterday. She sat down with her head in her hands and felt her headache returning. It was all she could do to stop herself bursting into tears. She was tired and sore and sorry for herself. She took a deep breath and sat up. There was nothing for it but to get on with it. On with life. On with death.

The body on the table was that of a young Caucasian male, Margaret guessed in his early twenties. He was short, only about five-seven, but powerfully built and covered with thick body hair. The hair on his head was already thinning. There was evidence of trauma around his face and neck. The knuckles of his right hand were bruised and deformed as though one or more might be broken. She would look at the x-rays in a few minutes. His penis had been severed, almost in its entirety, and was absent. There were multiple stab wounds in his chest and abdomen. Margaret counted thirty-three.

She looked at the photographs from the crime scene on the stainless steel counter behind her. It looked like someone's bedroom, but not that of the deceased, according to the report. There was a lot of blood on the floor around the body, but not much of it seemed to have come from the stab wounds. Margaret guessed that the penis had been severed first, and that the victim might have bled to death even before the frenzied knife attack.

She returned to the body, and Jack helped her turn it over. Jack Sweeney was one of her autopsy assistants. He was in his mid-thirties and of indeterminate sexual orientation. He had been working for the Medical Examiner's Office for nearly ten years. 'Be careful with this one,' he said. 'I read the report. Apparently he was a male prostitute.'

Margaret glanced up, surprised. 'He's not what I would have thought of as typical,' she said.

'Some men like them rough,' Jack said. Then added, smirking, 'So I've heard.'

Margaret found evidence of trauma and semen in the anal passage and immediately felt herself breaking into a sweat. She ran a sleeve across her forehead and found her breath coming with difficulty. 'Is it very hot in here?' she asked.

Jack shrugged. 'Usual, Doctor Campbell. Pretty cool.' He peered at her. 'You okay? You look a bit flushed.'

Margaret put both hands on the table to steady herself. She was light-headed now and starting to feel nauseous. The sweat turned cold on the back of her neck.

She made a dash for the sink and was violently sick into it.

Jack was at her side instantly, arms around her shoulders. But she shrugged him off. 'I'm sorry, Jack, I need a little space.'

'What's wrong, Doctor? Something you ate?' He was concerned for her.

She saw her breakfast in the stainless steel sink and turned on the tap to wash it away. 'Probably.' She took off her latex gloves, filled her hands with cold water and sluiced her face, then stood, leaning against the sink, willing the trembling in her legs to stop. She remained like that for several minutes, until she began to feel some control returning. She snapped on a fresh pair of gloves and returned to the table.

'You sure you're up to this?' Jack asked.

She nodded, but even as she turned her attentions back to the bloodless white flesh on the table, the sweat began beading across her forehead, and a further wave of nausea rose from her stomach. 'Jesus.' She made another dash for the sink and acid bile burned its way up her throat into her mouth.

Lucy looked up in surprise as Margaret hurried through the outer office, still in her green surgeon's pyjamas and apron, hair tucked away under her shower cap. She was deathly pale. She stopped in the doorway to her office. 'No one's to come in here, Lucy. And I mean *no* one. Lock the door. Do not leave the office. Stay at your desk.'

Lucy was alarmed now. 'What's wrong, Doctor Campbell?'

'Just do what I tell you, please.' Margaret slammed the door and crossed to her desk, digging out the phone list from her bag with trembling fingers, and snatching the phone from its cradle. Her breathing was tremulous and erratic, her body wracked by uncontrollable shivering. Fear and dread had balled themselves up together in a huge knot in her stomach. She listened as the phone rang twice at the other end before the operator picked up.

'USAMRIID Fort Detrick. How may I help you?'

'Doctor Margaret Campbell for Colonel Robert Zeiss. It's an emergency.'

'One moment, please.'

The one moment stretched into eternity. Margaret rounded her desk and dropped into her chair, but perched on the edge of it, only barely in control.

'Colonel Zeiss.'

'Colonel, I think I've got the flu.'

There was a brief silence at the other end of the line. Margaret could almost hear the colonel thinking. 'Why do you think that?' he asked.

'Because I've just had two bouts of vomiting, I'm sweating and shaking from head to toe.'

Another pause, then Zeiss said, 'Stay where you are, Doctor. I'll have a team with you as fast as I possibly can. We'll need isolation facilities. What's closest to you?'

'Hermann Hospital, I think. They have an infectious diseases facility and isolation rooms.' She could almost see the hospital, in medicine city, from her window.

'I'll alert them.' He paused again. 'Who have you been in contact with in the last few hours?'

'My secretary, my autopsy assistant. Li Yan, the Chinese

criminal justice liaison . . .' Her heart sank at the thought. Please, God, not Li as well. 'But he's on a plane to Washington, via Dallas.'

'Shit!' Zeiss almost whispered the oath. 'What airline?'

'AirTran.'

'We'll try to intercept him. Make certain that your autopsy assistant and secretary have no contact with anyone until we can get them isolated. Is there anyone else?'

Her mind raced. 'INS Agent Hrycyk,' she said. 'Councilman Soong, and about a dozen Houston police officers — but that was several hours ago.'

She heard Zeiss groan. 'Let's just hope you're wrong about this,' he said, and she wondered if he only hoped that in order to save himself trouble. 'Sit tight until the team gets there.'

He hung up, and she sat holding the phone, feeling like a criminal. As if somehow it was her fault that she had got the flu and had knowingly gone spreading it around. She replaced the receiver and sat numbly, wondering how she could possibly have contracted the virus. It could only have been during autopsy. Or could Steve somehow have passed it on to her? And, then, what had triggered it?

She looked around her office, her eyes lighting on all the little personal things she had gathered there over the months. The Chinese wall hanging she had been given by Li's former boss in Beijing, a soft woollen pencil case she had kept from her schooldays — sentimental value, something that connected her with who she had been in happier times. There was a paperweight that her father had given her. It was just a big flat pebble he had found on the lake, with the fossil of a fish clearly visible on the top of it. A photograph of herself sandwiched between her mother and father on the occasion of her tenth birthday. She looked at the chubby, round red cheeks and the bobbed hair, the shining blue eyes, the fondness in her father's gaze, the distance in her mother's. There was a pair of old shoes, moulded to the shape of her feet, that she kept for changing into on return from a crime scene. They seemed ancient and empty and neglected, and she wondered if she would ever put them on again.

Depression and self-pity descended on her like a chill mist on an autumn morning. All these things, she thought, belonged to someone else, someone with a life, someone who did not expect to die, at least not for a long time.

The phone rang, crashing into her thoughts like a bucket of iced water. It was an internal call. She snatched at it. Lucy's voice, small and scared, asked, 'What's wrong, Doctor? What's going on?'

Margaret said, 'I'm sorry, Lucy. It is possible I have contracted a virus. Some people are going to come and take us all into an isolation facility at Hermann Hospital. Even if it's confirmed, the chances are I won't have given it to you.'

There was a long silence. Then, 'What virus, Doctor?'

'It's the flu, Lucy. A particularly nasty form of flu.'

The team arrived in under half an hour. Margaret saw them from the window of her office. Three army ambulances, drivers wearing Tivek suits and HEPA filter masks. Three two-man medical crews wearing full protective STEPO suits brought out litters for carrying contaminated patients. The litters were hooded in clear plastic and fitted with their own filtered air supply. They were all part of the national biowarfare defence force put in place during the Clinton regime. The sight of them made Margaret shiver.

III

The army interception team missed Li at Dulles by minutes. He had called home during his stopover at Dallas and told Xiao Ling to get a cab out to the airport to meet him. He needed to talk to her, away from Xinxin. To his astonishment, he had been met by both of them, Xinxin laughing, delighted to see him, gambolling around her mother as if they had never been apart. The transformation in Xiao Ling, too, was astonishing. Something had breathed life back into her broken spirit.

Both were concerned by the state of his face; it was even worse than when they had last seen him. And the three of them had stood hugging on the concourse, wrapped in their unexpected happiness, for a long time. Half shell-shocked, Li had told their driver to take them to the Washington Harbour complex on the Potomac, down the hill from Georgetown. It was a stunning fall day, a warm wind blowing up from a clear sky in the south and softening the air. They could get a drink at Tony and Joe's and sit out in the sunshine and watch the roller bladers cruise by on the boardwalk.

The harbour was busy. The sun had brought the people

of DC out from premature winter hibernation to enjoy the warm autumn sunshine and make the most of this unexpected reprise of summer. Tables and sunshades were laid out along the waterfront, and people crowded the steps to the fountains. The traffic on the Whitehurst Freeway was a distant rumble. This had once been a derelict area of crummy parking lots and scrap yards, transformed now into an upscale development of restaurants and shops, and plush offices occupied by govern-ment lobbyists. Only the airplanes, threading their way along the curve of the Potomac, heading for Reagan, spoiled the peace. By law they could not overfly the White House on the DC side, or the Pentagon on the Virginia side. And so the river had become the flight path into the National Airport. But after a while you stopped hearing them. Li sat with his sunglasses on, watching the sunlight coruscating on the river, drinking a beer, and smoking a cigarette. He felt relaxed for the first time in days. Xinxin finished a tall coupe of ice-cream and persuaded her mom to let her go and watch the joggers and the kids on roller blades. Xiao Ling told her okay, as long as she stayed inside the fence. She took a sip of her Coke and for the first time allowed her anxiety about her brother to show.

'Are you alright?'

He nodded. 'A few cuts and bruises. I'll survive.' He took a pull at his cigarette and looked at his sister fondly. She was like the old Xiao Ling, the little girl he remembered as a child. Whatever scars the last few years had left were on the inside now. For the moment nothing showed on the outside except her smile, and her clear concern for Li. He leaned forward and took her hand. 'You're safe now, Xing,' he said. 'We've got the *ah kung*. He's in custody.' And he realised he had used, without thinking, the nickname he had given her when they were kids. Xing.

She squeezed his hand. 'I've been doing a lot of thinking, Li Yan . . .'

But he was anxious to hear what had passed between mother and daughter, and interrupted. 'What happened with Xinxin?'

She shook her head. 'I don't know. I woke up this morning, and she was in bed beside me. Curled into my back, fast asleep. I've no idea how long she'd been there.' There was moisture gathering in her eyes. 'It was like she was saying to me, okay, I don't know why you went away, but you're back now and I forgive you, so where were we . . . ?' Xiao Ling laughed as the tears ran down her cheeks. 'And, you know, now I can't for the life of me understand why I did leave.'

'Make that two of us,' Li said.

Shame fell across her face like a shadow. 'I'm sorry,' she said. 'I'm so sorry. It was like . . . like some kind of madness. I can't explain it. Something took over inside me. Something irrational, beyond my control. When I look back, it's as if I was another person.' Li wiped the tears away from her face. But she was determined to get it all off her chest. 'I'm a different person now. I know that. Different from then, different from before then. So much has happened.' She forced a smile. 'What does a farmer's wife from Sichuan know about anything?'

'A lot more now,' Li said wryly.

She nodded, and then suddenly she said, 'Li Yan, I don't want to go back to that immigration court.'

Li frowned. 'Xing, you've got to. They placed you in my custody. I have to take you back.'

She shook her head vigorously. 'No, you don't understand. I don't want to apply for political asylum. I want to go home. I want to go back to China with Xinxin.'

'Not to Xiao Xu?' Li said, concerned suddenly. He had always disliked his brother-in-law, from the first time Xiao Ling had brought him home. 'You know he's living with someone else now.'

She shrugged. 'Yes, I know,' she said. 'And, no, I would never have gone back to him. He was part of the madness, a part of what drove me away in the first place.' She hesitated for a long moment. 'When I told him I was pregnant again, he beat me.'

Li felt his hackles rising. Had he know that, he would have been on the first train to Sichuan to deal with his brother in-law himself.

'I didn't tell you,' she said, 'because I knew what your reac tion would be. You're like all men, Li Yan. You think the only way to settle a problem is with your fists.'

He smiled sheepishly. 'Not always,' he defended himself. But he knew that in this instance she was right. His smile faded. 'So where would you go?'

She tipped her eyebrows back on her head and made a face. 'I don't know. Beijing maybe. I'll need to find a job.'

And he understood then that his destiny had been decided for him. He could not let Xiao Ling and Xinxin go back to

China on their own. His sister was carrying the flu virus. She would need special care. 'I'll come with you,' he said. 'You will stay with me. Both of you.'

'But your job . . .'

'I will ask to be re-assigned,' he said. 'Back to Section One. In the circumstances, I don't think they will refuse me.'

She leaned forward and removed his sunglasses, and gazed into his eyes for a long time. She knew the sacrifice he was making. 'I love you, Li Yan,' she said, and she kissed him on the cheek.

IV

Margaret sat up on the bed in the small isolation room. Her sealed window unit looked out over the lushly watered Hermann Park. The midday sun had long since burned off all the dew, and she saw joggers, plugged into Walkmans, pounding their red-legged circuits around the park. She felt as if she were watching a movie, something unreal and unreachable. She had never had the least desire to go jogging, but suddenly it seemed like the most desirable thing in the world. Just to feel the sun on your skin, the air in your lungs, the ground under your feet. To be free simply to live.

She had been in a daze when they wired her up to the monitor and took her blood samples. She remembered a doctor in a space suit telling her that her temperature was normal, but they weren't taking any risks. They had stuck a needle in her left arm and connected her to a bag of Lactated Ringer's solution – salt and water to counteract the effects of any dehydration. Like Steve, they had also put her on a course of rimantadine anti-viral drugs. The thought of Steve conjured pictures in her mind of his last moments, writhing and manic, vomiting green bile. And the cold, steel fingers of her own fear closed around her heart.

She had been aware from time to time of people coming up to the observation window in the corridor and peering in at her, but she hadn't paid much attention. A near hysterical Lucy, and a very subdued Jack, were in rooms further along the corridor. She had heard Lucy's plaintive appeals to God as they wheeled her away. But Margaret had no faith that even if there was a God, He could or would do anything to change things.

There was a phone by the bed which she was told she could use to make calls through the switchboard. But she couldn't think of anyone to phone. She had wondered if they had caught Li at the airport in Washington, but when she asked, no one appeared to know.

She felt like an animal caught in headlights, frozen by her own fear, unable to move, unable to change or influence her own destiny. And something dark behind the lights was waiting to crush her.

The strangest thing was, she felt fine now. Physically. No more hot flushes or cold sweats. No more nausea. In fact, she was almost hungry.

She looked up as a doctor came through the 'airlock'. There was something very strange about him. His white coat hung open, a stethoscope dangling from his neck, dark, baggy pants belted at the waist, a pair of scuffed loafers on size ten feet. Everyman's cliché of a hospital doctor. For a moment, Margaret looked at him, puzzled, before she realised what was wrong. He wasn't wearing a spacesuit. She wasn't even sure if he was the doctor who had spoken to her earlier. He was about forty, sandy hair flopping across his forehead. And he was leaving the doors open behind him. His loafers squeaked on the linoleum as he crossed to the bed and disconnected her from the drip. He pressed a small bandage on her arm and drew out the needle from beneath it. Then he sat on the edge of the bed and looked at her curiously.

He said, 'Good news and . . . well, other news. I'll let you decide if it's good or bad.' He paused. 'You don't have the flu, Doctor.'

She stared at him, hardly daring to believe it. Other news, he said he had. Other news. What other news? 'What's wrong with me?' she asked, and her voice caught in her throat.

He raised one eyebrow. 'You're pregnant.'

She sat for a long time in her office watching the sun sinking towards the western skyline, a great orange orb enlarged and distorted by the pollution that hung above the city, starting to turn pink as it tilted at the horizon.

Lucy had gone home. She had told Margaret that she would not be in the next day, and that Margaret could expect to receive her resignation in the post. Jack had also gone home, but said he would be in tomorrow. He said he was glad Margaret was okay. He was glad they were all okay.

Margaret hadn't known what she felt. Numb. Scared. Confused. How could she be pregnant? She had blurted to the doctor that it wasn't possible. That it had only been a matter of days . . . He had just shrugged. If she was ovulating at the time, sperm and egg would have combined within minutes, or hours. Her body was simply reacting to that. Earlier than usual, but it wasn't unheard of.

Margaret ran her hand softly over her lower abdomen. She had Li's child in her. A tiny, fertilised egg that in the next weeks and months would take shape and grow in her womb. It would develop little fingers and toes, a mouth, nose, eyes . . . She wondered if it would have her fair hair, or Li's strong, black Chinese thatch, if it would have those beautiful slanted almond eyes, whether they would be dark like Li's or blue like hers. Would it be a boy or a girl? It had taken a long time, several hours, but all the pain and anxiety and uncertainty had slowly but surely ebbed away, and she found herself suffused now with an almost unbearable happiness. This changed everything.

V

Li and Xiao Ling and Xinxin were laughing together as they came up the path to the front door of Li's townhouse in Georgetown, Li chasing and catching Xinxin by the door. He wrapped his arms around her and tickled her feverishly. She squealed, laughing uncontrollably, and wriggled to try and get away. But he held her firm and breathed in the smell of fresh-baked bread from her hair. But it wasn't bread. It was just her own distinctive smell, sweet and clean and fresh. Bread Head Margaret had nicknamed her in Beijing, but the translation had not worked in Chinese, so they had stuck to the English – and the nickname had stuck to Xinxin. The scent, and the thought, brought Margaret flooding back to his mind, and for a moment his happiness was touched by regret.

The sound of the telephone ringing on the other side of the door snapped him out of his dream, and he released Xinxin to run giggling to her mother. He hurriedly fished the keys from his pocket.

He had spent two hours at the Embassy in the early afternoon. They told him that there had been some sort of scare over the flu and that the US authorities had been looking for him earlier. But apparently it was no longer an issue. He had spent an hour with the Ambassador, briefing him on developments in Houston. And then he had requested a transfer back to Beijing. The request had caused some consternation, and several other high ranking officials were brought into the meeting. Li had been asked to explain his position, and he told them about Xiao Ling and Xinxin. He had been left waiting on his own in an ante-room for some time while, he suspected, the Embassy conferred with Beijing. Eventually he had been summoned again to the Ambassador's office and told that he had been granted leave to return to Beijing. A decision on his future would be taken there in the next few weeks. But Li suspected that the PR value of Xiao Ling's high profile return to China was irresistible. The American Dream,

Beijing would tell the world, was not all it was cracked up to be. Li didn't give a damn about the politics. He just wanted to take his sister home.

To celebrate, he had taken Xiao Ling and Xinxin on a whistlestop tour of the Washington sights. The Vietnam wall, where the name of every American who had died in the South-East Asian conflict was etched in black marble. A sobering place. Arlington Cemetery, and the grave of the assassinated John F. Kennedy, fine words once spoken by him now carved in stone for eternity. The changing of the guard at the Tomb of the Unknown Soldier. The strange, mechanical, strutted ritual had fascinated Xinxin. The Lincoln Memorial. Another assassinated president, towering in white marble, seated in his temple and gazing out across the Reflecting Pool to the Washington Monument, and Capitol Hill beyond. He wanted them to see these things, to have these memories to take away with them, because the chances were they would never be back. Tomorrow he would pull some strings to get them on a White House tour. And the day after they would fly to Beijing.

The dying embers of the sun slanted red light into the hall as he opened the door, nearly falling over his bicycle in his rush to get to the phone. He had called Meiping earlier and told her she could have the day off.

'Wei?'

'Li Yan?'

He recognised Margaret's voice immediately, and his heart suddenly filled his chest and restricted his breathing.

'Margaret.' He waited a moment, but she said nothing. 'They told me there was a scare with the flu.'

'Yeah,' she said. 'False alarm.' More silence, that neither of them knew how to fill. Xiao Ling and Xinxin came in at Li's back and closed the door and went through, chattering, to the kitchen. Margaret heard the voices and said, 'How are things with Xinxin and Xiao Ling?'

So he told her. About them making up, about the long talk they had all had. About his decision to return to China with them. About the Embassy granting him interim leave to return to Beijing while they took a final decision about his position. Xiao Ling, he said, would receive the best of care if, or until, the flu struck.

Fifteen hundred miles away in Houston, Texas, his words fell like stones in a desert. An arid wind blew through Margaret's soul. Everything she had felt just minutes earlier, the hope and the happiness, withered inside her. Only his seed remained there, the one spark of life in a bleak landscape. He talked about their day, and she listened without hearing. For beyond his reserve in breaking the news to her, she sensed his happiness, something she had not felt in him for a long time. If she told him now about their child, it could only throw everything in his life back into confusion. He might resent it. Blame her. She didn't want to be the one to hurt him again, and neither did she want to be hurt by him.

'Margaret . . .? Are you still there . . . ?'

She forced herself to refocus. 'Yeah, I'm still here.'

He knew there was something wrong. He could feel it

reaching out to him over all the miles. 'Is that all you phoned for?' he said. 'To ask about Xiao Ling and Xinxin?'

For several long moments she did not trust herself to speak. 'Sure,' she said, finally.

He said, 'Margaret, is there something wrong?'

'No,' she said quickly. 'So you won't be coming back to Texas for the Immigration Court?'

'No.'

Silence.

'Well . . .' she said, '. . . I guess that's it, then.'

'That's what?' he asked.

'Goodbye,' she said.

And he realised that this might be the last time he would ever speak to her. 'Margaret . . .' But he stopped. He had no idea what to say. Then, finally, he said, 'I guess it is.'

Silence.

'Well . . . Goodbye, then.'

Her voice was so quiet he barely heard her. He had to clear his throat before he could speak. 'Goodbye,' he said, and held on to the phone until he heard her replace the receiver at the other end. And a part of him died in that moment.

Margaret's tears blistered the list of phone numbers on her desk, and she was glad there was no one in the building to hear her cry of anguish.

CHAPTER FOURTEEN

I

It was twilight by the time she got to Conroe. The last of the day filtered through the trees, and the lake lay still, like glass, reflecting a sky where the first stars were already appearing in a pale blue shading to dark. The blood had drained out of the western horizon, and the flat Texan landscape stretched away into a shimmering eternity.

Margaret's Chevy bumped up the long dirt track to the Mendez ranch, raising a cloud of orange dust in its wake. She had nowhere else to go. All her things were here, and she could not face a night alone in a hotel room. She felt safe enough in light of Mendez's remorse, and whatever uneasiness she had about facing him was nothing compared to the aching hollow space that filled her heart. The Bronco was parked opposite the garage, and as she punched in the access code to open the door to the house, she heard Clara barking on the other side of it, a scrabble of claws on floorboards.

Clara danced around her legs, jumping up, her paws punching into Margaret's chest. Margaret pushed the dog away and realised she could barely see. The house was in darkness. She caught her knee on the hard edge of the gun rack and cursed as she fumbled to find a light switch. Finally, her fingers stumbled on a panel of switches on the wall. The gun room and kitchen flickered into sharp fluorescence.

Nothing had changed. The kitchen was still piled with unwashed dishes. The smell of stale food and cooking oil hung in the air. Clara's food bowl was empty, and by her agitation Margaret reckoned she was probably hungry. Her water dish was also empty. Margaret had no idea where Mendez kept the dog food, but she filled the water dish at the sink and put it back on the floor. Clara slurped noisily, one eye on constant alert in case there was food to follow.

Margaret called out, 'Hello? Felipe, are you at home?' Her voice was soaked up by the house and there was no response. She went through to the sitting room and turned on the lights there. The ceiling fan stirred hot air. The door to the smoking porch stood open, the air laden with the smell of fresh cigar smoke, but there was nobody in there either. She passed through the dining room and out into the front hall. She switched on the stair lights and called up, 'Felipe?' Still no response.

She went back through to the kitchen and into the bar. She was tired and dry, and needed a drink. She took a bottle of tonic from the refrigerator, cut some lemon and put ice into a tall glass. The vodka bottle was already in her hand before she realised that there was somebody else to think about other than herself now. She hesitated for only a second, before pushing the bottle back on the shelf and pouring herself a plain tonic water over ice and lemon. It tasted good, sharp and refreshing.

She carried the glass with her as she went up the stairs to her room. In the hall, she stopped. The door to Mendez's study stood ajar and she could see the light of a desk lamp burning softly somewhere inside. Previously the door had always been closed. Curious, she pushed it open and walked in. It was a small room, smaller than she had been expecting. The walls were lined with bookshelves, and the shelves were groaning with books piled one on top of the other. The floor was strewn with papers and maps, and open books with pages folded to mark the place. A battle-scarred old mahogany desk was pushed up against the wall below a window with its blind pulled down. Layer upon layer of papers drifted across the landscape of its obscured leather top. Haphazard stacks of files rose in columns like cliffs. An old Macintosh computer was half buried in a gorge between them. A captain's chair was turned towards the door, as if Mendez had left it only moments before. A passport lay across the computer keyboard, pushed back from the front edge of the desk. It was the green-blue colour of a sullen tropical sea, with gold lettering, and an eagle crest. A number was punched, like Braille, along its bottom edge beneath the word PASAPORTE. Margaret picked up the passport, puzzled, and frowned. She opened it and saw a younger Mendez staring back at her, like a still from an old movie. She looked at it for some time, lost in thought and consternation, before dropping the passport back on the desk.

She flipped idly through some of the papers strewn across the desktop. Scientific stuff mostly. Notes and articles, several of them in Spanish.

A wicker bin was overflowing. Anything up to a dozen sheets of paper had been scrumpled up and thrown on the floor. Margaret stooped to pick one up and flatten it out. Her stomach turned over. It was an unfinished letter addressed to her. Handwritten. *Dear Margaret, I don't know where to begin, or how to express my apologies* . . . She started unfolding others. They were all addressed to her. Pathetic, inept attempts at apology. For a brief moment she almost felt sorry for him. She wondered if he had managed to complete one, if it was waiting for her in an envelope somewhere.

She heard a sound behind her and turned, startled. Clara stood panting in the doorway, looking up at her with mournful eyes, as if attempting to ape her master's contrition. Margaret smiled at her own foolishness and went through to her room, Clara padding at her heels. She looked around, checking in her suitcases, and the boxes of her stuff, for any sign that Mendez might have gone through them. But everything appeared exactly as she had left it.

She picked out some clean clothes and underwear and went in for a shower, locking the door behind her this time. She stood for a long while, letting the water wash away her misery, comforting herself with the thought that even if she never saw Li again, he had left a little of himself with her forever. And there was a powerful element of succour in the thought of the life that was growing inside her.

Towelling herself dry, she slipped into her fresh clothes and immediately felt better. Clara was waiting for her out in the bedroom and followed her downstairs to the kitchen. The back door was unlocked, and Margaret wandered out to a paved patio, moonlight reflecting now in the still waters of a small swimming pool. A security lamp, activated by a motion detector, flooded the back of the house with light. Margaret was momentarily discomfited, and wondered why she was so jumpy. As she went around the side of the house, and the open garage, another light snapped on, reflecting harshly off the metallic paintwork of Mendez's Bronco. Margaret frowned. He had to be around somewhere if the Bronco was there and the back door unlocked.

The meadow in which the two mares still grazed was washed in the colourless light of the moon. Beyond that, a path led around the side of a pond, a deep, dark pool of water choked by lilies. And beyond that, in a black stand of trees, a light shone in an outbuilding she had only vaguely been aware of in the daytime. It was an old wooden barn with an empty hayloft, and a tractor glinting darkly beyond a half-open door. She could not tell exactly where the light was coming from, or what was its source. She was uncertain if there was a window there. She hesitated to make the walk in the dark. It was, perhaps, four or five hundred yards. But the path shone pale in the moonlight. She could hardly lose her footing or her way.

It took her several minutes to cross the meadow, watched with interest by the horses, which seemed frozen in their dark-eyed curiosity. They returned to their grazing as she skirted the perimeter of the pond. The air smelled damp here, and was filled with the gentle screech of cicadas. As she got closer to the barn, sheltering in the shadow of its small clutch of trees, she saw that the light was coming from an unglazed window at the far end of it. But it was a feeble, reflected light, that appeared to be shining into the barn rather than out of it.

She slipped in the open door, squeezing past the tractor, with its smells of diesel and dried cattle dung, and saw that the light was coming up through a large trap door lying open at the rear of the barn, its wooden lid propped against the back wall. She crossed the dusty stretch of floor, compacted earth and dry, brittle straw, and saw a wide, wooden ladder leading down into a square pit lined with stout wooden planking. An electric light was screwed to the wall on one side. On the other, a deep, studded metal door set in a thick frame was not fully shut. From beyond it she heard the faint sound of music. She recognised the Intermezzo from *Cavalleria Rusticana*, a sad, bittersweet melody that raised goosebumps on the back of her neck and along her arms. She climbed carefully down the steps and stood on the concrete floor of the pit. Mascagni's Intermezzo died into stillness, and a sweet, plaintive soprano sang Puccini, *O mio babbino caro* from *Gianni Schicchi*. A haunting piece of infinite sadness. She reached out and pushed the door with the tips of her fingers. Although it was heavy, it swung open easily, and she blinked in the bright fluorescent light of a small underground chamber, concrete walls and low, slabbed roof, painted white. There was a wooden-topped bench in the centre of the room cluttered with all kinds of equipment; a couple of gel electrophoresis machines, a digital camera with UV light for scanning gels, an iMac and flatbed scanner. Two walls were lined with worktops set with stainless steel sinks, a small electric oven for doing blots, a couple more iMacs, a scanning electron microscope, a rack of test tubes, jars and bottles, piles of papers, books, a coffee maker, an ashtray overflowing with cigar butts. Against the third wall stood a couple of incubators, a home refrigerator and an ultracold freezer. A portable stereo, next to a small centrifuge, was playing the Puccini. Louder now.

Mendez had his back to her. He was wearing a stained white lab coat, and as he moved away from the sink she saw half-moon spectacles perched on the end of his nose, attached to him by a cord around his neck. He was wearing latex gloves and swirling a small quantity of blue fluid in the bottom of a test tube. He reached up and took something down from the shelf above his head, and then slipped the tube into a rack and wrote in a large notebook open on the worktop in front of him. The voice of the soprano fell away into quiet melancholy and Margaret said, 'Felipe?'

He was so startled, turning quickly, that he knocked the test tube from its holder and the glass smashed on the counter, spilling its blue liquid content across the top of it. Wide-eyed, barely able to believe what he was seeing, he took in the vision of Margaret standing in the doorway. And then, 'Shit!' he said, spinning around to pull paper from a roll and mop up the spillage. He looked back at Margaret, consternation in his face now, and a tenor began singing an aria from *La Bohème*.

He crossed to the stereo and turned it off, and its sweetness was replaced by the deep hum of electrical equipment. He frowned. 'Margaret,' he said, as if waiting for her to speak and confirm that she was not some figment of his imagination.

'I didn't know you had your own lab out here,' she said.

He shrugged and looked around, as if trying to see it through her eyes. 'The previous owner was convinced there would be a nuclear holocaust. He intended to survive it in here. I had it fitted out as a lab when we first bought the place. It's pretty limited. Just for my own personal researches. Any serious work has to be done at Baylor.' He paused, turning his eyes on her again, drinking her in. 'I wasn't expecting you.'

'I'm sorry about last night,' she said.

He shook his head vigorously. 'No, no, my dear. Please don't be sorry. It was entirely my fault. My behaviour was unforgivable.' He hesitated. 'Have you come to collect your things?'

'I was going to stay over, if that's alright. Tonight anyway.'

'Of course, of course,' he said quickly. 'Margaret, you have no idea how miserable I have been these past twenty-four hours. I can't apologise enough.'

'You've apologised more than enough,' Margaret said. She raised the flats of her hands towards him. 'No more. Please.'

He nodded, beaming, almost unable to contain his delight. 'Of course.' He snapped off his latex gloves. 'I hear the ringleader of the snakeheads has been arrested. Your Chinese friend has done well.'

Even the mention of Li clouded Margaret's thoughts. 'Yes,' she said.

'We should eat, and you can tell me all about it.' Mendez slipped out of his lab coat. As he hung it on the back of the door, the tail of it swept a pack of cigars off a gurney pushed against the wall. Margaret stooped to pick it up. She looked at the brand. It was unfamiliar to her.

'Mexican,' she said.

'Yes, I have them sent to me.' He took them from her and slipped the pack in his pocket. 'I prefer Cuban of course, but they are still illegal here. American cigars are too sweet, so I have these sent up from Mexico.'

She said, 'I don't think you ever told me whereabouts in Mexico you were from, originally.'

'No, I probably didn't,' he said. 'You would never have heard of it. A small town called Hermosillo, in the north-west, near the border with Arizona.' He laughed. 'But, of course, I was a perfectly legal immigrant. I didn't cross the border in the back of a truck. I came on a bus, with a scholarship to Cal Tech.'

'A long bus trip.'

'It certainly was.' He ushered her out, turning off the lights behind them. 'Come, my dear, I'm sure I have some pizza in the freezer that we can put in the microwave, and some good Chilean wine to wash it down with.'

'I've given up alcohol, Felipe,' she said.

He followed her up the steps into the barn and looked at her in astonishment. 'But the consumption of fine wine is one of life's great pleasures, my dear.' He dropped the trap door, raising a cloud of dust.

'Yeah, well, I think maybe I liked it just a little too much,' she said. She was not about to tell him that she did not want to damage her unborn child.

As they walked past the pond and across the meadow, he told her about his progress, or lack of it, in identifying the proteins that triggered the flu virus. 'The list of things that do not do it is growing by the day, but compared to those that might, it is still just a drop in the ocean. Currently, I am looking at fruits. In particular, those indigenous to North America.'

She let him talk, let the words float over her. She was tired, and although she would probably not admit it, even to herself, she was almost beyond caring. The chestnut mares broke from their grazing to stare at them. One of them whinnied, an apparent signal for them both to go skittering off into the darkness, shaking their heads and snorting their derision.

In the kitchen, Mendez surveyed the mess as if seeing it for the first time. 'Every so often I have a blitz,' he said. 'I spend a weekend clearing the dishes, cleaning the place. Then I turn around, and it's like this again.'

'You need a maid,' Margaret said.

'I have tried, believe me,' Mendez said. 'You have no idea how difficult it is to get someone to come all the way out here.' He cleared a space on a worktop and dug a frozen pizza out of the freezer and got it out of its wrapping. 'Ham and pineapple. Is that okay for you?' he asked. She nodded and he said, 'Go through and relax. I'll feed the dog and bring this in when it's ready. If you're not having wine, what'll you drink? I've got some apple juice in the refrigerator.'

'That'll be fine,' Margaret said. She left him to it, and heard Clara barking excitedly as he filled her food bowl. She sank into the recliner in the living room and watched the shadow of the fan circling the ceiling. She daren't close her eyes, or she knew she would simply drift away. It was only twenty-four hours since Mendez had made his clumsy pass at her. Only twenty hours since she had last made love to Li Yan. The events of the previous night at Enron Field seemed like a lifetime away – someone else's lifetime. She could remember running along the track above the baseball field, the huge replica locomotive looming over her in the dark, the roof shutting out the stars, the vision of the blood-crusted Li staggering down between the rows of seating. But it was as if they were not her memories, as if she had perhaps borrowed them from someone else, or seen them in some movie. She folded her hands over her belly. The only thing that felt real now was her baby, the life she carried inside her. Strangely it seemed to give her, almost for the first time in her life, a sense of purpose. And then she remembered the passport, and something else, something she had seen in the lab, and she came back down to earth with a jolt.

'Here we are, my dear,' Mendez said. He was carrying a tray with the pizza cut into wedges on a big round plate. There was a tall glass of apple juice and a bottle of Chilean wine and a crystal goblet. He placed it on a coffee table which he dragged to sit between the recliner and the settee so they could both reach it. The hot smell of the pizza was savoury and enticing. Margaret lifted a wedge, pulling it free of its trailing strands of cheese and took a large bite.

'It's good,' she said, and she reached for her glass and washed it down with a mouthful of apple juice. She looked up to find Mendez sitting on the settee watching her, his face slightly flushed. He was smiling oddly.

Margaret woke to moonlight flooding through her bedroom window. It was inordinately bright, and she had no recollection of coming to bed. She had a sense of breathing in slow motion, her chest rising and falling in slow, gentle undulations. She knew from the feel of the cotton sheet on her skin that she was naked, but could not remember undressing. But there was no alarm in it. She felt relaxed, her limbs heavy. So heavy she could barely move them. She fought hard to grasp conscious thoughts that seemed to slip through her fingers like the fluttering feathers of a bird in panic. She was scared to squeeze too tightly in case she damaged it. She frowned in confusion. There *was* no bird. Start again. She remembered eating pizza with Mendez in the sitting room. He had turned on the television and was chatting to her brightly, endlessly. Words following words. Words she couldn't recall. When had she come to bed? With great difficulty she turned her head and saw figures burning red lines in the dark. She blinked, eyelids like camera shutters set for long exposure, trying to make sense of what she saw. Two. One. Six. Revelation. It was two-sixteen in the morning. Hours since she had sat eating pizza with Mendez. There was something she had meant to do. What was it? Something important. When Mendez was sleeping. She had wanted to go back out to the lab. Why?

A shadow fell across her, and with a great effort she turned her eyes up to see what it was. Felipe was smiling. He was fully dressed, and she wondered, stupidly, why he had gone to bed in his clothes. And then, from somewhere deep in her subconscious, a tiny bubble of fear came fizzing to the surface, and she knew that somehow she had not undressed herself and come to bed, that Mendez was fully dressed because he had not yet been to bed. And that if she had not undressed herself, then he must have done it. More bubbles broke the surface. Something of it must have shown in her eyes, because his smile widened and he said softly, 'My dear, don't fight the Rohypnol. You know you won't win.'

Rohypnol. Rohypnol? The word meant something to her. There was a bird in her hands again, wings flapping, heart fluttering. This time she clenched her fists. Rohypnol. Clear. Tasteless. The classic date rape drug. Apple juice. Her mouth felt dry now, very dry, a strange bitterness in it. She wanted to touch herself. Down there. To know what he had done to her, but it was as if she had no arms, no hands. She could not move them, could not feel them. Instead, she heard his voice again, soft and hypnotic.

'I knew when I went into my study that you had been there,' he said. She forced her head around so that she could see him more clearly. She tried to focus on his lips. Important that she could understand what he was saying. He smiled. 'You saw my feeble attempts at writing you an apology. The trouble is, that to make an apology convincing it has to come from the heart.' He shrugged. 'Then I saw the passport, and knew it was not where I had left it. And I remembered you asking me in the lab where in Mexico I came from.' He shook his head. 'Not very subtle, Margaret.'

He moved around the foot of the bed to her left side, and the moonlight lay over her, unbroken, like a shroud. She tilted her head with difficulty so that she could follow him. He sat down on the edge of the bed and ran his fingers lightly over her forehead, and then with his forefinger traced the line of her nose and lips and chin. 'When I first came to the States, I had no reason to conceal the fact that I was a Colombian. I never have. But people always made assumptions. My Latin looks, my accent, my name. A spic. A Mexican. Only when all this blew up did it become convenient for me to go along with it. To put as much distance between myself and my roots as possible. I am, after all, a naturalised American citizen now. So no one who did not know that I still retain my Colombian citizenship would be any the wiser. No one would have any reason to make the connection.'

He slowly drew back the sheet to look at Margaret's naked form in the bed and trail the back of his hand down from her neck and between her breasts. He sighed. 'Such beauty,' he said. 'Such a shame to waste it.'

Margaret could only watch, and feel very distantly beneath the surface calm, a rising panic. Her breathing came a little faster. She made a small grunting noise. He said, 'Margaret, Margaret. I told you not to fight it.' He cupped one of her breasts in his hand and grazed the nipple with his thumb. He leaned over and kissed her softly on the lips, and then sat looking at her for a very long time before covering her with the sheet once more. 'Such a waste,' he said again.

He stood up and crossed to the dressing table. She could hear him opening something, laying things out on the polished surface. Hard things. Metal and glass. But she could not see. He said, 'A name like Mendez. An accent I could never quite get rid of, no matter how hard I tried. You cannot know what a handicap they have been in this great country of ours. Always an Hispanic. Always a foreigner. Never an American. Even when I got a passport. Everything I have achieved was in spite of my background, Margaret, in spite of the prejudice I encountered with every job application I made, with each board I faced. And then, of course, finally, they got their revenge. Some piddling bureaucratic oversight – not even mine – and I am forced into early retirement. Forced to abandon my career at the peak of my powers.' He turned around, and she could see the lights in his eyes, fuelled by anger and hatred. 'And then what do they do? This government of yours, this great country with its precious ideals of liberty and equality. They start dumping poison on my people. Spraying disease and genetic disorder on innocent women and children, poor Colombian peasants scratching to make a living. And why? In a futile attempt to stop the trade in a designer drug that your own President has confessed to taking.'

Even through her confusion, Margaret was aware that Mendez's 'we' had become a reference to himself and the Colombian people, and that his 'you' now applied to Margaret and the Americans, among whose number he apparently no longer counted himself.

Again, she heard him speaking and had to force herself to concentrate. 'No longer could I just stand by doing nothing,' he was saying. 'It was time to do something. Time to teach America a lesson. Time to show its politicians that they could not just stomp around the world trampling over other people's rights and sovereignty. Time to teach white Anglo-Saxon Americans that they could die just as easily as the rest of us.'

From somewhere Margaret found the strength to speak. The words bubbled out of her throat. 'You . . .' she said. And with another great effort '. . . you engineered the virus.'

He smiled. 'Of course. And don't you just love the irony? *Spanish* flu. A Colombian revenge. Oh, I'm sorry, I forgot. Americans don't understand irony.' Slowly, very slowly, the fog was lifting from Margaret's brain. Mendez said, 'When one of my students came to me with soft tissue, it was as if he had been sent by God. He was a volunteer with the expedition to recover the *Seadragon* from the Arctic. It was about eighteen months ago. You probably read about it. The submarine crew who died from the Spanish Flu in 1918. Their vessel became trapped under the ice pack, eventually coming to rest on the polar continental shelf. The boat was never holed. A couple of divers looking for another wreck found it, and some scientists figured that the crew had probably been preserved inside by the cold, and that if they could raise the sub they might be able to recover soft tissue and culture live virus. They failed, of course. Sure, they got the soft tissue, but they couldn't culture live virus. Wasn't cold enough, even down there.'

He turned back to whatever he was doing on the dressing table. 'My student managed to secrete a little of it away. He thought I might succeed where others had failed. I was flattered by his faith in me, and sad to disappoint him. I told him it was a waste of time. It couldn't be done. Which was true. What I did not tell him was that I could clone the virus from the viral RNA in the tissue he had given me. It was almost intact. As near to perfect as you could hope for. And then, of course, it was easy for me to engineer it to my own particular specifications.'

Margaret fought for breath to speak. 'You're . . . insane.'

He swung around. One eyebrow cocked. 'No, Margaret. Just smarter than the rest of you.'

'You won't . . . just kill white . . . Anglo-Saxon Americans.' The very effort of forcing herself to speak was clearing her mind. 'You'll kill Americans . . . of every race . . . every colour. And people . . . all over the world. Even . . . Colombians.'

He shook his head and smiled, as if saddened by her wretched stupidity. 'You don't really think I would create a virus without also producing the vaccine?' he said. 'After all, that's what made me able to sell the idea to the Colombians who've been bringing in the Chinese. Once the flu is out there, they can sell the vaccine to the highest bidder. Lot of money to be made. And, of course, the people of Colombia might just get preferential treatment. Naturally, I have already vaccinated myself.'

Margaret coughed the phlegm out of her throat. Her tongue was so dry it was sticking to the roof of her mouth. 'Can't work,' she gasped. 'You know it. No one . . . could produce enough vaccine . . . in time. Once the flu is . . . rampant . . . it will be . . . too late.'

He shrugged and turned away again, and when he turned back a few moments later, he had a syringe in his hand, needle pointed at the ceiling. He squeezed it gently until a spurt of clear liquid shot into the air, flashing in the moonlight, then he approached Margaret around the bed. Panic was feeding strength to her lungs and heart, and her breathing became rapid and erratic. She found movement in her arms and legs, but not enough to resist. She heard her own voice scratching in her throat with each breath, whimpering like a dog.

'Just relax, Margaret.' Mendez told her softly. 'I want you to know how it feels. To live with death hanging over you. To wonder when and where it will come from.'

She felt the cold dab of disinfectant on her arm, and the sharp bite of the needle. There was nothing she could do to stop him squeezing the syringe, forcing the virus through the needle and into her bloodstream. And with a start she realised that her baby, too, would be infected. An icy despair broke over her, like a wave in a frozen sea.

'Unless, of course,' she heard Mendez saying, 'you're smart enough to figure out what it is I programmed to trigger the virus.'

He withdrew the needle, dabbed her arm again and stood

up. He returned to the dressing table and started clearing away his things. She lay, under sentence of death, and saw poor Steve's haunted face in that moment when his resistance finally ended. And in her mind's eye she saw also the faceless faces of all those who would die just like him, just like her. Hundreds of millions of them. A tear forced its way out of the corner of her eye and ran down on to the pillow.

His shadow fell across her again, and she saw him silhouetted against the window. 'Goodbye, Margaret,' he said. 'Time for me to go home.'

When she awoke, she was not certain how long she had slept. Minutes. Hours. Moonlight still streamed in through the window, but the angle of it had changed, and half the room was now in deep shadow. She turned her head and found that it moved quite easily. The digital display on the bedside clock told her it was just after four. With consciousness came recollection, and an involuntary moan slipped past her lips. A deep, heartfelt moan of distress. She grieved more for her unborn child than for herself, a revelation to her that she could consider another life more important than her own. And she knew that it was only nature, what had been programmed into her. It was just that she had always thought that her conscious mind would always make decisions over her evolutionary one.

She figured that Mendez must be long gone, and she was lying attempting to summon the strength to try to get out of the bed when she heard a crash from somewhere downstairs, and a man's voice cursing. Then Clara started barking, and the voice shouted again and she stopped. Margaret lay still and listened for a long time hearing nothing. And then a car door slammed outside. Maybe he was still packing his stuff into the Bronco. Maybe his decision to run had not been taken until tonight, triggered by Margaret. Why had he not just killed her? And as soon as the question formed in her head she knew the answer. Because he loved her. Because he knew he could never have her. Because he wanted her to suffer as he had suffered with her rejection. She closed her eyes and was aware that she was breathing almost normally. But her mind was still fuzzy, not fully in control of her body. She turned her head and lifted her arm and saw the needlepoint where the virus had entered her. It gave her fresh impetus, and with an enormous effort she forced herself up into a sitting position, the cotton top sheet falling away to the floor.

It took another great effort to swing her legs over the edge of the bed, but when she tried to put her weight on them, they offered no resistance and folded under her. She collapsed into the thick piled carpet like a house of cards. Part of her wanted simply to close her eyes, but another, larger, part of her fought the impulse. Her muscles were like jelly. She had to put steel into them with her mind, and it took several minutes for her to drag herself, on her knees, to the door. She fell into the landing and found herself staring straight down the stairs to the entrance hall. She lay, listening, for a long time, but heard nothing. Even if she made it down there, she had no idea what she could do. She had no strength. But she could speak, she was sure. If she could get to a phone . . . She let herself go and half slid, half tumbled, to the foot of the stairs, carpet burning her legs and arms and chest.

As she lay in the hall, breathing hard, she heard the cough of a motor starting, and then the roar of it as Mendez gunned the engine. Suddenly she no longer wanted just to make a phone call. She wanted to stop him. Any way she could. Margaret had never suspected just how powerful a fuel adrenalin could be. A rush of it came with her anger and despair and powered her struggle to her feet, pulling herself up on the coat stand. She almost fell again as it tipped away from the wall and crashed to the floor. The door jamb saved her. She clung to it desperately, steadying herself before staggering off through the dining room, clutching at anything that offered support, and making it, finally to the kitchen. The lights had all been switched off, but the moonlight still poured in through the back window. She used the central island to support her progress around the kitchen and into the gun room. The gun cabinet, which had earlier bruised her leg, was there to keep her on her feet. Outside, probably no more than twenty feet away through the open garage, she could hear the Bronco's engine idling. Why had he not gone? And suddenly she was afraid he would come back and find her there, naked and helpless. How on earth could she have thought there was any way she could stop him? She heard him calling to Clara, the dog barking distantly at first, and then closer. A car door slammed. After several seconds, another.

It was in that moment Margaret realised what it was she was leaning against. She felt for the light switch, and blinked in the painful brightness of it crashing through the darkness in her brain. Six shotguns were neatly stacked along the rack. She snatched one down and broke it open on top of the chest, and with thick, fumbling fingers, pulled open the top drawer. The first box of cartridges she pulled out split open and spilled its contents across the floor. As she dropped to her knees, cartridges rolling across the floorboards away from her scrabbling fingers, she heard the whine of the Bronco reversing into the turning circle opposite the entrance to the garage. She let out a tiny cry, and her fingers closed around a cartridge. And then another. Using the gun to prop herself up, she dropped them one after the other into the two barrels and snapped it shut. She was on her knees then, swaying behind the door. She reached up and pulled the handle down, using it to lever herself to her feet and draw it open at the same time. It almost tipped her backwards to send her crashing to the floor again. But she caught the architrave and held her balance. She stood reeling there for an eternity, hearing the Bronco slipping into forward gear, its headlights swinging into the garage as it made its turn. She staggered out and was immediately blinded by them, caught in their full glare, stark naked and barely able to stand. Beyond the blaze of them she saw, palely reflected, the astonishment on Mendez's face as he jammed on the brakes. She swung the gun to her shoulder and pulled the first trigger, firing straight into the light. The force of it propelled her backwards, and the involuntary reflex of her finger emptied the second barrel. She heard the scream of the Bronco's engine and the blaring of the horn as she fell.

CHAPTER FIFTEEN

I

The first thing she was aware of were the voices. There seemed to be so many of them. She felt as though she were floating in an auditorium filled with people. She wanted to open her eyes. But the lids were so heavy she could not move them, as if someone had decided she was already dead and had placed pennies upon them to keep them shut. When eventually they snapped open, she was taken almost by surprise. The room was filled with sunshine, the shadows of people moving around in it. Where was she? Lying on something soft, staring at the ceiling. A fan was turning lazily overhead. She smelled something familiar. Something disturbing. What was it? She became aware of her breathing becoming more rapid. It was cigar smoke. Stale cigar smoke. Mendez! They were Mendez's cigars. She tried to sit up and pain closed around her head like a steel band. She heard a familiar voice. A man's voice. 'She's awake. Doc, she's awake.'

A face floated into her vision. A familiar face. But it wasn't attached to the voice. It was a woman. A doctor. Someone on her staff. A medical examiner. 'Elizabeth,' she heard herself say.

Elizabeth's warm hand gently brushed her forehead. 'Just lie still, Doctor Campbell. You're gonna be just fine.'

But Margaret knew she wasn't. She knew things they didn't. She remembered last night with a dreadful clarity. At least, she remembered some of it. Though not how it ended. How she had got to be here. She forced herself up on to an elbow and saw deputies from the Montgomery County Sheriff's department standing around looking at her with unabashed curiosity. There were forensics investigators in white Tivek suits, and men in plain clothes. One of them blotted out her view of the rest of the room. Mendez's sitting room. She had at least had time to log that. And she was lying on his settee, covered in a blanket. She refocused on the face looming over her, and connected it with the voice she had recognised earlier. It was Hrycyk.

'Jesus, Doc,' he said. 'What the hell happened here?'

She forced dry lips apart and became aware of her tongue seeming to fill her mouth. 'You tell me,' she said, and she allowed herself to drop back into the softness of the settee. He disappeared from her field of vision, and returned a moment later with the back of a chair which he leaned on, watching her closely.

'Neighbour about half a mile away down the road phones the cops. What sounds like a car horn's been going without a break for more than an hour. Cops get here just as daylight's breaking. They find Mendez in his Bronco, slumped on the wheel. What's left of his head is laying right on the horn. He's got a big hole in his chest. His right foot is jammed on the accelerator and the engine is gunning at top rev. There's a dog in back, behind a mesh grill, barking itself hoarse.' He paused and took out a cigarette.

Margaret heard Elizabeth saying, 'I'd rather you didn't light that, Agent Hrycyk. This is still a crime scene.'

He grunted and put his cigarettes away again. 'You god-damned people are all the same,' he said. 'So where was I? Oh, yeah. Garage door's raised right up in the roof. Headlights of the Bronco shining right inside. And you're laying there in your goddamned birthday suit clutching a double-barrelled shotgun. Mendez is dead as a dodo. And it sure as hell looks like you're the one who made him that way.' He searched her face for a long time, apparently looking for some response. Finally, he couldn't contain his curiosity any longer. 'Why'd you shoot him, Margaret?'

She was aware of a hush falling all around her. Hrycyk wasn't the only person in the room who wanted to know. 'Because he was the one,' she said eventually.

'The one what?' Hrycyk frowned.

'The one who engineered the virus,' Margaret said. She drew her arm out from beneath the blanket and held it out for him to see. The pinprick left by the syringe was still visible. 'He injected me with it.' And without warning her eyes filled with tears. 'I'm infected. The bastard infected me.'

Hrycyk's eyes were like saucers. 'Jesus, Margaret,' he said. 'Jesus fucking Christ.'

She pulled herself up on one elbow again and brushed the tears from her eyes. There was something else in her head. Something important. Something she had meant to do before. 'I need to get out to the lab,' she said.

'What lab?' Hrycyk asked.

Elizabeth said, 'Take it easy, Doctor.' And to Hrycyk, 'You're getting her excited.'

Hrycyk ignored her. 'What lab?' he asked again.

'Mendez has a lab. Here at the ranch.' Margaret fought to remember why it was important. She struggled to sit up, and the blanket fell away.

Hrycyk blushed, embarrassed by her nakedness, and quickly pulled the blanket up to her shoulders. 'For Christ's sake, someone get her something to wear!'

Elizabeth took over and wrapped the blanket around her until someone came with a towelling dressing gown and Margaret's sneakers. Margaret slipped the soft towelling around her and tied it tightly at the waist. Then she slid into her sneakers, and with help got to her feet. She staggered a little as she felt the blood rushing from her head. 'You shouldn't be doing this,' Elizabeth said.

'I need a drink,' Margaret said, and one of the deputies brought her a glass of water. She drained it in a single draught and stood gasping. 'Okay, let's go.'

'Where we going?' Hrycyk asked.

'Across the meadow. There's an old barn . . .' She grabbed Hrycyk's arm. 'Just stay with me.'

He took her hand, and put a supporting arm around her

waist. He appeared awkward, embarrassed by his own concern. It didn't fit, somehow, with his image — or the one he liked to project. Out of all context, Margaret wondered suddenly if he was married and asked him.

He looked at her in amazement. 'Is that a proposal?'

'You wish,' she said.

He grinned. 'Silver wedding anniversary next year. Got two kids at college.'

Margaret wondered why she was surprised.

The chestnut mares were frolicking at the far end of the meadow. Sunlight slanted across the grass, steam rising as it burned off the dew. In the far distance, two long strands of mist hung above the lake. Mendez's Bronco stood silent, its nose buried in the upright between the garage and the house, its windshield shattered. Margaret could see the blood inside. But the body had already been removed. Police vehicles, a forensics van, an ambulance, and several unmarked cars blocked the dirt track leading to the road. A couple of crows sat on the fence watching as Margaret led a small entourage of law enforcement people across the meadow, supported on the arm of Agent Hrycyk.

The barn was shaded by trees and dark inside. Margaret remembered from last night the smell of cow dung in the treads of its huge tyres. They crossed the dusty floor and she pointed out the trap. A couple of the sheriff's men moved forward to open it, and one went down the ladders to find the lights. When they came on, Margaret insisted on climbing down herself. They helped her from above and below, and she stood shakily in the pit where she had listened to Mascagni's Intermezzo from *Cavalleria Rusticana* only fourteen hours ago, when she still had a whole life ahead of her.

Fluorescent lights flickered to life as they went into the lab. It was just as Margaret and Mendez had left it the previous night. Hrycyk whistled softly. 'So this is where he did it, huh? Created a monster you can't even see. Jees. It's like Frankenstein's surgery.' He turned to Margaret. 'What is it you're looking for?'

She shook her head, eyes darting across every surface. 'I don't know.' She frowned as if in pain. 'I can't remember.' Whatever it was cast a huge shadow across her mind, but somehow she could neither see nor touch it.

She scanned the wooden-topped bench in the centre of the room, the gel electrophoresis machines, the digital camera, the iMac and scanner, then jumped focus to the far worktop. Something, she knew, had lodged in her brain. Something she had seen here. Something significant that had not immediately occurred to her. There was the small electric oven for doing blots, the other iMacs, the electron microscope, and all the detritus of jars and bottles, papers and books, coffee-maker and ashtray. She ran her eyes past the incubators and freezer to the stereo and small centrifuge. And then suddenly she realised what it was. She swung her eyes back to the worktop. 'The coffee-maker,' she said.

'What?' Hrycyk was nonplussed.

She broke free from the bewildered INS agent and made her way across the lab. There were cupboards below the worktop.

She eased herself down on to her haunches and opened the doors. The top shelf was crammed with vacuum-sealed packs of Washed Arabica Colombian coffee. A couple of packs on the bottom shelf were open, and some beans had spilled across the melamine. There was an electronic coffee-grinder with some grounds still in it. But the coffee had long since lost its freshness.

Hrycyk crouched beside her. 'I don't get it,' he said. 'So he liked coffee.'

'That's just the point,' Margaret said. 'He was allergic to it.'

II

Margaret and Hrycyk sat in silence in Mendez's office at Baylor. They had been there two hours. A secretary had come in and offered them coffee. They both refused and accepted an offer of water instead. Margaret felt like death. She had refused medical treatment, and after making her official statement, Hrycyk had driven her straight here with samples of the coffee. He had disappeared on several occasions for five minutes at a time, and come back smelling of cigarette smoke.

They both looked up as the door opened, and a young man in his thirties, dark hair flopping across a flushed face, came in. Unlike his former boss, the young geneticist's lab coat was crisp and clean and fully buttoned. He looked at them both, and then sat down and held up a coffee bean between forefinger and thumb. He nodded. 'You were right,' he said. 'That's what does it. Mendez spliced a promoter into his virus which is activated by a protein recognising the unique chemical flavour of Colombian Washed Arabica coffee.' He half-smiled, shaking his head in admiration. 'Brilliant. Absolutely brilliant. The man was a genius.'

'A dead fucking genius,' Hrycyk growled, and the young man flinched as if he had been slapped.

Margaret felt relief surge through her like a prescription relaxant. She could have wept. As long as she never drank coffee again both she and her child would be safe, even if she had to live with Mendez's viral contaminant for the rest of her days. She said, 'Colombian coffee. He had a finely honed sense of irony. He didn't figure we were smart enough to understand it, or figure out what it was.'

'Dead wrong, huh?' Hrycyk chuckled, as if he thought he had made a joke.

'The thing is,' Margaret said, 'maybe the Chinese *don't* drink much coffee. But I'll bet there's Colombian in most blends in most coffee shops in America. It can only be a matter of time. Somehow we've got to get that message across. Fast. It could take just a single case to start the pandemic.'

She stood in the phone booth at the end of the hall fumbling in her purse for the FEMA list. She was certain it was there somewhere. She found various pieces of paper, folded and crumpled and smeared with eye make-up, near the bottom of the bag. But no FEMA list. She cursed and flipped with trembling fingers through her address book instead, and found Li's home number in Georgetown where she had made the scribbled entry a couple of days before. She wanted to tell him that Xiao Ling was going to be okay. And somewhere, lurking at the back of her mind, was a hope she would not even dare to acknowledge, that somehow this might change things. She ran her credit card through the reader and tapped out the number. It rang in her ear. Long, single rings. Five of them. Six. Seven. After the tenth ring she reluctantly accepted that there was no one home and gave up. She had not made a note of his cellphone number. That was on the FEMA list which, in her mind's eye, she saw now lying on her office desk. She hurried back along the corridor looking for Hrycyk.

III

They turned the corner at the intersection of Wisconsin and M, and passed beneath a golden dome supported on Greek pillars. From here they had a view down M Street towards the bridge over Rock Creek. Tall narrow shopfronts in red brick, trees newly planted along the sidewalk still in green leaf. Xinxin, happier than Li could remember, kept running ahead, only reining herself in when Xiao Ling or Meiping called on her not to go too far. They were an hour ahead of Houston time, and it was a beautiful morning, more like spring than fall. The sky was painfully clear, and the warmth of the sun on their faces lifted their spirits. Their White House tour was in the afternoon, and they had the morning to kill.

Xinxin knew where they were going. Li had taken her and Meiping on several occasions to the M Street Starbucks, and she was salivating already at the thought of the hot chocolate slathered in caramel that he would get for her. Outside Johnny Rockets, Li led them across the road through traffic which had ground to a halt. For a moment he considered taking them into Café Häagen-Dazs next door for an ice-cream. But ice-cream wasn't on the list. They passed the Bistro Français and turned into the narrow rough brick doorway that opened into Starbucks Coffee Shop. A poster read: REMEMBER THE GOOEY, STICKY, BUTTERY-SWEET, LIP-LOCKING LOVE OF CARAMEL?

It was busier than Li had expected. People sat reading newspapers or talking in animated groups at tables beneath pictures of steaming mugs of Caramel Apple Cider and Caramel Macchiato. Li sat the girls up at the bar that ran along the window, and left them looking out at Ben and Jerry's Ice Cream Parlour across the street to go and fetch their order. He came back with tall cappuccinos for himself and Meiping, Xinxin's favourite chocolate and caramel, and plain bottled water for Xiao Ling.

They talked excitedly about their trip to the White House. Li had secured them a VIP tour, and Xinxin wanted to know if they would meet the President's dog. Xiao Ling watched Li and Meiping drinking their coffee and wrinkled her nose. 'I don't know how you can drink that stuff,' she said. 'It smells horrible.'

Li shrugged. 'An acquired taste.'

'Have you never tried it?' Meiping asked.

Xiao Ling shook her head.

'Mine's great!' Xinxin said.

Li laughed. 'Yeah, but it's not coffee, little one.'

His cellphone rang in his pocket, and for a moment he hesitated to answer. Only a handful of people knew this number, so it could only be official business. But that official business might include confirmation of their flight tomorrow, so he fished it out of his pocket and flipped down the mouthpiece. '*Wei*,' he said.

'Li Yan?' A group of people at the next table laughed loudly at some inane joke and he could barely hear her voice. But he knew it was Margaret and he was at once tense. He stood up and moved away towards the door, slipping behind the glass and pressing a finger to his other ear.

'Margaret?'

'Li Yan, it's coffee.' There was a strange urgency in her voice. 'Don't let her drink coffee.' And he did not immediately understand. How could Margaret know they were in a Starbucks?

'What do you mean?'

'The trigger. It's in coffee.'

And even as her words sank in and he made the connection, he saw, through the glass, Meiping offering her cappuccino to Xiao Ling to try. She was laughing. And he could see the words form in her mouth, almost hear them above the din. *It's only coffee. What harm can it do?*

Li's yell cut across the hubbub in the coffee shop. He heard it distantly, as if it were someone else who had shouted. His legs felt leaden as they carried him in slow motion past the astonished faces of Starbucks customers. A table went spinning away to crash against the window, hot coffee streaking the glass, condensation forming instantly like frost. Someone's angry voice burned his ear. A hand clutched at his arm. The cup was at Xiao Ling's lips as he lunged at her, knocking it from her hand to clatter away across the floor. She was frozen in astonishment and fright, uncomprehending. Xinxin's cries rose in her throat, giving vent to her fear. Why had Uncle Yan hit her mother? Li put his arms around his sister and drew her to him and immediately felt her sobs. He squeezed most of the breath from her and knew that death had been only a whisper away.

A member of staff was at his elbow demanding to know what he thought he was doing. Who did he think was going to clear up the mess? Someone stooped to pick his cellphone from the floor where it had slithered beneath a chair. He could hear Margaret's voice. Urgent and fearful. 'Li? Li? For God's sake, Li, are you still there? What's happened?'

He took the phone and put it to his ear, and with a voice that seemed so much calmer than he felt he said, 'I'm here, Margaret.'

'Is everything okay?'

'Everything's fine.'

And for a moment neither of them knew what else to say, or how to end the conversation. Then Margaret said, 'So ...' her voice trailing away, her sentence unfinished

Li said, 'So ... what?'

'So, you'll still be going back to China?'

'I have no reason to stay, Margaret.'

Another silence. Then, 'What if I were to give you a reason?'

He glanced at his sister. She and Meiping were staring back at him, fearful, curious. He was aware of Xinxin clutching her mother's leg, still crying. A girl with a bucket and mop was splashing the floor around his feet. 'What reason?' he asked. What reason could she give him? That she loved him? Well, maybe she did. And maybe he loved her, too. But they had been down that road before and it had not led to fulfilment.

'I'm pregnant,' she said simply. 'I'm carrying your child, Li Yan.'

And of all the reasons he might have imagined, that was not one of them. But he knew immediately that it was the only reason he would ever need.

Note: At the time of writing, the American federal government had not actually cleared the use of *fusarium oxysporum* for spraying coca crops in Colombia. But it *was* under active consideration.

ACKNOWLEDGEMENTS

As always, there are many people whose help has been invaluable in researching *Snakehead*. In particular, I'd like to express my deep gratitude to Dr Richard H. Ward, Professor of Criminology and Dean of the College of Criminal Justice, Sam Houston State University, Texas; Steven C. Campman, MD, the Armed Forces Institute of Pathology, Washington, DC; Professor Joe Cummins, Emeritus of Genetics, University of Western Ontario; Kong Xianming, Police Liaison Officer, Embassy of China, Washington DC; Caree Vander Linden, US Army Medical Institute of Infectious Diseases, Fort Detrick, Maryland; Sheriff Victor K. Graham, and Chief Deputy Jean Sanders, Walker County Sheriff's Department, Huntsville, Texas; Chief Frank Eckhardt, Chief of Police, Huntsville, Texas; Agent Mike McMahon, Immigration and Naturalisation Service (INS), Houston, Texas; Dr Richard Watkins, Governor, Holliday Unit, Huntsville Prison, Texas; Major Katheryn Bell, Texas Department of Criminal Justice; Dan Richard Beto, Director of the Correctional Management Institute of Texas; Jerrold Curry, Houston Food Bank; Desta Kimmel, Media Services Coordinator, Houston Astros; J. D. Perkins for his extraordinary knowledge of submarines; Bonni Hrycyk for her advice on ice and letting me borrow her name; Dick and Barbara Muller for their hospitality, and willingness to educate me on the history, geography and political vagaries of Washington DC; Sean Hill for being my Sherpa in Houston, and Michelle Ward for her kind hospitality and great sense of humour.

COMING SOON

THE RUNNER

Peter May

CHINA THRILLER 5

The fifth China thriller sees Li Yan and
Margaret Campbell uncover an insidious
conspiracy on the eve of the Beijing Olympics.

AVAILABLE IN PAPERBACK
24 AUGUST 2017

riverrunbooks.co.uk